THE DELPHINIUM GIRL

HARPER & ROW, PUBLISHERS

NEW YORK

Cambridge
Hagerstown
Philadelphia
San Francisco

1817

London
Mexico City
São Paulo
Sydney

THE DELPHINIUM GIRL

Mark Smith

Delphinium illustrations courtesy of the Granger Collection.

FIRST EDITION

Designer: *Gloria Adelson*

Library of Congress Cataloging in Publication Data

Smith, Mark, 1935–
  The delphinium girl.
  I. Title.
PZ4.S653Dg 1980   [PS3569.M53766]   813'.5'4   79–2660
ISBN 0–06–014018–6

---

80 81 82 83 84 10 9 8 7 6 5 4 3 2 1

Contents

The author wishes to express his gratitude to the Ingram Merrill Foundation for its generous support during the writing of this book.

THE DELPHINIUM GIRL

1 *Invitation to the Dance*

BY midsummer it had begun to look as though the Angles would never make up in time to have their party before the fall. And no lawn party at the Angles' would have been a crack in the social calendar of what had become their small set's little season. The Kubiliuses, who had a pond, had an annual skating party; and the Kevilles a Christmas party because they had an old Colonial house with a stairwell that would hold a twelve-foot tree; and Marco and Alexander seemed to have initiated a rite of spring at which they served a punch bowl of Rhine wine and champagne, woodruff flavored, and floating the first strawberries of the season. For five years now the Angles had thrown a lawn party for their friends.

Unfortunately their quarrel was over nothing definite, which put any resolution of it out of reach. It had also followed rules instead of passion, which meant that, unable to burn itself out, it had endured. Each night after the children were trundled off to bed, they would sit down at the kitchen table and in a silence that was mutual and absolute write each other the notes they would then exchange across the centerpiece of fruit. They would do this until their brains buzzed and their eyes glazed over with the strain of composition and the lack of sleep. Sometimes their notes contained well-reasoned arguments and five-point programs for doing better in the marriage. Too often they sank to name calling of a low sort—bitch! bastard! bugger! beast! He was fond of the rhetorical question, which, to his disgust, she often undertook to answer, although he was at his best when wielding analogy and metaphor, in his cruel but accurate use of which she could not compete. She preferred insinuation anyway, delighted in implication, her final sentences ending with multiple dots ending at multiple question marks. He thought her stupid, melodramatic, insensitive to the point of psychopathia. She thought him sarcastic, with a feeling for the jugular, the beating heart, the intestines, another person's soul! His strategy was: make everything as personal as possible and then attack! annihilate! destroy! When one of them announced I've had enough for one night, it was a surrender made on paper. Any exchanges of "goodnight" were written, too. Although some evenings had been known to end with one of them rolling the last note into a ball and bouncing it off the other's head. But in the morning at the same table when they took breakfast with the children they would speak to each other in friendly if weary voices of eggs and weather and the school bus and who was to be home when today. They had begun the practice of note writing in their first years of marriage, when they lived in California. They did it for the children's sake, they said.

When she had her fill of quarreling, she flew home to Oregon, where she spent three weeks with her sister, visiting relatives and looking up old school friends, leaving him to mind the three boys, the youngest of whom was still in diapers though he was nearly four. A tall man, he found himself spending the better part of the day in their company squatting on the floor. He treated them with a gentleness that appeared more professional than personal, and tried never to show impatience or raise his voice. The boys called him John. They called their mother Janet. When Janet came home, John went off for a week, backpacking in the White Mountains. There had been at least one time before when he had not gone alone.

He returned to find her in a good if slightly goofy mood, and dancing. It was a modern sort of dancing she had been introduced to out in Oregon, and she would be going down to Cambridge weekly for lessons—although not really lessons so much as sessions. The dance, as he understood it, was a mixture of self-expression, therapy and communication. Only incidentally was it exercise and art. She had come to the conclusion that she could not compete with him in "word language." And because of the tremendous advantage he had always had over her whenever they were forced to use it, he had smothered her, bottled her up. Her thoughts followed his thought patterns, she no longer knew how to express her feelings, her body motions were no longer her own. Hereafter she would communicate with him by dancing.

Originally he had only to watch her dance around their sunken living room while he sat in the little balcony affair above, his arm resting on the rail. Although she had no formal training in dance, she was trim, athletic, graceful. In black leotards, she kicked like a chorus girl, slunk catlike against the walls, ran in place, curled up in a fetal position on the floor. No music accompanied her performance. This was because she insisted you had to interpret and express your own inner rhythms and harmonies, not someone else's creation. He was not even allowed to clap or hum. When she was finished with a dance, and he studied her in that final position of kneeling with her long hair cascading over her face, or with her arms raised up as though in supplication of the sun, he knew she had just expressed something to him, even if he didn't know exactly what. He certainly didn't know how to answer.

She wouldn't let him try to, not in "word language" anyway. He tried to show her that he took it all with the same earnestness that she did. He even persuaded himself that her explanations and efforts just might make sense. After all, it wasn't as if her approach was all that alien from the way he thought himself. As the young principal of an experimental regional high school he had introduced into the curriculum not only such long-overdue innovations as sex education, gymnastics and girls' sports, but the far more exotic disciplines of yoga and judo, while promoting a theory of pupil-teacher relations he called, in the basketball jargon of the day, "one on one."

It was only a matter of time before Janet invited him to dance himself. He had balked at first; he couldn't imagine such silliness, he would feel like a goon. Finally, in the hope that such a sacrifice might end their differences, he attempted a little something in his stocking feet with the curtains closed. He tried to remember the moves and motions of ballet dancers, cheerleaders, go-go girls, although when in doubt he simply performed calisthenics interrupted occasionally by a running leap or his earthbound notion of a pirouette. He knew he was clumsy, unnatural, he could hear how his feet hit the floor. He had tried to balance himself on one leg, like a ballerina in *Swan Lake,* and found that to keep from falling he had to keep hopping one-legged around the floor. She was quick to congratulate and encourage him, saying, "Hey, that's good! It's really good. It's you. Do that again." And she had laughed with that patronizing innocence he remembered from a time before, when, in one of his baby pictures at his mother's house, she had recognized one of his "grown-up looks." When she pressed him, he told her he really liked the dancing, that he understood it now, that it was important to him, too. He lied, though. All he knew was that she excited him. She thought he understood those hand movements, rhythms, body positions, the storytelling choreography of her impromptu dance. What

he understood was legs and breasts and lips and flesh and dancing slave girls and a familiarity that bred desire. Soon they
were dancing at the same time and together, embracing in
what resembled the shuffling fox trot of exhausted dancers,
cheek to cheek. Early on in their marriage, he had learned
to equate the most passionate love-making with the hot, salty
taste of Janet's conciliatory tears.

Which meant they had the party after all. It took place upon
their lawn, which, although a rural lawn, was lavished with
an almost suburban fussiness, and if it didn't contain any fewer
weeds than the lawns of their neighbors, it was at least regularly
mown. For the past week the lawn had looked like a putting
green, and the giant marigolds, the only flower in the narrow
border along the barn, had reached their peak of color. What
was more, the Angles had just spray-painted white the wicker
they had been collecting all winter, and they wanted to see
their pieces set out in little intimate arrangements across the
lawn. As in summers past, John set up the badminton net and
chalked the courts, then laid out the croquet course, keeping
an eye open for the hidden dip and deceptive slope. The mass
of daisies that came up wild in the low spot behind the barn
was at its best that weekend, and he mowed a path through
it leading out to the old pasture, grown up in blueberries, into
which, it was hoped, the children could be induced every now
and then to go off and play.

Although they didn't need a reason for the party, they had
one anyway, and announced that they would honor and intro-
duce a newcomer to their midst, one Robert S. Stargaard, whom
they had met for the first time only the week before. Nine
years ago, at the age of twenty-five, he had published a novel
entitled *My Underground Self*, a copy of which the Angles
borrowed from him and now displayed on a coffee table for
all to see who went indoors. On the front of the soiled and
tattered jacket was an inexpert drawing of a youth's face, wide-

eyed with horror, one half of which was in light, the other half in darkness, the dividing line between them what appeared to be a thunderbolt. No one at the party had ever heard of man or book. He was a friend of the Orlovskys, who were in London, and was staying in their house for the summer. In order to begin a second book, he was taking a year off, although from what he didn't say, and told everyone he met that he was interested in staying on in this area of New Hampshire in the fall. When the Angles learned that Professor Renzi had just been awarded a grant to study and teach in Greece in a year's time from now, they decided, why not, they would honor Professor Renzi, too. Everybody knew who he was.

2   Dr. Gossip and Mr. New

BECAUSE Dr. Milton Cullenbine was a nuisance at any party, gossiping and picking quarrels, the Angles had been careful to make the Cullenbine invitation to his wife, knowing she would not come, and hoping she would forget to tell Dr. Milton, who would. In their innocence they had not foreseen that she was sure to tell him to get rid of him, and midway through the afternoon he appeared in brand-new tennis togs and tennis shoes, with a sprig of the yellow flower called butter-and-eggs inserted in the band of his tennis hat and drooping beyond the brim. This and the mincing way he seemed to spring along the ground made it appear that on the rise of any step he might continue up to make a kind of English morris dancer's leap. He was fiftyish, and had high cheekbones and a Hunnish color.

"Just our luck to catch him when he wasn't laid up with something," John said in an aside to Janet.

"Or locked up," Janet added. "After all, you would have thought the odds were with us."

In the many complaints of Cullenbine it was impossible to sort out what was cause and what effect. Addicted to both alcohol and barbiturates, he was also plagued by a host of emotional and nervous disorders and was so accident prone that he could have accurately described himself as an invalid. He had worn new leather shoes out onto the ice and broken his leg in the ensuing fall; had broken an ankle playing tennis, catching his foot on the tape; had been hit in the head with a golf ball when he was slow to leave a green, and once in the head with a driver when he wandered too close to the tee. He was an executive of a small chemical company of which he had himself been one of the founders, and would stay away from work months at a stretch, claiming one illness, injury and breakdown after another. At some point in each of these absences, his fellow executives would finally agree among themselves that this time he really had gone too far, that there was no putting off the decision that he had to go. But how to dispose of a man and keep your conscience clear when the poor devil was hobbling about on crutches, or limping with his foot in a cumbersome cast, or was shut up in a sanitarium where he was being inflicted with electrical shock treatments, especially when that man was as powerful and entrenched as Dr. Cullenbine? But just when they would set in motion some generous plan to retire him by buying him out, they would see him walk in the glass doors the first thing next morning with shiny face and shoes, briefcase in hand as though he had taken it home as recently as the night before. Sometimes his recovery would be incomplete, and he would appear on crutches, or using a cane, and once inside a walker, but if he was well, his flying feet would tap down the corridors on busy errands, his head, as likely as not, bound up in that mysterious and, some said, useless bandage. He would be full of boundless electrical energy and good will. It was as if the man could be heard saying, Step back! Make room! Let me pitch in!, and be seen squaring his jaw and rolling up his sleeves. He claimed he knew how to read the minds and faces of the men around him, and that this was the secret that allowed him to survive. Vita, his wife, said he merely had an inner sense that told him, invariably, when he had gone too far.

The first week back on the job he would work like one driven by genius, twelve hours a day, be down to eight hours the next week, and to four in the third, and coming in erratically after that, and then only when high on some narcotic or stimulant. Soon he would miss blocks of days at a time, and never once bother to call in to say that he was sick. Finally he would turn this unexplained and extended absence into yet another disappearance, leaving his colleagues to pick up the pieces of the many projects and appointments he had set up in those first enthusiastic days of his return, and to make another desperate attempt to find out where he was, what had happened to him and when, if ever, he could be expected to return.

Vita was like he was. Some said it had been a marriage of kindred souls; others that there was no way anyone could live with Cullenbine and not become infected with his hypochondria and goofiness. Twice they were hospitalized at the same time, but not in the same place or for the same reason. They had a stormy marriage full of drunken arguments that were like those great thundering mad scenes of Elizabethan theater that culminated in rape or murder, and both of their children, as soon as each was old enough to be on her own, had lit out for the West Coast, where they had remained with the obstruction of the continent between them and the chaos of their parents' home. It was common knowledge that Vita had not shared Milton's bed for several years. Janet Angle said, No wonder he was interested in other men's wives. No wonder he came to all the parties.

But more than women, new faces attracted him at the parties. Any newcomer he was quick to take aside, insinuating a collusion between them on the grounds that they were better than the others present. For Robert S. Stargaard he filled a paper plate with potato salad and one of the hamburgers that John Angle was cooking on his smoky grill, and sat beside him in a wicker chair while Stargaard sat cross-legged on the grass. From this seat he singled out most of their fellow guests and informed Stargaard who they were, what they had or hadn't done, and what he, Cullenbine, really thought of them, implying that this was what Stargaard would come to think about them, too.

Stargaard couldn't help but feel a bit flattered by such attention, even if he was made uncomfortable at hearing such private and scandalous information about people he had only just met, and from a stranger, too, an older professional man who was articulate and well read. What a fussy gossip the fellow was! That was not to say he was without his insights. Of his hosts, the Angles, he said, "Did you notice how they've been feeling each other up? Did you ever in your life see two people give each other such insipid smiles? And the way she cuddles up to him with her arm around his waist and—look there? did you see it?—she just slipped her hand into his pocket, I swear she did. And now he's slid his hand down her backside inside her pants and is feeling her bare ass—you can't see it the way they're facing us but you can tell by the faces they're making. They must have just come off one hell of a spat— and it's not over yet either. I wouldn't give their marriage another year. The next good-looking bimbo he meets can have him. And it's the next sweet-talking lifeguard for her."

Stargaard was impressed. With far less certainty, it was what he had been thinking, too. The couple's affection for each other was just too public and theatrical to be routine, or even real. Because of the problems he suspected his hostess of having with her husband, he thought she would be more accessible than the other women he had seen. He certainly found her attractive and sensual. Tall and long-legged and wearing halter shorts with white knee socks, she appealed to some perverse male appetite, best left unacknowledged, for young precocious girls; and Stargaard had been entertaining images of nutcrackers and scissors holds all afternoon. He wondered why he had really been invited to the party. Come to think of it, it was his hostess who had called.

Cullenbine pointed out a tall woman with salt-and-pepper hair up in a bun and wearing a gray-and-white-striped dress of a material like mattress ticking. "Pokey Kubilius," he said. "You're old enough to know the fifties type. Comes from money, went to a private school, probably went to Radcliffe, too. Tops in her class, and all she ever wanted to do was marry some Harvard man like Kubilius and live happily thereafter in a big suburban house with a big dumb dog and half a dozen kids. Life in four stages: wet nurse, kindergarten teacher, teen-age adviser, matriarch. Probably the last of her kind, too." Her husband, Cullenbine explained, was an anesthesiologist, and not a very good one either. "He'll put you to sleep, all right— with his cheap pessimism," he said. "Pokey calls hims 'Chaz'— short for Charles—but I call him 'Curare.'"

Stargaard didn't feel he had the right to ask what he meant by this, and so he said instead, "And what kind of doctor are you? A psychiatrist or psychologist of some sort would be my guess."

"No, no; but you're close," he said, pleased. And he explained that he was chief of personnel of a company he had helped to found, he and another scientist having made a discovery in the laboratory which they had patented and that the company, among other things, produced. It was possible he liked to talk about himself even more than he did about other people, and Stargaard learned he was born in South Dakota, a descendant of sod hut farmers, had gone to school in Wisconsin and come east as a young man. He had received both a religious and a humanistic education, and his doctorate was in biology. In his later years he had left the laboratory for the office. His company was burdened with incompetent young scientists in its laboratories, and spiteful executives, who were his enemies, in the offices upstairs.

He was in the midst of taking the young scientists to task when suddenly he stood up and bid Stargaard rise, too. "Time to meet Alexander," he said. "I see she's just arrived. And without her pretentious husband. You'll like this girl a lot."

They met her midway on the croquet court, where she had been handed a mallet and induced to play.

"Is it Alexandra?" he asked, thinking Cullenbine had mumbled the final syllable.

"Alexander," she corrected, explaining probably for some hundred thousandth time that it was the gift of an eccentric father.

"Don't let me interrupt your game," he said.

"Aren't you playing?"

He looked around. "All the mallets are taken."

She seemed to pose with her mallet on her shoulder. "Will you share mine?"

He begged off, grateful for her offer, which he suspected of being insincere.

That she should be so feminine and have a man's name excited him; somehow the name suited her as its feminine counterpart would not. She had kept her maiden name, too, which was Quen. Cullenbine was right; he liked her immensely, right off. If his hostess, who was all honey and girlhood, signaled good sex, this woman, who was cooler and more complicated, signaled good breeding, and he wasn't certain if this didn't arouse him all the more.

"Too bad Sarah Keville's not here," Cullenbine confided. "I like Sarah better than Alexander—and you'll like her better, too."

Stargaard wanted the chance to like her. By this time he was willing to trust the judgment of Cullenbine, and he promised himself he would not forget Sarah Keville's name.

Later in the afternoon, while he chatted with Professor Renzi on the man's plans to visit Greece, he watched Cullenbine, in those tennis togs, pay court to Alexander with a coyness that suggested he believed he had reversed the roles, and she was wooing him. Both Stargaard and Renzi were wearing garlands of daisies loosely interwoven with ground ivy that Pokey Kubilius had made in secret and placed with a shy smile of affectionate apology upon their heads. For her it must have been a reminder of a lost aristocratic childhood and some north shore garden party where young girls and matrons alike had dressed in white. Stargaard had worn his garland cockeyed from the beginning, while Renzi's had started to unwind, a coil of ivy spilling over an eye and ear. Janet Angle had taken their picture. "The artist-heroes," a woman called out in passing.

Just as the mosquitoes were about to make them adjourn indoors, a man showed up and made apologies for his absent wife, explaining he had himself returned from a business trip earlier than expected and had dropped by on his way home. He was big and rosy, and his hair was a Grecian mess of graying golden locks and curls. He made Stargaard think of beefeaters and yeomen and your solid English type. The man was obviously well known and just as well liked. It appeared that nearly everyone, upon catching sight of him, called out across the yard or room, "There's Toby!" or "Hey, Toby, over here!" He was not the sort of man you would ever see standing in a crowd alone. "God bless all here!" he called out in the Irish fashion, and put his arm around the shoulder of every man he knew and bussed the cheek of every woman. Stargaard did not doubt the genuineness of his affection or of the delight he showed at being among friends. The Angles called him Keville. Too bad, Stargaard thought, that Cullenbine wasn't beside him to tell him what he thought of this likable fellow. And too bad that Keville's allegedly attractive wife had not come with him, too.

Stargaard joined the group in which Alexander was talking. To his disappointment the conversation turned immediately to books and writing. He thought she looked at him more often than she did the others. She left early (which he took, mildly, as a personal slight), and apparently without so much as a good-by to anyone.

He moved off by himself and wandered down the path between the daisies, looking out beyond the pasture to the woods, and above them, to the small peaks of several mountains. This is a good place, these are good people, I could be happy here, he told himself.

3   *Marco and Alexander*

MARCO was Alexander's husband, and because he was not at home as much as she was, he was not as well known to their friends. He was originally from

Montreal, and his real name was Marcel, but Alexander had always called him Marco. They had moved from New York to the country to get away from not only concrete and shadows but the crippling expense of daily living on a grand scale, and the claustrophobia of their party-giving neurotic friends. Because those city friends who did not dream of living in Vermont dreamed of living in Maine, they moved up to New Hampshire instead. They had an architect build them a house on two levels with cathedral ceilings, balconies, skylights, a huge fieldstone fireplace and sliding walls of paneled glass that looked out upon birch and pine woods and the remnants of fieldstone walls. Where their country friends preferred to have their houses surrounded by fields, and to see woods in the distance, they had built deliberately in the middle of the trees, regretting the loss of those they had to cut down to make way for the house, and leaving others so close to the foundation that they would eventually encroach upon the shingled walls; others, the bottom of whose trunks would have been buried in the landscaping, were also spared, and now rose out of what looked like stoned-lined wells.

They had counted on Marco's eventually doing all his work at home, cognizant that before that day arrived he would have to return for brief work periods in New York. It had not turned out that way, though. With each year, he went away more often, and stayed longer, sometimes for months. Their friends weren't exactly certain how they made their money. Marco had been identified variously as photographer, stage designer and, more recently, illustrator, just the sort of professions in which a man might, if he was established, spend a month on assignment and earn a considerable fee. On the other hand, they could also be the hobbies of a wealthy amateur who received an income from a family source. Alexander never accompanied him when he went away, and since they were childless, she spent a lot of time alone. She was too busy to go anywhere. Besides, she had come to love the country and to be intolerant of the city. Usually she wore jeans and sweaters, although she could be fashionable and shocking, and sometimes wore a double-breasted blue pin-stripe suit, pinched at the waist, with high-heeled leather boots and a wide silver-colored tie. Marco's clothes were still stylish and urbane. In the summer he had been known to wear loose linen jackets that suggested Naples in the days of Mussolini, and sometimes a scarf and a soft white hat with a wide brim that he carefully bent over one eye.

When Marco was home they would dine at a late European hour before the fireplace, with candlelight and wine. Recently, when he had complained about the pushiness of a New York woman photographer they both knew, she had joked that he was probably still a little bit old-fashioned in his attitude toward women. He had been quick to defend himself. "I'm not at all competitive," he said. "I'm the last man to be uptight. If I were to marry again, I'd marry a professional woman, I wouldn't even consider another sort. Someone with her own office, and making lots of money. Like six figures of money. A doctor, a lawyer, maybe a banker. Someone on a board of directors would really turn me on."

"Why not an opera singer?" she wondered.

"You mean you don't see the problems you wouldn't have with a broker?"

"Sex is better with a broker?"

"I wouldn't be at all surprised. But I'm talking about ego, temperament, problems like that."

"And weight."

"Come on, I'd be big enough to overlook that. But now that you mention it, I wouldn't mind seeing my wife perform in costume on stage. The center of attention—a prima donna. I'd like to be watching in the wings, be down there in her dressing room before and after the performance. Imagine flying back and forth between La Scala and the Met. I like to see women haughty and arrogant—for a good reason, though."

"If the weight's a problem for you," she said, "why not concentrate on ballerinas?"

"If I were to marry an artist," he said, "she would have to be two things. She would have to be very successful. And she would have to be an interpretive artist, not one of your sullen creative types. But on the whole a businesswoman would suit me better."

She thought she knew him well enough to know that he was only partly joking. He had surprised her, frightened her a little, made her think. Were his remarks intended as a reproach? She was hardly a hausfrau. She had assumed that even the most sympathetic men were afraid deep down of emasculation by professional breadwinners of the sort Marco had just envisioned as his next wife. Marco was probably different, though. He had gone far to encourage her in her studies and activities. She had a darkroom separate from his, and a studio for her painting in a loft with a skylight, and currently she was relearning some Scott Joplin rags on the antique upright rosewood piano. Most of all, though, she spent her time in reading, at least a book a day, so that she was often seen with her glasses pushed up on her head, and Marco would tease her that someday he would buy her glasses that were suspended from a golden chain. She wasn't one for crewelwork, weaving, jewelry-making, throwing pots. She was fine arts, not arts and crafts.

And yet she looked robust enough to have been born to a rural sporting life. She could be pictured on horseback leaping through a flock of frightened sheep, running with a large leashed dog, casting a fly in soft weather into an Irish stream. She did none of these things, however. Except for the annual skiing trip up north she took alone, she was not much of a sportswoman. Neither she nor Marco had moved to the country to try their hand at breeding Morgans, Nubians, Newfoundlands, Black Angus. Nor did they care for husbandry, much less for outdoor gardening. Unlike their friends, they had never looked at country living as a chance to breed and sow. They had simply set themselves down in the middle of the country, without any plans to use it or make it give them anything, and liked the life immensely. Even the waxy, luxuriant greenery of Alexander's house plants in their hanging pots suggested a gardener in a high-rise.

When Stargaard, in the company of Renzi, called for the first time at her house, he thought she lived in a beautiful glass bubble full of shiny books and greenery set down in the middle of the woods. There were colorful extension lamps, an aquarium with a few exotic fish and a bottom of brightly colored pebbles, and bookshelves of expensive oversized art books, the smell from the high-quality paper of which was the dominant smell of the room. He was charmed by the modern kitchen, the studio, the piano, those trees. She knows how to live, he thought.

"And so you do whatever you want, then?" he wondered.

"And whenever I want, pretty much," she said.

"Then I like your life!" he announced. He felt more enthusiastic than he had in months.

"Good, I'm glad you do," she said. "Because I like it, too. As you can see, I know how to take care of myself. That's because I like to feel good about myself. And I like myself, too—just the way I am."

He wondered if she was joking, and when he decided she was serious, he felt a sudden loss of interest. He didn't like such narcissism. He knew her feelings about herself were much in fashion, having heard them expressed often enough by those handsome but vacuous sweet-natured acquaintances of his on the West Coast. Such narcissism said to him: psychoanalysis, yoga, health food. But the moment of repulsion passed. Why shouldn't she like herself and be honest enough to say so? What was he, anyway—some old-fashioned champion of unhappiness, self-hatred and depression?

"If I were to marry again," Renzi said, "I'd want to marry a photographer, like Marco—or whatever it is that Marco does—and live like you." Renzi had been divorced for several years, and liked to joke that Marco was probably a gangster's son supported by Mafia money.

"You don't believe I made myself," she said.

"I believe you spoiled yourself."

"It's true, I wasn't brought up to live like this. I was raised with obligations, responsibilities, a work ethic. I had to spoil myself because no one was nice enough to do it for me. I wish I could tell you I went through hell to do it, but I didn't. It was easy."

"A man like John Angle would claim you're still the product of your childhood environment," Renzi said, "no matter what you say."

"Only in the sense that I deliberately set out to become the opposite of what it had in store for me," she said.

"Maybe most of us have spoiled ourselves," Stargaard said. "Or maybe we were just people in the right time and place to be spoiled." He added, "Although few of us to your degree."

"When you look at the pathetic history of the world," she said, "you have to admit our generation has had life awfully good. Sometimes I wonder if future generations will have it as good as ours. It would be sad to think that our generation is the best of what's been and what's to come."

"There have always been leisure and professional classes," Renzi said, careful not to say who fit into which, "but never so many of us at one time, I dare say. Besides, Alexander, I don't know that you should create yourself. I mean, just look at you—you're already created. You should make something from yourself, it should come out of you and have an existence all its own. That's the ultimate test."

"A child!" she said. "You want me to have a child!"

"If that's all you can do. But it would be better if it came out of your mind, your spirit, what you will. It would be better if it was art."

She said, "I think so, too."

At home that night, Stargaard, still caught up in the mood of the afternoon, indulged one of his few luxuries: he put his bathrobe on over his clothes and sat down alone to a setting of red wine, fruit and cheese. Usually he lived like an Old Roman, dining on meals of stale bread, green olives and mugs of coffee, or he would boil up a pound of pasta and eat it plain. In his years of bachelorhood he had learned to count pennies, and even his best friends called him "cheap." Tonight he had a pomegranate, a chunk of stale Gruyère and a bottle of Cahors. He halved the pomegranate, which was so ripe it seemed to explode with juice, shaved off a piece of cheese and poured out a glass of wine. A pleasant jumble of geography and history tossed about his head: a Biblical landscape with palm trees; English and French knights warring in a medieval town; bucolic Alpine pastures overrun with great fat bell-clanking cows. And somewhere in this montage, Alexander was present, too.

Strange about Alexander, he thought. She was a loner and her own woman and yet, he was willing to wager she had always had a man in mind. She had made herself into a man's woman. The way she moved and looked at you and spoke all betrayed that underlying consideration. He guessed his interest in her was less infatuation than admiration and envy. He didn't think her life was leading anywhere, but then why should it? Why should anybody's life lead anywhere? Why couldn't it just stay at home, as it were, and enjoy itself until death do us part?

The wine was almost the color of the pomegranate and smelled, as he would soon confirm by taste, a bit young. He rolled it around the glass until it almost overran the rim. At the very top of the wine, where it flew around the glass, a narrow line of liquid, as clear as water, separated from the red it floated on, and just where it caught the light—or just possibly gave off some light of its own—"There! right there! That's Alexander," he said.

4 The Bean Supper Mystery

IN the hallway of the Orlovskys' house hung a small oval mirror exactly like the one that had hung beside the front door of Stargaard's parents' home. In it his reflection was like a cameo, a portrait bust and no more. When he was in his teens and, later, when he was home from college, he would often stand before that mirror and imagine his reflection as a photograph in the gallery of poets that were to be found in the front pages of an anthology of the greatest modern poems. It had seemed then that the photographs of poets were always oval-shaped, and he had come to associate the shape with both fame and poetry. That was the image he had carried within himself, his face in a photograph in an oval frame. Turtleneck sweater, a serious but youthful face. A clean-cut and handsome Anglo-Saxon countenance, hair parted in the middle. Or a softened and dreamlike Celtic quality, his hair a Medusa of messy locks. He had tried to look faintly injured, bewildered, sensitive, arrogant, bemused.

Rupert Stargaard.
Dylan Stargaard.

Wilfred Stargaard.

W. H. Stargaard.

Could he have ever been so innocent? he wondered. So optimistic? So young? Odd, how he had equated art not only with poetry but with being young. It had been a young man's calling. That was what he had believed, without knowing it, back then.

In college he had taken courses in existential philosophy and in modern literature that featured European novelists who were studied like existential philosophers, and he had abandoned poetry for philosophy. The novel, *My Underground Self,* written in the first person, and begun when he was nineteen, had been the consequence. It had sold less than two thousand copies, but had been favorably if randomly reviewed, and if there was a consensus among its critics it was that its young author was a man of promise. A few voices had hedged their bets, suggesting that after a brilliant if difficult beginning, the book had fallen down about halfway through. The old saying among editors and publishers that most people have only half a novel in them had been known to haunt Stargaard in his darker moods.

In the intervening years he had been sidetracked from writing the second book by interests in other quarters. He had received money to write a screenplay from his book and had spent two years on the film, one of them searching for locations in England, where it was supposed to be cheaper to produce even though his book had been set in an unnamed American city that probably most resembled Minneapolis. The film never came close to being made, and to this day Stargaard suspected the producer of using its budget for the sole reason of bilking the film company of the funds he needed to keep himself and his mistress living in a grand style abroad. Stargaard was supported by two grants; he had written journalism; he had moved around the country, teaching writing at colleges when he had to, driving in one of a series of battered Volkswagens from

Montana to Massachusetts to Arkansas; he had given of himself
to the peace movement, to the rights of artists behind the
Iron Curtain and to any number of political and environmental
causes, and had worked for liberal candidates who always lost;
he had spent a year living cheaply in Europe on an advance
for a second novel he was attempting to write only now. The
years had slipped by. He had lived without house or family
or occupation; he had lived with girlfriends and in other people's houses and apartments when they were out of the country,
"house-sitting" for low rent, or no rent at all. Usually he had
managed to fall in with a woman who became his lover.

Lately he found himself confronting the cameo of himself
in the Orlovskys' mirror. He looked detached, confounded, a
trifle blank. He also looked mad, legitimately mad, and this
frightened him. In his youth, he would have gloried in a look
like that. But these days he didn't want to look like a madman.
He wanted to look sane. Well fed. Happy. It occurred to him
that he no longer carried within him an image of himself. Certainly the youthful face in the oval frame was long gone. He
couldn't see himself as wanting to become someone or something anymore. Maybe he had reached the stage where at best
he worked for the sake of working, and at worst, to pass the
time. I should have been a gardener, he told himself. Or a
woodsman. Maybe a policeman. But a shepherd would have
been best of all.

He suspected he no longer daydreamed. At least those
dreams in which he found himself aggrandized and rewarded.
He couldn't remember when he had last caught himself at
it, and he felt saddened by the loss. He certainly didn't feel
privileged, lucky, special, heroic. Erotic and romantic fantasies
for a man as lonely as himself were not uncommon, though.
He thought of Alexander.

She had recommended the bean supper given Saturday night
in the town hall of her country town as a good opportunity

for him to see some local color. She would definitely be there, she went to all of them. He said he just might be there, too.

But she wasn't there. Not when he arrived, which couldn't have been more than fifteen minutes after the doors had opened, nor anytime thereafter. He was put out by her absence. After all, she had said she would come. When he was certain she was not at any of the tables, he sat outside in the summer twilight on the grass beneath an old elm and stared off at the mountains while keeping an eye on the locals and tourists who passed in and out of the screen door. Men in suspenders and straw hats—he hadn't seen that in years. When they took in the blackboard with "Bean Supper Tonight" chalked across it, which had been set out beside the road to draw the tourists, he entered, hoping she would come while he was inside. The crowd had thinned out and he had his choice of places at any of the long harvest tables. The meal was sponsored by a men's club, and friendly older men who were bald, bowlegged, lame, big-nosed, set up the tables and cleared away the dirty dishes. There were several kinds of baked beans and potato salad, but the ham had run out and bologna was made to do.

He was almost finished with his meal when a family sat down at the table across the way, a man and woman with two small children, a boy and girl. He recognized the man as Keville. What was more, Keville recognized him, and was the first to say hello. He introduced him to Sarah as a writer and friend of the Orlovskys, but had to ask his name. At first sight Stargaard was not that impressed with the woman. Maybe it would have been different if she sat across from him alone.

Immediately one of the waiters sat down next to her husband, while another came over to stand between the two, and the three of them talked of road agents, subdivisions, town warrants. Stargaard and Sarah talked about writing. She had assumed, for some reason, that he was a mystery writer. Maybe she thought all writers were mystery writers. She had been eager to share with him a plot she had dreamed up for a who-dunit. The setting, a small New England village, and the open-ing scene, a bean supper—not unlike this bean supper—with nearly everyone in the village present. Someone cries out, rises, clutches his or her throat and keels over backward. Dead. A poisoned pot of beans. Everyone in the village a potential vic-tim, everyone a suspect. The whole village gripped with fear: who was next?

"A poisoned bean pot." He laughed. "The ultimate New Eng-land whodunit!" He added a few touches of his own. "How about a tyrannical selectman as the victim, somebody every-body hates and fears. And let's have the church organist make the suspected pot—but the minister's wife herself warmed them on the stove at her house—"

"But the sexton set them on the table," she said.

"And the ex-selectman who had lost his seat to the victim was in charge of the meal!"

"And the beans themselves were bought at Caleb's store!"

They both laughed over this.

"I think women write the best mysteries, don't you?" she said. "English mysteries anyway."

"But that's because English mysteries are intellectual puz-zles, and women are more cerebral than men."

"But they're more than puzzles," she said. "They have a sense of evil to them."

"And women," he retorted, "have a better sense of that, too. I mean, in a world where everyone is a suspect, you have to think the worst of people, don't you? Now the best American mystery writers are men."

"Meaning that they're not cerebral and evil but sensual and good?"

"No, sensual and sentimental. And violent."

"And women aren't violent?"

"Well, you get poisoned in an English mystery. You don't get beat up."

He lingered over his coffee, which a waiter kept refilling from a big stainless-steel pitcher; he even ate a piece of squash pie.

At first he believed that Cullenbine was wrong, Sarah wasn't the equal of an Alexander. Later, at home, when he found her impression staying with him far into the night, he was willing to concede the wisdom of his mentor. For the life of him he couldn't see why, though. She provoked and puzzled him; he couldn't find a name for her attraction, nor for her strength. He even seemed to focus on a weakness, her eyes, which were blue and moist but weak-looking and squinting, as though she needed glasses, or wore troublesome contact lenses.

He had enjoyed her company and felt certain that if he knew her better he would like her more than anyone he had met since coming here. He recalled what Cullenbine had said about her, although he couldn't see how his definition fit her, personality or physique. With what Stargaard could best describe as affectionate condescension, Cullenbine had said, "Our *grande dame,* you know."

5   *The Grande Dame*

SARAH Keville was a freckled blonde who in summer tanned herself to the point of peeling and appeared in public with a smear of grease or a flesh-colored Band-Aid on her sunburned nose. "My only ambition in life," she would sometimes confess to a group of her friends, "is to become a *grande dame* before I'm dead." She might have said it, a cigarette and drink in hand, wearing bell bottoms, open blouse and Swedish wooden shoes. Her friends thought it an odd ambition for any woman, much less Sarah, who was only thirty-six. Not that they thought she was ever doing more than making conversation, or striking a pose.

To most of the women Sarah knew, a *grande dame* was more an intellectual than a social creature, and the consensus among them was that it would be nice to be a *grande dame* when the time came, but so much nicer not to be old too soon, or even old at all—and here death might be mentioned as an attractive alternative, possibly a godsend—and what one did in the years of one's relative youth was far more pleasurable and meaningful than what one did as a *grande dame,* and certainly one did not save oneself up, as it were, to become one, and even if one did aspire in that direction, it was an ambition more reasonably confessed to at the age of sixty. It seemed to these women that a *grande dame* was the best of a bad end.

"Do say you don't mean it, Sarah," Adele Fox said. "Because I don't see where there's room for such a woman anymore. Not in a world like ours. I'm in sympathy with your ambition. I find it admirable, but I must tell you, I feel so sorry for you, too."

Dr. Milton Cullenbine overheard them talking. *"Grandes dames* and whores," he said. "Gone. All gone now." This was a reference to an earlier conversation on the increasing promiscuity of modern coeds, which, Professor Renzi had claimed, would put the world's oldest profession out of business. The wives of the professors present had joined in, expressing their mock fears that their husbands might run off with one of these coeds, although there was usually a fresh enough example of a professor having done just that to legitimize their fears. At the door Cullenbine had taken Sarah by the shoulders. "Don't wait to be one of those old *grandes dames,*" he said. "It would be such a waste." He seemed to look her over. He was more than a little drunk.

Sarah herself did not take her ambition seriously. Her occasional confession of it at parties was only a reminder of her school days at a private women's college on Cape Ann, when she had, for a brief period one semester, dressed and acted out the role. It had been an unconscious piece of girlish theater, designed to make herself popular or, at the very least, known. Instead of coffee she drank only smoky Lapsang souchong tea, brewed on a hot plate, which made her room smell like a fisherman's tar-paper shack heated by a kerosene stove in rainy weather. Instead of beer she drank only martinis, and then with a slice of cucumber instead of lemon twist or olive. She smoked a cheap off-brand of cigarettes (with a picture of someone like a Turkish sultana on the package) sold only at one shop in town, wore make-up better suited for the stage and sometimes an outfit that made her resemble a small girl decked out in the old hats and capes she had discovered in her grandmother's attic. She would cut classes to play bridge, staying at it into the late hours of night, and always with that off-brand of cigarette in her mouth and with either a cup of that smoky tea or that martini with cucumber at her right hand, Debussy or Ravel playing on the phonograph in the background. Some of her favorite remarks, imitated by the other girls, were "Well-finessed!" and "Bravely bid!" To the girls' stories of staying out after hours on dates she was sure to have something matronly to say. Once she said, "Naughty girls, so wicked of you to do those dreadful things, but simply horrid of you to tell." The remark was repeated throughout the dorm, the girls imitating her *grande dame* voice. With the girls she earned the reputation of being something of a character. Some even called her "our Aunt Sarah." But it was not a role Sarah ever played outside the dorm. She never played it in the presence of men.

Since she was certain no one had ever really taken her ambition seriously—at least no more so than she did herself—she saw no reason to keep it a secret. Even so, she was careful to present it as a joke. She would make herself appear youthful and flirtatious, as though inviting not only disbelief but contradiction. Sometimes she would take Toby into her confidence, saying as they dressed to go out to dinner, "Will you love me when I'm a *grande dame?*"

"But you're a grand dame now," he would answer, giving the words an English pronunciation, or the mock-French pronunciation one sometimes gives the word "Garbage."

He put it to her this way once: "You'd have to have it all backwards not to want to stay young. Everybody knows you don't get any prizes for growing old. Not my Delft doll, though. Not my delphinium girl." (For he sometimes called her that because her eyes were the classic delphinium blue and he prized delphiniums above all other flowers.) "She can't wait until she has a dowager's hump and a whiskey voice. How come you don't know that when you're eighty you're supposed to look forty and make out like twenty-five? Who do you think discovered America? Columbus?"

"Erik the Red?" she said. "Some Irish monks? Phoenicians? Iberians? Indians? Who then?"

"Ponce de León. He found America when he found the Fountain of Youth—I think it was somewhere around Fort Lauderdale. He was the first American—metaphorically speaking, of course. What he found, we're all supposed to be looking for."

Before they were married he said, "You know, Sarah, life to you is long. To me it's short. That's the difference between us."

And it was true. Back then, with husband, house and children in the offing, she had no burning ambition, not even on their account. Nor did she have one now. She was preoccupied with nothing; she did not even have what could be called a hobby. She was interested in the restoration of old Colonial homes, one of which she lived in, and the refinishing of antique furniture, which she sometimes bought at auctions and stored in the barn. She championed the preservation of the landscape and the wilderness. But at this stage she was content to read about these subjects in illustrated books. She also wanted to take up the piano again, and she thought she would like to study ballet. But she didn't feel she was ready yet for either. It wasn't that she used the tender ages of her two children as an excuse, or that she blamed them for these delays. She simply believed she could afford to wait.

She was well read, and if she had a preference for anything, it was probably to read. Sometimes she pretended she was ill or cold so she could stay in her bed for the better portion of the day and read, snug beneath the covers. She associated books with privacy and blankets. She did entertain a vague desire to write a mystery, a whodunit more in the English manner than in the American, although she thought her setting might be Nantucket or Manchester-by-the-sea. But she could put off the thinking about it; she was a long way from any writing.

It was not easy to see how a desire to be a *grande dame,* half-hearted though it was, had come to her by the example of her mother, who had been friendly but reclusive, content to stay at home and keep up the house and grounds. As far as Sarah knew, her mother had never considered a career or a profession, nor had she ever confessed to any daydream or ambition other than to buy a house in the Bahamas. It was difficult to say what she might have done in her older years, since she had died comparatively young. Nor was her background "high society" or even, for certain, "old family." She had led a privileged life in the households of a pair of husbands, and was probably one of those women who had married well by reason of her looks, which were striking to the point of seeming grand, and apparently had been content to leave the evolution of her life at that.

Sarah's mother's family was said to be of old Yankee stock, with Maine sea captains and Massachusetts mill owners in the lineage, and her mother had mentioned an indirect ancestor who had been Rhode Island's governor and another who had been a member of its supreme court. But Sarah could remember as a child hearing her Great-Aunt Flora tell a story she claimed to have firsthand from some long-dead ancestor, of an impoverished emigration from England as late as the mid-nineteenth century, and a passage in steerage in a ship that had become becalmed off the coast of Newfoundland, where the passengers perished from hunger and disease. And Sarah's Aunt Olive used to have great fun with her anti-Catholic and haughty cousins by hinting that the family had the blue-green potato fields of County Kerry in its blood along with what she chose to call "the romance of bogs."

If Sarah's willingness to sit back and contemplate a late beginning to her life was in any way genetic, it was probably her father's bequest. He had been born in Florida, where he spent his early years, and maybe the slowness and patience of the Southerner that had been in his veins was equally in hers, although it was unclear whether either of his own parents was Southern born. More importantly, her father had put things off. Compared to most men, he had married late, had become a father late, and then only once, but had retired early. A lawyer with a large Boston practice, he had without warning given up family and profession and run off to Italy, where he spent the rest of his life alone in a small Tuscan village, painting local scenes. Sarah's mother had been quick to marry another lawyer, by whom she had two sons.

Sarah had often wondered if her father had been influenced by the example of his own grandfather, a nineteenth-century painter of ponderous and stolid New England landscapes who gave up a studio in Providence to spend the last twenty years of his life in Algeria, painting Arab oases and market scenes. Sarah had seen two of his earlier paintings, which he had done in Florida, of palm trees, shacks, swamps and black women with bundles on their heads. An associate of the National Academy of Design, he had signed them George Washington Smith, ANA. Like so many of the painters of his era, he had lived into his eighties.

Sarah's father, unfortunately, had died within a few years of his retreat to Tuscany. Sarah had never seen any of his paintings (probably because he never did any until he went to Italy), although her mother said he would sketch trees and animals for Sarah on legal pads when she was small. Sarah remembered him as being quiet but forceful. Her mother said he was stubborn. He must have been secretive; he had certainly led a secret inner life. No one, apparently, neither friend nor family, had foreseen his desire to paint, much less suspected him of latent bohemianism and wanderlust. Sarah had seen a photo of him at his little medieval house in Italy. He was wearing sandals, an immense straw hat and a tattered pair of shorts, and had posed bare-chested before a backdrop of cypress and between two potted lemon trees. He was bearded and so thin and tan he reminded her of an ancient beachcomber or desert wanderer, his skin hanging loose and wrinkled on his bones. He had looked eccentric and timid and "not all there." In both hands he was holding, absent-mindedly, the blossom of a sunflower. She wanted to picture him as someone who worshiped sun and wine and the smell of oil paints. But was he really an artist? she wondered. Or only a reclusive dilettante who used painting to justify the irresponsibility of making a change in his life? Or worse yet, as some of her mother's relatives had maintained, no more than a harmless and bewildered lunatic who was more to be pitied than condemned? Often she told herself that she, too, would blossom late in life, at which time she would at last reveal the nature of her true and secret self; and that she, too, possessed, as her father had, an unpredictable and daring spirit that would express itself in art.

6   *The Land Baron*

TOBY was a self-appointed real estate developer and land speculator. He hunted with Parker Fox and John Angle, invested in apartment buildings with Dr. Kubilius and had sold Marco and Alexander their land and the Orlovskys their house. That he was liked both by this crowd, who were, for the most part, conservation minded and college educated, and by his real estate companions, who were development minded and self-made, was a measure of his natural power to make himself agreeable. He gave advice and help to anyone who even seemed to ask for it, and over beers he would recount his own troubles with a bewilderment and candor that would make his listeners want to hug him. If he did well in life it would be due, in good measure, to the good will of others, since almost everyone who met him wanted to help him and be counted as his friend. If he failed he could probably blame himself. He was just too easily buoyed up and overpowered by the magic of his salesmanship, the product of which was often nothing more than his own unlimited reserve of optimism, which he could bring to bear, most successfully, upon himself. Stargaard had once caught Cullenbine in a rare moment when he was neither mean nor drugged and asked him what he thought of Toby. "Golden boy and loser all in one," was all he said.

Toby was the son of a wealthy Massachusetts contractor, who had encouraged him to ride and sail although he himself did neither. Toby, however, was too independent to heed his father and too good an athlete to be interested in any sport in which the nonathlete could excel. Instead he had played pickup Rugby and varsity lacrosse, apparently for the pure animal love of roughhouse he found in those sports. His father had sent him to prep school and to Dartmouth College, after which he had envisioned a career for his son in government service at a high level, ideally in the diplomatic corps. Failing that, he would have preferred to see him in the world of finance, just so long as it was high finance. He was prepared, however, to lower his ambitions and take Toby into his own business if he had to, which he did, starting him at a position near the top.

Sarah supposed she had assumed Toby would continue to work with his father, an arrangement that had allowed them to live comfortably from the first, and that he would someday inherit the company, which they then might sell. The attraction of Toby was that he already had a place in the world, and Sarah had not foreseen any risk or threat of change in the life she would have with him. On the contrary, if she had foreseen anything, it must have been herself luxuriating in a surfeit of unconscious time.

They had married when Sarah was twenty-two, and had lived the careless lives of newlyweds for five years in Manchester-by-the-sea, on Cape Ann, before Jessie, their first child, was born. They had set up house, rent-free, in a stone gate lodge with leaded windows on the grounds of an old estate, the land of which was now owned by Toby's father, the big house having long ago burned down. The winters must have all been short-lived or mild back then, because she could only remember summer, and an idyll of sailing, swimming, tanning, horseback riding against a backdrop of sea and flowers, of limes and lobsters and mussels eaten raw on the half shell on the beach with bottles of white wine buried upright in the sand at the edge of the tide. She remembered herself in Bermuda shorts and blond ponytail on a woman's bicycle with a wicker basket on the handlebars, and the Colonial atmosphere and architecture of the town as being almost more West Indian than New England. On warm Friday evenings one of their school friends, or her two stepbrothers, would take the electric train up from Boston to spend the weekend, and she would meet them at the little train station in the Jaguar Toby had owned back then. In those days Sarah's stepfather had called Toby "Apollo." His golden hair had lain straight on the top of his head but had curled around his ears, while his eyebrows appeared to be dusted with a fine white sand, and he had worn red bathing trunks with a white T-shirt top that had made him look like a lifeguard. He would take his kayak to the beach and, paddling furiously while the boat teeter-tottered, try to drive it over the white water of the incoming waves.

But Toby had not cared much for comfort and security. He didn't like working for his father; he wanted to make a million dollars of his own, and had at first planned on being a millionaire before the age of thirty, although reluctantly he had upped that figure to thirty-nine. He had struck out for New Hampshire, where they had lived for so long that Sarah had lost touch with almost all of her old Massachusetts friends.

Originally Toby had come north to get in on the land boom. He was busy purchasing large tracts of woodland in the mountains and in making preparations to construct condominiums on Lake Winnipesaukee. Sarah sometimes referred to him, jokingly, as "the land baron." He could be enraptured at the prospect of putting up a complex of prefabricated houses overnight, but his real love, right now, was land. "The time is right," he kept assuring Sarah, as though she worried about his investments and gambles, as though she cared. "The boom is coming. It has to, with the population explosion, and with the people screaming to escape the rotting cities, it figures they have to go somewhere." When he talked about land, and especially when he looked at land, it seemed to Sarah that he ate the land, and grew large upon it.

He spent many happy hours in his car alone, driving up and down mountain roads, a map open on the seat beside him, searching for parcels of land. He would put on a white hard hat when he visited a construction site and sometimes when he only went to look at land and there was no danger of something falling on his head. To Sarah, the hat said to the tall trees he stood among, I can fell you, I can bulldoze you away.

He also liked to talk business on the telephone, which he did with an ease and authority that continued to amaze Sarah, who did not like to talk on it at all. He averaged several hours a day conferring with bankers, brokers, buyers, sellers. He could spend half the night poring over topographical maps, blueprints, sewage plans, and in drafting subdivision proposals. Every morning he sent out and received a stack of mail. His favorite complaint was that there were not enough hours in the day to let him do what needed to be done. But to Sarah it was not so much work that he did as keeping busy. She supposed she was the sort who could plant a tree that would not bear fruit for a hundred years. But Toby had never been able to bring himself to buy any tree or bush that would not bear the first year. They had owned their house for seven years and had yet to plant their orchard.

He showed the same impatience when they went hiking in the White Mountains, Sarah's favorite recreation since those times when, as a young girl, she went with her brothers and their friends. Her pleasure was not so much in climbing as in lingering above the tree line in the wind and rocky desolation of the summit, and in taking excursions down side trails to springs and waterfalls. But Toby insisted on their taking the shortest route possible, turning the hike up and down into a forced march and finding his only pleasure in his merciless climb to the top. There, with his hands on his hips, he would confront the green wilderness below him as though it were a vanquished army prostrating itself at his feet, and say to anyone at hand, "Who says we're overpopulated? Who says we're overdeveloped? Do you see a house anywhere?" How hungry it made him. to see at one time all that wooded land. He would bite into the apples and celery stalks they brought along as though into the life stuff of the world.

If Sarah could still show, on occasion, a light-hearted interest in old age, Toby, she was convinced, had a serious love affair with youth. At the close of many of the parties they attended he could be found in the company of the other men, engaging in some sort of competition that, to Sarah, did not always seem appropriate to their years. A recent evening at the Orlovskys' had ended with Indian wrestling in the kitchen. Allan Orlovsky pulled a thigh muscle and went limping off on his wife's arm, while some friend of Parker Fox cut his knuckles on the kitchen table. A half-drunken Toby had won his share of matches, and she had watched him not only draw John Angle across the imaginary line on the linoleum but, in his enthusiasm, bounce him off the refrigerator and then the doorjamb as he pushed him all the way into the living room. On the way home in the car he confessed what he called the secret sorrow of his life. Did she know that he had dreamed of becoming a professional athlete since he was the smallest tyke? She said she was surprised he had ever wanted anything that wasn't land or money. "I've had this dream since I was little," he said. "And you know what's so pathetic about my having it? I was just about a strike-out king when it came to baseball. Oh, sure, I always told myself I'd hit the ball out of the park—all I had to do was hit it. I never even went out for the high school football team, never played basketball except in driveways and alleys, never played hockey—at least with skates."

She wanted to interrupt, saying, Oh, come off it, you're over-dramatizing. She knew very well he had been a better athlete than that.

"And then it came to me all of a sudden," he said. "I'm older than any player on the Red Sox roster. Not only that, but there can't be more than a handful of players left in both big leagues that are older than I am right now. In a few years I'll probably be older than any player in the history of big-league ball."

She must have smiled at the absurdity of this confession, because he cut her off before she had a chance to speak, saying, "And calling it silly and immature won't make it go away in the morning. You have your fantasies, your little daydreams, I don't ask you what they are. But so do I, and believe me, they're nothing to joke about." He went on to insist he had it worse than she did. Her ambition to make a great lady of herself, or a *grande dame,* as she chose to call it, was still possible because it was in the future, and couldn't happen until she was older. His secret ambition, however, had already passed him by. She said she didn't want to hear about it. He said that was because she could not understand the depth of his feelings in this matter, that maybe only another man could.

She was tempted to reply that maybe only another woman could understand her feelings since, for so many of them, their ambitions by necessity had to be "put off." But she would have used this argument unfairly since it applied only incidentally to herself. She preferred to let the matter drop. She was embarrassed and a little angry that he would take her ambition so seriously. It was the first time that he had done so, and it was wrong of him to take hers as seriously as he took his own. You could not equate the two at all.

At the parties she had observed the men surrender to the youthful fashions of the times. Gradually their hair became longer and shaggier and their sideburns heavier until, after Christmas or summer vacation, they would appear with drooping mustaches that made them resemble Texas cowhands of the last century. Then one night, as though touched by a magic wand, they would appear in striped bell bottom trousers, shoes with heels like flamenco dancers', a pink shirt, the wide decorated tie, a belted jacket with immense lapels, gray-haired forty-year-old imitations of the students many of them taught. Not Toby, though. He grew fatter instead of thinner, kept his hair, which refused to gray, shorter than was presently the style, and continued to dress as he had in college, which was in seersuckers, blazers, corduroys, chinos and narrow striped ties, an imitation of the professors he had studied under then. She had hoped that in these rapid-changing times this was his way of insisting on stability and tradition, proving that in at least this one instance he could not be tempted by the call of youth. But one evening as they sang folk songs at a party, Adele Fox pointed out the large woman sitting on the floor beside John Angle, who was playing the guitar, so close to him it appeared they were a duet in which the others merely joined. She was dressed like a college coed of the 1950s, in knee socks, baggy sweater and wool tartan fastened by an enormous safety pin. Adele whispered that the woman was in her mid-fifties and a grandmother several times over. Later, when the woman stood up, Sarah saw that legs, breasts, buttocks, were all enormous. So was her face, which was lion-sized, the cosmetics on her sagging features looking less like shadows than like lumps and bruises. She thought the woman's husband could have been a grandfather; he was dressed in a conservative "old man's" suit. She had understood Toby then. He wanted to stay young, but not by trying to keep pace with the present.

His plan was to stay behind in the happy youth of his own past.

It explained his taste in reading, too. If Sarah preferred Elizabeth Bowen, Katherine Mansfield and the mysteries of Dorothy Sayers and Margery Allingham, she also made certain she read the best seller of the season if it was written by a respected author. But the only books on Toby's shelves were those he had owned in college, textbooks mainly. His favorite writers were still Wolfe, Hemingway, Fitzgerald, O'Hara. Apparently he had reached not only his sartorial but his intellectual pinnacle during his freshman college year.

At a late hour when the men at a party would be huddled in the kitchen, he was certain to deliver his oft-repeated remark, his voice aquiver with regret. "Oh, to be sixteen again!" he would say. "If only we knew now what we knew then!"

7 *Still Lives*

IT used to be that Sarah looked forward to the dinner parties given by her group of friends. She could be counted upon to bring a special dish, and if she was to have the dinner in her own home, she would spend a happy day cooking and cleaning in preparation. But lately she had come to take them too much for granted, and had gone so far as to beg out of a few upon occasion. Maybe it was too much of the same food, the same faces, the same old conversations.

But for Stargaard these parties were all so new and different.

He was surrounded by new friends; he had never been to so many parties! They were given by turns and seemed to come in bunches, with the people present taking so obvious a pleasure in each other's company that they were like the far-flung settlers of some frontier outpost where house parties were the only means of companionship and fun.

They were certainly informal enough, a couple arriving with lift tickets pinned to their skiing parkas, or the men in flannel shirts or camouflage jackets and setting their fly rods or shotguns just inside the door, and the women in hiking boots and long Finnish dresses. On arrival they made sure to greet each other with hugs and kisses, a demonstration of affection they did not appear to come by naturally, and therefore practiced self-consciously. Or so Stargaard thought as he dutifully returned a peck or squeeze. He guessed that their parents, like his own, had shown their children little physical affection. Only the Angles seemed to throw themselves effortlessly into the hugs and rubs of such a welcoming.

There would follow an evening of gourmandizing and conversation, and afterward of singing to guitars and banjos or playing electric football or table soccer on the floor, or the parlor games of fictionary and charades.

Stargaard had found himself the guest in dining rooms lit by candlelight and open fires, in the company of primitive oil paintings and fresh flowers; and in bright kitchens with walls of Delft frying pans, copper fish molds, heavy French and Belgian cookware and Swedish breadboards, and ceilings hung with strings of garlic and drying apples and mushrooms and upside down bouquets of drying herbs, and shelves that read like a travelogue of international cuisines. At the Kevilles' he had been served an eye of the round from a side of a beef "critter" they had purchased from a local farmer; at the Foxes' a poached salmon that Parker caught in Newfoundland; and at the Kubiliuses', pheasant that had been shot and given to them by a neighbor. For first courses he had dined on the following homemade soups: sorrel, puréed oyster mushroom and one made entirely from yellow tomatoes. The cooking, he noticed, was most often French—Cordon Bleu or the country cooking of Gascony. As a professor recently returned from a sabbatical in France had said, the best French cooking to be found nowadays was in the New England homes of professional men, prepared by their wives.

But it was the large potluck buffets, "like a smorgasbord out of the heroic past," as Renzi called them, that impressed Stargaard the most. They had impressed Sarah, too. She would come to one bearing a platter of the grape leaves she had picked and preserved herself and stuffed with pilaf and a touch of mint, a favorite of Renzi, who would himself bring a moussaka of sorts; and Colleen Orlovsky might appear with a platter of deviled eggs made with a dash of curry and chopped lovage; and Adele Fox with her specialty of fried chicken wings rolled in coconut that Toby favored so; and Parker Fox with a platter of smelts he had caught with a dip net and fried in batter and then chilled in a basil vinegar with white peppercorns and onions, sliced thin; and the Angles were sure to bring a gumbo, perhaps the one made with oysters and shrimps and dosed with Tabasco, and for sure another guacamole, along with the twin bowls heaped with fresh grapes, red and green, for the Angles were devotees of the vine; Cullenbine, whose wife disliked to cook, could be counted on for a tray of cheese— Swiss Emmenthal, native blue, double Gloucester and a gigantic wedge of Brie; Dr. Kubilius would contribute half a dozen warm loaves of the French bread he baked himself and seasoned with his own home-grown herbs, while Pokey would bring not only the Swedish meatballs in a chafing dish, but a great wheel of tart, apple or pear, glazed with apricot; and Alexander a Danish baked raspberry and apple compote, and Sarah a deep dish of rhubarb pie, with a thick crust; and the hosts, whoever they were, would likely supplement the board by opening tins of fish and shellfish from Scandinavia and Japan, and perhaps some pâté from France. These dishes would then be laid out on dining room and living room tables and kitchen counters or, if the weather was warm, on old oak tables covered with tablecloths and set out beneath a shade tree. They would be eaten with Scandinavian stainless-steel silverware from white Finnish china or Mexican earthenware, and washed down with bottles of Dutch and Norwegian beer, the necks of which were wrapped in tinfoil, and strong German or Alsatian spirits distilled from raspberries or pears, and Polish vodka flavored with buffalo grass. For wine they tended to drink jug wine, including retsina, although lately a group of them, led by Orlovsky, had championed good wines, and California wines at that, especially the reds.

In protest, Toby had quoted Hemingway: "The best wine is *vin ordinaire.*"

"Nonsense," Orlovsky countered. "It's only the best because the time of your life when you drank it was the best."

Toby said, "I think that's what he had in mind."

"Besides, you had to drink it then," Orlovsky said. "You couldn't afford any better. And even if you could, you wouldn't have been able to tell the difference between an Algerian and a Châteauneuf-du-Pape."

"Remember the cheap Yugoslavian and Chilean Rieslings we used to drink in the old days?" Parker Fox said. "The Yugoslavian came in a tall green bottle and the Chilean in a small green flask, and you could buy them for seventy-nine cents each."

"And the Moselle was ninety-nine cents a bottle," Orlovsky said. "Zeller Schwarze Katz. Kröver Nachtarsch."

"I remember that," Parker said. "Wasn't that the one with the label of the old wine *Meister* in his wine cellar spanking the bare ass of the small boy with his pants down?"

"You can't afford the Moselle today," Orlovsky said. "At least I can't. Not even in Germany."

"Two marks to the dollar soon," Parker said. "The first time I was over there the exchange was nearly five."

It had struck Stargaard that to an outsider, these people might be taken at first glance for a wealthy class of epicurean aristocrats. But most of them, he had discovered, were not even from the East originally, and were children of mechanics, farmers, factory workers, small-town businessmen, although a few of the women came from families that were established and well off. As far as he could tell, all the men had married "up." That they were conscious of where they came from and what they had acquired in taste and privilege he knew from their conversations, but he doubted if they quite saw the irony in their singing of sentimental folk songs that celebrated the lives of coal miners, railroad brakemen, dirt farmers, impressed sailors, slaves. They had been raised on Swiss steak, pork and pot roasts, potatoes in half a dozen different forms and the seasoning of salt and pepper. They had found themselves at a young age in Europe, soldiering, studying, traveling, living cheap, and there they had acquired European tastes and appetites along with a sense of savoir-faire and privilege. At home they had settled into positions and professions that were reasonably secure and paid well while the goods of the world were delivered up at bargain prices to their doorstep. They went almost exclusively to European movies, drank European wine and beer, drove European cars, ate European meals.

Only lately had they begun to appreciate the expense and scarcity of things, not only imported goods but many of their own. At the same time they had discovered that the world itself was becoming depleted and polluted, and were apprehensive that life would not continue in the old way. The conversations around the table, usually light-hearted, could take an ominous turn.

Kubilius liked to say such things as "Our grandchildren won't eat lobsters or haddock. Probably not even clams."

"They won't eat meat at all," Adele Fox corrected. "Not when it takes ten pounds of grain to make one of meat, and with half the world starving."

"They'll probably get their protein from plankton in some form," Parker said.

"Do that and you'll unbalance the food chain," Adele protested. "What will the little fish eat that are eaten by the bigger fish?"

"Already I find myself telling my children, 'Better give this a try,'" Kubilius said. "'You may never get another chance if you wait until you're grown up.' And their kids will see a word or picture in a book and ask them, 'What's that?' 'That's a steak,' they'll say. 'It's something you eat. And those are spare ribs, and that's a kidney chop.'"

"Like the Orientals, we'll eat only soybeans and rice," Adele Fox said. "For a treat we'll throw a few roots and greens into the pot."

Alexander, inadvertently perhaps, had caught this new mood in a painting she had done from memory of one of the more lavish parties. The vision owed less to the influence of Flemish still lifes than to German Expressionism. The dishes were done in silver and looked, strangely, like bones, while the foods on them were messes of green and red, and the tablecloth they were heaped on looked like yellowed silk that had gotten dirty. Across from the table and surrounded by a sea of blackness waited a fleshy but faceless crowd that looked at once sinister and formal, the men appearing to be dressed in ties and tails, and the women in outmoded velvet gowns. If the table said to the viewer: plunder and carrion, the people said: greed, cigar smoke, fat fingers, apprehension. The blurred food and people were not helped by the heavy varnish, which made the scene too glossy for much to be seen of it in any light.

For years the evenings together had known only the most minor interruptions and distractions. There was always the chance that the radio Kubilius wore on his belt would beep and that he would have to leave for the hospital to assist in an emergency operation on someone just injured in an auto crash. "Off to put someone else to sleep," Cullenbine would say then. There had been a pair of quarrels between the Cullenbines, and once sharp words between the Angles, and someone remembered a fight between the Orlovskys, of all people, and their leaving early in a huff. No one could remember when a baby-sitter had called.

But one night the previous summer at the Angles', an incident that unsettled everyone occurred. They were playing a happy but violent and half-drunken game of croquet into the twilight hours, whooping and cackling as they knocked each other's balls into the brambles that grew beyond the grass, when a haze that at first went unnoticed, it mingled so completely with the dusk, drifted across the lawn.

A woman said, "What is that awful smell?"

"Strange smell, strange twilight," said Parker Fox. "I don't know if I can see the wicket. Janet, I guess I'll have to head for your ball instead."

"The air's yellow," the woman said. "Don't tell me—that's no sunset."

"I don't know what else it is. There's a sunset out there somewhere."

For the next few minutes there was only the sound of wooden mallet heads being socked against solid wooden balls.

"Good God, isn't anyone going to tell me what is that smell?"

"Must be someone burning something."

"Probably just a brush fire someone started with gasoline and rubber tires."

"More like rubber tires and dead dogs. No wood smells like that."

"Could be a mink farm on fire. Maybe a tannery."

Parker Fox put his foot on his own ball as he prepared to send Janet Angle's ball into the "boonies," and then hit himself in the instep instead. "Can't see a thing!" he complained, hopping.

"Maybe it's the town dump."

"It can't be. They haven't had an open fire all year. Against the law now."

"It's the smog," Toby said.

"Can't be."

"Smells like smog to me," Toby said. "I just came through Portsmouth, and it was all along the coast. I thought it thinned out, though, a few miles east of here, but it must have spread inland just since then."

They had all read about the smog in the papers, heard about it nightly on the news. An immense belt of polluted and stagnant air that stretched along the eastern seaboard from Atlanta, Georgia, to Portland, Maine, it had combined with a big Bermuda high, and with no upper loft winds to disperse it or blow it out to sea, had been sitting there all week. In some cities the people had taken to wearing masks, and a public health officer had estimated that, directly and indirectly, it would be responsible for somewhere in the neighborhood of ten thousand deaths.

"It's the first time I've smelled smog in town," Archie Auden said, "and I've lived here for sixty years. I didn't believe I'd ever smell it, either. I've always had the theory that the local air currents kept our air about the cleanest in the state. That's because the mountains to the south there shunted the polluted air from Boston up the river valley to the west, and the rest of it went up the coast there to the east, leaving us alone here in between."

"Looks like you'll have to change your theory," Parker said.

"Stop burning at the dump after all these years and for

what?" Auden said. "So we can breathe New Jersey freeways, I guess."

"For three hundred years this area's been settled," Adele Fox said, "and this is the first time anyone ever smelled anything like smog."

"Four billion years of prehistory," Renzi corrected. "It's a bigger first than that."

"An historical moment," Orlovsky said.

Some woman said, "Oh, it makes your eyes water, it actually sears your lungs!"

"Indoors, anyone?" John Angle said.

But for a few moments longer they stood dumbly about the lawn, mallets idle in their hands, watching, as darkness settled, their simple world of blue sky, green forest, gray stones, white houses, become streaked and indistinct, like a badly varnished painting. The landscape seemed to be smoldering. Finally it disappeared.

8   Codeine and Campari

IT was the heavy summer weather more than anything, Sarah convinced herself, that had given her such dreadful moments in recent nights. A week of nights that were overcast, breezeless, the air humid to the point of becoming a suffocating fog that seemed to come through the screens. Under the cover of so dense a fog and darkness, wild animals encroached upon the yard as though they were disoriented, or had reverted to the old ancestral trails. All night she heard their footsteps on the grass. Without warning, large winged insects made loud rattling, clacking Oriental noises as they attacked the screens. Whippoorwills called suddenly at all hours from as close as the foundation. Raccoons grunted beneath the open windows and squatted on the window sills, looking in. They got into the cellar, where they overturned trash cans and dragged off sacks of garbage, the underside of which they ripped open like a belly, so that most of the insides spilled out in a trail of refuse leading to the woods. They came onto the porch and carried off the litter of Jessie's cat that had been quartered in a cardboard box and ate them alive in the foggy landscape of alders that lined the creek below. And Archie Auden told of his neighbor who in the morning had confronted the mystery of a pile of feathers and a pair of webbed feet on the outside of his locked duck house, which was walled with one-inch chicken wire, and a drake's head on the inside, and was forced to conclude, after much scratching of his head, that the raccoon had worked the fingers of his human-looking hand through the wire, grabbed a duck by its tail feathers and pulled it through that one-inch opening, eating it bit by bit as he pulled it through.

For the first time Sarah could remember, a toad got into the house and hopped around the living room; he was sand-covered, as though he had just risen from the earth, and too big to hold in one hand. He was followed by the usual chipmunk, which perched on a wicker basket or peeked out from beneath the sofa and scolded them with impunity; but this one acted deranged or diseased, and actually ran toward Jessie's cat, who quickly caught and slowly killed it. Almost nightly one or more bats flew in, a passing shadow more sensed than seen, and a spooky silent beat of wings followed by the outcry of "Bird inside the house!" Strange bird. One that did not crash against the windows or beat its wings against the panes but was jerked up and down in flight like a dark, fluttering kite on a string. "It's no bird, it's a bat!" This discovery followed by the mad chase with brooms and fish nets and the shutting of doors and the turning off of lights until, trapped in a small room, the creature, as though supernatural, simply disappeared.

Sarah lost track of how many nights running she woke up after midnight, unable to understand how Toby, uncovered and restless at her side, could stay asleep. The fog seemed to get into her eyes, her mouth, her whole system. Her flesh looked white and luminous in the dark, and felt clammy, cold but wet. She had a headache and indigestion. She had heartburn so bad it crushed her chest, and she had already eaten a roll of antacids and taken one of the codeines she usually reserved for cramps. Now she fetched a water glass of Campari, which she drank undiluted and warm, savoring the bitter taste like medicine. She lay down, pretending she was drugged, but was so overwhelmed with forebodings that she was afraid to sleep. And she didn't dare to move for fear of the harm it might provoke within. She had heard that such awful feelings could signal that a heart attack was imminent, or that somewhere inside you a cancer had begun its slow and secret growth.

At a recent gathering the women had stood around the buffet, eating off their plates in candlelight, and again spoken of the high incidence of cancer among younger women in the local towns. The area around the university seemed hardest hit, favoring Hodgkin's disease; whereas the Angles' country town was notorious for leukemia, with three recent cases along a single mile-long stretch of road; and the town next door to Sarah's for breast cancer and tumors. The disease, if you counted it in all its forms, had reached epidemic proportions, and the women spoke of it with the dread and resignation they would have used for Black Death and plague. It was as though they believed a skeleton on horseback and swinging a scythe had been set loose upon the earth. Or maybe some lizardlike demon like those seen in medieval woodcuts haunting the foot of a canopied bed. To each other, they recounted biopsies taken, ovaries and breasts removed, cobalt burns, the nausea of chemotherapy, the loss of hair. They exchanged theories for the causes: birth control pills, an overdose of roentgen rays, air pollution, impurities in drinking water, hormones in the feed of beef cattle and milk cows, preservatives in foods. Or a virus you were born with. And might possibly communicate. Adele Fox told the story of a woman—unnamed but herself a registered nurse—who had volunteered to drive a neighbor with Hodgkin's disease to the clinic for chemotherapy but, after explaining that her disease might be communicable, asked her if she wouldn't mind riding in the back seat.

They cornered Dr. Kubilius in the kitchen, where he was busy with a pair of clippers, trimming the stems of an herb bouquet. He came close to stating that any woman's death from cancer, unless she was very young, was an act of carelessness bordering on suicide. "With the methods they have for detecting cancer early in women," he said, "breast and cervix cancer especially, and with the success they have in curing it, there's not much excuse for a woman dying of it these days. All you have to do is take the tests. Most of your cancers can be cured in time." He turned to the men who had been listening. "But if you're a man, don't even bother with the checkups. Why waste the doctor's time? Most of your cancers can't be cured, even if they can detect them. About all you can hope for is grandparents who lived to a hundred and lots of luck." It was an example of the man's sardonic sense of mischief, for he must have known how this advice could only inflame the hypochondria and self-pity of his friends. As likely as not, he would finish up his warning by telling stories of patients who were dead two months after feeling well, or of men who had dropped dead of heart attacks as they were leaving a doctor's office where they had just been given a clean bill of health.

What if I should die? Sarah began to ask herself. From cancer, or something worse. What if it should be me? After all, it was happening to others all over the landscape, taking them by as much surprise as it would her. No doubt those women, too, had believed they were special cases, deserving to be overlooked, or made immune. Her case really was special, though. She had known from the earliest, with an instinct that was as powerful as simple faith, that she would live to an old age. She was too young and incomplete for such a fate as early death. She hadn't become anything, not even herself, not her real self, never mind anything else. She was a fetus—her death no better than an abortion! It would be stupid, cruel—it wouldn't make sense! No, something other than disease explained her apprehension in the night. Something that had less to do with the body than with the mind. She had problems. She had problems with herself and with her family, that was the simple explanation for her present state. She had to focus on these problems, discover what they were, face up to them, root them out!

Whatever the answer, she felt she was being made to admit that over the course and outcome of her life she no longer exercised control. And more: that perhaps she had never exercised that much control. What were her expectations—what was her notion of herself—before she married Toby and had the children? Surely they had been very different from the way her life had, in fact, turned out. But she was uncertain what that earlier image of her life had been. Once upon a time she had spun her girlish fantasies of the life that lay ahead of her, but the monotony of marriage and motherhood had pushed them too far back into her memory for her to recollect—or want to recollect. But think of it: there had been a time when all possibilities had been open to her! To think that she had not known that such an irretrievable moment had been there before her! And now to be carried onward, if not exactly against her will, then because of her failure to assert that will. How ignorant and slothful she had been! Life had swept her along to insignificance without her delivering one whimper of resistance! She knew it could have been so different, too. She couldn't say how or why exactly. But the awfulness was in knowing that because she had missed her chance, her life could never be other than what it had become. And yet, strange to say, until this series of sleepless nights, she hadn't known she was that dissatisfied, or unhappy.

Toby had read the snail-like pace and deferred ambitions of her life. "Life to you is long," he had said. "Right you are," she answered then. But now time no longer seemed to stretch ahead of her like a milky way of stars. It had become like a small farm that needed endless pondering and tending. She was no longer a child. She could no longer think like a child, she could no longer ignore time, could no longer take the future for granted. Hereafter she would have to reckon with the hours. She began to scold and inspire herself, and to flirt with the vague and fragmentary notions that filled her head. She would leave house, husband, children. Take a job in Boston or New York, sign up for courses in philosophy and psychology. She would understand things then. She might make something of herself then. Might find out who she was. But there was a great danger in attempting this. She had always been afraid that she would someday learn she did not have a good mind. She could almost admit she had designed her life so as to avoid the risk of so crushing a discovery. Perhaps the time had come for her to find the courage to test herself and manifest the truth, no matter what it was.

But these resolutions gave way so easily to that daydream in which she would see herself as a great lady, wearing ankle-length dresses, slacks, shawls, a big floppy hat, and in her colors of purples, dark greens, black. She was adorned with strings of pearls and heavy medieval-looking jewelry. At times she used a cane, a walking stick. Her hair, which had always been long and a source of compliments and which she had always wanted to cut, was now short and almost mannish. She began to resemble a picture she had seen once of Isak Dinesen. She would spend her summers in a large Victorian cottage on Nantucket or at Seal Harbor; it would have numerous gables, blackened shingles, diamond sashes. Inside there would be white wicker furniture, blood-red Orientals, marble mantels. She and her houseguests would dine on freshly dug clams, freshly caught lobsters. On rainy days she would hold court in her brick town house in Back Bay or on Beacon Hill. She would curl up in a rug beside the narrow hearth and the fire of white birch logs; she would reread Jane Austen, or write letters at her club-footed desk, erudite and entertaining letters. She would have Orientals on Orientals; she would make a specialty of Caucasian Orientals and be famous for them. In her salon she would be known for smoking a particular brand of small cigars that came in a tin, and famous for her chartreuse, green or yellow, depending on her mood. She would learn about wines. At her dinner parties she would surprise her guests with a magnificent but inexpensive *cru bourgeois* she had discovered by herself. She would surround herself with fresh fruit until her tables looked the models for Dutch paintings. Her kitchen would be a market of fresh vegetables. She would peel pears and apples in one peeling with her knife—a special knife— an accomplishment she had perfected in college and which she performed to the astonishment of those girls who had just noisily bitten into the apple they held in hand.

Finally, during one of the long nights, she got outside her dreams and watched them from a distance. Why, she was dreaming the same dream, night after night, and it was the same dream as her daydream! For years she had fooled herself into believing that her ambition to become a *grande dame* was frivolous. Her knowledge of psychology alone should have told her that the dream would not have stayed with her if it had not been fixed to the ground rock of some truth. She did have an image of herself. And it had nothing to do with *them*. It had everything to do with herself. Toby was right: her obsession really was as serious as his. And he was right about another thing: she could still become her daydream. The future was still before her. Too bad for Toby then, destined to daydream about the past!

From here on, she had only to imagine herself as a great lady to free herself of apprehension and put her mind at rest. It was like a tonic. It was better than any codeine and Campari.

9   The Mother

WITH the daylight came the simple contradictions to her make-believe. There had been a conversation at breakfast. Ned had asked his sister if you were old when you reached the age of twelve.

"Old enough," said Jessie, two years closer to twelve than Ned.

"Old enough for what, Jessie?" Ned said.

Toby was reading the paper. "You're old enough to drive a car when you're twelve, aren't you?" he said. He was amused.

"Sure," Ned said. "You can."

"No, sir," Jessie said.

"You can if you're old," Ned said, fighting his way out of

the trap. "And remember? You said twelve was old."

"I didn't either. I said twelve was old enough. I didn't say for what, though."

"I suppose you can get married, too," Toby said.

"I'm going to," Ned said, puffing out his chest.

"No, sir," Jessie said. "He can't either, Dad, and you're teasing, aren't you? Tell the truth."

"Yes, sir, I can, too. I can if I want to," Ned said.

"No, sir!"

They began to poke and punch each other, and it was impossible for any outsider to know who hit first or last or landed the hardest blow. Ned screamed at the top of his lungs.

"It was an accident!" Jessie said.

"No, sir!"

"I said it was an accident!" Jessie said. She pretended to cry herself.

"You can cry louder than that," Toby said. Ned could, and he did, too.

"Stop it, both of you!" Sarah said. She wanted to yank them out of their chairs and shake them until their teeth rattled in their heads. "How can you quarrel over something so stupid?"

"Oh, calm down," Toby cautioned. Displeased with her show of temper, he meant her more than he did them.

"You're as bad as they are," she said. "Egging them on."

"You're the ones at fault," Jessie said to Sarah. "If you and Dad didn't fight we wouldn't fight either."

"That's right," Ned said. "Where do you think we learn it?"

"We'll have no more of that, old pal," Toby said.

Even so, Jessie managed to get in, sotto voce, "If you guys don't behave, how do you expect us to?"

Toby was amused, although he tried not to show it. Sarah said nothing. She knew they were wrong to be disobedient and insolent, but right in the charge they made, even though her arguments with Toby were few and far between, and never lasted long, or got out of hand. The scene was typical of a hundred others in a day. She could not make them eat their suppers without bribing them with dessert, and when she punished one with a spanking for striking the other, both were quick to point out the irony of her action, an irony with which she secretly agreed.

Jessie was eight, Ned was six. She supposed they were both healthy and bright enough to satisfy an educated mother. They were near the top of their classes in school and gave every indication that they would continue to do well academically, but she couldn't help but wonder how they would do in a good suburban school in Massachusetts where they would have to compete among the children of families more like their own, or in the university town among the children of professors. Friends and family had predicted that Jessie, with her long hair and delicate features, would become a great beauty in her day. But Sarah was only certain that she would be good-looking, and feared that as she grew older she would become less so. She thought her awkward in the social graces, and much too shy, and at other times, loud and forward to the point of rudeness. She also tended to be devious, a trait Sarah did not associate with little girls, much less a child of her own. Several times she had caught her keeping back her Sunday school money, and once stealing candy from the local store. Jessie often blamed her brother for her own misdeeds, and apparently felt no remorse when her ruse succeeded. Because she lied, he often lied in self-defense, and it took a Solomon to sort out the smallest quarrel between them. Ned had a tendency to whine and wheedle, "to keep it up," as Toby called it, behavior Sarah thought was alien to a real boy. He never let up until Sarah gave in and he got his way. He had no sense of self-denial, no quality of patience. He was also too credulous, just as Jessie was too cynical, to suit her taste. Granted, these were small faults in the children, and it was petty of her to hold them against them, but she couldn't keep herself from asking how they came to be that way. Every day of the year they were before her in flesh and blood, as solid and irrefutable as mountains. And there was no remolding them either, as those Africans did with the human neck, lips, feet, the shape of the head. If she had ever imagined what her children would be like, she was certain she would have expected better. Even if she didn't deserve better, hadn't she at least imagined better?

She often came across stories in her magazines in which a suburban wife would wake up one morning and realize she did not know her husband (doom), did not know her children (doom), did not know herself (doom). It made her laugh. Her own case was different from that. Although she might concede she did not know herself, she was absolutely certain she knew her children and her husband, and with a clarity that even if they suspected they would not acknowledge. It was just that knowing them as she did (and she was focusing on the children now), she couldn't see how they had come to be hers. Or that there was no alternative to the way they were. Or to her being bound up with them forever. They would always be hers, she could never disown them or revise them. Her blood would beat in theirs, and in that of their own, for generations untold.

She couldn't imagine them grown up; she had no reckoning of their successes. She had no dream of Jessie descending, in her bridal gown, the spiral stairway of their house, as Toby had and could be counted on to mention, birthdays and Christmas or whenever he was in a slightly drunken sentimental mood. Nor of Ned in gown and mortarboard, graduating from college, or residing in his own office, pursuing his own profession, whatever that would be. If that happened to them, she would be there, that was all.

Although she had spent by far the better part of every day since they were born in taking care of them, she had almost never thought of them. They simply were not a part of her inner and more important life. She was a somnolent cook, maid, laundress, chauffeur; nor was she much more than a babysitter when it came to performing the more exacting and sympathetic roles of nurse and governess. She could hardly blame Toby for this state of things, much less the children. She had let this happen herself. So what right did she have to complain about their failure to measure up to some vague notions of good behavior that, considering how little she thought about them, probably were not her own? She had loved them from the start, wished them the best of everything, had tried to give them what she could, or thought she should, but it wasn't as if she wanted a voice in their development. Although she accepted this development as her responsibility, it had never been a part of her ambition.

Their schoolteachers, schoolmates, the television set they had watched transfixed before they could walk a step (and most of all those kindly pied pipers in costumes on the kiddy shows who assured them they were all good children who were loved), and Jessie and Ned themselves were far more in control of shaping their personalities and destinies than was their mother. Sometimes when she thought of her own indolence in conjunction with the rush of time, she became panic-stricken. She should instruct them in the art of drawing—didn't she have some skills with pen and sketch pad? She should be reading to them, too, better books than the badly written things they were reading on their own. She should have done so years ago. And now was the best time for them to learn a foreign language, or even two languages (and this was not only her own fault but that of the schools for not teaching them, although she had done nothing to change the schools), and she would remember the little Swiss girl, seven years old, she had met in England, who could speak five languages. Already it was too late for them to pick up a language as quickly as they would have had they had the chance when they were younger and could have learned to speak it fluently and without a trace of accent. She should have started them on gymnastic lessons, ballet lessons, music lessons; one should be playing the violin, the other the flute; at the very least they should begin piano lessons. Here they were, wasting their best years when their minds were the keenest for learning and remembering, and she wasn't doing anything about it. Even now she could see the consequences of the weak example she had shown, because what did they do in their free time? They made little nests in closets and corners, using sofa cushions for walls and stringing a blanket from one chair to another for the roof, and inside them, and away from her eyes, they performed the whole litany of domestic chores. Playing house because what else had they seen their mother do?

She wasn't one of those girls who had majored in elementary education and ran her household like a kindergarten, always soft-spoken, kindly and understanding regardless of the provocation or the way she felt. She didn't have the patience or the sympathy of a Pokey Kubilius, who did for her five children what Sarah could not do for two. Pokey spoke of other mothers in terms of their "mothering," by which she meant their ability "to mother," making a point of leaving "instinct" off "mothering" because she insisted it was an art you could always learn. Nor did Sarah show the appreciation for her children that Janet Angle showed for hers. Janet would complain about her sons to anyone who would listen, and had been heard to state in public that the last child had been a mistake to have conceived and later to have delivered, but she also loved to labor her friends with stories about them that always ended with her laughing first and loudest. She was amused and fascinated by the things her boys said and did. She called her oldest "Tiger," which suggested intimacies and expectations that Sarah could never dream of entertaining for Ned. And Sarah never re-counted anecdotes about her children to anyone but family, and rarely then.

Only now did she begin to understand the reasons for her weakness with the children. Given who she was destined to become, how could she expect to have a rapport with small children? She would just have to get through these difficult years as best she could, suffering with her own incompetence and failures until the children were grown up and gone and she could at last become her dream.

Her restlessness began to wake Toby in the night, and he scolded her for those long naps she took now every day, saying this was what kept her awake at night. Sometimes he kept her company until just before the sky lightened, lying beside her on his elbow. But the small talk he made in his attempt to comfort her would turn eventually to his own dreams, which were of land. His talk was full of fields overgrown with juniper and blueberries, large tracts of acreage grown up in second-growth maples and evergreens, whole mountainsides, lake frontage, road frontage, so many thousands of board feet. Now was the time, he said, to buy more land.

But she had her own dream. And the more serious that dream became, the more secretive she became about it. She no longer mentioned it at parties; she had no wish to share it with Toby, even though he pestered her to learn what dark thoughts kept her awake at night. She tried to shut out his voice and to see herself instead in cape, straw hat and walking stick, strolling alone along an isolated beach against a backdrop of falling surf; or presiding in a velvet gown at a dinner party, candlelit like a Degas painting, that was catered in her small wainscoted dining room; or seated at her small desk fit into a narrow win-dowed dormer, writing letters to her many friends.

But, she reminded herself, there would be work and responsi-bilities in this new life, too. She would engage herself in meaningful social causes; she would support art and artists by being at once benevolent, munificent, tastefully acquisitive. She would be respected, she would have a presence, people would *feel* her.

One night Toby suggested she see a doctor. He wanted her to put an end, once and for all, to her restlessness, pain, insomnia. He made it plain he thought her trouble could be either physical or mental. She thought he leaned to the latter. So did she.

10   *Red Hollyhocks and Blue Delphiniums*

LATER, doubts that she could become the woman she dreamed about began to worry Sarah. Although she believed a *grande dame* was a creature more of the spirit than of the flesh, she could not deny the flesh. She questioned if she had the face or figure, the physical presence, for such a role. Such women had to be big-boned, handsome to the brink of ugliness, with a touch of both the crone and the matron about their character. But her full-length bathroom mirror mocked this image. She was so short, so freckled, so thin. She had always looked like a little boy, had always been her most attractive in sailor suits. What would the years do to such a body? to such a presence?

Her worst doubts, however, concerned her knowledge, her

wit, her ability to make conversation. She had come to realize that whenever she spoke at parties on any of the pressing topics of the day she inevitably referred to a recent television news program she had seen or a newspaper or magazine article she had read. Apparently she had no knowledge of the world outside these sources, and could not make serious conversation without repeating their information and echoing their editorials. She had wanted to keep abreast of political and social problems and to sound informed in company, and the television especially, with its special programs on national and world affairs, had spoken to her so privately and intimately that she sometimes mistook its information and opinions for her own. It was equally true of the other women she met at the parties. They spoke a kind of scholarly argument, brought in their authorities from the popular press to substantiate their points of view, seconded a news commentator's editorial with a magazine article, refuted a television special with a newspaper series. Surely these could not be the conversations of her dinner parties and salons of the future? The men, however, were a little more experienced than the women, and must have had some of the information firsthand, or at least from more direct and personal sources. How ashamed she felt to remember the way she had pontificated, parading her television and best-seller knowledge before these men. How indulgent they had been of her, treating her like a child by favoring her remarks as though they really were her own! Did she have any views of her own on important affairs? One could only get them, she supposed, through experience. But how in these times was she to learn about life on her own? Maybe it wasn't possible to think originally anymore.

To Sarah, a great lady delighted in people, thrived on company. She fed on gossip of a high order as it concerned the social lives of worthy men and women, and kept up an avid appetite for psychology. She was found not only in the brick

town houses of the best section of the city in the company of
foreign statesmen, philanthropists and artists, but in the tene-
ments of the poorer quarters, where she was busy with charities
that demanded organizational skills and a personal contact with
the poor. But until now Sarah's favorite activity had been
climbing in the White Mountains, and her preference had been
to climb alone. Even when she had hiked with her brothers,
and more recently with Toby, she managed to block out their
presence. She didn't want to hear their voices on the trail,
wanted to hear only the heaving of her own lungs and the
scrape and smack of rocks beneath her boots. In the best of
these moments she had never been happier. Just herself and
wilderness and heights and the punishment and victory she
felt inside her body. Admittedly, she preferred self and wilderness to society and people. And she couldn't help but wonder
if this contentedness with isolation wasn't really misanthropy
in thin disguise.

But, she consoled herself, people weren't all one way. They
were a bundle of contradictions. Take Toby. He liked to travel
up and down the roads daily in his car and could buy wood
lots and cutovers, sight unseen, but he also liked to garden.
For a few hours or for only minutes, he could forsake that
immense landscape of lakes and forest and abandoned farms
and exchange the long shot for the close-up, focusing on an
area of earth no bigger than a few square yards. Although
he had a modest vegetable garden, his special fondness was
for delphiniums, the only flower that he grew. He had a large
bed of a belladonna variety against the house, all the classic
delphinium blue. He had sent away to England for the seed,
and she remembered how they had come in a plain packet,
and he had put them in the freezer because Archie Auden
said this might fool them into feeling they had been in the
ground all winter, and that ought to make them germinate
quicker and produce a bloom or two that first year. Auden

had wondered why he didn't try the Connecticut Yankees that were so popular with his neighbors. Others suggested white delphiniums with black eyes, blue delphiniums with white eyes, yellow delphiniums, dwarf delphiniums, but he was interested only in the one variety he grew. The only time she recalled him showing interest in another flower was when he said, Wouldn't those delphiniums look good against a background of red hollyhocks? She suggested a border of red geraniums planted in front of the delphiniums, but he wouldn't hear of that.

Once he confessed that as a child he had seen a bed of his delphiniums in the front yard of a house he admired, but he couldn't remember where the house was, or even if it was a real house or only the picture of one in a book.

It was in a book. By chance she came across it in a box of children's books at a yard sale. An old grammar school reader for an early grade with illustrations that looked more English than American. The boy in the story was curly-headed and wore knee socks with short pants and sandals. His companions were a puppy, a red wagon and a goose. His house was a small cottage with diamond-pane windows and the suggestion of a thatched roof. Inside the gate and picket fence was a bed of old-fashioned blue delphiniums, and behind them, against the cottage itself, a pair of tall red hollyhocks. She didn't show it to him. She didn't buy the book either. She knew that having glimpsed into his secret, she understood better than he could the contradiction between the uncertain and careless way he lived his life and the small perfect world of his deep-rooted dreams. Poor Toby. He didn't know why the picture of the house he carried around inside his head was so important to him. He didn't have an inkling as to why he grew the flowers.

His first set of hollyhocks had come from a nursery, but they had turned out to be hybrids with showy double blossoms that were cherry red. Then he found an old-fashioned rose-red flower with an open bonnet growing wild, and transplanted it in his border, saving the seed. He had his specimens of hollyhocks, but from the beginning his delphiniums had failed. For years now the bed had been plagued by microscopic mites that, like a cancer, turned the blossoms into blackened dwarfs and misshaped the leaves grotesquely. They didn't kill the plants, only ruined them for flowers and foliage. Because of his new-found concern for the environment, he refused to use pesticides, preferring old-fashioned remedies, which always failed. He still weeded and fertilized and separated the crowns each spring, but when the first signs of the disease appeared, he lost faith and ignored the bed entirely, refusing even to cut off the old blossoms, so that the bed grew rank with quitch grass and burdock, and became an eyesore beside the house. Auden said the mites were common in the East, and that Toby's problem was likely a matter of poor "air drainage." He himself grew half a dozen Pacific Giants, and he wasn't bothered by any mites. He claimed the trouble with having a large bed like Toby's was that it became infected so easily. Better to have a few specimen plants in the border as he had. He advised destroying the bed and starting over. But if Toby could not bring himself to help the plants, he could not bring himself to destroy them either. It would be an admission of his own defeat and of his misplacement of a trust in nature to cure its own. Besides, he didn't want to spend the time it took in starting over. He would wait another year.

11   Old Beaux

OF all her friends, Sarah believed Archie Auden was the most sympathetic, and that he genuinely liked her for who she was. Since his wife had died of cancer two years before, his neighbors had gone out of their way to keep him company, and Sarah especially had adopted him. She had to be careful with him, though; he wasn't a man you could provide with charity. His family had been in the state since the seventeenth century, and he owned both a nursery and a large apple orchard. A sophisticated countryman, he was a Harvard graduate, and years ago had taught agricultural courses at the state university; Sarah was surprised to learn from Renzi that as a young man he had lived and studied in Italy. He was tall, with fine, straight snow-white hair left just long enough to part and comb to one side, and Sarah judged him to be the handsomest man in town. He looked patrician, and at the same time like one of those big gardeners in their soft caps and Wellingtons she remembered working in the cottage gardens of the Cotswolds. He kept bees, too, because of the orchard, and he smelled of apples, cider, burning apple wood.

Sarah had many talks with him on gardening and hiking in the mountains, both of which Auden pursued with passion, and she believed he recognized in her a fellow nature lover and mountaineer. Recently when they had discussed his taking up cross-country skiing, he confessed to her what she believed he would not have told to just anyone: his giving up of downhill skiing. "For the first time in over forty years I was scared to death on skis. I said to myself, What in hell's name are you doing here, tearing down this slope like a fresh kid? You're sixty-one years old, too old for such foolishness. Just like that, you see, I'd lost my legs, lost my nerve. If a tree had been in the way right then, I'd have hit it for sure. If I'd taken a spill, I would have broken my back. It came to me then: I didn't want a broken leg—I didn't even want a sprained big toe! I didn't even want to chance it happening. I figured mountain, skis, common sense, were all trying to tell me something, and that was the end of it, I hung up my skis."

"What about climbing in the mountains?" Sarah wondered. "Will you give that up, too?"

She might as well have asked him if he didn't think he would soon have to be bathed and fed. He had been laughing at himself; now he looked angry. "I hope I'm never so old I can't get myself up into the mountains," he said. "Because if it ever came to that . . . Oh, I'm down to a pilgrimage or two a year, and lately I ask myself halfway up, a lot more than I used to, Auden, what in hell are you doing here, you don't have to put up with this, but then I catch my second wind, and I'm glad I don't surrender to temptation and turn back, because it's always worth the effort to reach the top. If I couldn't get above the tree line, if I couldn't get up there in the wind and rock . . ."

Toby and Dr. Kubilius joined them, beers in hand. Toby said, "I just read somewhere that they've discovered that if a man has a strong sex drive when he's young, he'll have a strong sex drive when he's old."

Auden laughed. "I wouldn't know," he said. "My field is stamens, anthers, pollen."

Kubilius said, "They used to think a man could use himself

up by overdoing it when he was young. The theory was that a man had only so much to give."

"Sounds like Aristotle," Auden said.

Toby gave them both a wink. "Those poor guys," he said, "who thought they were saving it up for old age."

Auden still supervised the operation of his orchard, in which he also labored, and Sarah did not see much of him in the busy days of summer. But come October and he would show up at her kitchen door bearing a gift of several bushels of his best Cortland drops, and a little later, with a bushel of his best McIntosh, and he would supply her with as many Baldwins as she thought she could keep in the days ahead. She would have liked to see more of him, to know him better, to learn the secret of his quiet dignity.

She had always seen too much of Dr. Milton Cullenbine. At times the man came close to being a nuisance. Not that he made indecent proposals, or was anything but courtly and polite. More than once he had confided that he and Vita, his wife, had not slept together for five years. She wondered why he told her this. Did he want her pity? Or did he mean to announce that he was faithful to her to the point of staying chaste? She sometimes compared notes on Cullenbine with Alexander, who said that he told her Vita would only let him make love to her twice a year, and then only in winter and months apart.

Both women's husbands he delighted in belittling, referring to them as "boys." He told Alexander that Marco was a dilettante and an amateur, and suggested that he wouldn't have moved to the country if he had been good enough to make it in New York. Also, he was really a selfish-bachelor type who thought only of himself and would eventually leave her to make it on her own. He called Toby a "fatso" to Sarah's face, and pointed out how slim he was in comparison. It was true, Cullenbine wasn't fat so much as thick around the middle, but his skin was loose. He predicted that Toby with all his land schemes would overextend himself and end up losing everything he had, or thought he had, to back taxes and a rat's nest of litigation. He would separate Marco at parties and ask him interested and flattering questions about his recent work and then respond by arguing the value of painting over photography and illustration. Of stage designing, he liked to say, "If a play's any good, give me the bare boards!" He would waylay Toby with some question about real estate or taxes, and then attack his plans for land development, arguing in favor of strict zoning, land use and restrictive conservation laws. Both Marco and Toby had been known to drive home talking to themselves and ordering their wives never to accept any invitation to a party that Cullenbine had any chance of being at.

Once Cullenbine, having taken Sarah aside with his usual "Let's have our little talk, shall we?" confessed that in his mind he saw himself as having the face and physique of a man— oh, say, thirty-five. But in the mirror, you see, he looked maybe as old as forty. And yet he knew he was fifty-five, and that other men of that age looked to him like fifty-five. Older, sometimes. What did he look like? he wondered. Thirty-five? Forty? As much as fifty-five?

"I think you like me because I'm younger than you are," she said.

"Of course I do," he admitted. "You're a spring chicken, and when you're as old as I am you'll develop an eye for the young boys. Oh, not that you'll be brave enough to do anything about it. But you'll look and dream. A man would have to be hard up or a fool to desire a woman my age. I'm not saying it's fair, but that's the way it is."

To him, a woman was someone a man did favors for. "If you were my wife," he would say, taking her hand in his, "you wouldn't want for anything. You'd have the best house, the best clothes, wouldn't do a lick of housework. I'd send you roses every day, I'd pamper you, I'd spoil you rotten. It's what you deserve, my darling, it's what you were born to have in life." The implication was that Toby failed to appreciate her, and quite possibly abused her—at least in comparison with the promises of Cullenbine. She was amused by his innocence. He seemed to view her as a high-priced concubine, or as a piece of treasure in her own right to be shut up in some splendid castle keep. What an old-fashioned notion he had of what a woman expected of a man!

She teased him, too. "And would you make me a money tree?"

"Birthdays and Christmases."

"Fifty . . . ?"

"Hundred-dollar bills!"

"And a fur coat?"

"The most precious for my precious. To keep my precious warm."

"And diamonds?"

"On every finger!"

And his favorite enticement: they would cruise together through the Orient on a big white liner, or steam down the Nile to see the secret cities, and Sarah was sure he had a vision of them in pith helmets on top of camels, photographed against the backdrop of the giant pyramids.

Sarah was surprised that his romantic fancies could be so outmoded and commonplace, and that his notion of a woman had never gone beyond a stereotype he had probably acquired in early youth. A woman, by his definition, talked too much, spent too much money, lacked business savvy and was ineffectual with machines; she was also irrational and capricious and, what was more unbelievable, he wouldn't want her any other way. In return, he was to protect and baby her, making himself subservient to her whims, while complaining, with mock exasperation, "That's a woman!" It was doubtful that Vita had ever allowed herself to be put in so stultifying a mold.

Usually Sarah's tête-à-têtes with Cullenbine did not last long. The drinks and drugs that had emboldened him in the first place would soon take their toll and, after once again complaining that the universities weren't training young laboratory scientists of the caliber to be found in his own day, he could be counted on to doze off, smiling with his dreams.

Unlike Cullenbine, Auden did not treat women differently from men. When she pointed this out to Kubilius, he had remarked, yes, he was equally aloof from both. When he spoke with someone, he honestly did not take into account that person's sex, nor did he appear to differentiate between anatomies and clothes.

Cullenbine didn't interest Sarah much, but she often thought of Auden, and in terms almost too large for life, so great was her respect and admiration for him. He was like her grandfather Bingham, in whose form she had imagined, as a small girl, the likeness of God.

She pictured him in his own apple orchard, where he could be seen walking, especially in spring and fall. He had a theory he never tired of putting forward, in your dining room if he had to, but preferably as he strolled with you through his orchard. He believed that if you walked a small child through an apple orchard at blossom time, such a subtle but powerful impression of peace and beauty would be stamped on his subconscious that it would influence his character for the rest of his life. He would grow up to have a pacific and aesthetic nature, with a good chance of wanting to become an orchardman or a gardener himself. "Imagine yourself as a small child again," he would say. "A whole orchard—a thousand trees or more, all in bloom at once! Big trees, too, and not your modern dwarfs. And the child—just a toddler—walking through this canopy of giants. The colors—those pinks and whites—that fragrance, the sunlight, a gentle breeze, the hum of bees, petals falling like a spring snow and covering the orchard floor." All his life the child would measure beauty against this experience.

He believed that ten thousand years ago in prehistory there had existed a place in the Near East, an oasis irrigated by a river, inhabited by a group of orchardmen and gardeners who lived in peace with one another and in perfect harmony with their environment. They didn't know the meaning of war or violence. And this time and place were the origin of the myth of the Garden of Eden that had remained imprinted in the collective subconscious of Western man, including modern man, so called, today. It was that lost perfect world for which mankind was destined to pine. Thirty years ago he had written up his theory and had it printed privately in a small volume by a vanity press. Recent archaeological excavations in the area, he liked to say, were continuing to prove his thesis right.

Both of his own children were active conservationists and pacifists. His son was a professor of archaeology, whose specialty was the identification of the seeds and pollen of prehistoric plants, and his daughter a civil rights lawyer in the justice department of the government. His son had married a Quaker, his daughter another civil rights lawyer.

Once in the late fall after a spectacular sunset behind the western mountain, Sarah had gone out walking on the hilly road before her home. Suddenly the sky went dark, the wind came up and the smell of unseen apple smoke sweetened the chilly air. On an open ledge of the apple orchard that sloped below, she had seen between the trees a small fire in the brush pile of apple branches that Auden had been pruning from his trees. A tiny furnace of red fire whipped back and forth by the wind. And the silhouette of Auden like a watchman beside the fire, larger than life, alone.

12   *Old Women*

ONE warm midsummer night at the Kubiliuses', Sarah left the kitchen and the conversations of the other women and went outdoors to watch the men play a ragged game of basketball in the floodlit driveway beneath the backboard on the garage. They used their hips and elbows when they went up for rebounds, slapped the hands of shooters and dribblers, bickered loudly over the accuracy of the score. Every few minutes someone would take time out and huff on the sidelines, hands on his hips and head lowered as though hacking blood. Dr. Kubilius, who was waiting for a chance to get into the game, drifted over to Sarah. He wanted to talk, she could tell. Earlier in the day he had gone to a nursing home to examine an old woman who was to have an operation on her fractured hip. "She told me she was ninety years old and what did she have to live for? 'Everybody I know is dead,' she said. 'I've lived my life, why can't I die?' She didn't want us to operate on her hip, and who can blame her? Then she asked me if I'd give her something to make her die. 'You're the anesthesiologist,' she said. 'Just put me to sleep, only don't let me wake up.' Don't think I wasn't tempted, either. Why should we put her through the misery of an operation on her hip? She'll probably never walk again no matter what we do."

He seemed to admit to a confusion and helplessness Sarah had not seen before, and she was flattered that he would confide to her so personal and professional a secret. More than most men, he intimidated her and made her feel uncomfortable. He didn't seem to be in any way attracted to her, a passiveness in a man that Sarah sometimes interpreted to mean he didn't like her. "She really asked you that?" she said in disbelief.

"These old people are always asking me to give them something," he said. "In the old days most of them would have been long dead of pneumonia. And they weren't being sarcastic or ironic, either, when they used to call pneumonia 'the old man's friend.' It's a quick and easy death. But now we know how to cure pneumonia. And of course, we do. But it's not just their age and illnesses that make those people want to call it quits. Those goddamn nursing homes are the best argument I've seen yet for euthanasia. It's a real effort for me to make myself go into one of those places. All those old people propped up like dummies against the walls, and a staff that either ignores them or treats them like they're lunatics or little kids."

"After all these years it still depresses you?"

"Why do you think doctors have the highest suicide rate of any profession?" he asked. It was a question she had heard him pose before.

Toby, who was taking a breather, had overheard them. "Those old people," he said, "they're probably so old or sick they don't know what they're saying. You can't just let them die. You certainly can't kill them. Who knows, maybe while they're being kept alive, science will discover some new cure."

"For longevity?" Kubilius said.

"Someday even for that, for the miseries of it anyway."

"Maybe," the doctor said. "But not in our time."

"You have to respect human life," Toby said, as though this were a moral certitude that put an end to the discussion.

Sarah thought about the nursing home. She said to herself, I don't want to end up in one of those places. The next day while she did her housework she caught herself saying, "No, sir, not me."

Her Great-Aunt Flora had been obsessed with nursing homes. A "Swamp Yankee," she had feared the county poor farm with a passion. Even after her advantageous marriage to a Boston Brahmin from "old money" and long after the institution of the poor farm ceased to exist, she had lived in terror of the place. To her a nursing home was a palace that would let her escape the clutches of the poor farm once and for all. She would take Sunday drives in her big Packard into the countryside to "pick out my home."

That weekend Sarah went to an auction in a nearby town. It was too "country" to suit her taste, useless clutter that seemed to be all cardboard boxes full of Mason jars, broken lamps and plastic dishes, and Victorian veneer furniture with a bubbled varnish sold by the auctioneer, in straw hat and bib overalls, to the poor locals and blue-collar Massachusetts summer people furnishing their camps. She preferred a tent set up in the garden of a big house where only the best antiques were sold. On the chance that a good piece or two had not been brought outdoors, she went through the house, the entire contents of which were to be sold. Someone mentioned that the house, just an average-sized Victorian farmhouse, had been a nursing home. She almost said aloud, Oh, that can't be so. Small dirty rooms, in one of which there appeared to have been a fire, the timbers exposed and charred and the plaster blackened. The dirty linoleum, worn black in places, the purple doors and woodwork, the smell of an oil stove in every room. In the barn she came across the sign. It had been taken down. It said "Birchcroft Nursing Home."

She couldn't believe it. Old people who were sick and helpless had actually lived here; their children had knowingly condemned them to such a fate; the state had sanctioned it. She could not imagine ending up in so grim a place. She who had tramped alone in the high mountains. Even one of those white Victorian mansions with the green awnings and trimmed hedges was no less a degradation, a defeat of the soul.

But what guarantee of good fortune did she have for her future? What she assumed would be the certain realization of her character might only be a wishful dream she would see contradicted by the outcome of her later years. What if Toby should become an invalid or, God forbid, die young? He hadn't made his fortune yet, and given the way he speculated, he might lose his nest egg overnight. Already she had heard that condominiums were in trouble. She could end up not only old but ill and poor, living on a monthly social security check. And alone, too, because Ned and Jessie, with their own families to think about, wouldn't have her—although she wouldn't live with them in any case. She would become hardened and embittered by her failures. She would become timid, a case for charity, visited by well-meaning strangers. She would become eccentric, but only in mean ways and for desperate reasons.

And if she refused the nursing home, it would probably mean she would have to move into a house trailer. It was what had happened to many of the older women in town when they could no longer manage their big Colonial houses. To live in a trailer—she who had waged a private war against the ugliness of trailers! Or else move to a city where she had neither family nor friends, living in a slum apartment she could barely afford.

No doubt about it, she concluded, to be old was to be helpless, more often than not. Old people were betrayed by family, employer and government alike. She had watched a television special on their plight. They were no better than victims. They were without hope. They had no dignity.

There was the old woman the locals called "the dog lady," accusing her of stealing and selling dogs. She lived behind drawn shades in a one-room shack that starving, barking dogs of all breeds, half-breeds and sizes were chained around, each dog having its own radius of bare dog-fouled earth to guard. Occasionally she could be seen in men's shoes and a housecoat clutched at the breast, darting from door to dog. Sarah had gone there once to see if she had come into possession of Ned and Jessie's puppy. But she couldn't make herself heard above the din of all those dogs. Nor could she get within a hundred feet of the door.

And the old woman they called "the butter lady," who lived in a big run-down farmhouse where Sarah sometimes bought the homemade butter Toby complained was rancid. Lame, overweight and in her seventies, the woman would be found lying on a couch in an old dress, a hair net and gray stockings, complaining of swollen legs. She was looked after by a half-wit, a man young enough to be her son, with gapped teeth and blond hair that had been cut with a bowl. He milked her cows and turned the hand churn. They both appeared to live in the one-room bedroom-kitchen of the house, with its sooty plaster walls, unvarnished floor and potbellied stove. The few times Sarah was there, they had quarreled with the pettiness and subtlety of lovers.

In the past, older women in bad health and with limited means had been something of a blind spot in her vision. Now she saw them everywhere. As miniature zombie-like passengers in the front seats of incredibly large cars; or in groups at the local restaurants, blue-haired, eating lunches of steamed clams or batter-fried fish in a cloud of powder and a war of sour flesh and sweet perfume. And the old woman she remembered from last winter inching along an icy side street behind a walker. Like a figure in some early Netherlandish painting, she seemed about to raise up her blind and toothless head and cry out in pain.

When Sarah learned of the new organization in town whose members visited shut-ins and senior citizens, she persuaded herself to volunteer. Her first assignment was a Mrs. Colley, aged seventy-three, who lived alone in a new turquoise-colored house trailer. Sarah found her sitting at a chrome bar, smoking a cigarette and drinking a glass of whiskey and Coca-Cola. "I'm just having my highball," she said. She was dressed up in slacks, high heels and a pullover sweater, and seemed to expect that Sarah had come to take her out somewhere. To make simple conversation, Sarah asked about her family, where they were, and if she saw them often. Mrs. Colley replied by telling her that she had had a child at the age of forty-nine. And then had added, as though it were the punch line of a joke, "And with a husband dead for five years! Wished I'd done it earlier— I wasted five years!" And she greeted her own confession with an outburst of baritone hilarity that had her coughing. Then she tried to talk Sarah into the two of them going out to a bar—she knew a good place where there was dancing and hillbilly music and a lively crowd. When Sarah declined, she said, "Well, dearie, you getting any?" And as Sarah looked at her in her innocent confusion, she said, "Why, sure you are— when you walked in here, I didn't hear you squeaking any!" Sarah had planned to stay an hour. She stayed fifteen minutes instead. She forgot she was supposed to remind the woman of her liver and her doctor's orders not to drink.

That she would not live long enough to make something of herself no longer worried Sarah. It was that she would grow old and become nothing much at all. It was that life could pass her by and she would miss her youth and middle years in anticipation of a later blossoming that might, in the end, turn out to be the worst years of the lot. She could not take chances. She had to prepare herself to meet the future. Best of all, she had to make the future happen. In either case, she had to develop herself every step of the way. Only then could she be certain that when the time came she would be ready to assume her role.

13   *The Fantasy of the Harpsichord*

MOST of the women Sarah knew were accomplished and creative mainly in their kitchens. All of them, however, had voiced ambitions beyond the watching of the foreign cooking shows on educational television and the preparation of a special meal. They did not want to be housewives dependent on their husbands' money; they wanted their own work, to make their own money. They often spoke of opening French restaurants, tearooms, organic food stores, art galleries, real estate agencies. They sketched out schemes for writing children's books, and insisted that all one needed was a good illustrator and a gimmick or slant that had not been used before. They also discussed the mystery stories they might someday write, exchanging plots and detectives. They all agreed that successful mysteries depended on original plots with surprising turns. Over the years Sarah had read hundreds of mysteries. She was convinced she could write a detective whodunit every bit as good as the best of them. She had the time now that both children were in school. But sometimes she thought she ought to have an ambition that was grander and more difficult than this.

She supposed she had considered herself the equal of her friends. But they seemed to possess an intellectual status that was foreign to the social world that had been the cornerstone of Sarah's upbringing. She wondered if they felt intellectually superior to her as she could not help feeling socially superior to those real estate associates of Toby's she was forced to meet at business parties: the clubby men in crew cuts, bow ties and plaid slacks and their tight-lipped, hard-faced young wives in their preposterous wigs. Now she found herself taking stock of her friends and suspecting that once again she was coming up short in comparison. They did more than she did; they could do more, too. Alexander had her obvious skills in music, painting and photography. Janet Angle had her folk singing and her recent interest in dancing (about which Sarah knew little except that it was modern and self-interpretive and that John had said she was very good). Now she had taken up weaving as well. Sarah had been invited over to see her new loom, a monstrous wooden contraption that filled the bedroom, giving the impression the room had been built around it. Both Angles showed her how they used the shuttle, banging and clacking with their hands and feet. They planned to weave their first design, a Navaho blanket, together, taking turns.

And Vita Cullenbine was an artisan in leather, designing and making belts, purses, armbands and vests, which she marketed herself from a booth at craftsmen's fairs. She had her workshop in what had once been their daughters' bedroom, from which she rarely ventured, and where Sarah could imagine her, small, slight, dark and handsome, with a face that had been prematurely lined, tinkling away with a small hammer like a Nibelung on buckles and silver studs, and busy with her knives, needles and punches upon an assortment of hides. She wore a smock at home, and her face and hands were often dirty, and she sometimes smelled, like a shoe repairman, of oil and leather. All of which had seemed to Sarah incongruous and even a bit improper, married as she was to a well-to-do executive like Dr. Cullenbine.

And just the other night, Adele Fox, who researched and wrote feature newspaper and magazine articles on New England subjects, ceremoniously announced that she had just been given a contract on a book. For years she had suggested: "A Shakespeare cookbook! All you do is collect all the references to food in Shakespeare's plays and then research their recipes. Then you present them in old script along with the relevant quotation from Shakespeare. What a marvelous Christmas gift it would make!" Sarah had thought the idea foolish, but Adele had sold it to a small publisher, Neptune House, that Cullenbine claimed was in the business of selling large printings of new titles as discontinued remainders at cut-rate prices. Sarah didn't think she came off too badly against Colleen Orlovsky, who was addicted to golf, having been runner-up two years in a row to the state women's champion, and champion herself three years ago, but lately Colleen had shown some interest in environmental causes and local politics. Even the late Polly Auden had been a selectwoman of the town and a partner in her husband's orchard. Only Pokey Kubilius seemed to have no interest outside her home.

For years her best friend among the women had probably been Colleen Orlovsky. Now she decided she would make a special friend of Alexander, whom she admired. She would learn from her; Alexander would get her into good habits. Alexander had begun to give piano lessons to a few of the local children, and Sarah persuaded her to take on Jessie and Ned. Alexander was patient and innovative, and the children practiced faithfully and learned quickly. Sarah was encouraged for her own sake to discover that Alexander had never given piano lessons before. She liked going to Alexander's house, and after the lessons the two women would visit over coffee while the children looked at photography books, or painted with watercolors, in Alexander's studio. Sarah would have liked to take lessons herself, to pick up the little bit of playing she had been able to do back in her teens. At first she was too proud and embarrassed to ask, and too fearful of Alexander's turning her down. But when at last she did approach her, Alexander was elated. Of course she would help her. Come the spring they both would be playing Mozart again.

"But I never played Mozart to begin with," Sarah confessed. "At least not that I remember."

"For the first time, then!" Alexander said. "He wrote so many beautiful but simple pieces. They're not difficult to play."

Sarah felt she owed her an explanation as to why she had not continued with her childhood lessons. "I always had this wonderful fantasy about playing a harpsichord," she said. "I felt the harpsichord was me, somehow. It seemed such an unusual instrument. I didn't know anybody who had one, or who could play one, or who could give lessons on it, which was why there wasn't any chance that I could play it. I probably couldn't really become interested in the piano because of that fantasy about the harpsichord."

During one of their talks together, Sarah discovered that Alexander spoke some French, and seemed to be more proficient in it than she was. They decided they would help each other's French. From now on, every time they met for a piano lesson and chatted over coffee, they would speak in French.

"And let's go to Paris and speak it, too," Alexander said. "We'll go in the spring, just the two of us." Marco was gone more often than not, and Toby could look after the children when they were not in school, and if not Toby, then Toby's mother, someone like that. They would only be gone ten days. Why, a round-trip air fare, if you stayed ten days, hardly cost any more than the fare for one way. Or better yet, they would go over on one of those cheap package tours and then ditch the others once they were there. Just think, the two of them in Paris, strolling the boulevards arm in arm.

At first Sarah hesitated. She wasn't certain that Alexander's invitation was altogether sincere. But the more she considered it, the more possible and desirable the trip became. "We can really try out our French then," she said. "And spend afternoons at the Louvre."

"And suppers at great little restaurants," Alexander said.

In Sarah's mind it was settled then: they would go to Paris in the spring. But that was such a long way off that she had plenty of time to think about it before they made their plans.

The Kubilius children had been the first to take lessons from Alexander, and some days, when their children's lessons overlapped, Sarah met Pokey there. Pokey had been helping her children with their lessons on the piano at home, and Alexander, complimenting her on her achievement, asked her how she came to know so much about music.

"Oh, I used to play the cello," Pokey said.

"Used to?" Alexander scolded in a tone that was meant also to say, Shame on you, why don't you still?

"I mean I used to play it well," Pokey said. "Or certainly better than I do now, because I don't play well at all now. And only then when Chaz wants me to join him on some piece he's playing on his viola."

Sarah knew that Dr. Kubilius's two passions in life were herb gardening and the viola. Until this moment she had pictured him alone evenings in the little glassed-in conservatory off their lounge. Now she had to put Pokey in there with him, seated, a cello between her legs.

When she was a girl in high school, Pokey confessed after some hesitation, she wanted to be a concert cellist. She went to summer festivals, played with youth orchestras, gave a recital or two. But she developed other interests in college, and knowing she could not achieve the excellence at the cello she demanded of herself unless she devoted herself to it completely, and no longer willing to make so painful a commitment, she gave it up. She started to speak of these new interests, but perhaps because she felt this would lead her into listing her accomplishments, she broke off and returned to her usual shyness, seeming to apologize for having gone as far as she did.

When Sarah told Pokey of the plan she and Alexander had to practice French and visit Paris in the spring, Pokey said that was an excellent idea, only she said it first in French, which both women, caught unawares, failed to understand. After this, Pokey, who was not oblivious to their confusion, grew even more reticent. She had revealed too much of herself to these women, had called attention to the differences between them, and her life in this community, Sarah realized, had been built around her never doing that. Alexander, however, was persistent, and pried more information from her, piece by piece. Apparently Pokey had lived in France on at least two separate occasions. The first time for several years with her family after the war, when they had lived in an apartment in Paris and vacationed on a farm in Cantal in the Auvergne and at the seaside at Menton. Her father had been an American commissioner of some sort. When she was older she had herself gone to the Sorbonne. Sarah assumed she spoke fluent French.

Later Alexander told Sarah that Pokey had a doctor's degree in education, but didn't want anyone to know about it, and had been employed, before her marriage, as the director of an experimental school.

Sarah's piano lessons didn't work out. On more than one occasion when she showed up, Alexander wasn't home, and if Sarah thought this irresponsible, she didn't complain. There were times when she herself didn't feel like taking a lesson, usually because she hadn't gotten around to practicing. Whenever she didn't come herself, she made sure to phone beforehand. The fantasy of the harpsichord returned. Nobody she knew around here played that. How wonderful if she could play it in her little music room! Oh, not necessarily Scarlatti or Bach, but old airs and simple minuets. And carols at Christmas, when Toby and the children would crowd close and sing. More than any other instrument, the harpsichord spoke to her of poetry and magic. Compared to its courtly elegance, piano playing was all pounding and banging, like dancing in big boots.

Now when Sarah and Alexander talked over coffee they spoke in English instead of French. They didn't mention Paris either. Sarah recalled that everyone she knew who had gone to Paris in recent years had complained of high prices and unpleasant experiences; none of them had cared for the Parisians.

One day Sarah ran into Renzi at Alexander's, where he had come to ask for advice on the purchase of a camera he wished to take along to Greece. He wanted a library of his own color slides to illustrate the new series of lectures he planned to give on his return. In passing, Sarah confessed that she and Alexander probably needed a more formal and disciplined approach to their education.

"Why not take a night course at the university?" he said. "There's an adult education course in the late summer term on Italian opera, and there's supposed to be a very good course on film. And if you're in the mood to brush up on the classics and the Renaissance, well, I'm teaching in the summer session, and you can always sit in on one of my spiels. I'd fire you up, if nothing else."

They audited the film course. They saw, on alternate evenings, *Nanook of the North, The Gold Rush, Rules of the Game, Citizen Kane.*

Sarah decided she would do well to concentrate on intellectual and artistic efforts. She saw herself more inclined to this direction than to social works and acts of charity. A great lady, she had concluded, was not born to the role, but earned the attribution. It didn't happen to you simply because you were starry-eyed enough to hope that was who you would become.

It was instead a matter of acquiring experiences and refining sensibilities and tastes.

She felt so lively and optimistic about herself that she asked Kubilius to recommend a doctor who specialized in giving thorough physical examinations. He gave her the name of Dr. Durr, saying he didn't know much about the man but that he had heard he was good.

Dr. Durr wasn't any older than she was. He was big, well scrubbed and freckled, a heavy asthmatic breather with enormous hands. She couldn't say his examination was especially thorough. She wasn't put in the hospital, she didn't even have to report there for tests. It was a routine examination—heart, blood pressure, blood sugar, urine, Pap smear, breasts. He said she seemed to be in good health. Now they would wait for the results of the tests.

As she sat up on the examination table, and he towered over her, handsome and snorting in his white gown, she confessed to having strange feelings in the night that made her manufacture the strangest dreams and daydreams, there was no difference between them really, they were so much alike. She was not specific, and he didn't ask her to elaborate. Instead he looked confused and embarrassed as he stared at one of the small windowless walls, deep in thought. "That happens to me when I eat lasagna," he said.

"No, that's not it," she said. "I mean something else."

He was quick to retreat. "I know you do," he said. But he frowned and shook his head. No, this was meant to tell her, he couldn't fathom what the trouble was.

"Could my problems be mental?" she wondered.

He laughed. "You're not the type," he said.

In the weeks that followed, the envelopes from the laboratories came one by one in the mail. All carried the same one-word message. Negative.

14 The Courage to Create

RENZI was short and wiry, with black coarse wavy hair that had begun to recede and thin, and a fellow professor had once remarked that he looked the way the early unadulterated Britons must have looked. Usually he favored baggy pants and heavy crew-neck sweaters, moth-eaten and unraveling at the sleeves, which gave him the appearance of having just stepped out of a cool room in which he had been working on a book. Even when he was fussy about his appearance, he managed to resemble some small dark mountain farmer who had come down in his Sunday best to preach a hellfire sermon in the hollow's church.

The humanities course he taught was famous at the university, and was a potpourri of philosophy, the classics, architecture and art. He began it with a long stay in classical Greece, touched briefly on the Etruscans and the Roman Empire, skipped the so-called Dark Ages altogether, and finished up with a long stay in the Renaissance. He celebrated the greatest artistic monuments of Greece and Italy, and little else, and in his mouth the letters of the words "art" and "man" were invariably high case. His classes were combination pep rallies and slide shows, and he specialized in showing color slides of antiquities and paintings. Much of his effort as a teacher went into the purchase and labeling of slides, so that he had become almost more of a technician than a scholar, and he looked forward to his year in the classical world as an opportunity for him to take his own set of slides. Such an acquisition would allow him to add that personal and authentic touch to his running commentary which, so far, had been sadly missing. ("Now, when this particular shot was taken, we had just passed this old shepherd, who I'm sure, couldn't have changed an iota from his ancestors in the days of Euripides.") All summer he had been busy consulting photography catalogues and manuals, and eliciting the opinions of local photographers, in an attempt to determine the proper equipment for him to take along, and the technology and cost of range finders, lenses, automatic winders, light meters, flashes, film and filters had filled his mind far more than any dreams of the Temple of Zeus at Olympia, or approaching Rome via the Appian Way.

And yet his lectures, when he abandoned the projector and turned up the lights, championed human imagination and spirit over matter, and he was famous for an incident in his classroom when a student had dared to ask him for proof of this "universal creative force" he had a habit of referring to, and in reply he had wandered over to one of the high windows that overlooked the campus lawns and the masses of lilacs that were then in bloom, and after a dramatic pause, and with a look upon his face that said he was infinitely sorry for this student, had asked, "But can't you *feel* it?" And shaking his head with the anguish of his disbelief, had prematurely dismissed the class.

To him the most ennobling philosophy was that which championed human creativity, especially as it was manifested in the best of Western civilization, and in the advice he offered his students in regard to its application to themselves he had never quite been able to reconcile two opposing notions. One had it that the world was akin to a great creative democracy in which all men were poets, although not equal in their poetry, and at the very least were capable of creating within the limit of their abilities. Here he was apt to inform them that in classical Greece all makers were poets, regardless of what they made, the word "poet" coming from the Greek for "to make," and equally apt to quote Carlyle: "A vein of poetry exists in the hearts of all men." The contrary notion claimed that a few men were poets whereas the mass of mankind were not poets, but it was the duty of anyone who had been given the intelligence and the will to try to create, if only to demonstrate that he was not one of the sterile, middle-class mob. And in support of this elitest notion, he might quote Nietzsche: "Before God we are equal, but before the mob we do not want to be equal," while addressing those unknown talents in his audience as "You creators, you higher people!"

For years he had presented these ideas to young students, in whom he hoped to awaken an enthusiasm for art and to inflame their latent spirit to create. His duty was to quicken the heartbeat, open eyes that had been blinded, raise up the sleeping soul. To this end he was a powerful and theatrical lecturer, and he would often act out a dialogue, moving from one side of the rostrum to the other, taking different voices while, like a preacher, he would thump and gesticulate with his hands. He had been known to shake his fists before his face in a kind of creative frenzy, and to throw out his arms as though to embrace the "All," and on more than one occasion he had ended a lecture worn out and like some black-faced singer or a man about to be knighted, on his knees. He had a trained singing voice, although it had the vibrato and lackluster of a church soloist, and if he touched on music while in the Renaissance, he just might, to illustrate the point, break into triumphant Italian song, which his students, over the years, had become accustomed to reward with an outburst of applause.

These performances would likely end with what had become his battle cry: "You must find the courage to create!" And

again, but more softly and with reflection, and only seconds
before the bell would ring to end the class, so perfectly could
he time his performance, "The . . . courage . . . to . . . create."

His lectures were open to the public, and were held in a
large hall, like a theater, with a balcony supported by white
columns. Sarah, who had attended several, thought them evan-
gelical, and the man himself more prophet than professor. He
left her awed and shaken, and she found herself note-taking
even though she intended only to listen. She couldn't catch
everything he said, she couldn't always grasp the logic of his
argument, or see how it all coalesced into a system, but to
her surprise she understood him intuitively, meeting his ideas
halfway with an intelligent outpouring of her own feeling. Or
so she told herself.

To Renzi the universe was a work of art, the ultimate masterpiece, although it was still in the process of being created by
the greatest of artists, the Universal Creator. And men, who
were His agents, so to speak, were lesser artists engaged, on
a smaller scale, in the same universal task. He spoke of "the
divine creative principle of the universe," and of will (how
he underscored and repeated that word), which was fundamen-
tal to all creation and which he defined, in human terms, as
"the deliberate action by a human ego," and in terms of the
creative universe as "the unexhausted procreative will of life."
"The human mind," he proclaimed, "is in the highest stage
of evolutionary development because of its self-consciousness.
Unlike the other animals of the earth, man is Godlike because,
like his Creator, he can himself create. In other words, man
himself is the universe, only greatly reduced. And if the evolving universe is to realize the utmost outer limits of its creation,
each unit of the whole, each ego, each man and woman, must
create to the limit of his or her potential. With this in mind
I invite you to look more deeply into yourselves than you have
ever dared to look before, and to ask yourself this question:

Am I one who wants to familiarize himself with all the fantastic dimensions of the universal naturalism? Am I one who wants to seize the tiller of the world and lay his hands upon the blueprint of the evolving universe? If you answer, Yes, I am he! I am that one!, prepare yourself for a lifelong and superhuman effort of investigation and construction!

"And he who creates the new life," he went on to say, "will become Godlike through the existence of his creation, will become immortal through the timelessness and perfection of that creation! And let me emphasize the sense of newness and originality of that creation, of the making of the new thing which you, as young Americans, as the new people living in this, the new place, you above all other races and nationalities should appreciate and grasp!" "Newness" and "becoming" were the key words in this portion of his oration. To make the new thing was to engage in the process of becoming. The increased power for active creativity, coming from the will, meant an increased state of "becoming," which in turn meant, ultimately, increased *being*. Like the universe itself, man was in the process of becoming. "The River of Becoming," as he chose to call it. For a man, to stand still was to die. It was to have been; it was worse than that: it was to be one who never was.

"Universal and personal growth are always in the same direction," he proclaimed, "and culminate simultaneously in each other, and the oneness of the vast universe is reached through the power exerted from the will of the single ego. To grow personally is to make the universe itself grow—it is to contribute to the continuation of its creation. And when you understand that, you will be seized with the ultimate creative passion! You will have realized yourself in the experience of that extraordinary passion! You will have become one in synthesis with the almighty and endlessly evolving universe!"

At this point, Sarah, like the others around her, almost wanted to stand up and sing. They were all artists then, or potential artists; that was central to Sarah's thoughts. She was herself an artist. Or a poet, or a maker, as Renzi chose to call it. To be an artist was to create, and to create something was to create yourself; she made that connection so easily. One had to make. And the choice to make depended on the power of one's will, and the success of one's creation upon the power of one's originality. One needed courage to create; she had never thought of it in such a way. And wasn't the implication then that one was cowardly who did not create? She stared at the statement she had scribbled down from his lecture: "[We are] not free until [our] actions spring from [our] complete personality [at which time] these actions are to the creations of ourselves as the works of artists are to the artist." She felt an overpowering urge to create, to make. Something inexpressible, something grand. It was like hunger, it was like a need.

She hadn't planned to see Renzi after the lecture, but she ran into him in the spacious corridor outside the hall as he stood between the Georgian columns, babbling to the crowd of students he drifted back and forth among. He had worked himself up to an incredible pitch, and the wonder-filled faces of his audience, and the applause they had given him at the end, told him he had never lectured better, had never delivered with more heartfelt passion. As always after a good lecture, he was euphoric, light-headed, full of himself. He was certain everyone admired him and knew, even more than he did, just how good he was.

He had trouble focusing on Sarah and at first couldn't place her face or recall her name. She had the flushed and excited look of a schoolgirl, which he interpreted as proof of her admiration and infatuation. She admired his learning, his erudition, his performance, the power of his personality. On a young man such a look would have only told him that he had inspired him intellectually; on a young woman that same look told him that her excitement was more physical than intellectual, and was directed less at the realm of great ideas than at the man himself. She had been stimulated, she had been aroused, he had excited her romantically. Suddenly at the highest pitch of his own excitement and self-congratulation, he threw his arms around her and squeezed her tight. "Sarah—what are you doing here? But what a foolish question—so good that you could come!"

She embraced him, too. She felt elated for his sake, as though she were congratulating him on the news of a great victory. "The courage to create," she said.

15   *My Underground Self*

WITH the Orlovskys home from London, Stargaard had been forced to seek new quarters and had sublet the apartment of a woman mathematician who was teaching for the year in Texas. If he stayed in this area until next summer, he thought he might be able to rent Renzi's apartment, or possibly caretake for the Kubiliuses, who were now talking of spending as much as a year in France. For nearly a month he had forced himself to stay inside those rented rooms with their flamingo wallpaper and smell of bath powder, working on the book. He had a title for it now, *Ground Level*. Or possibly, *Sea Level*. It had turned out to be a sequel to *My Underground Self*.

Recently it had come home to him that he did not live easily or well in the present. He did not enjoy it, he may not even have been completely conscious of it. One half of him had always hung back in the past while the other had daydreamed about the future. The past was the material of the life that he had lived, observed and felt and often stuck en masse and unrefined into his books, the ubiquitous "I" in the past tense. The future had simply been the reward of the good life and quiet spirit he would have earned for having written the book. The present was no more than the medium in which he did his work. He began to suspect that his recent preoccupation with the events of protest and politics had been an attempt not so much to be a man of the moment who participated in a corner of real history as to escape his miserable course of living only in the future and the past.

The center of *My Underground Self* had been the story of his love-hate relationship with his father, a vice-president of an insurance company who had secretly longed to be a newspaperman, and had committed suicide when Stargaard was eighteen; it was also about his last year in college, when he became discouraged with the pedantry and pettiness of the academic world; and about his failure at a job in the advertising world, which he had taken, he supposed, in a foolish attempt to become his opposite, along with the breakup of an affair with a wealthy girl he had hoped to marry and who had aborted their child without telling him she was pregnant. The book had ended with its antihero on a Greyhound bus at night, traveling across the continent to a small town in Idaho, a destination he had, in his youthful madness, picked blindly from the map. If the book had been nothing else, it had been honest. Oh, perhaps romanticized, overdramatized, and he had perhaps pretended to descend to depths of the human condition that were not really within his reach (he could make that judgment now); but honest nonetheless. Its failings were the strengths of youth.

Now he had discovered that the new book, *Ground Level*, was to be a chronicle of all those failures and inadequacies and awful wastes of time and spirit and love that had crowded the incidents of his life since the writing of *My Underground Self.* God, it was painful. And boring. It was as if he were under a sentence of doom to relive the past and, what was worse, to wrestle with it until he understood it, until he knew what he had done, and what had happened to him. And he expected other people—hundreds of thousands of them if possible—to be interested in the product of this process. It was unreasonable.

In the past his fantasies of the future were often silly and romantic, but they had served to encourage and sustain him. He would win prizes, he would be praised by the best critics and writers of his and other generations; he would write a bestseller, would sell a book to Hollywood for a fortune, and on Academy Award night he would be seen in his tuxedo taking the steps three at a time on his way up to receive the award for the best screenplay adapted from a novel, in this case, his own; he would have an affair with a German actress; he would begin to write and direct his own movies. ("Have you seen the latest Stargaard?") He would consort with the international set on the Riviera, for he had always known that success in art could be a ticket into the upper class. He saw himself at an outdoor café in a small Mediterranean town near Marseilles, eating raw sea urchins and drinking the local white wine they called Cassis after the town; he was in the company of his small, trim French girlfriend, who sunbathed topless beside him on the beach. He bought a big white estate in Bermuda; he lived tax-free in a big Georgian house in Ireland, where he rode with the local hunt and owned a thousand yards of fishing rights on a salmon river. And none of this would deter him in the slightest from the high seriousness and integrity of his work. On the contrary, it would allow him to write whatever he wanted without his having to scramble, scrounge and leech.

He could also acknowledge his having had the adolescent

dream of himself as the troubadour who, by the magic of his art, would somehow win the girl. The princess. The Ideal. He didn't know what. Except that it was a mystery probably acquired in childhood and that he related to the cruel and ecstatic melancholy of convertibles, moonlight and placing his hand, for the first time, on a woman's breast. Now the dreams were gone, and how much his ambition depended on these dreams, he discovered only now. He said to himself, I don't want fame, praise, money, fine houses. I don't want women—not even *the* woman. I don't want to write this book. I want to live, want to enjoy life, want to be happy. Which meant he had not come to terms with his book so much as he had with himself. He could discover no other reason to write the book than to put it behind him, once and for all. And yet he suspected that even then he would not be free, but that in another ten years he would be driven to write a third book and make the whole into a trilogy. *On the Way Up*, perhaps. Or *Up and Out*.

One afternoon he dragged himself off to a pizza parlor, where he had a half-dozen draft beers as he sat around a table with a red-and-white-checked tablecloth, talking sports with a sweaty bunch of young men in gray T-shirts who had just finished a game of touch football. When he came out it was evening, and he ran into Alexander on the street.

"I'm supposed to be in Renzi's lecture," she explained. "But I decided to do some shopping instead."

"Cutting class—naughty, naughty," he said.

"Sarah will let me know what he covered. We're sitting in on his course together."

"Really? I wouldn't think Sarah would be interested in that." Alexander he could envision in such a class, although he would have thought she would be beyond Renzi's instruction at that level, which probably explained why she had not gone to class.

"I suppose you're working hard."

"I'm afraid my daydreaming interferes with that," he answered. "You see, I keep imagining this kingdom where the best men are not only poets but slaves—of the most beautiful women, naturally."

"Does that mean you're looking for a patroness with money?"

"I guess I have someone more like a cruel, barbarian princess in mind. Someone handy with chains and whips."

"You'd work then?"

"I'd sing like a nightingale."

He wanted to invite her home. *(Home,* he thought sarcastically.) He suspected that she and Marco, who apparently was away for months at a time, must have some understanding between them when it came to outside interests. But he was half drunk, unshaven and he didn't think he had changed his clothes all week. The next time, he promised himself. And not at his apartment but at her house in the woods.

She was artistic and intellectual—along with possessing what he suspected was the dose of artificiality and thoughtlessness that those two talents often implied—and yet, unlike himself, she knew how to live well within the given moment. With her he could have both art and the pleasure of the present tense. Or such was the solution she provided in his fantasies. When you anticipate the two of us together, she would tell him, learn to let that please you; enjoy the thrill of expectation for its own sake. And as she embraced him, she would ask, What could be better than what is happening to you now? And when that moment was finished, she would say, Learn that what you have now is as good as any other moment. The best moment is always the one you have at hand.

If his fantasies of Alexander always came quickly to a sexual adventure that was at once satisfying and profound, his fantasies with Sarah never quite came to that. Not that he hadn't tried to go beyond simple companionship, or that he failed to find her desirable. But notations of her flesh gave way so easily to more homely pleasures. Maybe the presence of Toby, whom he liked and envied, was responsible for such an inhibition. Unlike himself, the man knew what it meant to be male and hearty and to live in the world, doing ordinary worldly things. He lived on land, bought and sold land, real land, not paper land. Grass you could mow, trees you could sit under or chop down, clay you could put your shovel into, ledge you could break with a sledge hammer. And Toby knew the clubby camaraderie of other men and the satisfaction of a family at home. Sometimes Stargaard went so far as to believe he wouldn't mind taking over the man's life and stepping into his family and business, ready-made.

With Sarah he saw himself set free of the demands of writing, for he was certain she lacked his brand of ambition that was made all the more painful by his compulsive laziness and misdirection. His life with her would be athletic, domestic, full of friendly give-and-take. She had said she liked to hike in the White Mountains. Well, he would go with her into the mountains. He would spend a week with her in the mountains; they would sleep in a tent. He would grow a beard, wear a red bandanna on his brow. She probably knew how to sail, too, was likely a first-rate sailor. With such a woman you could find the time to build yourself a sailboat and thereafter sail your life away. Together you could take a week to reach an island—you could take a year—two years! You could sail around the world, dropping anchor wherever and for as long as you pleased!

They would cook and garden together in their home. He would learn to know the land and read the signs of weather. He would do things with his hands other than type and scribble; he would carve, sand, fit, join, whittle, he would hack away at clods with a hoe. He would learn how easy it was to look up and watch the changing cloud patterns of the sky. He would chop chives and parsley, he would slice meat from the bone. And when he was not with her in the cool farmhouse bedroom beneath a goose-feather comforter and log-cabin quilt, shut off from the silent house and surrounded by the darkened countryside, they would sit at the kitchen table and work a crossword puzzle together by the light of a kerosene lantern; they would play a series of cribbage matches that lasted all winter, with the score in the hundreds; would play, with the help of a dictionary, an epic and endless game of Scrabble. They would read detective novels side by side on the screen porch. "I had the one you're reading figured out about halfway through," she said. "When he said high tide wasn't until late that evening, and the body wasn't found—"

"Stop! Don't give the end away!" he said.

16   *Children*

SO far in her resolution to be creative and courageous, Sarah had been able to bring forth little more than raw emotion. She didn't know the direction her work would take, couldn't find the medium of its expression, didn't have a glimmer of its form. At this stage she saw it best as an impression of light and color, but whether such a vision would yield eventually to ink or paint or even music, she didn't know. It was like a tremendous if abstract cloudscape that kept sailing off and changing form, often so quickly that it disappeared from her altogether, leaving her elated but exhausted, as though the strain of inspiration alone was enough to use her up and leave her satisfied.

In part she blamed the children for the slowness of her start. Only now could she see the unreasonableness of the demands they made upon her, and how they consumed so carelessly what she had come to view as time that was her own. She envied Alexander, who had neither the encumbrances nor the failures and disappointments of children. She also envied Stargaard, who had no family at all, neither wife nor girlfriend, and was free to pursue his life's work, living where he pleased. Of course you could make things when you were footloose and childless. And she grew bold and self-possessed enough to view herself and someone like Stargaard as equals—she, the woman who had accomplished nothing, equal to the man who had. If she had been given his chances, she would have done as well as he had done.

She wanted her own place in the house. A studio like Alexander's, or an office like Toby's. Years ago she had set aside a sunny room as a combination sewing room and nursery in which she had imagined herself reading or sewing on the window seat while the children played silently with toys and dolls upon the floor. But she had never repaired the plaster so she could put up the wallpaper of her choosing, and now the children were too old for such a room. It was this room that she decided would soon become her room. She would tell the children she was not to be disturbed when she was inside it, nor were they, under any circumstances, to pass through that door. As if that would stop them, though.

She had come to see their lives as anarchy and license. They wouldn't pick up after themselves, ate whatever they wanted when they wanted, walked through any door. She had learned restraint as a child along with obedience and responsibility. She had asked for very little, but she had asked first for everything. Why hadn't her children learned the same in turn?

"Go to your room," she would order Jessie.

"No," Jessie would say. "Make me."

"I said go to your room."

"No, I won't go. You can't make me, either."

Her own mother had been able to wither her with a look, shame her with a tsk-tsk. How she had dreaded her mother's disapproval, and when it came, it had oppressed her like the weight of sin. But with her own children she had neither authority nor presence. They couldn't care less what she thought of them.

Apparently the worst was still to come. The Foxes had complained about their daughter's recent boyfriend, who, like his two predecessors, had been in trouble with the police. He had set fire to a church—well, the rug in the youth canteen in the basement. To the Foxes he was impudent and surly. "And if we say anything against the dear boy it only puts her more in his corner," Adele said.

"Count your blessings," Orlovsky said. "At least you get to see your daughter's boyfriends. All I get is bold-faced lies and sneaking out the back door after dark."

"Just wait until the boys start hanging around your Jessie," Adele warned. "With that long blond hair of hers."

"They'll be there on their motorcycles," Parker said. "I'd start her early on birth control pills if I were you."

"Drugs and alcohol scare me a lot more than sex," Colleen said. "After all, sex is normal. But these days they're even doped up and drunk in grammar school. And I'm a nervous wreck whenever one of the girls is out with some new boyfriend in a car. How do I know they're not speeding down some back road with the kid throwing down the whiskey behind the wheel?"

Sarah was certain that she would never control her children when it came to alcohol, drugs and sex. She tried to imagine herself counseling Jessie on such matters, or supervising a party for her friends, serving out small rations of wine. She could never bring it off! She had no control, would never have it, and had no excuse for having lost it. She hadn't had a career, or a major responsibility outside her home.

"What hurts me most about my children," Adele confessed, "is the smug way they sometimes seem to genuinely dislike me." In a moment of weakness she had once confessed that their teenage son, whom even Parker could not handle and therefore ignored, had actually struck her during a quarrel.

"It's their sense of righteousness and superiority that gets me," Colleen said. "The way they won't talk to you for days. To hell with them, I want to say. But then I try to tell myself it's just a stage."

"And the embarrassment they have for you," Adele said. "We can't get our oldest to be seen in public with us. And we can't go anywhere without her because we don't dare leave her alone for fear of all the mischief she'd get into at home."

Janet Angle wondered if they had seen the television report on the problems of growing up as a ghetto child. Then Adele asked if they had been following the series of articles in the paper about the problems the American-Chinese were facing with their offspring, who, until this generation, had always been obedient, law-abiding, respectful. Sarah wondered if anyone had read anything about these new private schools where the children were taught the old-fashioned curriculum of the three R's and treated with an iron-handed discipline. Could this possibly be the answer?

Allan Orlovsky, puffing on his pipe, was amused by this. A small man with a big beard and bushy hair, he was soft-spoken and easygoing, but he seemed to let it be known, albeit kindly, that Sarah didn't know enough about the subject to even ask the question. He himself knew the woman who was the founder of the most famous of these schools, and he had been instrumental in getting a grant for a young educator to make a study of this philosophy in practice. "I doubt very much if that kind of school is the answer," he said. "In fact, I'm sure it isn't. This generation of parents is weak, that's the problem. We know the old values won't hold water, but at the same time we're smart enough to mistrust the new. That's why these kids are a special generation. It's not that they're stronger, or better; we're just more vulnerable. And it isn't that they're more tolerant; it's that we're more tolerant, at least where they're concerned."

Sarah was not ignorant of his rebuke. Unlike herself, he had direct access to information, he didn't have to speak from second- and third-hand sources. After all, he was himself an educator-sociologist, and the New England director for the International Education Committee. He arranged and supervised conferences and symposiums at various universities and centers not only in the East, but around the world as well. He exchanged views with foreign scientists and scholars, advised foreign governments, and was accustomed to hearing the best and most recent thinking on the subjects of education and social change. If he wasn't hosting a group of Eastern European language teachers or graduate exchange students from the Philippines, he was traveling to far-flung places like Finland, Japan, Brazil. He could read and speak numerous languages, and Colleen claimed he could pick up a new language in a month.

In an attempt to save face, Sarah said, "But haven't parents always rebelled against their parents? I saw someone read a letter on television from a father to his son complaining about the behavior of the younger generation, and it was written two thousand years ago, but you'd swear that it could have been written today."

Auden seemed to come to her rescue. "You worry about your children if they don't rebel against you," he said. "Still, when they reach their twenties, or become parents themselves, it's the same old story, isn't it? They take another look and decide that the old gentleman and lady weren't such fools after all. I know I thought that of my father. My boy and girl thought that of me."

But Sarah didn't think that her boy and girl would think

that of her. They had witnessed too many outbursts of her fishwife's rage, had caught her in too many acts of contradiction, intolerance, sloth, had seen her too many times in stances that were irrational, ineffectual, indifferent. They knew how to make her bribe them, not for anything as important as their affection, but only for a moment's good behavior. She was convinced they knew, beyond the need for words, how she faulted them for what she had become. And knew, too, that she had abandoned them to other forces, having sensed correctly that she had a secret life that took precedence over their welfare and affection.

She had made mistakes with them she could never put right. They would never think her wise; would never, except for the most selfish reasons, submit to her authority. They would always view her as a figure smaller than life. They would never forget what they knew about her, and she would never forgive them for possessing so cruel a knowledge.

Now in the middle of those nights in which she awoke with pain and apprehension even though the weather was cool and airy—was the best weather in the world for sleeping—she saw herself in the consolation of a time that looked beyond her children to her grandchildren grown into their young manhood and womanhood, a generation as yet unborn. University students in the Boston area, or recent graduates starting out in their life's professions, they would gather in the company of their many friends and cousins in her Beacon Hill apartment, the doors of which were always open to them. She would be their compatriot. She would listen to their fresh winds and fashions, and they, in turn, would heed her counsel. They would be clever, witty, they would be world travelers, they would be involved in art, gambling, love-making—they would tell her everything! They would go to plays and concerts. They would read poetry out loud from small narrow books of verse, and she would know the younger poets. One of their friends would ask to paint a large portrait of her. She would be posed in a summer gown and seated in the garden among the spikes of foxglove or delphiniums. They would call her Grandmama and sometimes Sarah to her face, and each would think of her as his or her good friend.

Selfish Ned and devious Jessie would speak of her as that tyrant, that iron-fisted, cold-hearted matriarchal bitch. So be it. They would be irrevocably "out." While she and her coterie would be hard at work aiding cultural events and supporting liberal and charitable causes, they would be spoiled, reactionary dullards, living off the income derived from their father's speculations and investments. ("Look here, Mother, Jessie and I really must insist you set a better example for the children.") Except they wouldn't dare. Given her posture, her bearing, her generous but firm control of the family purse strings, they wouldn't dare.

Such fantasies, she knew, were stupid, despicable, far-fetched and cruel, and when she caught herself enjoying them she wondered whether she was sane.

She began to wish she didn't have children, though.

She thought it would have been better if she had never married.

17   *The Twilight of the Species*

POKEY Kubilius tended to stand aloof from any discussions about the problems of raising children, smiling—or so Sarah thought—indulgently. Although Pokey had her own theories on "mothering," which she believed she could be so authoritative on such a subject. On her face in absolutely, she also believed in the natural right of women to choose their own role in life, and she never went so far as to suggest that other women imitate her, even though she knew, as she knew they knew, that she was good at what she was. Cullenbine had once remarked that Pokey's children were too good to be natural, and had malevolently predicted that they were the sort of family that would end up with that oldest boy who played the recorder hanging himself in his closet or taking a .22 rifle to the whole family in their beds. Sarah thought this was nonsense, and said so.

Unlike Sarah, who had neither planned a family nor avoided having one, but had let it happen to her with all the accident of falling down a hole, Pokey had chosen motherhood, and had pursued it with all the dedication of a life's profession. Nevertheless, Sarah believed Pokey acted naturally with her children and that she was, genuinely, their good friend. Sarah wanted her advice and sympathy, and was tempted to demand even more by confronting her with a candid confession of the dissatisfaction and desperation of her feelings.

She cornered Pokey at the Orlovskys' after dinner, asking such questions as "How do you make your children mind you?" by which she really meant "respect you," to the more profound "What do you do if you don't really feel like a mother?" and "But isn't there sometimes a conflict between who you want to be and who they are, and I don't mean just their presence, but their personalities?" to which Pokey, who had a habit of answering a question with one of her own, had responded, saying, "If you're upset because they're not who you thought they would be, wouldn't you do better to accept them as themselves?" These and other questions Pokey answered reluctantly, in a manner that was at once pontifical and apologetic, as though she wanted Sarah to know that she was sorry that was the amused but sympathetic look of worthwhile suffering.

Oh, that's all right for you to say, Sarah wanted to tell her. Her children would never think ill of her, would never consider rebelling against her in the first place; if by any chance they did, though, she would know exactly how to handle it.

At the same time she found herself thinking: Maybe Pokey doesn't run as deep as I do. Maybe I want more, maybe I demand more, maybe that is why I'm so confused. Maybe because I know less about myself I know more. Or will. Someday. Although she didn't really believe this would be so.

Pokey advised, "Just don't be so down on them—and try not to be so down on yourself either." She recommended several books on parent-child relationships and on modern woman's role in the home.

Later that same evening Sarah sorted Stargaard out of the crowd. She wanted to talk to him, too. She not only wanted to make him understand the sincerity and passion of her envy; she wanted to wound him with it, if she could. "You don't know how lucky you are not to have children to rob you of the precious minutes," she said. "No wonder you can write a book."

Adele Fox intruded. "They make the babies," she said, "and then go off into their little rooms and make their precious poems."

Stargaard protested. "I make neither babies nor poems."

Now Kubilius got in on it. "Surely you knew about birth control, Sarah," he said.

"She knew about it," Toby joked. "Her problem was she married a man who hadn't a clue."

"I don't think that's funny," Janet Angle said.

"All right, I knew about it," Toby said. "I just didn't believe in it."

Which really set Janet off, and she again made her announcement that she should have aborted her third child, which again shocked Sarah, and again elicited from Colleen Orlovsky, a practicing Catholic married to a nonpracticing Jew, the prediction that when it came down to doing it, she wouldn't have had the heart.

"And I would have had my tubes tied after the second," Janet said, "if I could have gotten the permission of three doctors. You know who I didn't ask, don't you?"

Kubilius, who was the answer to this question, tended to keep his own counsel on such issues and to be conservative in those rare moments when he didn't. "If it's a choice between mass starvation and the destruction of the planet through over-development and pollution of the human population, and controlling the growth of human population by abortion," he said, "then it seems to me that abortion is the lesser of the two evils. If abortions are performed to save the world from us, and specifically from so many of us, then I'm all for it, I suppose. I don't hear of many women having abortions for that reason, though. In fact, I haven't heard of any."

Janet, feeling she might have been attacked, said in her own defense, "But I wouldn't have needed an abortion, and I wouldn't have needed to have my tubes tied, if John would have been willing to have a vasectomy. Or don't you think I would have preferred that?"

"All you men should consider that possibility more seriously than you have," Adele said, "if for no other reason than to keep women like Janet from being faced with such a lousy choice."

There was near-unanimous agreement among the women in support of this.

"It is a whole lot easier and safer than a woman being sterilized," Kubilius agreed.

"And safer than practicing birth control with pills, IUDs and jellies that contain who knows what poisons," Janet Angle argued. Which led to another discussion of the various cancers in women they probably caused, and then to an exchange of rumors about those local men who, allegedly, had had vasectomies performed. Vita Cullenbine said Renzi had had one. Renzi wasn't there to say yes or no.

Colleen turned on Stargaard. She looked flushed, a bit drunk, unusually belligerent. "Probably the only man in this room who doesn't need to have one has had one," she said.

Stargaard, caught by surprise, blushed.

Colleen turned her attention to John Angle. She got close enough to bump him with her chest; she had her hands on her hips. She was in her golfing clothes, a headband around her hair, a sweater tied around her neck, and that miniskirt that made her legs seem straight and her waist thick. Even the smallest movement of her muscular body said power and good form. "It wouldn't have hurt you to have had one, mister," she said. She looked as though she wanted either fun or trouble, and she didn't care which.

Adele Fox sauntered up beside her. "You'd still be a man," she said. "A real man. It doesn't even cut down on the old sex drive."

"You act like we want to cut your whang off," Colleen said.

"You're educated, you know you're one over the limit now," Adele said. "You and Janet aren't having any more children, so why the reluctance? You're aware how dangerous it would be for Janet to become pregnant a few years from now. Why not make certain it will never happen?"

Vita Cullenbine came alongside to make a threesome of John's tormentors. She wore a gray caftan of a kind a woman might slip on after a shower. It had a deep V-neck which revealed her small breasts when she bent over. Her slender arms and neck jangled with a savage display of silver and turquoise. "Think about all the affairs you could have without worrying about knocking a lady up," she said. "All you have to do is pass the ladies notes—like this ship's officer did to me back when I was in college and sailing to Europe for the summer. Come to my cabin, it said, it's safe, I've had an operation. I hadn't the foggiest notion of what he meant." Sarah was surprised at Vita's forwardness. Usually she was so quiet and withdrawn.

Janet Angle snuck up on her husband from behind. "All men think secretly they might divorce you sometime in the future," she said. "Or that you might drop dead. And that's when they'll run off with some young chick who'll want them to have a second family, and they'll have one, too, just to prove that in their old age they've still got balls. It's in the back of John's head, it's in the back of all their heads."

"Not in mine it isn't," John Angle said, trying to keep his eye on all four women as simultaneously they began to circle him. "I can't speak for the other men."

If this was an attempt to shift the women's attention to the other men in the room, it didn't work. However, if he hoped to throw a scare into those same men, he probably succeeded. Already the men were clustered in a bunch against the farther wall, as though to remove themselves as far as they could from the plight of their comrade and still be in the same room. They looked relieved that it was Angle and not any of themselves that the women had singled out to ridicule, and in order to ensure that the women did not abandon him for someone else, they not only supported the women against him, but egged them on. John, it doesn't hurt any, they said. And: They say there's a fifty-fifty chance the operation can be undone. And: Let's hope they haven't confused sterilization with castration. To which Kubilius commented, Well, it does the job either way. At the same time there was an uneasy look about their faces. Angle himself was doing his best to see the joke in his encirclement, or at least to make the women see it.

Then either Colleen or Vita, the two ringleaders, or both

in concert, gave him a push or blow that sent him down, although there was the possibility he simply fainted. He had
appeared to lean backward as though attempting to perform
that West Indian dance they call the limbo, and had continued
backward in this fashion, with his knees bent and eventually
higher than his head, until he was down, disappearing before
the women, who fell forward into his space, which suggested
that, in going down, he had managed to pull them in on top
of him. For a second Sarah caught sight of one of his legs,
the foot of which was shoeless and the cuff of his pants somewhere above his knee. The women on all sides of him looked
as though they were sorting frantically through a pile of clothes.

"A darning needle!"

"A hatpin!"

At this, the other men, who were already cowering, could
be seen to bunch even tighter against the wall, reminding Stargaard of a herd of docile game animals abandoning a straggler
to a pack of wild dogs. The men who had wives in the middle
of the mayhem looked as though they were in shock.

After a brief spell of sluggish self-defense, in which he must
have believed the assault was only play, Angle suddenly was
giving combat. He kept trying to sit up and wriggle free, while
his attackers, using the weight of their numbers, kept throwing
him back. By the time he was free and no longer restrained
or pawed by female hands, he resembled some popular singer
who had been mobbed by teenage girls. His slacks had been
pulled down without first having been unbuttoned, and he
complained, as he held them up, that they had broken the
zipper on his fly. Vita he accused of pulling the hair on his
chest and of scratching his midriff in her attempt to raise his
shirt around his chest, and Adele Fox, of all people, of snapping
repeatedly the band of his jockey shorts. What other than this
had been done to him when they had him in their power,
he could not name in words. He appeared bedazzled, disillu-

sioned, violated, amused. He had the enormous eyes of a drugged and befuddled bull. Although he was laughing now (they were all laughing now), there was still a look of surprise about him that said he would never be the same.

18 *Doomsday*

 "AM I going to be dead in seventeen years?" Ned asked.

Toby, who had been scrambling eggs, looked up alarmed. "Why do you ask that?" he said.

"Because that's what Jessie said."

"Why did you tell him that, Jessie?"

"Because it's true," Jessie said. "We learned it in school, and heard it on television, too, lots of times. And that's because of all this pollution and overpopulation and because we're such big wasters. The world—the whole world!—has only seventeen years to live. After that everything on earth will be dead. And that includes Ned."

"It doesn't include me," Ned said, spooning up his cereal.

"Yes, sir, it does too. You're part of everything." She couldn't see how anyone could dispute this logic.

"Well, it includes me," Sarah said in an ironic attempt to comfort Ned.

"Sure, you," Jessie said, pouting. "It isn't fair. Because in seventeen years I'll only be twenty-five. You guys are older than that already. And it's your fault I'll have to die then, too. I'd like to live, you know."

"I'm not going to die, am I?" Ned said.

"Yes, sir," Jessie said.

"No, sir," said Ned.

"Yes, you will," Sarah said. "Someday. But you won't be the only one."

"See?" Jessie said. "What did I tell you?"

"Not me," Ned said. "I'm not old. I'm not going to die." He sprinkled sugar on a second bowl of cereal. "I'm not sick, either."

Their selfishness surprised Sarah. And their apprehension concerned her, although she didn't know how to calm them. Toby, however, prided himself on his ability to bring them out of their unpleasant moods and to make them little instructive speeches. It didn't matter if these were on subjects he knew little or nothing of, or if he had his facts and figures wrong, which was not to deny the genuineness of his compassion. "Correct me if I'm wrong," he was saying, "but some scientists, but not all scientists, have said the earth will be dead in seventeen years, but only if we continue our present rate of destroying the environment and increasing our pollution. But if we start to clean up things now, we can reverse the trend." And he reminded them of the report of salmon returning to the Maine rivers and of the potential use of pollution-free windmills to generate electricity that they had recently watched on television with the rapt attention they usually reserved for cartoons. It was true, he said, that men in the past, including their own father, had treated the environment carelessly, but that wasn't necessarily because they were bad men. Even the scientists who invented such things as pesticides, food additives, fertilizers, hadn't known the damage that many of them would cause. They had really been humanitarians, who had viewed these discoveries as advantages for mankind as a whole. More food would be grown, diseases would be prevented, transportation would be made safer and faster, etc., etc. But now these same men, and men everywhere, were aware of the problems of pollution and contamination and were working hard to solve them. Their own father's mission, as he explained it, was not only to save the land but to improve it by using it correctly.

Sarah had noticed that his recent interest in ecology and conservation had given his own projects a kind of moral legitimacy, and he now pursued them with an almost missionary zeal. He saw no conflict of interest, or irony, in his being a real estate developer and a member of the town zoning board and now a member of the town's newly formed Land Conservation Commission.

Maybe he was right, she thought, listening to him. There was still so much wilderness left around them, most of it in private hands. His optimism was easier to take than all this talk of Prepare to Meet Thy Doom and The Judgment Day Is at Hand, as if some sun-sized planet was on a collision course with the earth.

But the smog they had encountered that evening at the Angles' had returned a second time, and lately she could smell auto exhaust fumes even though the highway was several miles away, with hills between.

"It's an awful paradox," Archie Auden had said recently. "The interest in preservation and ecology, I'm afraid, has come a bit late. For up here anyway. Just as quick as you have an old Colonial house renovated so that it's looking good and proper after a hundred years of abuse, you have a pink house trailer set down next door. People finally pick up cross-country skiing and they have to fight the snowmobiles for the trails. There are those pushing blindly ahead and creating all kinds of future mischief, and those stepping carefully backwards and rediscovering what was best, and they're both using the same road. They can't help running into each other."

"We're stuck in the same old world together," Toby said, presenting the argument he had given the children. "We just have to take better precautions than we did before."

"Maybe it's already too late for that," Kubilius said. "They're saying now that life expectancy in the most industrialized countries has turned the corner and is going down. A child born today won't live as long as one born five years back."

"That won't keep the population growth down, though," Orlovsky said. "And the more people, the cheaper life will become. We'll become more and more like India and China and Latin America. The concept of the individual doesn't work very well in those countries. Neither does democracy, or Western humanism."

Renzi argued against this possibility. "The mind of man and the human creative spirit," he maintained, "will be put to the test and emerge triumphant. Man will simply undo the worst of what he's done. And I wouldn't count humanism out, not yet."

"It's swinging the other way," Orlovsky insisted, "against us." And by "us" he meant the liberals, the democrats, the intellectuals, the humanists. "We want to return to democracy at the grass roots level at a time when such a form of government isn't practical or even possible. We've discovered what we might have had when it's no longer possible to have it. And I'm afraid it's the younger people who will have to learn the bitter truth of this, and suffer accordingly."

"And we haven't prepared them for it either, have we?" Sarah ventured. "We haven't taught them responsibility, restraint, sacrifice."

"Oh, they'll do all right," Pokey said, winking. "We haven't been so bad as all that."

But Orlovsky's pessimism was not easily dismissed, and many of them suspected unhappy changes in their future. Maybe it would only take the form of some impersonal dictatorship, a bureaucracy run by bad laws and machines. More likely it would take the form of some great disaster and catastrophe that could happen in a flash, or take as long as millenniums. Not nuclear war or accident necessarily. It could be something far more insidious than that. Some massive annihilation by disease or human carelessness or by nothing more complicated than the massive human presence. At the very least, life as they had known it, as man had known it for thousands of years, would be altered, and for the worse. The irreversible process, whatever it was, had already begun.

For some time now there had been this vague dissatisfaction and apprehension, and the conversations at the parties had revealed a premonition of doom and danger, along with desires to move elsewhere. To a newcomer like Stargaard such longings seemed neither realistic nor reasonable, and he went so far as to view those who had them as being ungrateful.

After one of these conversations he had gone out onto the darkening lawn that overlooked the river behind the Orlovsky house. "You don't want to go somewhere else, Allan?" he said.

"Never."

"Of course. You're gone somewhere across the world as often as you're home."

"Just about," he admitted. "But this is still my home. I'll never live anywhere else, at least until my kids are grown."

Stargaard was surprised to hear him say he was so settled down and rooted in one spot. Orlovsky had always impressed him as a man who was at home in airports, conventions, hotels and conference centers, where he could be found in a three-piece suit with a plastic name tag on his breast, puffing on that pipe of his and speaking Portuguese or Japanese as easily as French.

Below them the mud flats and sandbars were rising and taking shape in the wide tidal river as the tide went out with the fresh water; a blue heron that had posed on the shore like a statue suddenly labored into flight, looking in blue silhouette like some prehistoric reptilian bird. "You don't want to move back to New York?"

"I don't have any ties to New York," Orlovsky said. And he told how he had been the only child of parents both of whom were the only members of their families to emigrate from their small village in Russia. They had married late, had had Allan late; both were dead now. They had spoken little English and had lived in New York not among their fellow Jews but, stubbornly, in an Italian neighborhood. "I never had a blood relative in this country other than my parents," he said, "until I had children of my own."

Stargaard thought now he knew why Orlovsky collected Shaker pieces and American primitives, especially farm tools, and decorated the house with them. In contrast, Colleen treated the house like a motel, did a minimum of housecleaning, and couldn't care less what it looked like or how it was furnished.

"And when your kids are grown," Stargaard said, "where would you think of going then?"

"Probably nowhere. Although maybe the south of Spain, if I could afford it. Funny, how we always look towards Europe. I bet you were like I was, and couldn't wait to finish college and go abroad. The kids don't seem to be like that today. They want to travel out west to states like Colorado or Montana. Or to Latin America, and places like Guatemala and Yucatán. My daughter wants to go to Ecuador."

On the far bank of the river, the pine forest seemed, in the blue of this darkening, to stretch as far away as Canada. In the river itself a man in a launch with an outboard was trying to pick his way slowly, without the help of any light, between the rising bars and the narrow pine-covered islands.

Orlovsky had brought a bottle out with him and, unseen by Stargaard, had filled his glass. It was an extraordinary young Napa Valley Cabernet.

"They don't know what a good life they have," Stargaard said to himself.

19 Emigration

RECENTLY two prevalent but contradictory blueprints for disaster had taken hold among the
men. One theory had it that all the carbon dioxide produced
by burning fossil fuels would act like the glass of a greenhouse,
trapping the sun's heat it had allowed to enter and turning
the earth, in consequence, into a gigantic hothouse, with the
continental glaciers melting and the sea level rising until all
the low-lying coastlines were flooded, including most of the
major cities of the world. The answer to this threat was simple:
move to higher ground. The second theory claimed that because of the dense concentration of dust in the atmosphere—
volcanic dust in combination with that raised by so much industry and agriculture—the sun's heat would be screened out,
and a new ice age, with the glaciers advancing southward instead of retreating northward, would result. A move to southern land was the answer to this threat. Regardless of which
theory would be proved right, it was agreed that the north
near the sea, where they lived, was the worst possible place
in the world to be, and that the wise man prepared for either
eventuality with a single move. Mountain land in the south,
it was argued, was the perfect solution and would turn back
either flood or ice. The land they hoped to buy, besides satisfying these two requirements, had also to be cheap, for they
wanted to buy in quantity. This was to thwart still a third dan-

ger, that of the future scarcity of land, the lack of which might
mean, in future times, starvation for those who didn't own
it. Some of them had gone so far as to maintain it was their
duty as parents to leave their children land since they could
afford it, and that such an investment in their children's future
was even more important than a college education. If the worst
happened, it was argued, they could always support themselves
by subsistence farming, a possibility Parker Fox especially rel-
ished, imagining his children as settlers once more in the wilderness, living off the land from hand to mouth. It was an
idea that Toby also promoted, although he had no such dooms-
day vision for the modern world. Only high land in Arkansas
and West Virginia seemed to fit all three requirements of being
high, southern and cheap, and Parker Fox wasn't all that sure
that either state was far south enough, or that the land there
was all that tillable or fertile, if it ever came to clearing it.
He received real estate brochures from agents in both states,
and actually made a trip to West Virginia, where he purchased
fifty acres of a slope that was too steep for him to walk up or
down, even though he hadn't cared for the area with its strip
mining, coal towns, poverty, squalid architecture and bad
roads.

The notion of buying large tracts of land cheaply anywhere
was attractive to everyone, and Kubilius, unlike other doctors,
who invested in apartment complexes in suburbs and cities,
had bought as much as a thousand acres of wooded bogland
in northern Maine. There was also talk of leaving the area—
this great good place—entirely. In part it was to escape the
Massachusetts and New York people, who were themselves
moving to escape the crowding and pollution of their own
states, although the dissatisfaction ran deeper and was less focused than merely that. Maine wasn't far enough away from
them, and was already contaminated. The Maritime Provinces
of Canada were mentioned as an alternative, but Parker Fox,

who used to champion them, finally made an exploratory trip to Nova Scotia and returned disenchanted, dropping the subject he had bored his listeners with for years. He hadn't liked the stink of the pulp mills, the junked cars abandoned in clear streams, the way the English and Scots abused the French Canadians, and Adele had been appalled at the dullness of the people, who were all for development without controls. Parker had also given up on the possibility of homesteading in Alaska now that so many local families were going there, not to escape the development of New Hampshire, however, but to participate in that of the wilderness up there. He had transferred his dreamy allegiance to New Zealand, expounding on the glories of its unspoiled fjords and glaciers, which, according to him, were a paradise for skiers, trout fishermen and hunters, and about as far removed as you could get from everywhere else. He could still be receptive to the possibility of Newfoundland. The Angles answered by dreaming out loud about the West Coast and British Columbia. Toby brought up the idea of moving to Australia, but the real estate potential of the Maritime Provinces, with the predicted boom of Americans buying land there, really interested him more.

It was also fashionable to insist that there were areas in Europe less spoiled than over here, and the possibility of a reverse migration was often seriously considered, from the New World to the Old because, in this age of American technology with its companion doctrines of consumption and waste, the New had become the Old. Get yourself to these places in Europe, it was counseled, if you want a few years of grace before the sprawling American culture catches up.

Adele Fox favored the western islands of Scotland, Skye and Harris, whereas Parker allowed the possibility of Ireland. In this he was supported by Stargaard, who believed that, as a writer, he could live tax-free. "All I have to do is make some money to make it worthwhile," he joked. He and Parker took to calling Ireland "God's country."

For several years Kubilius had made a study of Galicia in northwest Spain. It was his dream to visit there the next year, and possibly even to retire there after the children were grown. "You have the Irish weather and landscape, but the Spanish culture," he would argue with Parker. "In other words, the best of both worlds. Gallego cuisine instead of Irish. A light wine they call *ribeiro* served in earthenware bowls instead of stout. And the best selection of seafood in the world. And who do you know that ever went there?" He would also point out that the Gallegos lived harmoniously with nature, or so he had read and heard. It was a poor country, but every piece of land was utilized in some way, nothing was ever wasted, a perfect ecological system had been evolved. He would say this for Auden's benefit, painting a picture that was meant to make Galicia an answer to his theory of the perfect orchard in prehistory.

Pokey would listen to him with that amused and weary smile of hers. "Places off the beaten track are usually so for some very good reasons," was all that she would say. Everyone knew, without her saying, that she was perfectly happy where she was, and if she spent any time elsewhere, it would be in France.

Renzi was appalled that anyone would want to go to such remote and uncivilized places. "Literally to Land's End," he told Kubilius. "That's what the Romans called your fantasy land. *Terra Fina.*"

Auden took Adele and Sarah aside. He didn't approve of this preoccupation with traveling. Didn't they detest the summer travelers clogging their highways in the summer, just passing through?

"When we lived in the Midwest," Adele said, "we knew people who would spend their vacations driving in a big car out to Arizona or Wyoming, only to turn right around and drive home. Then they'd brag how they never put less than six hundred miles a day on their speedometer."

"No question about it," Auden said. "We do far too much

traveling for its own sake. I'm afraid it's gotten into our skin, or our souls."

"Sometimes I think we'd do better to return to the turn-of-the-century notion of vacations," Sarah said. "You know, when the whole family would stay on the seashore or in the mountains in a big white hotel with a big veranda, or in their big shingled cottage. And year after year they would go back to the same place, do the same things, see the same people. Like they used to do in the White Mountains, or on the Isles of Shoals."

Auden was sympathetic to this proposal. "We certainly have to hurry up and change the way we think about land and travel," he said. "And about the way we use our time, too. We'd do better to stay right here at home and clean up our mess instead of sneaking off in the middle of the night and leaving it to someone else. I've always thought we could learn a great deal from the Japanese in the way they make and appreciate those miniature but perfect gardens in their back-yards. If you do it the way they do, you don't need to go any-where, wasting time and fossil fuel, and paving over the land-scape. You never have to leave your yard. The whole earth, in all its varieties—mountains, lakes, forests, beaches, water-falls—can be represented and symbolized right there in that one little garden right off your back doorstep. Imagine a conti-nent where everyone had just such a little garden, and just imagine a race of people who knew how to see and find peace of mind in a world like that. We wouldn't feel this awful com-pulsion to race off to somewhere else in the world if we could see the whole in a little plot of ground like that."

"Maybe," Adele said, "but it hasn't kept the Japanese at home."

"That's because they've become like us," Auden admitted. "Maybe it's time we became a bit more like them—or at least like the way they used to be."

But when Auden drifted elsewhere, Adele said to Sarah, "A little backyard garden reflects the whole world, all right. Poisoned air, poisoned soil, poisoned water, poisoned plants, poisoned you. The problem isn't learning how to see the world in your garden. It's how to keep the world out of it, paradox though that would seem to be."

20   Wilderness and Sisyphus

PARKER Fox was a small-town lawyer who was far more interested in the out-of-doors than in his practice, and was therefore incompetent if you listened to Cullenbine, but only lazy and irresponsible if you listened to his friends. He wore tweed jackets over flannel shirts and duck-hunting boots to his office, and if he didn't greet you like Lincoln, with his huge booted feet on his desk, he was likely to do so from the small messy table he kept beside the shelves of lawbooks where, with the aid of a microscope, he tied his own trout flies. As often as not, his office would be discovered empty, his secretary explaining, with that look that said she had long since given up caring what his clients believed, that he was off to the county seat to register still another deed.

An avid hunter and fisherman and expert with either rod or rifle, he was, by preference, a food gatherer. "You are looking at man in his most primitive stage," he liked to announce about himself. He was hardly a sportsman. He would have preferred to catch trout by rolling up his sleeve and sticking his arm into the pool of the state hatchery, or to get himself a deer by chasing off the dogs that had just brought it down. Once he brought home and ate a beaver he had seen the car ahead of him run down, and he was the man to call to get rid of the woodchucks in your garden. He admired stories of old Vermonters who had a salt lick in their barn, the back door of which was always open, along with a secret horse stall that was heaped with antlers. As though they were poor country people, he would collect his family together and pick strawberries and raspberries in season, and take Adele out for a last gleaning of the high blueberry bushes, where, like a child, he ate as many as he consigned to his bucket. He had frogged the local ponds for years, and several times came near to drowning, and many times came home covered with leeches, and it wasn't his fault if you could hear a frog croaking in any of the ponds within five miles of his house.

A woodsman by birth and instinct, he had come late to the knowledge that there was food for the taking along the seashore. He had never seen such abundance, although his recent expeditions had been curtailed by the repeated visits of the mysterious and deadly red tide that made shellfish poisonous to eat. But when he could, he dug clams, collected mussels and lately had developed a fondness for periwinkles, which he ate by the panfuls, fighting off the children; he had been known to look longingly at the bands of seaweed at the tide line, which he nudged with his toe, vowing he would learn to tell the edible weeds. He had made friends with lobstermen, who delivered to him the crabs and whelks they found in their traps, although their munificence did not prevent him from raiding their traps that washed ashore in storms. He was a famous freezer of foods, and was often at the sink at home, making up and labeling little plastic bags of future meals.

He was fond of teasing Auden and Kubilius. "It doesn't seem

right," he would say, "that a man ought to have to raise his own food. A man shouldn't have his food tied down all around his house so that when he's hungry he just goes out and breaks off a hunk. Seems to me he ought to be able to go out and find it, root it out, grub it up, pick it up at his feet. Wild things taste better than tame things anyway." Naturally he championed the preservation of the wilderness.

Toby always supported him in this, using much the same argument he gave the children, although he didn't think we needed quite so much acreage set aside as we had at present. "Alaska is the perfect example of overdoing it," he said. "That's just too much land going to waste. After all, you can't turn back the clock. As much as you might like to, you can't deny progress."

"The return of trees and grass and wilderness," Parker said, "that's progress."

"I'm not against wilderness," Dr. Milton Cullenbine said, "but I am against this pernicious American doctrine of preserving it. It's always been a perfect dodge and cover for developers. Believe me, if I were a developer like our friend Toby here I'd want the wilderness preservation concept implanted in everybody's head. As long as you can believe there are wilderness areas set aside where life goes on as it has since the deluge, you can justify doing all sorts of tasteless and destructive things to the landscape everywhere else. If you get tired of looking at your mischief, or living in it, well, go take a peek at the wilderness. Get away from it all."

"By God," Auden said, "there's something to that, all right."

For Parker the solution was simple. "Let's have all wilderness then," he said.

Cullenbine said, "I'd rather have a continent that was one vast suburbia, if well done, like the very best of the English countryside, than have a few wilderness areas sandwiched between junkyards and shantytowns. No question but we'd be a lot better off with the English idea of small villages. Then all you'd have to do is watch the landscape gradually become a massive but handsome suburbia with green belts in between the towns. That takes planning, though. That means putting the real estate fellows in their place. Which is under a rock. Besides, when you developers want some more land for a ski lodge, or you tourists with your big campers want a parking space, you just change the rules and nibble away at the wilderness anyway. No, better to have development, and have it everywhere, only make certain that it's all done well."

"I suppose it all goes back to man's mistaken notion that he's inherited the earth," Parker Fox said. "That he's right there at the center of things. It used to be that the laws were only made to protect men, and the property of men, from the willful acts of other men. What we need now is more and stronger laws protecting the rest of the world from men."

"Crimes against nature are worse than the murder of any man," Cullenbine observed. "Although I suppose there are some who would say that homicide's a crime against nature, too. But I can actually foresee the time when a man is executed for polluting a river."

Adele Fox, who had tried on several occasions to break into the argument, now found enough silence to say, "There's absolutely no question but that man cheats himself when he destroys the countryside and kills animals wantonly. So many people don't understand that they're enriched by natural beauty and wild life."

"To hell with what man needs," Cullenbine countered. "I'm saying the rest of the planet has intrinsic rights of its own."

"Still, it's man's duty to protect the lower forms of life because he's intelligent enough to know they have rights to exist and should be protected," Adele said. "Granted, protected from him."

Sarah had observed that, unlike herself and the other women, the men seemed to regard Adele as an equal. She suspected it was because of the contract she had been given on her cookbook.

"They knew what they were doing in the olden days when they executed a man or woman for bestiality," Cullenbine announced, becoming progressively more outrageous. "Unfortunately they also executed the violated animals, who were innocent. And by the way, who says they're the lower forms of life?"

Toby wanted to return to the original subject. He said, "Aren't you admitting, though, with your green belts and model villages, that man is going to alter the face of the earth, like it or not?"

"Don't tell me what I'm admitting," Cullenbine said.

Auden entered the discussion now. "The mistake is in man seeing it as his duty to remake the world," he said. "I've always maintained it was his duty to tend it. I don't see man as a bulldozer or a builder, but as an orchard keeper, or a shepherd."

"We'll remake the earth because we're here, because we can and probably because we have to," Toby said. "But I think we should do it fairly and correctly. And we should hold ourselves in check, within reason."

"What's fair for a man may be awfully unfair for a woodchuck," Parker Fox acknowledged. "Much less a clump of grass."

"Or a ledge of granite," Cullenbine added. "We don't think anything about blowing one of them to smithereens."

"You're not saying a granite ledge has as much right as a man, are you?" Orlovsky wondered. He sucked on his pipe, amused.

"I am saying it," Cullenbine said. "And I want to mean it, too, I know I ought to try very hard to mean it. We've given rights to blacks, women, children; why not give it equally to animals and rocks, not to mention all those gases in the atmosphere?"

"Sure you're not playing the devil's advocate?" Orlovsky wondered.

"I'm the new man," Cullenbine said. "I speak for the democratic planet, I know the true meaning of human humility. So there is no cerebellum in the rock; let's give it equal rights regardless, what do you say? Do you seriously think the universe distinguishes on such a lowly level as self-consciousness between animate and inanimate, between the other animals and man? Do the cogs that move the great machine distinguish between a man and a rock, composed, as they are, of the same elements? Or, if you believe in a God, that He loves man more? He made the rock, too, didn't he? What's so special, what's so precious, about life? It's a chemical accident, that's all."

"That's a very dangerous doctrine to go preaching," Renzi said. "I don't think we need any more philosophies that promote the worthlessness of human life."

"Not just human life, all life," Cullenbine corrected. "And I didn't say it was worthless, only that it counted for as much as everything else. A scientist knows there are no clear boundaries between the living and the unliving. We're simply organizations of molecules with chemical origins. It seems to me I see life for what it is, no better and no worse. Show me the man who says he's better than obsidian!"

This flew in the face of Renzi's humanism, and Sarah secretly cheered Renzi on when he argued that the human spirit surmounted the purely animal, the purely physical, and that man was continuously engaged in the process of becoming.

"Becoming like the dinosaurs," Cullenbine said.

"All right, then I'll speak on your scientific level," Renzi said, "and grant you that man's destiny probably isn't divine in origin but only the product of evolution and natural selection. But the dinosaurs ruled the world in their day, and I'm sure they did a nasty job on the vegetation. Now it's man's turn. Call him the King of the Mammals in the Great Age of the Mammals if you want. But it could very well be his destiny to inhabit the other planets and colonize the universe."

"Christ, I hope not," Auden said.

"Who knows what man's limits are," Renzi posed, "or where he will end?"

"Listen to him," Cullenbine chided. "He'd be the first to claim we're not the equal of Athens or the Renaissance."

"Man's becoming, all right," Auden put forward. "Becoming wasters and polluters. I say it's time to sit back and *be* for a few centuries. Let the world go by instead of us trying to turn it. We can't afford to become anymore. The world can't afford it either."

Renzi answered this by launching into a lecture, in which he acknowledged at some length the victory of Sparta over Athens, the long stretch of the Dark Ages, the horrors of Nazi Germany, while insisting that finally, for every step backward man took, eventually he took a step and a half forward. During this lecture Cullenbine's mind could be seen to stray.

"But it's only a scientific progress that we've made," Orlovsky countered, "not a moral or humanistic one. I don't think there's been much progress lately in human nature."

"None to speak of in ten thousand years," corrected Auden.

"The last sixty years, anyway, haven't counted up for much," Orlovsky said. "I'm a humanist myself, or used to be, and I say it's a great pity there isn't progress. But how can there be? The biological and sociological survival of the fittest doesn't depend on such qualities as sensitivity, fair play and compassion. It's more like it that a humanitarian and altruist flies in the face of nature and, given the way things are, has the least chance of survival. I mean, the man who lays down his life for his fellow man isn't going to be around to reproduce."

"I don't see how anyone could argue that we haven't been

making moral progress," Toby said. "A hundred years ago we freed the slaves, we abolished child labor, we've as good as written off the death penalty—"

Kubilius, who had been waiting impatiently outside the circle, now leaped in. "What are you saying—that we have a society that legalizes abortion, and is about to sanction euthanasia, and at the same time will allow madmen and dangerous criminals to live at great expense to the taxpayer? That doesn't make sense. When there's not enough to go around, we're not going to kill off the unborn innocent and then share our rations with chronic troublemakers. They eat food, they take up space, they cost money, they demand services; set them loose and they'll steal our goodies and cut our throats. No, we'll get rid of them, all right. The death penalty will come back, and it will be used, although we'll kill the condemned man humanely, probably with a shot in the arm that puts him to sleep, like an old dog. And we're also going to kill idiots and serious malefactors. It's the next step after euthanasia. Already we've started up the executions again."

Orlovsky, who had admitted to some unhappiness with his old humanism, was not willing to go so far as this. "To kill, for whatever reasons, debases us even further, and opens the doors to the worst of evils," he said. "Which I would define, I guess, as indifference to suffering."

Kubilius struck back as though he had been set up. "How can you justify keeping a mad-dog killer alive when you're quite willing to abort what may become a Saint Francis? Or not even that, but just another ordinary good citizen?"

"But I thought you favored abortion?" Adele Fox said.

"As a matter of necessity I do," Kubilius said. "But do you seriously think that abortion will make us more unselfish and humane? I think it will have a terrible effect on us—although we won't realize it right away. But I don't want to get side-tracked on abortion." He turned again to Orlovsky. "How can you justify the expense of keeping that same killer alive when you let a small girl live in abject poverty in Mississippi? When the money you spend on him, but refuse to spend on her, could feed her, raise her up, give her a chance, make her happy, keep her from losing out in life?"

"I believe we should do both," Orlovsky said. "And I think we can, too. I'm convinced we dehumanize ourselves by killing criminals. Maybe we should keep them alive for our sakes as much as theirs."

"We dehumanize ourselves by letting the innocent child lose out because of poverty and malnutrition," Kubilius countered.

"Which is it, an innocent child or a crazed killer? If it comes down to a choice, right now we choose the killer. Think of it in those terms and then tell me that's not insane."

"My God," Renzi said, "human life is already cheap enough, and that kind of thinking can only make it cheaper. We all know about 'body counts,' the forty million dead in World War Two, the starvation in Asia and Africa."

"What I'm saying," Kubilius said, "is that it will become even cheaper."

The two instigators of this argument, Parker Fox and Cullenbine, had long since wandered off in pursuit of other pleasures, and now Orlovsky and Kubilius, having expended their passions, departed, too. Despite the absence of the most vocal members of his opposition, Renzi took up the discussion, and whenever he appeared to be isolated or attacked, Sarah tried to break into the discussion in his support. She saw the two of them together, even if she did have to admit she found some merit in the gloomy predictions of the opposing point of view. The argument made strange bedfellows, because, for the most part, Toby and Auden were on her side, while Stargaard took up the positions established by Cullenbine and Kubilius. Gradually even these principals excused themselves, and Sarah suddenly found herself alone in uncertain argument against two other women, the three of them embarrassed that they hadn't had the foresight to move off earlier.

Later that evening Sarah strolled with Renzi out onto the lawn, where they encountered Auden, Stargaard and Orlovsky, all of whom appeared to be gazing at the stars.

"It's hard to believe," Auden said, "but when I was a college man and reading poetry, it seemed to me that if we had a hero, it must have been Prometheus, who stole fire from the gods and gave it to mankind—along with knowledge, of course. That was what we wanted to give humanity. I don't know that we wanted to come to his bad end, though, chained to a rock with his liver eaten eternally by a vulture. When we saw ourselves in those days I suppose in some way we had the Promethean image in mind." He laughed.

" 'Thus alone man grows to the height where lightning strikes and breaks him, lofty enough for lightning,' " Renzi quoted.

"An attractive myth," Orlovsky said. "You could see how it shaped so much behavior. Rebellious, individualistic, altruistic, fatalistic. The Romantic hero."

"By the time I was in college, Prometheus had given way to Sisyphus," Stargaard recalled. "Or so our professors told us anyway. I wonder if we really did see ourselves as Sisyphus, eternally pushing that large boulder up the slope, only to see it teeter on the summit and tumble back down to the bottom."

"And punished not for giving a gift to man," Renzi mused, "but for cheating death. I wonder what the significance is in that?" And he walked off toward the house as though his comment could only be the climax and termination of the discussion.

"You have to admit," Orlovsky said, "that Sisyphus was much more the appropriate myth for man in the industrial age. The meaninglessness and boredom of the assembly line. Up and down with the rock. The patron deity of factory workers."

"Still, in our private and Romantic moments," Auden said,

"we must have imagined ourselves as being heroic like these figures. They must have worked their way into our psyches somehow."

"I wonder if men see themselves these days as isolated heroes?" Stargaard said. "As existential figures, as 'man alone'? I know I don't, and I don't see how anyone else can either. From my present perspective, it's ludicrous."

"It does seem a bit remote, doesn't it?" Auden agreed.

There was a reflective lull in the conversation until Sarah spoke hesitantly. "I wonder what we see ourselves as being now? I mean, the world is moving so fast, and that was who we thought we were then, but who do we see ourselves as being now?"

"Not as man alone, that's for certain," Orlovsky said. "Probably as a man in a group, a collective image of some sort."

"Edward Lear's Jumblies gone to sea in a sieve," Stargaard said.

21   *Keville & Keville*

IN the face of such pessimism, Sarah wondered if she wasn't preparing herself for a destiny that could not exist. What good would it do to finally become that complete creation of your dreams and possibilities if you found yourself in a paved and blighted landscape where the lakes were swamps of algae and the rivers boiled and burned down to the doomed and oily seas, and you were crammed with

billions of your fellows in the cubbyholes of the massive bee-
hives that had become the endless cities where, already deformed by radiation, famine and pollution, you awaited some
new mutant form of microscopic life to crawl out of the historical sludge with its final gift of plague? Given this Armageddon
for the species and perhaps even for the world itself, what
was her life, much less her ambition, worth? Could she even
count on a generation of children after her own? Wasn't it
possible that her own children, never mind some future generation, would perish in catastrophe? Best make of herself what
she could, then, while the world was still the sort of place in
which she could shine and say her piece. She had been slow
to start on her projects, but now no longer. She would get at
them immediately. Do something before you were destroyed
would be her motto. If her father was an example of a late
start in life, he was also an example of dying early.

But despite these frequent resolutions to get going, she still
had to drag herself to breakfast, and as often as not, she returned to bed as soon as the children were off to school. Sleep
did not revive her but seemed to take its toll of her instead.
Several times Toby suggested she go back and see the doctor.
She protested she didn't need a doctor. What she needed was
a good night's sleep.

Maybe she should keep busy, Toby told her, she should do
something, she had gotten into careless and depressing habits.
He didn't care for her inactivity and these prolonged bouts
of unhappiness. It was his way of saying, You have put things
off long enough, and since you haven't come up with any plans
or interests of your own, I'll have to supply the direction myself.

"Why not come into real estate with me?" he said one evening. "Take the real estate course when it's offered, take the
examination and get your broker's license." Until now he had
been content to have a wife who cared for house and children,
and he had given Sarah this world without complaint or ques-

tion; in turn he had kept to his own. Now he had offered her a merger. Although he actually referred to them as "a husband-and-wife team" (Keville & Keville, she supposed), she couldn't see how he could mean it. He was too determined to serve as the president of a company of his own founding to offer her, or anyone else, a footing equal to his own. Maybe he thought she would simply return to answering his many phone calls, as she had in the earliest days of his business, before he had a phone in his office and used an answering service when he was out. Maybe he saw her manning the office herself in his absence, greeting and talking business with the occasional house-hunters and Sunday drivers who happened by. Maybe he even saw her sitting in that small office with him and his associates and cronies, talking properties, banks, taxes, zoning, percentage, contractors, builders, contracts, loans. Men who were in real estate because, as she remembered Cullenbine saying once, they were good at nothing else. "Like morticians," he had said, "without shame or honor."

Although she could acknowledge that by far the larger portion of his offer was a gesture of concern and help, she was insulted all the same. And the more she reflected upon it, the more insulted she became. Is that who he thinks I am? she asked herself. It made her feel ashamed. His offer was unacceptable, it was unforgivable. Did he actually believe she could be persuaded to participate in the tasteless transformation of the world she depended on for her own self-creation, self-fulfillment, salvation? Didn't he know that she had chosen to stand apart from this destruction, and that what he asked of her was outside the direction and parameters of her character? Do something now, he argued. Stop putting things off so much. *Now,* she thought. Of course she would act now. Only it wouldn't be as he wanted.

To celebrate the sale of a large tract of land that abutted an area that had just been declared national parkland, Toby and his co-brokers of the sale were to meet for dinner with their spouses at a new restaurant on the coast. Toby wanted Sarah to get together with his business friends, the women especially. Some of them, like Maurice LaBlanc, Larry Golden and Tom and Mary Cahoon, she had met before.

It was an early autumn evening that felt more like summer, and the white gravel of the restaurant driveway crunched underfoot while ahead of them they could hear the flapping of flags and sails. The men in the party looked proud in their white plastic shoes, white vinyl belts and cream-colored or plaid jackets, while the women in their long evening dresses of chiffon might have been on their way to an inaugural ball. The walls of the dining room were prefinished panels hung with clipper ships and Andrew Wyeth prints, but those that opened on the dockside were glass and looked upon a harbor crowded with sailboats and a few cabin cruisers, the crews of which could be seen in that pale early evening light where sea, sky and nightfall are all blue alike, having cocktails on deck. Three tables had been moved together to accommodate so large a party, and they dallied for two hours over several rounds of drinks before they remembered to order dinner. They were loud and happy, with everyone except Sarah leaning across the table and exchanging shoptalk and in-jokes all at once. One of the women told Sarah how her daughter had become expert in dressage this summer, and that her son, who was at camp, had learned to water-ski. Two of the women worked for their husbands, and one woman, who had brought her husband along, was a broker herself. Her name was Betty Widjak, but for business purposes she called herself Elizabeth S. Cole. Sarah remembered that she used to wear glasses in frames that came to points, like a cowl; now she wore huge aviator lenses. She spoke of money in six figures.

The good humor and cordiality of their table was just too outgoing to be contained, and the attempt was made to incorporate all other tables within easy hearing into the merriment of their own. Larry Golden and Toby, who sprawled in his chair with his blazer open and had his arms around those who sat on either side of him, couldn't get enough of teasing the college-girl waitresses in their neat blue pinafores with the white anchor sewn on the breast, a half dozen of whom kept appearing and reappearing at the table, squeezing in between two seated men. The others made friendly exchanges with the diners at the smaller surrounding tables, including some of the owners of the moored boats and a friendly party of older men who all had either blond or snow-white hair and were dressed identically in the seedy, ill-fitting blazers and striped ties of the local yacht club. The talk was of tides, types of sailboats, knots, shipwrecks, storms and sea lore, even though it was apparent that Sarah's table knew very little about those topics. Then the innkeeper himself, in a paisley jacket, joined them for half an hour. He knew both Toby and Larry Golden. When at last they ordered dinner, the men wanted prime rib or an entree called "surf 'n' turf," which was shrimp and steak, while some of the women, after asking the waitress what it was, thought they would try the bouillabaisse.

A three-piece band of stooping, balding men in their fifties, with neat little mustaches, and dressed in green Scotch-plaid jackets, played old-time dance favorites and new popular music, but in the old style. The piano player was blind, the drummer didn't do much more than brush cymbals, while the vocalist doubled on saxophone and muted trumpet and, during the more Latin numbers, shook a pair of castanets. A middle-aged couple danced a slow tango by themselves on the open stretch of floor between the tables, going from one end of the space to the other, and many took time out from dining to watch. The couple was light on their feet and showed off a dance studio expertise.

Then Sarah herself was dancing with the cherubic and chatty

Larry Golden, moving her feet in a daze, stiff-legged, their hands held formally, her hand on his shoulder as though to push him off. Maurice LaBlanc wanted to dance with her, too. So did the husband of Elizabeth S. Cole. After that she was just too tired to take the floor. I don't belong here, she kept telling herself. She couldn't seem to drink enough to escape the show and noise.

She took to staring out the glass wall at the line of large shingled summer cottages perched along the shore across the harbor, with whole wings, or even whole houses, lit up like great ocean liners in a splurge of light. She could picture rooms of white wicker, Kazaks, Canton china, with China-trade paintings of sailing ships upon the walls, and the houseguests for before-dinner drinks in the apselike porches that seemed to go out over the water like the quarterdecks of ships. Houses where there was always salt and splash in any kind of weather, and the breeze and mist blew through the rooms as though you were on the deck of a ship at sea.

As the first course of their meals came, their table drew in upon itself. The men took to playing poker with dollar bills and insisted that the women play, too. They dealt out one to each and then went around the table, each calling out in turn the best poker hand that could made from the serial number on the bill. After several hands they had used up all their dollar bills, and Tom Cahoon gave the waitress a pair of twenties and asked her to have the bartender change them into singles— and oh, to keep a couple for herself.

"And give a couple to the bartender," Larry Golden said.

"That's not going to be enough," Maurice LaBlanc said, digging into his pocket and bringing out a roll of twenties, from which he peeled the top.

They were having so much fun that they barely touched their first courses, and, to the consternation of their young waitresses, the plates and bowls of soups and salads were piling up around the table.

One of the houses across the harbor began to send up a small and noisy display of fireworks from the rocks that jutted out in front of it, probably in celebration of a family birthday or marriage. Or perhaps for no better reason than that someone liked to hear the bang and see the bright colors explode against the sky and then, in falling, light up the fleet of idle boats.

"Over there, that's where I belong," Sarah said.

22   *The Salon*

AT the small dinner party Renzi gave in honor of a visit from his old friend and professor, Harcourt McDonald, Sarah had been quick to notice the common denominator among her fellow guests, of whom only Stargaard and Marco and Alexander were known to her. It would appear that Renzi had tried to invite a sampling of those he judged the local creative personalities. Apparently Adele Fox had not been invited. Neither had the Kubiliuses. Nor the Orlovskys. Sarah had maneuvered Toby into confessing that he did not really want to go, and he had stayed home instead, baby-sitting. On her own, if only for the evening, she began to envision a life apart from him.

The floors of Renzi's apartment were covered with Anatolian scatter rugs, bright but worn down to the threads in places, while a pair of Turkish kilims hung on the walls, as did rows of small English watercolors of landscapes and coastal scenes, matted and behind glass, and running, in some places, from floor to ceiling. His best books were locked up behind glass doors.

The party was catered by two women graduate students, only slightly younger than Sarah. They had filled the rooms with vases of fresh flowers and had prepared a menu that was perhaps their notion of what was eaten at a literary salon. Cheese omelet followed herb omelet, the one girl cooking while the other served, with a main course of linguine and clam sauce, finished off with a simple salad. The women were tall and swanlike in build and did not seem sensual so much as oversexed. They acted nervous and uncertain of their roles. They were studying for their doctorates—would be doctors, both said, before the end of the year—and yet here they were, showing deference to Sarah, who had what amounted to little more than a junior college education but was the fellow guest of artists and scholars, with whom she was conversing on equal terms. At the table Alexander was seated next to the guest of honor, but Sarah was put at the foot of the table, facing her host.

Professor McDonald was both formidable and unforgiving, with a streak of humorless mischief and an appearance that reminded Sarah of a combination Punch and Moses. He spoke grandly, in the Oxford manner, delivering even the most mundane observation as though he were a prelate in a large and ancient church. He had retired early and gone to live on a houseboat in the Seine, for which, his wife said, they had been written up in several magazines, and Alexander said was he *that* man because she remembered seeing one of the articles. The first time Sarah spoke to him directly she mentioned that she had attended several of his former student's lectures and even at her age had found his message to create exhilarating.

She was certain he not only woke up but inspired the younger students.

"I must confess that I've never been able to determine whether Renzi's guff is harmless twiddle-twaddle or doctrine of the most pernicious sort," McDonald said in a voice loud enough to make their conversation the table's conversation. "Everyone an artist, indeed! If you ask me, we have enough people trying their hands at so-called art these days. Our culture is in the process of being buried in third-rate artifacts. And why? I ask you. Because the standards are much too low. And still these third-raters keep crying to the government, Give us more money for the arts! If I had my way, the government would give people handsome subsidies not to create. I've never understood why people would want to waste their time making bad things. Heaven knows, the great artists already make enough of those. I mean, how many masterpieces can a man make in his lifetime? You notice, don't you, that Renzi here doesn't believe his own nonsense. You don't see him creating. He devotes himself instead to his private scholarship and to his teaching, and a good thing, too—with the sole exception of some of the nonsense he preaches. It makes a good deal more sense than his writing worthless and unreadable books that only a handful of pedants would ever trouble to read. Let's have only the great artists devoting their lives to the service of art. Hasn't history proven that only a few gifted men and women in each generation are capable of producing great art? Surely the best works of these geniuses are more than enough. We wouldn't want to be at sea in great art, wouldn't want to wallow in it. I mean, how long can you stand watching a glorious sunset? How many times can you read a Keats sonnet? It seems to me the rest of us would be far better served if all inferior artists became carpenters and soldiers. That way, you see, we would have sturdy serviceable cabinets and benches and we could rest easy in our beds knowing that our borders had been made all the more secure against our enemies."

Although this speech had the ring of a set piece, he had seemed to become genuinely outraged as he spoke, and Sarah looked to Renzi to defend himself by arguing a position she had heard him proclaim in public with such sincerity and passion. But to her surprise he passed her a look she read as saying: Better humor him.

Marco, the first to respond, changed the subject slightly. "If I couldn't be an artist and have complete freedom in my work and life to do whatever I like, then let me be a prisoner or soldier. Let society take care of me."

"At least you would know what was expected of you," Stargaard quipped.

"And you'd never want or go hungry," Marco said.

"Or depress yourself by worrying about your having to make something that no one needs or wants," Stargaard added.

McDonald thought this discussion frivolous and went on to make a series of assertions to the point that the period of great art, and of great artists, was long since past. The last great poet he allowed might have been Yeats, and the last great painter Van Gogh, although he let it be known he would be much happier if he could push the date back even closer to the eighteenth century, and to names like Turner and Baudelaire.

"There, you see, we're not so far apart after all," Renzi said to him.

Now Stargaard picked up the gauntlet Renzi had refused, and Sarah, who didn't dare enter the argument herself, cheered him on. "We simply don't know who the great artists are in our time yet, but they're there. And with so many people working at art, my guess would be that the general level of competence has never been higher, and that we're bound to produce even greater artists than in the past because of the competition, the body of knowledge about techniques, the simple mathematical odds—"

"But the concept of art has nothing to do with odds," McDonald said, pronouncing the latter word with an English accent and with the distaste he might have shown for any of several slang words meaning excrement. "Neither is it democratic. It's the province of the exceptional man and woman. The hero, the genius—or the madman."

At this, the little curly-headed painter they called Cambria (and Sarah didn't know then whether this was his surname or his only name) clapped his hands. "Hear, hear," he said, cigarette dangling from his mouth. Sarah thought that with those large button eyes in which a ring of cornea always showed around the blue iris, and with his chalky coloring, he resembled a mime in whiteface. He and Stargaard had known each other in New York.

"We don't need artists counterfeiting genius," McDonald continued. "We don't want artists counterfeiting insanity. We don't want sane men whose poetry is an act of madness. We want mad men whose poetry is a desperate and courageous attempt at sanity. We don't have great art today because we simply don't have the heroes to make it."

Surprisingly, Cambria came left-handedly to McDonald's defense. "Of course art is dead," he said. "Or at least dying. And I mean art as we've always known it. Today's artist has to see himself in perspective against the theory of relativity and against the flood of modern mass culture of which he is a part, and face up to his ultimate insignificance. He has to know his place—if he wants to survive. Already there's no pejorative difference between Haydn and jazz, and I can envision a time when the popular culture will overwhelm the exclusive culture. Everything will be done for the moment then. No more concepts like 'immortal,' 'classical,' 'lasting.' Music will be recorded rather than performed, and on recordings that will either be erased or wear out. Photography will replace painting, and every man will be his own photographer. The prints and negatives, however, won't last more than twenty years. And no more novels either, just television shows that will be made on celluloid that will rot and disappear like the films. The paints and canvases I use myself won't last fifty years. You won't be able to preserve them, and once they start to go you won't be able to restore them either. Let the next fellow have a chance on the museum walls. After all, art can't outlive the world."

"Maybe some forms c f art are dying in our time," Stargaard conceded, "the novel among them. At least I'm coming reluctantly to that conclusion. The history of art does have its graveyards of mastodons. Epic poems, sermons—"

"I suspect we're saying pretty much the same thing although for different reasons," Cambria objected. "You've likely become disillusioned with yourself and with what you're doing, and because you've reached the conclusion that you're dead, you want to take art and the novel and the rest of us with you. Sorry, we can't accept that. It's not a position you can support with a sincere and thought-out theory." Sarah suspected he was teasing Stargaard.

"There's more truth than you know in what you say about me," Stargaard admitted.

"But what you said just now," Renzi said to Cambria, "it comes to the same thing, though, doesn't it?"

"But it's the theory behind the work that's become important," Cambria explained.

"I should think it was only the work itself that mattered," McDonald said.

"But you should be able to see the theory in the work itself," Cambria countered, "and enjoy it for its own sake. Which came first, the work or the theory? And who can say which is more beautiful?"

After both Stargaard and Cambria had left, each pleading he had to work early next day, Sarah overheard McDonald telling Renzi and the others that this Stargaard fellow wasn't a real writer. When challenged by Alexander how he knew, he admitted he hadn't read his book, but then he didn't have to. He could tell a man's ability simply by talking to him for a few minutes and judging the quality of his mind. Sarah recalled that Dr. Milton Cullenbine had dismissed Stargaard in similar fashion. He had tried to read his book, he said, but it was impossible. Vita, however, had read it and faulted it on any number of counts. Not a bad fellow, had been Cullenbine's assessment, but definitely only an average writer of the second rank.

To Sarah's surprise, Renzi looked as though he agreed with McDonald's assessment of Stargaard. But then, she knew from his lectures that Stargaard couldn't possibly measure up to his definition of the artist. Maybe Stargaard wasn't as good as she thought he was. And this painter Cambria—well, obviously he was a fraud.

Sarah stayed behind with the two women graduate students and helped Renzi wash up the dinner dishes and clean up the ashtrays and drinks. McDonald and his aristocratic and alcoholic wife, who had about her the sad air of having to dress nightly for dinner in English manor houses that had been converted into country hotels, lingered over cognac by themselves while the three women worked around them. He was reminiscing about a trip they had made to Egypt years ago, and she was agreeing, with one- or two-word answers, to everything he said. When he had nothing more to say, or she to agree to, they said goodnight and went back to their motel.

The graduate student who did not have a language examination the next morning was still there when Sarah left.

23   The Conference

SARAH had never once imagined herself as a
great artist, had never even viewed herself as
having an attitude she could really call professional. She had
yet to commit herself to a project. But she was well aware
that there had to be tangible proof of who she had become.
There had to be a thing made. She thought she would do drawing or writing, or a combination of the two, for although she
had training and practice in drawing, she had an interest in
writing. Writing didn't require the formal skills and training
of the other arts; you needed experience, feeling, you were,
from the beginning, on your own; you didn't have to study
anything but life itself. Perhaps she would write a book she
would illustrate herself. Perhaps a group of poems. Haikus.
Or nursery rhymes for children.

She had seen a simple solution for herself in the world of
primitive painting. It was attractive because one could simply
sit down and paint away, and there it was, playing by its own
rules; by definition it was untutored, natural, and anyone who
felt pressed for time, as she did, could begin immediately. But
she was drawn to the works of more academic painters, and
admired Whistler, Mary Cassatt and Childe Hassam. After all,
her great-grandfather had been an academician, and she suspected her father's attempts had been impressionistic, if not
abstract. Whatever glimmer she had of the work itself, it would

surrender eventually to an image of herself as that woman she would become, the one leading inevitably into the other.

To create something and, in so doing, create herself, that was all that seemed to matter now, and she held on desperately to the good news and promise of salvation in this position. She simply could not justify herself without it. She mustn't ever doubt her ability to prove it true. All it took was concentration, industry; above all, courage.

She was determined to try to talk to Renzi about this, and she went to his office after sitting in on the last half of his slide show. But students had made appointments to see him, and she had to wait out in the corridor, standing against a wall among undergraduates who sat on the floor or on their books. She overheard his enthusiastic and musical voice as it delivered both anecdote and instruction from behind the door, and saw the students leave beaming as though they had been praised and loved. He was in no hurry to move them in and out, and she let several get ahead of her; she wanted to see him when no one else was left in line. She wanted to exchange ideas, confess to elevated feelings. Above all, she wanted to be moved.

"Sarah," he said, when it was her turn. "I didn't know you were waiting; why didn't you make an appointment?"

When Renzi was in his classroom or office he tended to treat the few social friends he encountered there like students. On his own grounds they just did not meet on equal terms. Sarah was here because she had put herself in his trust, and he automatically assumed the role of teacher and guide while ascribing to her that of his disciple. Besides, he suspected that women, like Sarah, who sat in on his lectures and visited him in his office were attracted not so much to his ideas as to the man himself. He himself could not easily separate the two, and he interpreted their interest as a rather bold declaration of their infatuation. He had had enough experiences in the past to justify his making such a claim. Oh, they talked art and ideas and culture, but all along their interest was in the man at hand. With most women it was embarrassing, but he liked Sarah and was pleased with himself that he had touched her spirit. What he knew of her present life he judged uninspired and ordinary. A life without insight or observation, much less contemplation. She had been shut up in a country house with children, married to an extraordinarily handsome and pleasant sort of Babbitt.

"I want to do something," she began. "I want to make something."

"Then do it," he said, patronizingly. "I've always maintained that the worst sin is unfruitfulness. Your power to create depends ultimately on the power of your will—"

"And on patience, too," she added.

"All right, that too, but I said most of all on will."

In his professional role he did not care to be corrected or contradicted.

"But you see, I'm not sure I can do anything—or that I should even try."

"The waste of potential, that's an even greater sin. You don't get a second chance to show what you can do. And the creative spirit doesn't necessarily stay with you forever."

"But the other night, your friend McDonald, he seemed to say I'd be foolish, I'd only make myself ridiculous if I even so much as tried—"

He interrupted. "You shouldn't have paid any attention to him. Why let him tell you what to do? You're responsible only to yourself." He was aware he hadn't exactly addressed himself to her question, just as he was aware he hadn't replied to Mc-Donald's argument at the dinner party. They would have only rehashed old positions if he had, resolving nothing while boring the guests. And he wasn't about to answer McDonald's argument now. Besides, he was put out to learn that after hearing his own statement on the subject of creativity, Sarah should so easily give credence to an opposing view. And that of his old teacher, no less.

"Oh, I agree," Sarah said. "Shouldn't we each try to realize ourselves within the limits of our potential, even if that potential, in some of us, doesn't really amount to very much, compared to what some others have? You yourself almost said as much. That was our purpose—"

"That's right," he said, coolly. "I did say something along those lines." Although he prided himself on his Socratic ability to examine and debate, in truth he had no such inclination or skill. And he didn't care to be taught, not even with his own words.

"It's come down to this for me," she confessed. "If I don't create, I don't make myself into what I want myself to be, what I think I should be. I can't tell you what that is, exactly— I mean, I don't want to tell you. But it's important to me, it's all I seem to have right now. I mean, if I don't do that, I don't know what to do, I don't know what I am. Because I have this feeling—an inclination, if you like—that if it doesn't happen pretty soon, it will never happen. . . ."

He didn't care for the direction of their conversation. It had become too personal and serious. He would have tolerated this at a party, but not in his office. He saw his role changing against his will from idol to sympathizer and counselor. He had never been good at handling unexpected confessions of pregnancies, incest, family deaths, and he hated it when his students tried to use him in this way. With Sarah, he was determined to put an end to it before it got out of hand. "But what you want to happen to yourself happens naturally, or not at all, as a natural consequence of your being driven to create. One can't go about it as deliberately as all that. You can't make yourself into an artist, or into a better person, or a different person, or whatever, simply by trying your hand at art. True, it may happen, it does happen, but creativity isn't therapeutic, it isn't a character builder."

She tried to explain, then to make excuses, and he was surprised to realize that he had hurt her. He didn't see how he had any choice, though, but to set her down and put her straight. Like slapping a hysterical patient. Still, he felt a bit ashamed of himself. He had gone too far. He would raise up her spirits again in compensation. "It's too bad you can't come with me to Greece. I bet you'd be a great help in the photography project. Be a great help in other areas, too, I'm sure. You have good instincts, I know. I think you'd enjoy Greece." It was an offer of sorts, and certainly an attempt to feel her out. Suddenly he felt daring and sensed he could go even farther in his declaration. "The other night at my place," he said hesitantly, "I was hoping you would be the last to leave . . . that the girls would have gone home first."

He felt good now, he had brought things around to where they should have been, and their talk could proceed along the lines he liked. He continued on the subject of Greece and cameras, believing that she would be interested in this. He showed her the new hiking shoes he planned to use in the Greek mountains. Brought his new range finder out of his desk drawer and extolled its virtues over other types and brands. Then he went so far as to favor her with confession and intimate self-revelation. He told her all about his ex-wife and how they had come to part amicably; he had become so absorbed in his own work that he neglected her, and another professor had stolen her away; he had lived with the affair for months; she finally divorced him and married the other fellow; his ego had been hurt terribly but he had survived—he had to—and she still lived in town and the fellow taught in the same school, and they often ran into each other on the street. By the way, what did she think of the slides of Rome he had shown in class today? What, she didn't see them? Oh, missed the first half of the lecture, did she?

Meanwhile Sarah had been thinking: He wants a companion who will flatter him. He wants to talk. He knows how to talk but he doesn't know how to listen. Range finders, lenses, meters, automatic winders, tripods, flashes, film and filters—what did she care about them? And you would have thought he was speaking Japanese with his Mamiya, Konica, Nikon, Fujica, Asahi, Yashica, Zuiko. He was a strange mixture of conceit and vulnerability, the latter breaking through when you least expected it, such as when he recounted the beauty of Greek townscapes and countrysides only to confess to having never been to Greece, and wasn't that outrageous with his teaching "Greece" for all these years? It was as though he wanted her to admire and pity him in the same breath. And it occurred to her: He doesn't know who he is either. And what is more, he will never know. And never know he doesn't know. He did not see her as being special in any way. She could have been one of a hundred. But her overriding thought was this: He wants to sleep with me—but not too much.

24   *Being and Becoming*

ALTHOUGH it was Alexander whom Stargaard planned to encounter and take out for a carafe or two of wine, it was Sarah who had the pleasure instead. He met her in the local bookstore, where she was browsing in the children's section, and when she said, I've wanted to talk to you, I've something I have to ask you, he said to himself, This is it, you are about to make a fool of yourself. He was clean-shaven, freshly showered, well dressed in a white turtle-neck sweater and blue blazer. He had just come from a tennis match with Cambria and some of his friends, in which he had not only expended himself but lived up to his small talent. He had leaped and bounded about the court, bullying his partner, annihilating his opponents. Take that down the alley, effete watercolorist! And now that passing volley, you out-of-shape dentist! *Olé,* Stargaard! Bravo, Stargaard! Serve and smash! Stroke and slash! Not only that, but he had played and sunbathed the whole week. He had frolicked in pools, and the mindless laps of his ferocious butterfly had displaced gallons of water and made a small tempest out of the pool. He had been among friends who made gin-and-tonics in great silver pitchers whose outsides became beaded with the chill and in which floated a sea of ice and limes. He hadn't written a word, and didn't feel bad because he hadn't. He told himself while he lathered his muscles in the hot shower, I could give it up for good. I could change my ambitions, lower my standards, live a healthy and happy life, in touch with the earth. He was some nude blond Nordic sun worshiper. He was aglow with an outdoor and athletic eroticism that had nothing to do with big cities, window shades or lingerie; he was arm in arm with Olympic champions and plowboys.

They went for a midafternoon beer.

She wanted to talk about "making." Not him, but books, writing, pictures. She was interested in creating, she wouldn't say exactly what, and he couldn't get her to be more definite. For a while he played a guessing game. "What is it? Landscape sketches? Abstracts? Something other than painting? Nursery rhymes? Tapestries?" But to each question she bit her lip and shook her head.

"One thing I've learned from listening to Renzi," she said. "He doesn't do what he preaches. I admire you, because you do create, you make things. There are those who make and those who only talk about it. You're a maker. I only hope I am, too. It's important for me to be like you."

But what was this? Stargaard asked himself. He didn't want to hear this, he hadn't asked her to come here so he could hear this. "You mean you want to write that whodunit we used to joke about for fun and profit," he said hopefully.

She looked surprised. "No, I would hope to do so much more—and I wouldn't want money to be the reason."

He insisted upon the mystery, in a light vein, though. "Why not write it?" he posed. "Nothing wrong with fun and profit. We mustn't ever think we're too good for that."

He was peeved that she would think herself above such a subject or ambition. "Careful," he warned. "You wouldn't want to turn into a dilettante or, heaven forbid, an amateur. And I can't see you, somehow, as being anything but honest and natural." What he meant was that he did not want her to become like Alexander. In a way he did not really understand, he wanted her not only different from but better than Alexander, for he judged her by higher standards. He had come to enjoy his little fantasies of the two women, and he liked the notion of their being opposites. In Sarah he saw a kind of upper-middle-class domesticity, without the pretense of intellectualism. With Sarah life would be life, not art, and you would take it as it was served. "Besides," he added, "this art business isn't a healthy occupation. It's probably a sickness of some sort. Speaking for myself, I don't want to paint a landscape, I want to be part of the landscape scene the other fellow painted. Let someone else paint me. Let him catch me doing what he'd be doing if he wasn't so sick in the head. Better yet, put me in a genre painting. A cottage with a thatched roof, a muddy courtyard, maybe a well, a window seat, a picket fence, a mass of sweetbrier—"

"And there you are," she said, "a hay swain." He suspected she had spoken with contempt.

"And there you are," he heard himself saying. He tried to speak kindly, knowing it was both a declaration and, he hoped, an invitation. "A girl at the open casement, waving a handkerchief—or is it reading a letter?"

"Oh, we're in this together, are we?"

"Why not?" he posed.

And when she continued to look at her hands, he said, "I'd like that, like it a lot."

"And I suppose I'm wearing a kerchief and laced-up bodice," she said, "with my bosom peeping out. And I have a wooden bucket in my hand—or is it a pair of buckets on the yoke I carry across my shoulders? And what about one of those little white Dutch caps and wooden shoes that go clop-clop?"

"Maybe a shepherdess was more what I had in mind."

"Little Bo-Peep?"

"Well, nothing as frilly and citified as all that."

It was true that he had often pictured her in his fantasies in fresh air and big barns full up with hay, bright kitchens and feather beds, especially in his weakest moments, which had been many lately, and that picture had seemed to him both a solution and a consolation. He was aware that he was botching it, that she hadn't cared for what he had said to her, that she would likely reject any overture he was foolish enough to make. He felt the conflict of wanting to both help and injure her. Usually he made it a point not to interfere in other people's lives; also never to give advice. But he was so certain that this new interest of hers was artificial and wrong, and a waste of time besides. "This making—whatever it is you're up to— I don't think it's you."

"Who do you think I am, then?"

Now he was angry. He would give her a little lecture, for her own good, and by God, he would show his anger and disappointment, too, so that she could see for herself the sincerity of his concern. "It upsets me," he said, "to see you trying to be something you're not, and shouldn't be. I mean, why be so damned self-conscious and intellectual? Oh, I know I'm out of line, but goddamn it, I can't help feeling the way I do, now can I? You'd be better off just living your life. You're so good and right the way you are. For better or worse, people should be content to be themselves." By the end of this little sermon his anger had left him and the feeling he hoped to show her had sounded forced.

She said nothing in her defense, or in argument against him. Although he couldn't bring himself to really look at her, he was certain he had hurt her. He was quick to apologize and castigate himself. "You should have told me off," he complained. "Should have told me to mind my own business, should have told me to shut up."

But he knew that what had been the better half of his dreams were gone. So was half of his real possibilities. It wasn't only her insistence on this new and wrong direction in her life, but her unhealthy pallor that went far to cool his athletic enthusiasm.

When she left him alone in the booth with the remainder of the beer, he thought of Alexander. He was in that woodland house of hers. A chilled bottle of *Spätlese* and twin bowls of strawberries with *crème fraîche* on the white square plastic coffee table. He could see himself thumbing through a portfolio on American Impressionist painters, inhaling the aroma of heavy paper. For a while he watches the Siamese fighting fish in the aquarium, then observes the blue jays at the bird feeder through the glass-paneled doors. Just when he thinks he can wait no longer, she comes barefoot from her studio in the paint-smeared smock. Touches him with fingers that are messy with bright chromatic colors, yellows, reds, greens. There is a slash of blue across her cheek, a streak of green across her forehead, she leaves a smudge of yellow on his chin. She wears nothing beneath her smock, which he removes. What an erotic sense of privilege in the love-making that follows! What high style and impeccable taste! As though he associated sex with high-society women and high-fashion models more than he did with belly dancers or the fleshy and abandoned models of pornography and cheesecake, much less the wholesome housewife-athlete of his idle dreams.

Strange, unlucky Stargaard! Alexander drove him to sensual distractions, she gave him headaches and made his own flesh too sensitive for him to touch, while Sarah, whom he was still certain he liked better, left him cold.

25 Death Has No Mercy in This Land

IN early autumn, the Kevilles, along with the other country families, made sure to watch the television weather report around suppertime each night. Was there a forecast out for a general frost? they wondered. And if not, how low would the temperature be by morning? Would there be a wind? A cloud cover? And that frost line there on the weather map—was it far enough east and south to put them on the side that was to get the killing frost? Already there had been a few close calls. The Italian tomato plants of the Kevilles were so laden with fruit that each plant looked like some multibreasted cult statue of a fertility goddess, and twice in the past week Toby and Sarah had gone out in the dark after supper and covered them with leaf bags of black plastic, turning them into rows of hooded victims, waiting to be executed, or already dead. Twice the Angles covered their tomato plants with newspapers that, in the morning after the wind picked up, were scattered over the yard and garden, catching against the roadside weeds. Three times Auden draped his few plants with old sheets, and a small clan of ghosts appeared to stand watch beside his house throughout the eerie starlit night.

In the early mornings, just as it was becoming light, there it was—a patch of white on the lawn. This followed by the usual report of a man a mile down the road in a notorious low spot whose garden had been wiped out while those of his close neighbors had all been spared. As early as two weeks ago, Dr. Kubilius had a touch of frost behind his barn, and the rangy borage plants that grew wild there were flattened against the earth in blackened pieces as though smashed by a giant hammer.

It was amazing how these affluent and privileged people loved to exaggerate and even manufacture their helplessness and desperation before the annual onslaught of frost! It was as if, at this one time of the year, they could make themselves believe they were prehistoric farmers and food gatherers living on the edge of the great glacier, dependent on the comings and goings of the season.

Townspeople like the Orlovskys and Stargaard were oblivious to their country neighbors' vigilance and worries. To them the visitor they scraped off their windshields in the morning was nothing more than what the children called him. But in the country, although they called it frost, they meant ice. Primeval, timeless ice, that half degree of cold that was the difference between life and death. And they meant death, too, although they never called it anything but frost.

But just when it appeared that this year they might pass

over into those smoky, bronze-colored days of Indian summer that sometimes go on and on into November, allowing the old-timers to regale the newcomers with tales of that "Golden Age" autumn when they could not make green tomato mincemeat or relish because every tomato stayed long enough to ripen on the vine, the night of reckoning came after all. Once again they had been taken by surprise! How cruel and senseless this early coming of the cold! Why, if they could just get through this one night, there would be weeks of sun and warmth ahead! But all the weather signs were unfavorable. Windy at sundown but still as death by dawn. No garden would escape the frost tonight. Not those on the sunny southern slopes. Nor those protected from the north by a building or a wall. Take what you can tonight, and give up the rest as sacrifice.

After a quick supper, the Kevilles hurry out into the garden, where they work by flashlight, feeling among the tomato vines as though for udders, picking every fruit their freezing hands can find. Bushel baskets and then cardboard boxes are filled with green, pear-shaped tomatoes. "The melons," he says. "Go get the melons." The three or four melons, and not ripe yet. She says, "I forgot about the melons."

Dr. Kubilius, on his way home from the hospital, hears the forecast on the car radio, and dashes from the car into the house, then, pausing only long enough to change his clothes, he dashes out into the garden, where he works by porch light, grateful that tonight he is not on call. He forks up several scented geraniums, now scraggly and unwieldy, along with a lemon verbena, almost as tall as a small tree, a tender lavender, a few seedy basil plants, and tips them carelessly into big clay pots he lugs down into the cellar, where he will pot them tomorrow after work, or on his next day off. His oldest boy, after he has finished practicing his music lessons, the recorder solos of Elizabethan airs that have accompanied the doctor's desperate digging, comes outdoors to help without being ordered or asked. But he is first sent back indoors to put on a sweater and, if he can find them, a pair of gloves. Pokey, in a parka and bandanna, has taken the oldest girl with her to hold the flashlight, and gone down into the vegetable garden, where she rummages among the half-dead bean vines that have already dragged down their poles, searching desperately for a few misshapen beans. Now her flashlight can be seen roaming through the pepper plants. The youngest girl comes out and wants to pick cabbages, but her mother says, No, they'll be all the better for a touch of frost.

Even Janet Angle spades up the best of her showy marigolds and pots them to bring indoors, and Adele Fox picks a last bouquet of zinnias. And Parker Fox, who is no gardener, congratulates himself as he ties trout flies in his study for the foresight he showed in talking Adele into making a French-style "pic-nique" and going with him today to glean the high-bush commercial blueberries of their neighbor.

A night of suppers of steaming parsnip stew or red-flannel hash taken at a late hour around the stoked-up stoves, and of nestling into comforters. When the lights go off indoors, the musty smell of elm smoke mixed with the sweet of apple spreads out upon the quiet air.

The long night of black and silver begins.

In the darkest hours before the dawn, when it is still too early for the early risers and too late for the insomniacs, who are at last asleep, the hour of execution is at hand. The visit occurs. Death as whiteness, death as ice. It is on the lawn and weeds, on the vines and leaves. A death that passes, with the first touch of sunlight, from white to black. Death as the black spot. As the white visitor who blackens life. Death, once again, as ice.

26   *El Tango del Mercado*
Frio

"TODAY'S a shopping day," Sarah said at breakfast to no one in particular. She wasn't fully
awake yet, and her head hung over her mug of coffee, which
she held in both her hands, her face warmed by the steam.
"I've got to do some grocery shopping." She went as soon as
the children were off to school, which was too early to make
sense. She had wanted to go back to bed, but the house felt
too cold for that. The car was just as cold, however, and the
heater didn't help. The sky was low and slate-colored and made
her feel as though she were on the edge of the Arctic, at the
edge of the tree line.

She didn't know why she stopped at the supermarket in
the new shopping plaza. She had watched the bulldozing of
the pine trees that were later burned in huge piles, and then
the paving of the sandy soil, and she had sworn that if they
were actually building a shopping center miles from any good-
sized town but close to her house in the country, she would
never shop there. The plaza looked as though it were in the
wilds of Newfoundland. From the highway you saw miles of
pine trees and suddenly a huge parking lot and long storefront,
and immediately after it, nothing but more pine trees. All the
shops except the supermarket still had For Rent signs in their

windows, and the parking lot was so deserted she thought at first the store was closed. The employees' cars were huddled together on the far side of the building, looking sinister somehow, and forlorn. She sat in the car, couldn't seem to get out of the car. She knew she shouldn't have gone out today, she hadn't felt up to going out today.

Inside, she went blank. She couldn't find her shopping list, couldn't remember if she had made one out. She hadn't a clue as to what she was supposed to buy. Probably something the children wanted. Some after-school snack. A kind of bread, perhaps—or was it fruit? They were both so fond of tangerines. She searched her bag to the bottom and all her pockets thrice over for the shopping list.

She decided that as long as she was here she might as well pick up some sliced almonds. She was always out of sliced almonds. She found cans of almonds, but they were salted and unsliced. Elsewhere she found bags of almonds, but they needed to be sliced and blanched. Where could the sliced almonds possibly be stocked? She didn't see anyone she could ask. She was out of capers, too, and every now and then she needed capers for a sauce. But where would they keep capers? With the pickles? In the gourmet section? Did they have a gourmet section in this store? She went up and down the dozen long aisles aimlessly, pushing the empty wire cart before her, hoping she would recognize what she was looking for. Arrows indicating the one-way direction were painted on the polished floor, banners advertising cereals and coffees hung overhead and signposts at the intersections marked the goods along each way. The shelves were so well stocked it appeared that not so much as a can or box had been sold.

She came upon the produce section and was startled to find it placed differently from the one in her customary store. She searched the bins heaped with fruit and vegetables packaged in plastic, where she smelled nothing unless it was a trace of celery. She stood, trancelike, for several minutes before a mound of oranges until she remembered it was not the season for tangerines.

The milk cooler was also misplaced. It should have been beside the beer cooler, across from the meats. Milk spilled out of the plastic jug she lifted with difficulty into the cart; milk was on her hands and dribbled down the front of her coat. With its cargo of milk, the cart was almost too heavy for her to push.

Frozen turkeys were on sale, and were especially large. She reached into the freezer, took a carcass in both her arms and rolled it up against her breast, trying to lift it out. But it was too cumbersome for her to manage and too cold for her to touch, and it tumbled back, a solid turkey shape of ice among the heap of others in the locker. She shivered, leaning over the frozen food, trying to clear her head and catch her breath. She had been shivering since she had come into the store. The air conditioning had turned the place into a refrigerator. A drafty bone-chilling cold that felt unnatural and got up under your clothes. Her hands were like ice, the metal of the pushcart was ice cold. You could perish, she thought, in such a cold.

The delicatessen counter behind the glass case was crowded with silver trays of salads and cylinders and rectangles of cold meats and cheese. None of the salads had been disturbed, none of the cold cuts had been sliced. No attendant was behind the counter. She would try the Genoa and muenster, a sliced half pound of each, and punched a bell like those used by desk clerks to summon bellboys. But no one came. She wondered if she had seen anyone else, clerk or shopper, since entering the store.

The meat section began where the delicatessen ended, and ran almost the length of the store. Heaps of gray plucked fowl, chickens yellow with their fat, rows of bright fatless meat, all wrapped in cellophane and piled every which way, as though they had been sorted through by frantic shoppers. The blood trapped inside the package she picked up squished back and forth behind the plastic, then bubbled up and leaked out, the wet cellophane unraveling from the meat when she let the package fall.

On the other side of the long glass partition behind the meat case, a man and a woman in white aprons and white hard hats stood at a table, wrapping meat. She could see but couldn't hear them talking. They were laughing, fooling around; the man threw a piece of fat he had trimmed from a steak at the woman, and then ducked when the woman threw it back. The next time she caught herself looking at the glass, the table, which had been heaped with meat, was empty and the pair were gone.

The cold was worse near the refrigerators and freezers, and she went back into the aisles as though she thought the high walls of goods would keep out the drafts. She couldn't seem to find her way out of the aisles; they were like some modern indoor notion of a maze. She came across a grocery cart abandoned in the aisles. It was heaped with frozen pizzas, boxes of detergents, sacks of dog food, kitty litter, cans of cream soda. Whoever had collected them was not in sight. She thought she heard someone in the next aisle over, but when she turned into it, no one was there.

She hadn't known there could be so many kinds and brands of bread. Nor of bottled soft drinks. They extended down one whole aisle. She found herself walled in by huge boxes of soaps and detergents, cardboard boxes and plastic bottles of no value, where the smell was of soap instead of food. She was in a world of phosphates, artificial colors, preservatives, retardants, supplements, additives. I want to shop in a French market, she found herself thinking. I want to go to a boulangerie, patisserie, charcuterie, I don't care if it takes the whole morning. I want to go to the square on market day and shop by the fountain under the plane trees where the farmers and their wives are selling fresh flowers and live rabbits and chickens. I want to see tables of figs, grapes, corn salad, homemade preserves. Or if she couldn't be in France, she would telephone her order to the gourmet grocery on Beacon Hill, and a man in an apron and straw hat would deliver it on a little dolly to her town house door. . . . She leaned forward on her cart, which almost wheeled out from under her. What's wrong with me? she wondered. I can't go on like this. Her hands were gripping the handle of the cart as though it were the crossbar of a Ferris wheel.

She was at the meat section again. At the far end of the case, the man in the white hard hat had come out from behind the glass and was rearranging some packages with his hands. She started toward him, but just then he disappeared through a swinging door. The voice of a woman came over the loudspeaker. "Can I help you?" it asked. The woman in the hard hat was looking at her from behind the glass panel, holding up a large old-fashioned microphone. Sarah shook her head.

She looked down the aisle to the front of the store. A long line of empty silver grocery carts, pushed into each other, and a girl in a blue dust coat leaning with her arms folded against the empty checkout counter beside the cash register, looking bored and cold.

She became aware of the music then. Strange, how you took the music, like the cold, for granted. She had been hearing it all along. Piped-in, it seemed to come from cameras trained on her from as many as a dozen hiding places along the upper walls. Latin music. Tangos wrapped in aluminum, bagged in cellophane. Tango followed tango in an endless string of tangos. Castanets and strings, but never a voice heard singing—and was the melody played on a piano or a marimba? The background music of a suburban cocktail lounge, already dark in midafternoon. Be wrong, be false, be nothing much at all, the music said. Be out of place, unconscious, packaged, soothed, confused. She was shopping to tangos in the early morning in a huge walk-in refrigerator where nothing spoiled. Bananas, pineapples, avocados—*caramba! olé! Señoritas* and *gauchos*, too. *La luna, la guayaba, la noche, las naranjas, el mar, el limón.* Look sharp! Here comes the dark handsome man with slick black hair and a bolero jacket, and the girl with high heels and a dark curl pasted to each cheek, dancing down the aisles between the canned vegetables and fruits. *La Calle Loma de los Riscos, El Lomo de Cerdo, El Amor.* Palm trees in moonlight along the *playa,* and fishermen in small boats who cast their nets into the elusive moonlight of the shallow sea. She was dancing on a warm evening on the veranda of an old seafront hotel in Buenos Aires. Or was it in São Paulo? Or on the deck of a great white cruise ship moored in the harbor of Montevideo, having steamed up the river Plate?

Wherever she was, she had never been so far away from home. Nor so cold and desperate either.

She told herself she was about to be sick. That it would explain everything if she were sick.

27   The Hands of Dr. Durr

WHEN Kubilius came into the equipment room of the hospital to get dressed for the surgery he had scheduled that morning, Durr told him, "We could lose your friend." And when Kubilius looked in on Sarah for himself after he was through with his surgery, he caught himself saying, "She could be dying." And he went storming off, in search of Durr.

Durr could not remember seeing so fast-acting and virulent an infection. Nobody knew what it was, or what it was doing. She had been barely examined and admitted before she was delirious in her room and then unconscious, near death. The emergency room staff had at first guessed the gall bladder, or a severe influenza in the lower intestinal tract. Although a bacterium or virus of some sort was the most obvious answer, Durr suspected poison, and wanted to know where she had been recently, and with whom, along with what she had had to eat and drink. "I almost hope it is poison," he said. "I'd hate to see an epidemic of this." Until the laboratory could isolate and identify the cause, it was a matter of finding the right antibody by the old-fashioned empirical method of hit or miss. Durr was worried about the liver, though.

She responded the second day and improved slightly on the third. When Kubilius looked in on the fourth day he said to Toby, in Sarah's presence, "When she first came in here I gave her even odds at best." He was aware that Toby believed he wouldn't dare to show such gallows humor unless it was a gross exaggeration of the truth. If anything, it was an understatement of the way he had felt. Not that Sarah was in any condition to be cognizant of what he said. Or to care much, if she was.

Her life had become a dream state, and her dreams were pleasurable or horrible, depending on the time of day. At night she was victimized by nightmares, remarkable for their horror and absurdity. While she was dimly conscious of the advancing and retreating flashlight, the spongy footsteps around her bed and the whispering of plotters in the darkened corridor outside her door, she dreamt she was a French army nurse who lay feverish with malaria beneath a mosquito net in a jungle hospital in Indochina, awaiting capture and presumably torture by

guerrillas who were about to besiege the camp; and another
time, that she was an unwilling witness to voodoo ceremonies
around a campfire at midnight in a steaming jungle in Haiti,
a dream that ended with her attempt to flee an army of moldering zombies she had watched break through the clay of their
sunken graves. And the terror of these fatiguing nights would
not end until the morning sponge bath, which would begin
while she was still asleep, her limp arms raised one at a time
and washed so that they were barely wet, with the water cool-
ing quickly along her flesh, and she would think, As though
I'm already dead, and what does it matter if I am?

But in the daylight came the dreams that were like an album
of snapshots she opened and studied at her pleasure. She drove
a sports car with the top down, with the windshield down,
through the winding and hilly roads of an English countryside;
she helped to sail a boat into a bay studded with islands and
surrounded by a bowl of blue hills; she made love with Toby
and several handsome but nameless men of her choosing, including, best of all, a mystery man she did not wish to name
or identify although he resembled John Angle, doing it with
them below deck of the boat and in a secluded pasture with
the sports car parked beside the road; she planned a meal in
her kitchen, consulting a cookbook at the table before the cut-
tir ; board heaped with fresh okra, eggplant, a yellow onion,
bright red peppers, each in its certain place, and once she
saw herself, for what seemed hours, snapping beans. And the
subtle pleasures of these dreams was not interrupted so much
as complemented by soft footsteps, smartly done; the silver
wheeling of a cart into the room; the gentle voices of women
above her head; the awareness of a warm hand that held her
wrist; the sudden welcome and overpowering smell of alcohol;
the fluff and thump of pillows; the snap of clean, unwrinkled
sheets and the sliding of hands beneath her backside, gently
rolling her over.

How quiet her room was at almost any hour! The building itself seemed asleep—the whole world was napping! She became her earliest memories, drifting in and out of sleep. She was a baby napping in daylight in her crib, staring at the wall, at a patch of sunlight on the ceiling, fascinated by the pink bars of the crib and the decal of the golden-haired girl with the short blue dress and watering can surrounded by geese and flowers. She was out of body, out of time, suspended in a dreamy infant state. She didn't have to worry because she wasn't doing anything, wasn't becoming anyone. She was sick, confined, drugged, and there was nothing she could do but wait and dream.

She would wake to the surrounding images of white uniforms in motion and the flash of flapping sheets that in her dim and blurry vision seemed like the distorted and floating portions of a ruffling sail. Then it would be summer in Dark Harbor, in the big white cottage of her Aunt Olive, with its baronial and timbered library and the paneled dining room with the low row of casements with diamond lights that overlooked Penobscot Bay, the walls hung with the large marine paintings by William Stubbs and Antonio Jacobsen that her late husband, the Oklahoman who had come east, had collected. And the Oriental rugs with the geometric designs on which Sarah would sit as a child, picking out with her finger the small strange shapes of animals and people. The blue lupines on the lawn, and the old abandoned garden that was a ruin of escaped flowers, overgrown paths and tumbled walls. She tried to see herself at some time in the future in that summer house, playing her aunt's role, but she found herself looking backward into the past instead, to that summer when she and Toby and the children had used the house for a month after the death of her aunt, just before the estate was sold. She remembered the path to the pebble beach, which wound through the wild raspberries that had scratched the children and made them cry, and how they had stood on the ledges and jigged for mackerel while the children at the big Georgian-looking estate beside them jumped and somersaulted on the large white trampoline that was set out on the lawn above the sea. And the afternoons they would walk along the road with the ice cream cones they had bought at the Blue Heron, which Jessie called the Red Herring because the store was painted red, and Sarah had caught little Ned's ice cream in the nick of time, and he had eaten from the melting dip of strawberry she held before him in the palms of both her hands. . . .

In the middle of such reveries she had been known to open her eyes in response to some premonition and confront the same man in a wheelchair in the corridor outside her door, looking in. A gaunt, whiskered, hunched-up man whose bony knees pushed up his robe. Their eyes would meet; and in a lazy silence she associated with those shadowless, hot summer hours that belonged to the sun-flash and buzz of flies, he would study her as though trying to determine if she shared with him the secret and disappointing knowledge of his end. At first his look had been skeptical and faintly disapproving, but lately it had said that they were equals and that she understood him as no one else had. Strange how he never continued on past her door but always wheeled himself around and then away, returning in the direction from which he came. It was as if she marked the limits of his exercise, or was herself the reason for his venturing out.

Sometimes she would be startled awake by the sudden closing of her curtains by so firm and quick a hand that it seemed the hooks would tear through their eyes. It was a sound she had come to recognize as a prelude to some new violation or pain.

But this time it was no worse than the massage, the probe, the crush of Dr. Durr. The sensitive but ruthless hands of Dr. Durr. Like baby flesh, those hands. He could heal her with those hands. He was a faith healer, possessing such a pair of hands. And the big man himself snorting above her like a winded stallion. "Doesn't hurt down there today . . . huh? That tender . . . huh? Not so bad . . . huh?" Then the sheet brought up across her waist and the man making his exit through the gap in the curtains, the hem of his laboratory coat flying behind, while, exhausted by his visit, she settled back into that sleepy oblivion that had become her routine.

The next time she yawned and stretched it was early evening. The lights were on and Toby was in the room, and she was hearing in midsentence, as though she were being roused from anesthesia, "—the bus this morning but just barely." Some evenings she would learn from the older woman in the adjoining bed that he had been and gone, having kept a patient vigil beside her while she slept.

She received notes from both her half-brothers. Dean worked for a bank in England and mentioned a recent hiking expedition into the Pennines. Marshall, who worked for an airline in Hawaii, said he hadn't had a chance yet to go up any volcanoes, but would let her know when he did. Neither of them had married. She received a telephone call from the woman her stepfather had married after the death of Sarah's mother. Then her stepfather himself, who wasn't well, got on the line and wished her a speedy recovery. For the last six years they had lived in Florida.

Most of her friends and neighbors had paid her a visit early in her stay when she had been unaware or heedless of their presence, and were not coming now, Toby said, because they believed, as she did, that she would be home any day. She was surprised by their absence all the same. Auden, she knew, was too aloof and reticent for any demonstration of concern, and Adele Fox was busy with the manuscript of her cookbook, but why hadn't she seen Cullenbine bounce into her room, bearing flowers and chattering away until the nurses had to tell him it was time to leave? Probably he was bedridden with an injury or breakdown of his own. Kubilius, who admittedly was already in the hospital on other business, stopped by at least twice a day. She would often stir and see him standing beside her bed. His elbow would be in one hand and the other hand would hold his chin.

On the day of her discharge she asked Kubilius, and not Durr, if they knew yet what had been wrong with her.

"Nothing that rest won't cure, I imagine," he answered.

She let it out then, the fear she had repressed from the beginning. "It isn't cancer . . . ?"

For a moment he looked both touched and amused. "I can't imagine anything less like cancer than what you had. Unless it's a broken leg. No, whatever you had has paid its nasty visit and gone on its merry way. You won't see it again. All you had was a very bad case of something like the flu—although, don't misunderstand me, that was bad enough."

The flu! That's all it was, the flu! She couldn't believe her good fortune! Even when she slept and dreamed, she was sure she had not been unconscious enough to sublimate her fear of cancer. From the beginning she had feared that this attack was the first and fatal sign. When all along she had had to contend with nothing worse than a bad bout of the flu. She had done so much better than she had any right to expect! "The flu?" she said. "What kind of flu was that?"

"Better ask Durr," he said. "I can get rid of your pain, I can give you a good night's sleep, but a diagnosis isn't one of the things I'm supposed to be good at." Somehow the way he said this, or tried not to say it, made her suspect he knew about bad news. Still, it was understandable that he would be evasive and uncomfortable at such a question. After all, Durr was in charge of her case. I guess I've learned enough, she told herself. I don't have to ask any more questions.

How strange to come home empty-handed. She had been

in the hospital only twice before, and both times had returned with a baby in her arms. Now those she had brought home were waiting for her, standing in the living room with what would have been a Victorian formality if Ned hadn't been leaning against the back of a chair and Jessie hadn't kept sneaking looks at the television show her mother's entrance had interrupted. They were too intimidated by her return to speak, and when they did not approach her, she went to them instead, kissing each lightly on the cheek. "Did you miss me?" she said, asking the ritualistic question that in no way revealed the way she felt, or allowed them to respond with what she was certain was the apprehension and joyfulness of their real feelings. And when in their embarrassment they only nodded, she gave the ritual response: "I missed you, too." Although it struck her with a sense of guilt that, except as a presence in the memories of herself, they had not been much in her thoughts. "Let me look at you," she said to each in turn, holding them at arms' length. She was surprised that they didn't look at all as she remembered them.

By suppertime they came close to treating her as if she had never been away or ill, demanding those small favors and services she had always given them. Although she had been told to stay in bed, she was up and down all day, keeping busy. When she looked in on the children at bedtime, they were shy of her. They preferred the silence and the dark and the drawing in upon themselves. Something as important as life and death and as incapable of expression as love had come between them.

28   *Adieu, Cullenbine*

ALTHOUGH Cullenbine's friends were fond of observing that he was infatuated with Alexander and enamored of Sarah, the love of his life had always been Vita, his wife. Classmates in college, they were married in the final days of World War II. On the mantel of their living room was a studio photograph of the young curly-headed ensign from South Dakota in his dress whites, and his small dark bride from Nebraska in a simple broad-shouldered dress. A similar photograph was in their bedroom.

While Sarah was in the hospital, Vita had again moved out of the house without first saying where she was going or how she could be reached. As usual Cullenbine was quick to lose all sense of shame and reason and, after working himself into a frenzy with the help of pills and vodka, took to making midnight phone calls to their mutual friends. He would begin by listing his grievances against Vita, then beg his listeners' sympathy and support against her, and in the end berate them all for always taking her side of the quarrel. He was convinced that Vita had told Adele Fox of her whereabouts, and demanded she tell him where his wife was hiding, goddamn it, he knew she knew, why wouldn't she say? Was Vita living with another man, a young man? Come on, you can tell me, Adele. Some kid who got her drunk and gave it to her in the hay? Or was it several men, and were they all in the sack together, taking turns or intermeshed in some baroque, contortionistic daisy chain? Christ, Adele, how could he prevent such scenes from happening when she wouldn't even tell him where Vita was? When she wouldn't so much as take a message and pass it on? The least she could do was tell him who Vita was shacking up with. Nothing would surprise him, he knew what people and the world were like, but it was this not knowing what she was up to that drove him up the walls. So who was it? Some muscular kid with a shaggy head of hair and drooping mustache, who had her ass pinned to a bare mattress in some unswept cellar flat? Horny young bastards. Potters, blacksmiths, jewelry-makers—he knew the good-for-nothing types. Levi's, sandals, beards and leather vests, with a big medallion on a chain around their necks and leather wristbands and maybe thick leather belts that could really raise a welt across a woman's ass. Hirsute animals, hung like savages with their big sausages. Or was she in the company of some big black painter of acrylics, rubbing his bull-like bulge against her bush? Or maybe sixty-nining with some big dyke bitch? There she was, out on the town, drinking cheap sweet wine and smoking pot with her friends and making it with a lover all night long, night after night. While here he was at home—their home!—ill and all alone every night, all night, night after night, and knowing she was hiding out among her so-called friends, knowing that even their old friends, so called, were on her side, no matter what she did, knowing she was getting it every night, too, taking it all night long. . . . He wanted to kill her! He'd never let the bitch inside the house again, it was no use begging him to take her back! She had made her choice, she'd have to live with it, she could get on her knees before him and make him a million promises; he'd never take her back. . . . On the other hand, for Christ's sake, have a heart and show some pity, Adele—he desperately wanted her back! He'd do anything to have her back! Walk from here to the Vatican on his bloody kneecaps if it would bring her back!

When Adele took to hanging up on him, he called Sarah instead, certain she could be reached at home at any time of night or day. With Sarah he kept the worst of his ravings in check and confined his chatter to a catalogue of complaints and fears, concerning not only Vita but once again the fellow executives and young incompetent chemists of his company.

He even told Sarah why he had always liked and trusted her, unaware, apparently, that this confession might affect her in any unhappy way. He had judged her neither so successful nor ambitious in her life that she would ever rival him. Nor was hers a personality to patronize him. Nor were her good looks so glamorous as to mock him. And she was not so innocent or ignorant that he had no choice, given the uncompromising nature of his judgments, but to hold her in contempt. She had always been his favorite, and he admired her even more than he did the lovely Alexander. If he had felt safe in the allure of Alexander's playful insincerity, he had been all the more comfortable in the solid honesty of Sarah's character. (He meant that, he hoped she appreciated that.) Come to think of it, maybe it was Sarah's youth, more than her honesty, that attracted him most of all. Not that he was so foolish as to believe she was a fortress that could hold back his years. Nor was she in any way to imagine him as some sort of centenarian vampire sucking at her life-giving blood. Maybe (and he was thinking out loud now) he believed that when he was in her company he could maintain the illusion that he was not so old that his life's work in the laboratory was behind him. With Vita, however, there could be no such illusion. She knew what he had become, what he had been, she knew all his weaknesses and secrets.

Adele was outraged to learn he could be so full of his own problems that he had taken to pestering Sarah with his non-sense, and she called him herself, ordering him under no circumstances to call Sarah again. "You're a sick man," she said. "Have I ever denied it?" was his reply.

However, he did call Sarah one more time to tell her he was going into the hospital for a combination rest and checkup and that he wanted her to visit him there. But when she telephoned the hospital the next day, they told her no Dr. Milton Cullenbine had been admitted. Nor was he scheduled to be admitted. Sarah was later to learn that when she had called, he was home in bed.

As Adele and the others saw it, in his attempt to get Vita back, Cullenbine had devised an insane scenario that owed more to theater than to life. First he sent Vita an urgent letter through Adele, who, it turned out, had known where Vita was after all; and against the instructions of Vita, Adele passed it on. (Later she would claim she never told him she had done so, or admitted that she knew where Vita was.) In the letter he asked Vita to come to the house for nothing more than a brief meeting. After all these years together, surely she wouldn't deny him a last chance to bring about a reconciliation and make amends for any wrongs?

Next he took an overdose of barbiturates, and since he was both addict and chemist, he must have known how to gauge the dosage so that he would be unconscious half an hour before she was scheduled to arrive. She was to let herself in through the front door he purposely left unlocked and discover his unconscious form upon their bed. She was also to find the poetical note that both celebrated and blamed her. She was probably to read it while biting on her handkerchief and waiting for the ambulance to arrive. He was to be rushed to the hospital, where, after a few dangerous and unpleasant hours while she watched over him, he would recover. At that time they would be melodramatically reunited in each other's arms, her tears falling on his face. Once again he was to have used his illnesses and a hospital setting to his advantage.

Unfortunately his plans went wrong from the beginning. Although Vita received his message, she had no intention of showing up for any tête-à-tête. She knew his tricks too well for that. She could predict from past experiences that any meeting at this stage was likely to end up in his trying to keep her home by locking her inside her room. Which would result in the pair of them wrestling and rolling back and forth across the floor after first standing and delivering blows, using sofa cushions and house slippers as weapons. She insisted she gave him no hope at all. As always, he had understood human nature—up to a point. He knew Vita well enough to know that she would not go off without telling Adele where she was, and Adele well enough to know she would pass on his note to Vita. And some portion of him must not have been entirely certain that Vita would come, because it was said he arranged for a local woman who did housecleaning for Vita to come by to do some vacuuming only an hour after Vita was expected to arrive. Silly Cullenbine! He who had complained so often about the irresponsibility of the modern worker might have known he needed yet another safety valve. He had envisioned a play with two scenes, home and hospital. It was home and mortuary instead. Three days later an officer in his company got in touch with Kubilius, who he knew from past experiences was both a doctor and a neighbor of Dr. Milton. They were worried, he said; they could get no answer at his home. With that, Kubilius had gone over to the house, expecting the worst. He found Cullenbine in bed in the downstairs bedroom, the door of which had been left open to allow anyone to see him upon entering the front door. The note was beneath a vase of roses. He was said to have been smiling. No one who knew him could doubt that he had died believing he was a clever man.

Adele Fox, who told Sarah most of this by telephone in those first weeks that she was home, had other news as well. First, about the Angles. John was alleged to have had an affair with that girl named Miranda Sales, a promiscuous Californian who had left her two children with her long-suffering husband and returned to college only to drop out and work for a while (it was rumored) as a go-go dancer at a topless bar. The romance had started not long after Janet had hired Miranda to baby-sit for her while she went down to Cambridge to dance. Supposedly Janet had even caught them in the Angles' bed. Miranda was famous for her legs and miniskirts, which were the size of handkerchiefs, and she showed off her ample chest like an old-time "sweater girl." The men had taken to teasing the women at the recent parties by suggesting that their husbands were infatuated with her, or worse yet, that she was interested in them. Adele was surprised Sarah hadn't heard of her before. She was a cocktail waitress at one of the bars Toby was known to frequent, and Adele knew for a fact she had gone to him for information on buying a small house in the area as an investment. "If that's true," Sarah said, "I don't remember Toby mentioning her."

Not only that, but Marco had left Alexander. Really, when you thought about it, it seemed so inevitable, why hadn't they seen it coming? Marco had gone off to New York for one of his extended stays, only this time the months had multiplied and he never did return. He had taken an apartment in Manhattan close to that of the woman he planned to marry as soon as the divorce went through. She was the head of her own consulting firm and had recently been put on the board of directors of a New York bank. According to Alexander, Marco was the sort who could not long abide girlfriends or mistresses but had to have wives, seeing in them some complementary reflection of himself. They were like houses, automobiles, paintings—although to be fair to him, it was more complicated than that. It now came out that he had been married to an airline stewardess in Canada before he married Alexander.

Sarah remembered a conversation she had several years before with Janet and Alexander about the unfaithfulness of husbands, a mutual friend having just lost hers to another woman.
"I won't deny that my marriage hasn't had its problems," Janet
confided, "and we've come close to separating a dozen times,
but it's never been because I thought John was playing around.
I've had to worry about a lot of things, but that, I'm glad to
say, isn't one of them."

"That's not a worry of mine either," Alexander said. "If Marco
and I break up—and you have to be realistic, you have to
realize that that could happen—I know it won't be for that
reason."

But neither of them could be more certain on this score
than Sarah. "Maybe I'm naïve," she said, "but the possibility
of Toby fooling around has never entered my head."

29   *Business as Usual*

FOR Toby the times were hard. The condominiums on the shores of Lake Winnipesaukee
weren't selling, and the company that was building them, in
which he was a partner, could no longer meet the bills of the
contractors, who were suing. Then the small land corporation
he had helped form to develop a ski area declared bankruptcy,
and the subdivision of another large land investment was de-
layed because of the legal actions of conservation groups and
the stringent demands of new state conservation laws. As if

this wasn't bad enough, mortgage money was tight, and houses weren't selling. He was already overmortgaged and "land poor" with taxes and had become so deliberately, maintaining you were a fool not to be in debt beyond your means if other people were willing to lend you the use of their good money so that you could make good money of your own. The secret of success was to do as much business as you could on credit. That and to take great risks. His cash reserves, which were never much, had been long exhausted, and his credit was already dangerously overextended. For the first time he could imagine himself as bankrupt. What if the work of all these years was to come to nothing, he asked himself. What if he was brought down just when he was on the verge of his great success, only months away from making his first paper million!

Until now he had seen himself and land on the scale of Cecil Rhodes and the Louisiana Purchase. But as his financial position worsened, he subscribed to goals and schemes that were far less grand. He talked a man into giving him a sixty-day contract on a parcel of land, the sale contingent on his acquiring financing; but he gave the man no option money after leading him to believe that was little more than a formality, his credit was that good. He did this to keep the man from selling to another party. After sixty days he had not only failed to raise the money to buy the land but had sold the seller's other prospective buyer a large wood lot of his own. Next he misrepresented the foundation of a cottage, saying it was sound, and then the boundary line of a lakefront lot, because he desperately needed the commission those sales would bring. He sold the timber rights off a section of land he had agreed to sell, and then passed papers on it without informing the buyer of the timber he had lost in the interim to Toby's loggers. He who had dealt in hundreds and thousands of acres could now count the acres of his transactions on his fingers; who had dealt offhandedly in five and six figures of money now dealt desperately in three and four. He had become small-time. His daily ambition was no more than to avoid or satisfy his creditors. Which meant that he stayed away from home as much as possible. When he was home he would not answer his phone, and when he saw a party come up the driveway to his office, he snuck back into the house and stayed there, refusing to let Sarah or the children answer the door. His shoulders slouched and he passed on tiptoe. He had heard a rumor that he might be investigated by the state real estate board.

At the end of winter his luck turned. Against what had been all the prevailing financial forecasts, condominium sales picked up and then took off. The state water commission approved his plans to develop a campsite, and he sold a large and expensive tract of land. Not long after that, mortgage money loosened, and it seemed that everyone was in the market to buy a house. There was no explanation for any of this. He had passed through a dangerous period where cheating and getting by had become a guilty obsession, like an addiction to roulette. And yet he had not only survived, he had prospered. All the same, he had been shaken by his close call. He promised himself, I won't do things like that again.

It was during this period of depression and recovery that he began to think of younger and more active women. Sarah, he saw now, had always been too reserved and insular, her head full of dreams. Not that he had anything against dreamers. He was one himself, but his dreams took the shape of plans that usually found their way into the world as deeds.

He wanted the company of someone more robust, jolly, outgoing, aggressive. A young girl who liked to work up a sweat. The image of a woman athlete hurling a javelin or leaping hurdles was enough to make him feel aroused.

He took to slowing down his car to watch young women in baggy sweat suits jogging along the roads, sometimes looking like boxers with towels draped over their heads. There were the lumberers and strugglers, who appeared to pull themselves along; they were all right. But he liked best those who wore only the T-shirts and shorts and whose slim calves descended, sockless, into their track shoes, and who could fly like winged Mercuries, their feet seeming never to touch the ground.

He also took to stopping to watch the women's field hockey practices at the university, where he was sometimes the only onlooker on the sidelines. He admired the stamina and roughness of the players, liked to hear the crack of the crossed sticks and to see the plaid skirts flaring out and the braids of hair flying behind the running girls. There was a timelessness about them; they seemed no different from the girls of his own college days.

His favorite was the more handsome of the two best players. Her name was McAlpin, and the girls called her "Mac." She was fair-haired and broad-shouldered, with legs that looked powerful in her thick knee socks, and he was surprised that up close she was almost as large as he was. Once after defending successfully against a goal, she came off the field hurt and sat down in the grass, leaning back on her arms, while the student manager cleaned the wound on her knee.

"Nice play," he said to her.

Although she said nothing then, a little later she approached him on the sidelines. "Are you a coach?" she said.

"I used to help out with the lacrosse team," he answered. Adding, "A few years ago." It had been more like ten. "I'm not on the staff here, if that's what you mean."

"Are you a graduate student?"

"Not really." Then, afraid that he would lose her, he said, "But I have been thinking about coming back to school."

If he was attracted to girls like McAlpin, he was also leery of them. They wielded such terrible power: a slip of the young tongue and they would make him face the truth of who he really was. Already he suspected they thought him old, out of shape, ridiculous. A spectator, in short.

This attraction to younger and more active women he did not keep to himself but talked out with almost anyone he sat next to in the quaint seafood restaurant-bars of the coast that he would frequent when he was lonely, and had gone to almost daily during his long spell of avoiding the office at home.

"How old would you say I look?" he would ask his old business associate and fellow heavy drinker Tom Cahoon, unaware that he might have asked that same question as recently as yesterday.

"Twenty-nine?" said Tom, who had to know how old he really was.

"Two years ago I could have passed for twenty-four. I've aged five years in two."

"Beats me how you can lust for younger girls," Tom said. "Your wife looks even younger than you do. All you have to do is see her to know what she was like when you met, and what she'll look like twenty years from now. Neither of you will ever show the years. I'll always call you two the golden kids."

"Five years in two," Toby repeated. "At that rate it won't be long before I look older than I am!"

At night Toby would lose himself in the seed and plant catalogues that he found crammed daily in his rural mailbox. He would fall asleep reading them and dream of landscapes like Iowa, the San Joaquin Valley, Kent, the Golden Vale, and in the middle of the night awake and read some more. Outside there could be snow and ice and howling wind, and in his hands a world where there were fields and slopes of flowers, every kind of flower, and all in bloom.

What did it matter that he would do as he did every winter and order a tenth of the seeds he planned to, and plant only a fifth of those? Or that after he planted the seeds he would lose interest in the garden until the catalogues came the next winter, although when the fancy struck him he could be a ruthless weeder, at which time the garden could be turned overnight into a grid of green and black.

All winter he would compare varieties, quantities and prices. Which variety of early cabbage should he plant, which variety of late, when should he start each as seedlings, when would they be ready for harvest? And in the end he would be lucky to plant the one variety. It would be the same with beans. Fresh lettuce, he vowed, he would have every day of the growing season; he would make frequent and staggered sowings of half a dozen kinds. Far more likely that he would plant only bibb and limestone, and that in a single seeding in the spring. He drew maps of the garden with the care of an architect, laying it out in neat rows and labeling each vegetable in its special place. With a ruler he designed orchards, placing dwarf trees between the standard sizes. He laid out vineyards on the southern slope, hedgerows of multiflora roses along the drives, wind shields of poplars to the north. He consulted Auden and Kubilius and others, but in the end could never bring himself to order stock.

Again he would consider starting several new varieties of delphiniums from seed. He could imagine the beds of stately and triumphant stalks with their open bells of sky blue in place of the diseased plants that now grew shriveled up and black. Again he would decide against it; it would take too long.

When he read the catalogues he didn't worry about making or losing money; he didn't think about young women either.

30   *The Sensualists*

ON the first convincing day of spring, Sarah and the children spent a morning planting seeds in peat trays and shallow clay pots. The children had never worked harder, or better together, or shown more interest in a project of her choosing. Ned wore a big apron and, with his sleeves rolled up, stood on a chair and scrubbed the terracotta pots in the laundry sink with a big brush, while Jessie knelt on the floor and measured out sand, peat and humus in handfuls that she then mixed in a bucket, digging in her arms up to the elbows. Sarah planted the seeds and watered the pots from the bottom. She had been so slow to recover from her illness, and was still so easily fatigued, that she was surprised at this show of stamina. It could only mean that she was getting stronger. From now on she would make certain she kept active.

In her orgy of sowing she planted gourmet vegetables like lamb's lettuce and watercress, along with flowers that were Mediterranean, Alpine and even Himalayan in origin. Naturally Toby complained of the impracticality and exoticism of such plants, many of which he claimed wouldn't do well in this climate and had no place in his garden. He missed the point, though. She didn't care if her seeds sprouted, died from damping off or failed to survive transplanting. She hadn't imagined them waxing luxuriant in the garden, or as delectables on her plate. The moment of the planting had been enough. So what if the children had finally gone off, to leave her to finish on her own? To have breathed the greenhouse smell of soil, sun, green and wet and to have felt the thickness of the dirt caked beneath her fingernails had been reward enough. She was counting time as it came to her in moments, had learned how time could be ticked off and valued in portions smaller than a lifetime, and that the body kept time as well as the head. In the hospital she had been made aware of the possibilities of her body for strength and weakness, ease and pain, and she had come to recognize and savor the goodness in the commonplace sensations of the moment that could be as pleasurably intense as that deliverance one felt when, after a long and fatiguing trauma, the body was finally free of pain. Strange. She would have thought that lying ill and bedridden would have forced her even deeper into the reservoirs of her intellect. But just the opposite had happened. She had become aware of her body instead.

In this she believed she had become like Alexander. Once again she had taken Alexander as her mentor. Who, of Sarah's friends, lived more sensuously than Alexander? Or more faithfully on her own terms, and in a time scheme that was day-to-day? Like the Alexander she imagined, she, too, would greet the mornings in a silky Chinese gown by throwing open the drapes of her picture window and, with arms outstretched while continuing to hold the drapes in either hand, welcoming the sudden blinding flash of sun.

When Alexander, accompanied by Renzi, paid a visit to her convalescing friend, Sarah thought: Everything about her— face, hair, physique, make-up, clothes—is exactly right!

"Hasn't Alexander taken her separation well?" Renzi said.

"But I haven't let you see the sad state of my ego," Alexander confessed.

"It's true," Sarah said. "You've never looked healthier, or

better." She wondered if Alexander was sleeping with anyone. Renzi would appear to have become her escort, but she doubted there was much romance between them. The impression they made was of a divorced woman who preferred the harmless companionship of an elegant and interesting homosexual—although Sarah knew that Renzi was hardly gay.

"It's all this freedom to do as she likes," Renzi said.

"I can't see that I'm any freer for being divorced," Alexander said. "I've been alone a lot, and I've always been free."

"I don't care to be alone," Renzi admitted, having first reminded them of his own divorce. "The trouble with me is that I've been alone for so long that I've picked up intolerant and selfish habits." He leaned over to confide in Sarah. "Alexander would never put up with me. Still, that doesn't keep me from trying to persuade her to come to Greece with me. Don't you think it would be good for her? I do. She'd learn a lot, and she'd bring an artistic sense to everyday things."

Sarah was startled. Could he have forgotten that he had once made the same half-hearted invitation to her?

Alexander ignored it in any case. "It's funny that I never asked myself what I would want to do if my marriage broke up," she said. "Even though it didn't really make much of a difference in my case, because I've just gone on doing what I already did. But wouldn't you think I would have been clever or scheming enough to have daydreamed some alternative, or sketched out some little plan?"

Sarah wondered what it would be like if she was ever left alone. She was not unmindful of Toby's recent distraction and estrangement from her. He almost acted like a man left impotent by the disastrous end of some passionate love affair. Maybe he was put off by the state of her health. Maybe the worries of his business had drained him emotionally. He seemed so much older, heavier, sloppier. He sighed often, and he had only to carry a piece of furniture to be short of breath. Maybe she was losing him—although to whom or what she didn't know. She wasn't even certain that she cared.

On the morning of the Saturday they had been invited to spend the evening at the Angles', they quarreled. He had showed her the wasteland she had made on the table of the sunporch, the rows of seed trays she had planted with the children but had forgotten to tend. A blasted landscape in miniature had confronted her. Long, threadlike seedlings that should have been transplanted, or moved into a cooler spot weeks ago, and in any case should have been watered, lay all in the same direction, looking like an army of tiny collapsed parachutes across the dried-up peat cubes of hardened soil.

"The children forgot to water them," she explained.

"And you didn't?"

"I lost interest."

"What a waste."

Later in the afternoon he called from Portsmouth to say that she should go to the Angles' if she wanted, he might meet her there later, he had to go up north to close a deal. He sounded as though he had been drinking. She knew he had no intention of showing up. She went anyway.

The Angles, it turned out, had quarreled, too. Only John was there to greet the guests. "Janet's run out on me again," he explained. "She took off about an hour before you all were due."

If he was embarrassed by her absence he didn't show it. But then, it wasn't the first time that Janet had run off and left him to face their guests alone.

John gave Sarah, whom he hadn't seen in months, an especially warm welcome, hugging her as though they were not so much long-lost siblings as old lovers. It was a welcome he repeated, with variations, throughout the evening, usually coming up on her from behind. He would put his arm around her, squeeze her, kiss her cheeks, and only reluctantly let her go. People had come to expect such public demonstrations of affection from him. After all, he was an advocate of a school of teaching that had as its hallmark tenderness and sympathy, along with such notions as "openness," "touching," "eye contact." It was not unusual for him to take hold of a woman in passing and ease into an embrace that was far more intimate than any ordinary greeting, and to do so in company, without arousing any more notice from those present, including the husband of the encircled woman, than the comment: There's old Angle, harmless hungry lonesome John, at the girls again. "The Feelies," Cullenbine had called the Angles. More than once over the years John had given Sarah a friendly hug when they were alone in some part of a house, and surprised her with a kiss.

Although Dr. Durr had warned her that under no circumstances was she to drink alcohol, she drank vermouth. She was the only one drinking it, and she was confused when she picked up the bottle and saw that it was three-quarters down. She had been such a good girl up to now! She felt self-destructive and invulnerable, as only the young can feel. Kubilius was present and he had seen her drinking; she had caught him watching her as she filled up her glass. Why should he care about her drinking? He had joined his host in smoking pot.

Fortunately Janet had not left before making several dishes of Mexican dips and salads and fixing a long dish of crudités, which lay in a pool of melting ice. While the others were grouped around them, eating, Sarah asked John if she could see his new shipment of Swedish stoves.

He took her onto the glassed-in porch that served as the display room for the business he had on the side. The new models were in bright red and green enamels with bears and reindeer embossed upon their walls. With his arm around her waist, he guided her through this and other stock, explaining the slow-burning and efficient flue system to be found in each.

Of all the men she knew, he seemed least to have a firm profession. He could glide so easily from one interest to the other. She had always been attracted to him.

He came around in front of her and held her close, his hands clasped against the small of her back. Slowly he buried his face in the side of her neck. With a thrill, she recognized him as the mystery man of those frozen and erotic moments of her sickbed dreams. Man of fields, sea and sun, he had pleased her in those unhappy times far more than Toby or any of the faceless others had. He had held her close in meadow grass, sandy beach, forest glade. In his arms she had heard boat creak, fly buzz and splash; had smelled pine scent and mown hay; had watched sails fluff and seen, close up, insects on a blade of grass.

"I know who you are," she said, reaching up to touch his cheek.

"Who? Tell me."

"I know who you are, but I'm not telling." Her voice was sounding childish and drunken now.

She knew that this moment as he held her and she pressed close to him, like all those moments in her dreams, went neither backward nor forward in time but existed for its own sake, without consequence or meaning. Funny how, until her illness, she had never seen time in such insignificant and sensual terms.

"You smell of pot," she teased. "You're a pot head."

"And you're drunk," he said. "You're a booze breath."

And didn't he know how to communicate with his hands all those good things he could do for you? He was therapist and lover, both in one. He was the athlete-guru with the blond beard and the muscle tone of the rock climber and the manic jogger. Together they would carry umbrellas up the steep paths that meandered through the rainy Himalayas, passing through a high green world of mists and flowers, waterfalls and dreams.

"You'd be good for me," he whispered. "I'd be good for

you—I'd do nice things for you. I'd make you happy, make you smile."

She did smile. At being made the object of so modern an approach to seduction. "As I remember it," she said, "the men used to say, 'Be good to me, do it for me.'" Now it was the bold-faced assertion: Let me be good to you, I can be good for you. As though he were an instrument to give a woman pleasure. Well, what was wrong with that?

"Your pleasure's mine," he said.

"And I suppose you'll tell me next you've had, you know, the operation?"

"I didn't think I had to," he mumbled. "I thought you knew."

"I don't believe it." She laughed, pretending to retreat. "You never told me—no one ever told me anything about that."

"We were in the hospital at the same time," he said. "Only I was an outpatient. In and out. But I was very brave."

"You're joking; you couldn't have, the way you fought." She held him off and looked up into his eyes, which were soft and moist and incapable of dissembling.

"But you saw them," he said. "They were all against me, the whole world was against me."

"And so you did it." Beyond that, she didn't know what to say.

"Does it make any difference between us?" he joked.

His news was of no consequence to her. It was a matter between him and them. Why, then, did it affect her so? He had become pot smell, beads, sunburst medallion. He was useless as a seed pod or a shell. He was empty, scooped out, done in.

"We're in the mountains," he whispered against her ear.

"What did you say?"

"Let's go in the mountains someday, Sarah, you and me."

"Whatever you say."

She felt the hard cobralike surface of his body curve around her and saw herself as shrinking and giving way. The late hour and drinks, the disappointment and fatigue, had caught her all at once. Inexplicably she became afraid. "Shall we go back?" she said.

And just before they parted and returned to the hubbub of the living room, the messages within the body that had told her recently of pain and pleasure told her with a greater certitude than the judgments of either mind or medicine, that she, who had come so late to life, was doomed.

31 Murder in the Herb Garden

KUBILIUS had never shown patience with those who insisted they were ill or wanted to use medicine when the natural healing processes of the body would do as well. Surgery and internal medicine only when absolutely necessary, he would himself claim, served him for a motto. But he contradicted himself in practice. He prescribed anesthesia and painkillers beyond the common practice or what, as Cullenbine, who had so often been the recipient of his largess, maintained, was healthy for his patients. His duty, as he saw it, was to kill pain. And what of those whose life was pain? A dangerous equation.

His work at the hospital tended to send him into mild bouts of depression, during which he had been known to remark, "A professor used to tell us in medical school that we'd each kill five patients in our lifetime, and I've already killed four."

Today he left the hospital early and in an unusually dejected mood. The results of some of Sarah's tests were in and he had had a talk with Durr. "If a patient asks me how long do I have, I tell them the truth," Durr said. "At most I'll add a month or two. If they don't ask, believe me, I don't volunteer the news. I figure they don't want to know. What I do is try to give them enough information to figure out the bad news for themselves. Then they can ask the tough questions if they want to. That way it sure lessens the moral dilemma for me. You can tell her husband. I won't unless he asks."

Although Kubilius couldn't say he was surprised, he was heartsick all the same. What terrible news! He took off his surgical cap and blouse and threw them on the floor with all the force of a man who might also stomp on them or send them flying with a kick. A dramatic action for such a slow-moving and easygoing man. More in character, he collapsed in his chair and made a cat's cradle of his hands.

When he was low in spirit, he had three means of solace at his disposal: his music, his garden, his family—and all three of them were at home. Although his friends regarded him as a famous family man, the children were really Pokey's responsibility, and the cohesion of the family her creation. In the company of his family he was more the delighted observer than a fellow participant, and sometimes he wondered if his children weren't a wonderful show put on for his own pleasure and sense of satisfaction. Even when they were babies and would lie upon their backs inside their cribs, fascinated with the miracle of their own small hands and feet, which they would examine, wide-eyed and smiling, he was content to do no more than hang over them and watch, letting them grip his finger in their small fists. In the years that followed it was rare that he imposed his will upon them or exercised the authority that Pokey seemed to grant him absolutely.

Today he went home early and donned the khaki shirt and

trousers and visored cap that were his gardening clothes. They made him look less like a gardener than the naval officer he once was; or better yet, like a fellow who hung around a boat-yard, or the caretaker of a big estate.

Once inside the garden he performed his spring chores with the unwasted movements of choreography. He knew how to pace himself, and could reduce his pulse rate by a simple act of will. Even so, he would often lay down his tools and sit on one of those turf seats of his own making out of which grew dandelions and foxglove and sometimes, to his annoyance, this-tles, and smoke a cigarette in a holder, his long legs crossed. At his college there had been a sunken garden around the library with small stone statues of mythical characters and ani-mals set out among the shrubbery against the walls, and he used to lie down among them, worn out with the nights of studying, and go to sleep. Unknown to him, apparently, while he slept, the spirit of the place had crept into his soul. He had learned to blend with nature, and his collar and sleeves could sometimes be seen to carry bees, and Parker Fox could recount the time he had a long conversation with him in the garden, during the length of which a large hornet had perched on the tip of his nose.

His garden bound him not only to the earth but to the past. It had taught him how to use his hands and senses, and gave him the illusion of stepping outside the present moment into what was for him the best approximation yet of something timeless. Hospital, news, wars, pain, death, all were centuries away from here, and he prided himself that during the political and social upheavals of recent years he had been doing some-thing every bit as important as demonstrating in the streets.

He grew most of his herbs because of their fragrance or flavor (although he was often extravagant on the latter account, having, for example, a dozen sage plants when one would do); others he grew simply because they belonged by tradition in such a place. He did not grow the plants in neat rows in raised beds, in the medieval fashion, nor in a formal design, as in a sundial, hedged with germander, but let them wander as great clumps in massive beds and borders, where they grew rank and wild as thickets, with only rough and narrow paths between that wet you to the waist after rainy weather, and that he had to take his hoe to in order to keep free of stalks and vines. The children had been known to have their secret hideaways within the larger, thicker plants, and he was forever finding their rain-damaged toys and the wooden and cardboard remnants of their makeshift houses. They preferred the area of the artemisias, which they called "the ghost garden," or the mints, whose runners intermixed to give birth to new crossbreeds and waged war with the adjoining bouncing Bet, which would have taken over if he hadn't used a spade on it in spring, digging what amounted to a trench around its roots. At the height of summer his own privacy within the foliage was complete, and he could walk about in it as good as unobserved, his presence betrayed only by the patch of swaying stalks and rustling leaves.

What an overpowering confusion of aromas! The sour-apple smell of the sweetbrier in the rain, and the cloying perfume of valerian and heliotrope, while the gardener himself deliberately brushed against the lavenders and santolinas, trod on bee balm, slid his feet across the thyme and with his hands bruised the mints in which he sometimes ran the hose. Add to this the almost sickening fragrance of the sumac and bramble blossoms near the barn, and the dry, sunlit pine smell of the forest that grew beyond. Bees droned in the heavy, drug-laden air, humming like some ancient motor for the universe. On cool evenings or mornings great fat bees could be discovered trying drunkenly to walk the paths or drowsing in the heads of the wild marjoram, tame enough to touch. Toads and field mice in great numbers traveled about in the shadows of the larger plants. As did the small hopping birds that also flitted back and forth in the foliage, shaking the branches as though in anger when they took to flight. Garden snakes wound their way high into the tansy, where they draped themselves in the jungle of pungent, fernlike leaves. An old adder lived here, too, so enormous a snake that the first time Kubilius encountered it he mistook it for a child's monstrous stuffed toy until, at long last, and to his astonishment, it moved, turning away and sidewinding into the overgrowth of herbs. It had kept Pokey, who usually feared nothing, out of the garden all one summer.

He had a secret garden within this garden, too. There, in a small space, he grew, for his own amusement, Oriental poppies and celandine, among other plants, including some rare and outlawed species from which could be extracted the raw materials for soporific and narcotic drugs. He never pointed it out to friends, and even his own family didn't know the nature of the plants.

When he was through with his chores, he washed up carefully and went into the conservatory, leaving the French doors open to the garden. He picked up the viola and, after the ritual of tuning and resining and tightening the bow, put on a mute because it seemed to fit his mood, and ran through "Humoresque."

He remembered the evening last fall when he had looked up from playing the same piece to see Auden standing in the middle of the garden as though listening, his head sticking up above the giant stalks of mugwort. He had set down the bushel of apples he had been carrying toward the house and wandered out into the maze of narrow paths. What was he listening to or looking at? Kubilius wondered. "You ought to put one of those silver balls in the middle of your garden," Auden told him when, with viola tucked beneath his arm, he stepped outside to greet his guest. "It would bring all this together in a single bright image. Why, you could stand right here and see the whole surrounding world reflected in that little ball."

He ran through "Humoresque" a second time, and then "Beautiful Dreamer," which he judged as good as any Schubert lieder. But as he played it, he thought of Sarah, and his earlier depression returned.

He had known of the damage done to Sarah's liver in the early days of her illness, and that the question, after that original insult, was whether or not the liver—which was an amazing organ—would restore itself. Now they had learned that the damage was progressive. The prognosis of cirrhosis was certain. The normal liver cells would continue to be necrosed and then replaced by fibrous tissue until, eventually, the liver would be unable to carry out its enzymatic functions. Liver failure would then result, and the patient would become lethargic and jaundiced until she lapsed into a hepatic coma that would end in death.

If this course of unhappy events was clear enough, the cause of the illness that had done the damage was still a mystery. It was reasonable to suspect a virus of some sort, perhaps a new and rare mutant of a common form that was acting in synergism with some unidentified toxin, perhaps a chemical compound from a common manufactured substance that was to be found all over the landscape in the water, food chain and air. There was no telling where it came from. Maybe from the air pollution that drifted up the industrialized Atlantic seaboard; insecticides that had run off the land into the drinking water; the unburned carbon particles in the exhaust of diesel fuel; paint fumes, insulation fibers; or any of a thousand other sources, including a miracle drug she had been given in childhood, or during pregnancy, the side effects of which were showing up only now. Nor was it understood how organism and toxin interacted. Maybe they came together and formed a new organism entirely, part biological, part man-made chemical, with a new molecular structure, a new chemistry. A new disease of these modern times. Or such was Kubilius's imperfect understanding of it anyway.

He set the viola upright on his knee and plucked at it absently with his fingering hand. Necrosis! Profound coma! Strange words. Tragic-sounding words. So full of mystery. And doom.

32   The World Is Too Much With Us

"MAYBE what you had will never be identified," Durr told Sarah in his office. "Maybe you were the first and last person in the world to come down with it. Or maybe thousands are yet to have it. Maybe there have been thousands of isolated cases all over the world, only the disease hasn't been correctly diagnosed yet, or the information on the cases coordinated and analyzed so that we know we're looking at the same new disease."

In this and other brief and fragmentary talks Sarah had with both Durr and Kubilius, the doctors presented only possibilities, alternatives, theories, committing themselves to none, nor really satisfactorily explaining any. She had thought them enigmatic and evasive, and this had gone far to frighten her. But in the days that followed she recalled their reluctant explanations as having been not only definitive and exhaustive but finally optimistic.

And yet there had been a length of time that may have lasted as long as several days when Sarah understood, if not exactly the cause, then the effect of her disease. The hypothesis that her sickness could have been the result of some microscopic virus working in conjunction with some toxin made sense to her, and she extended and embellished the idea until she understood it completely, at which time it became an irrefutable scientific truth, as certain as if the doctors had not only championed it themselves but supported it with laboratory proofs. In this she was helped by those special television shows that reported and discussed the newest medical discoveries in the diagnosis and treatment of disease, and the friendly and talkative doctors she saw on the news programs, applying much of what she learned from them to the explanation and elaboration of her own condition. She had survived, but not without further risk and cost, apparently. There may have been some permanent damage to her organs—one of them anyway—and no one seemed to know for certain what the long-range effects would be. If there was still a mystery about the nature of the disease itself, there was nothing much mysterious about this sort of injury. The organ in question would malfunction and finally fail. She understood all this only to forget about it overnight, as it were, and never really think about it consciously again.

In time she came to focus not on the illness itself, or its aftermath, but on those symptoms she believed preceded it and quite possibly predicted it. "But why did I feel so bad so long before I actually became sick?" she would ask the doctors. "It wasn't only premonitions that I had; I did feel sick. Looking back on it, I know I was sick. Those awful feelings in the night, those awful dreams. And I had a complete physical, remember? And you found nothing wrong. Nothing showed up on the tests."

Durr couldn't tell her why; it wasn't a question that interested him, although he was relieved, for his own sake, that she was asking this and not more important questions.

Kubilius, however, was willing to go along with her. "Maybe, as you say, it is a case of your mind being ahead of your body," he conceded. "Or of being tuned in to your body some way. But it seems more likely that you had the virus in you a long time before you were seriously ill, and that was the cause of those early bad feelings. Who knows, maybe the virus had learned to mimic your white corpuscles so that your body was fooled and didn't destroy it, or there was simply a checkmate between the virus and the defenses of your body. When the toxin entered your body, it joined forces with the virus, which may then have mutated, creating a new and deadlier organism that really made you sick. Or it could have happened the other way around, I suppose, with the toxin present first."

But she had a theory of her own. Maybe her illness was a case of mind over matter. If the body could not quarantine itself from the poisons and infections of the modern world, neither could the mind. If you could be destroyed physically, you could be destroyed psychologically, and who could say that the two did not go about their business hand in hand.

She would have liked to use the free time of her convalescence to reread Henry James and at least a dozen new Simenons, but she couldn't concentrate enough to read anything more difficult than the newspapers and the women's magazines. Most of all she watched television. News programs, interview shows, talk shows, all with their never-ending reports of bad news from around the world that she was sure affected her as invisibly and lethally as x-rays. Oil spills off the New Jersey and Cornwall coasts, and dead wild fowl in the thousands; a nuclear power plant in Colorado blamed in the deaths by leukemia of local children; an earthquake in Turkey and the bodies of thousands of women and children, whose dusty protruding arms and legs you could actually see, buried beneath the rubble; a mother and seven children dead in a fire

in a cabin in rural Quebec; five teen-age sisters burned alive
in a second-floor fire in West Virginia; an escaped convict kid-
napping and murdering ten people across the state of Okla-
homa; an Israeli bombing raid on a Lebanese village and the
photograph of the children's bodies laid out in a long row and
the bearded father waving his hands and weeping; three hundred coal miners buried alive in Japan; a sex murderer killing
his ninth young girl in California; a war between two African
tribes, one massacring the other; a hotel fire in São Paulo, and
people seen jumping to their deaths from the top of the burning
skyscraper; a nursing home fire in Idaho and thirty old people
dead of smoke inhalation; a terrorist attack in an airport in
Rome, and thirteen people machine-gunned to death; starvation in the sub-Sahara, gaunt faces, stick figures, bloated bellies,
flies and corpses, dust and sand; an atomic test in northern
China and the wind currents carrying the fallout above the
United States and contaminating the milk supply; the deformed
babies of mothers who had been given a miracle drug during
pregnancy; one hundred and thirty dead in an airplane crash
in the Azores; a tidal wave in Bangladesh, and the casualties
in the hundred thousands; children murdered in the most sadis-
tic fashion by their parents and foster parents; special articles
and programs on child abuse, incest, drug addiction, venereal
disease, rape, hired killers. It occurred to her that all her life
she had been bombarded and imprinted with bad news. And
that for years now the conversations at the parties and dinners
she had gone to with her friends had been not only serious
but morbid. Abortion, sterilization, cancer, pollution, destruction, violation—such topics had become the normal social chatter of the day. What had happened to the stories, anecdotes,
dirty jokes, puns, bons mots, witty insults and flirtations of the
earlier days? She wondered what her parents had talked about
with their guests after dinner in their living room. Or her
grandparents at the turn of the century in their parlor. Did

men and women, when they came together over food and drink, talk about such subjects in other countries, other cultures? In Portugal, or Thailand, say? What a strange culture, that was so determined to broadcast disaster and discuss bad news. She mentioned this to Toby, and he had given her the stock response: "Well, it wouldn't be very interesting to watch a fireman rescue a cat, or learn how a third-grader in Detroit finally passed his math exam."

"And precisely because it isn't," she had countered, "doesn't that say something about who we are?"

Several tragedies struck close to home, and the immediate effect they had upon her was horrible. A girl in kindergarten was thrown at night into a swollen river by her stepfather, and Sarah could feel herself falling from the bridge into the icy currents that carried her along through the dark; by a miracle this child was saved, fished out by a chance passer-by who waded in from a bank. Then a toddler wandered off into the large swamp behind his house where, stuck in the freezing mud, he had spent the night. She imagined she could hear his cries coming from a long way off—she remembered how small children cried! Poor little fellow, he was barely old enough to talk. He had died. When an airliner crashed upstate in the mountains, and everyone aboard was lost, she found herself strapped in her seat, her hands clutching the armrests, the sensation of a diving roller coaster in her stomach. It was all too miserable! If you took all the tragedies you were told about into yourself and felt them with your heart, you would spend a lifetime grieving, and if you didn't feel them, you became inured and might as well be stone. Either way you were destroyed. It seemed to her that all the mischief and misfortune of the world had been brought to focus on the tiny living thing that was herself, and she wanted to cry out, Enough! She was too weak and insignificant for such a weight. Life wasn't worth living if you could be made to feel guilty for simply being alive.

In a more bitter mood she would wonder what any of this had to do with the town house on Beacon Hill, and its library with the old Bokhara on the floor. Or with the lodge in the White Mountains. Or the summer cottage on the Maine coast. Nothing, she would answer. Nothing at all.

She began to grieve for nothing in particular. She wept so easily, and for the slightest reason, too. Sometimes it was for no reason at all.

She would never accomplish anything for herself, or by herself, she knew that now. Even if she could have, the accomplishment would not have been important, and the effort itself would have been a shot wide of the mark. If she could not create, then she would devote herself to doing good for others, sacrificing herself until she lost herself, although she was still not certain she had been made along these lines. She would not give up like the soldiers and prisoners of Marco's metaphor, but would dedicate herself to service. She would begin now. As soon as tomorrow. As soon as she was well. So what if it was an exercise in futility; what choice did a woman of her sensibilities have at such a time?

33   *Youth*

BEFORE Sarah caught herself in the act of looking backward at her youth, she would have said such an interest for her was impossible. She had never dwelt upon the past, had never relived it, had never made a special effort to remember or recount events. Recollections and nostalgia were for her new experiences of uncertain merit. Oh, she had been nostalgic before, but only for that future life she had imagined she would someday have, as if, somehow, she had already had that life, or as if she suspected, even then, that such a future belonged only to the past. Now it was as if, having acknowledged she might not grow into that woman she had foreseen and fancied, or even grow old at all, she would move to safer, surer ground. As if, having found the way ahead of her blocked off, instead of staying put, she had turned back, saying to herself, If I cannot grow old, I will be young again. Wasn't it as valid as daydreaming about the unknown that lay ahead? Besides, she had before her the example of Toby, who had chosen to stay behind in the happy repetitions of his youth and appeared to take great comfort and satisfaction in his delusion. She would be one with Toby, then. After all, they were of the same generation, had spent much of their youths together, they even looked alike, could pass for brother and sister, someone had said.

She made references to their early dating, the years at college, the first years of their marriage, engaging him in tests of memory and nostalgic quizzes. Did he remember that girl— what was her name?—who introduced them at Perry's wedding in Beverly? He didn't know who she could have been, and he was surprised that she would believe that was where they first had met. And what about that friend of his who got drunk at some football game or other, he had brought a pint of whiskey, and there was trouble with some people who sat behind them, what was his name? He hadn't the foggiest notion, unless it was a fellow named Jack O'Hare. And that girl he had dated when they had broken up that summer, she went to Mount Holyoke, didn't she, oh, what was her name? He thought it was Lou, but he didn't think he dated her more than once. Well, did he remember her camel's hair coat when it was new, and the night she wore it when they raced in his black Jaguar through a stretch of the Essex woods? He remembered his Jaguar, of course, and knew the woods.

"I wouldn't mind hearing Dixieland music again," she said one evening. "Remember, back in college, it was all the rage? They used to go to bars to hear it, and weren't there a lot of college bands around playing it, too?"

"The Dixieland revival," Toby said. "It started out in San Francisco. Everyone was playing the banjo."

"I didn't like the music then. I thought it sounded trashy and unrehearsed, although maybe I really didn't like it because it was so popular with everyone else. I used to like French music—French classical music. But I bet I could warm up to Dixieland now. There was one song I liked. Could it have been 'Muskrat Ramble'?"

"Could be, Sarah. That was the name of a song."

"I know there was an animal in the title somewhere."

" 'Wolverine Blues'?" he wondered.

"And there was another song, too. 'Mama Don't 'low No Banjo Playin' Around Here.' The instrument changed with each verse, and while they sang it, they pretended to play that instrument. It seemed so stupid and childish then. Now it sounds like it might have been a lot of fun."

She was surprised at how little he remembered about the past. Why, she had a better memory than he did, and far more interest in the subject. Finally she understood why this was so. She should have known! He preferred the illusion that the past was not past, but present. No wonder he often winced and ended their talks abruptly; she was reminding him of his greatest loss.

Thereafter she continued the exploration on her own, focusing most often on her college days. She was unmarried, had her own car, almost all the clothes she wanted, and more than enough pocket money sent from home. Time, aging, death, they had meant nothing to her then. She could have died the next morning and not have cared one whit—would have been grateful to have lived as long as she had, would have been elated to have lived at all! How safe she had been back then.

It was difficult for her memory to particularize, and her images tended to be archetypal, while the feelings she brought forth were predictably romantic. She did remember the building on the campus that was like an English castle in orange and yellow sandstone, and another with tan stucco walls and a red tile roof that looked more Floridian than New England, so that she expected palm trees in place of the usual rhododendrons; and the glenlike setting of the grounds, the moss-green outcroppings of granite ledges and the shady spruces, an inland woodland setting that went, surprisingly, down to the sea, where there were rocky offshore islands and a harbor full of sailboats and the town of Marblehead across the bay. And she recalled a young pipe-smoking professor who wore tweed jackets with leather patches on the elbows and with whom she fell hopelessly in love, probably because he was already married. And there had been lawns and paths and falling leaves from the great wineglass elm trees, and gray squirrels and even ivy on the walls, and weekend parties with bonfires on the beach and beer drinking in the woods when the nights turned cool. In the winter the tower bells would ring out with Christmas carols, and you bundled up in fur coats and the cars were so cold, with steam or frost on all the windows, and you skied even though you didn't know how to ski, and climbed in the mountains in the spring when there were both snow and alpine flowers, and wasn't there a supper one snowy evening at an old inn in the Berkshires and they had sat at a trestle table before a blazing log fire?

In the spring you were overcome with *Weltschmerz* and wanderlust in those long twilights that were redolent of lilacs, and you couldn't wait to finish your exams and sail to Europe on one of those small Dutch liners that all the students traveled on back then. You roamed through the old quarters, which were the student quarters, of the older towns and cities (Amsterdam, Madrid and Lisbon had been "in" that year), making friends of other students of a dozen nationalities, exchanging folk songs in the evening around the Danish girl's guitar. Then you went into the countryside, hiking or hitchhiking with your knapsack, if you didn't go first to Amsterdam and buy an old used car. You took tea in Tudor inns, picnicked on Alpine slopes, slept under a bridge in Belgium, and in a youth hostel in the Schwarzwald, drank beer in an outdoor restaurant in Munich—or was it Salzburg?—where the trellises were draped with grapevines and thunbergia and there were gas lamps and you sang the sentimental songs in your high school German. And in the late hours as the couples danced to the old waltzes played by the small orchestra of violins and cello, you raised your stein and shook your head, wanting to weep with the wonder of the simple oneness of poor long-suffering and lonely humanity. O mankind! O sad and lovely world!

But gradually her recollections—if they were that—came to be haunted by the same long shadow. At some point a college classmate by the name of "Bones" Ragnar rode her monstrous black English bicycle across the scene, her long black cloak and skirt, the like of which no one else had worn, billowing out behind her. She was a genuine eccentric and outsider, and her tall body gave the impression of being all shoulder, cheekbone, chin and tooth. She was a brilliant student, at least by the standards of their school, and the girls had wondered why she was not at Radcliffe or Wellesley. Someone said she had grown up in Switzerland, where she had had a series of private tutors instead of attending school, and in consequence was forced to do well for a year in a school like theirs before she could be admitted to a university.

She never went to parties or dances, never joined in the impromptu gatherings in someone's rooms, never had a close friend. Still, it was impossible to know if such omissions disappointed her. Maybe she had suffered for her integrity and difference, although Sarah suspected she had been too remote and self-possessed for that.

For Sarah, her presence had pointed up the sameness of all the others, a uniformity Sarah herself must have remarked and disapproved of or she would not have tried to distinguish herself by playing the silly *grande dame* role. What was it that she used to scold her roommates with when they rattled on? Don't be so soporific!—that was it. And when they refused to confide in her what had happened on a date, she had ordered, Come on, expectorate! Saying it with a theatrical accent and smoking a cigarette dramatically while cupping a martini glass and probably wearing an outfit of gaudy and mismatched clothes. Such remarks had brought tears of laughter to the girls and given her something of a reputation as a wit and phrase-maker throughout the dorm. She had only pretended to be different, though. She had neither stood apart nor wanted to. Nor had she paid any penalties for her eccentricity. On the contrary, she had been taken all the more deeply into the bosom of the club. What an artificial ass she had been!

She wished she had not ignored Bones. Certainly the few times she had occasion to speak to her, Bones had been friendly enough, but Sarah would have been embarrassed to be seen regularly in her company. She wished she had spoken to her more often than she had, that they had gotten together in the library and over coffee after classes. She was sure they would have so much in common now. She would have loved to write her a brilliant and moving letter full of insight and passion, renewing the old friendship she wished they had had, and to receive a reply in kind. She would fill Bones in on the last dozen years of her life, which culminated in what she was feeling and thinking about herself right now. Do you remember, she would write, when we stayed up until the cock crowed and you helped me crib for that important French exam? Of course, you spoke the language like a native, having grown up on the shores of Lake Neuchâtel. That was the night you said, I predict that someday we'll both live in France, and we'll both have good husbands and be good mothers and— oh, yes—we'll both be doctors. And I wanted to give you the book of Elizabeth Barrett Browning poems that had been my father's and you said you could not accept a gift that meant so much to me as that, and I pressed it on you anyway, slipping it into your suitcase on your last day of school. . . . Bones, dear old friend and compatriot, she would begin the letter, where are you now? And how does one address you now? Are you Dr. Bones? Professor Bones? Madam Ambassador or Secretary Bones? Lady Bones and Dame Bones seemed to suit her better. She was probably a lawyer defending poor people in the rural South; a doctor in a small field hospital in the hinterlands of Somalia; a teacher of handicapped children in the highlands of Colombia. Dear old Bones, you were sure to be up to something that would meet the test of the good soul that you are!

She hunted up her old college yearbook and was surprised from the first at not only how old-fashioned her classmates looked but how old. There was something arrogant and sensual about the short hair styles and hard-looking hairless faces of the men pictured in the candid photos of the school socials, while the graduation photographs of the women, with their bright shiny mouths, uplifted chins, profiles bathed in light and complexions smoothed out with an airbrush, reminded her of the portraits you saw standing on a coffin that was closed. Almost against her will, she found her own picture and discovered that she looked like them. She had looked older then, somehow, than she did now. She would appear as antiquated to her children as her own mother, in those gray snapshots from the twenties and thirties, had appeared to her. As I saw my mother, she said to herself, my children must see me now. For the first time she felt a part of history. She could foresee a time when she would exist only in a record of those photographic moments. Already her life had become a document that could support the past.

She turned to Bones's picture, to see if she had been touched as the others had, but the square reserved for her photograph was blank. She had not bothered to have her picture taken. How typical of Bones!

It was not so long after this that Sarah decided she would give up this thinking about the past. If the future was impossible, the past was painful, and besides, both came to the same bad end.

34 *Harvard Square*

TOBY surprised Sarah one day by insisting that they go together on a shopping trip down to Cambridge and Harvard Square, apparently in the mistaken belief that she was still nostalgic about the "good old days." She would have preferred the elegant shops and outdoor cafés of Newberry Street, or the antique shops with their black English storefronts on Charles Street, but she knew he preferred Harvard Square. Unlike the other places, the Square was young and masculine, or had been, in the old days.

On arrival, they went their separate ways, Toby in the direction of his tobacco shop while she shopped for a car coat and dresses at Design Research, a glass department store that made her think of futuristic prewar Berlin. The racks were full of bright materials with polka dots, sunbursts and stripes. But she couldn't bring herself to buy anything. She wasn't certain of her size anymore. She thought she might take a smaller size now, but she didn't want to be measured to find out. It seemed a waste to buy for herself, although Toby had insisted that she should. So she bought for the children instead, a bright Finnish smock for Jessie, a set of wooden Swedish tools for Ned.

What a change had come over the Square since the Kennedy years, the time she remembered best. The Yard was the same with the old clapboard Colonials mixed up with the buildings of institutional red brick, and the grounds an Old World system of lanes and gates. But the Square itself was full of new stores, and concrete and glass highrises towered above the old churches. There were still too many cars, and the sidewalks were still crowded, and the crowds were still composed of young people. But the atmosphere had changed. It was like a carnival sideshow. Young vendors squatted or sat cross-legged on the sidewalk, selling beads and jewelry; in the shady tunnel of a new mall a girl played a Bach violin partita that echoed through the modern spaces; on a safety island between two avenues another girl piped Scottish tunes on an enormous bagpipe to a crowd of half a hundred, while a group of mimes and jugglers stood on the outskirts, waiting impatiently for their turn; a banjo player and a fiddler played classical Irish tunes on the sidewalk before a bookstore; a pack of Hare Krishnas with shaved heads jogged off, chanting, looking, despite their sandals and saffron robes, like a company of Marine recruits; at a busy corner a man in a black suit and a black vandyke, in the company of two women dressed as witches, handed out leaflets on Satan worship. But it was the change in the ordinary people on the street that struck her most of all. So many of the men were bearded, and the women had such frizzy and mousy hair, and so many of them seemed to wear bits and pieces of costumes or secondhand clothes. They seemed to her like immigrants. Maybe drugs or radicalism or disillusionment was at the root of it; she didn't know. But they no longer walked with that breezy confidence and vigor she remembered from before, when her generation had taken up the sidewalk, underdressed for the brisk weather with at most a long scarf wound once around the neck. Now they seemed to slouch and move not so much forward as sideways, using the narrowest edge of themselves to get by, to ease through things. There was no hurry in them, and no impatience. Something had gone out of them. It wasn't exciting to be among them anymore.

She met Toby at a German restaurant known for its selection of a hundred different imported beers, where he presented her with half a dozen cut belladonna delphiniums, all cobalt blue. He had discovered them at a nearby florist, the first time he had seen the variety for sale.

"They call me the delphinium girl," she said, accepting them.

"You're my delphinium girl," he said.

She said, "That's because I'm so blue."

They had a simple lunch of sandwiches and drank *Berlinerweisse.* He had bought some topographical maps at a bookstore. They were rolled up like tubes, and she could tell he was anxious to consult them over lunch.

She thought that with his ruddy face and cheeks and jacket of Harris tweed he could have passed for an Irish poet. He hadn't changed, he was out of place here, he was an anachronism. He still exuded the optimism of the era in which they had lived their youth, that sense of pride and luck and self that was to be their weaponry against the problems of the world. He still saw man as becoming better. Ask him, and he would likely tell you becoming was the definition of the species.

So different from now, when people were stopping in their tracks, or were trying to. Or were going back to the old ways, or were trying to. Or were looking after themselves, getting theirs before it was gone, and succeeding.

"Let's plan on going to Europe in the fall, what do you say?" he asked suddenly, springing it on her as though he was convinced that this would be the best of all surprises. She couldn't remember mentioning a trip to Europe to him in almost eight years.

"Renzi, Chaz and Pokey, probably Allan and Stargaard, they're all going to Europe," he said. "Why not us, too?"

"What about the business?"

"What's the good of being your own boss if you can't give yourself a holiday for three weeks? My mother will take care of the kids, I've already asked her. The airlines have these three-week packages that make it cheaper to go abroad than stay at home."

"Where would you want to go?" she wondered.

"France first," he said. "And then into Spain." His tone said they were the only possible answers to such a question. To him Europe was France and Spain, the countries he and his friends would have visited fifteen years ago, having read about them in the literature of the 1920s. She would prefer to return to England and, after that, to visit more exotic and remote places, like Romania or Turkey. But to Toby, England would be dull and unromantic, an extension of Boston and Cambridge. And the Balkans, about which he knew nothing, would be difficult and strange.

"You wouldn't think of going somewhere else?" she said.

"In Spain I'd be a millionaire."

"What's the exchange rate?" she said. "Sixty pesetas to the dollar?"

"A millionaire ten times over, then," he said. "How would I do in France?"

"I think there's less than five francs to the dollar."

"Then we'd be millionaires in France, too!" he said.

He sensed her reluctance. "The kids are old enough to leave," he argued. "There's no reason why we shouldn't go. Weren't we planning to take a trip back then when Jessie came along?" He gave her a pep talk, lapsing into nostalgia for their previous outings in Harvard Square and finally for his own trip to Europe in his college days, when, on the crossings back and forth, there had been all-night parties in the lifeboats.

At the end of his presentation, he unrolled one of the topographical maps, sneaking a look at the big green sheet. More land, she thought. In all that greenness he was seeing big hotels, shopping malls, thousands of small chalets. He was not without imagination or a vision. Unfortunately he did not have a vision of a great city, but of the suburbs. He did not aspire, he sprawled.

"Cheers," he said suddenly, as if he had remembered her. He toasted her with the preposterous schooner of *Berlinerweisse*.

Later, from the sidewalk table of a secondhand bookstore, she picked up a thin travel book on Wales published in the 1930s. It contained half a dozen gray photographs. It cost twenty-five cents and was the highlight of her trip. She thought it might come in handy as a reference for the mystery story she had taken to pondering during her daily rests. Solid background, authentic detail. Names like Bettws-y-Coed, Llandudno, Clynnogfawr. The writing of a mystery had come to seem appropriate for who she was. She wasn't fooling herself: it wouldn't teach her anything, wouldn't make her into someone she wasn't, wouldn't take her beyond the range of who she was, it wouldn't mean anything either; it wasn't even necessary. It was a diversion, something to keep her entertained and occupied. There was nothing shameful about it. On the contrary, maybe she should congratulate herself for having found her own level at long last.

At home she sat down at her desk and copied the descriptions she liked best from the book, the half-dozen belladonna delphiniums in a vase before her. Then she set aside a new page for her notes. But she wasn't ready yet to transfer the pictures she was forming in her mind to paper.

She was reading the book on Wales when Toby confronted her the next day. He wanted her to see the doctor; she hadn't seen Durr in a month. If he was no longer satisfactory, she should see someone else. They couldn't very well plan the trip to Europe if she didn't, and took care of whatever it was that ailed her. But it was more than that. They couldn't go on like this, surely she could see that. She was upsetting him, the children were on edge, the household was in chaos. Most of all, it wasn't fair to her. She was being self-destructive.

She said nothing in reply, only stared at the pages in the little book on Wales, smiling at the blur of print that met her eyes. He stomped out of the room. Only to immediately return and seize the book from her hands and throw it against the wall across the room. She sat as before, as though still reading the book, her hands folded in her lap. She had never seen him like this. Out he stomped a second time. Only to return and apologize. He was embarrassed, he was ashamed of himself. "What will we do?" he said.

She saw now that the shopping trip to Harvard Square had been a preparation for this confrontation; he had meant to put her in the proper frame of mind; the trip to Europe was an attempt to force an appointment with the doctor. Perhaps he had even planned to broach the subject at the German restaurant but had lost his nerve. She couldn't say she cared for the way that things were working out.

216

35 The Delphinium Affair

AS Sarah pondered the nature of her detective, she decided against a policeman or a private investigator, since those professions seemed to belong more creditably to men than to women, and were too professional to make her feel at home. She wanted her detective to be a woman, and it struck her that a woman detective had to be an amateur to be plausible. She preferred this in any case. Her detective would be a marvelous old lady with an extraordinary presence and sharpness of mind. She would be eccentric, a bit dotty perhaps, but also witty and with her feet on the ground. She would possess great powers. She would be able to see through people, she would know people inside out. Nothing would escape the keen powers of her observation, nothing would be beyond the scope of her many interests. The name Miss Cavanaugh came to mind.

Possible titles for the book itself were *Death Darkens the Village* and *Miss Cavanaugh Discovers.* First off she had to settle on her plot. Something baffling but comprehensible and, most of all, original. With a solution a reader would not guess along the way but would say, when the denouement was at last set out, was not only satisfactory but exactly right. Once she had settled on the plot, she could begin.

Her skill at drawing was much greater than her untested ability to write, and as she pondered the beginning of her story she took to sketching a map of the locale she planned to use as the setting for the crime. The map was like those found on the frontispiece or on the back cover of some mysteries. At first she tried to set the book in America and had drawn a map of a Maine island and a New England coastal village, but they were too close to home to hold her interest. She kept returning to a village in rural England or Wales. On her maps she drew and labeled, at one time or another, the inn, the post office, the green, the manor house, the maze, the river, the old mill, the right of way, the copse, the ford, the bog, the farm, the abandoned cottage, the pond, the rose garden, the gazebo, the church, the stile, the gate, along with paths, woods, bridges and ruins, and drew the dark shadow of a man with his arms and legs spread, which she labeled "dead man." Sometimes she simply marked the same spot with a cross.

To accompany the map she drew up a list of characters such as is sometimes found in the front pages of a mystery. She titled it *"Dramatis Personae,"* then crossed that out and wrote instead, " Persons This Mystery Is About." There was a publican who owned The Green Man, a thatcher, a gardener, the vicar, the vicar's wife (who was busy planning a bazaar on someone's lawn), the postman on his bicycle, the local constable on his bicycle, the doctor in his old car, the retired major, the daughter of Sir Richard Vane in the manor house, where she arranged cut flowers in a vase. The time was in the past although she chose to call it the present.

Gradually Miss Cavanaugh took shape. An avid birdwatcher and mountain climber, she was also an Oxford don. Sarah dressed her in tweeds, a man's shirt and jacket, big necktie and slouch hat, gave her a walking stick and a good pair of brogues and sent her on a walking tour in the mountains. She goes through misty mountain passes. Descends a narrow winding road where she is overtaken by a honking sports car with right-hand drive that has to stop for the flock of sheep in the road ahead. Then passes an abandoned cottage with house leeks and foxglove growing on the rotting thatch. Enters a village. Half-timbered and crooked houses that look, head on, like reflections in old imperfect glass; terraced mews of local stone. Lavender growing over the walls, with clematis and wisteria around the dooryards, and small lanes with hedgerows draped in woodbine. The church in transitional architecture and a ruined Norman tower with red valerian and ivy growing out of the rubble of the top. And nearby the manor house (fourteenth century with fifteenth- and sixteenth-century additions), with tree-sized rhododendrons lining the driveway to its door. She stops for tea at the inn. Lovely tea! Hot buttered scones and marmalade. And in the distance the steady noise of a mill-race, or is it a waterfall, and out the leaded windows, the surrounding mountains in their mists. An herb garden behind the big Georgian house next to the inn, the woody plants set out amid the ancient flags, and rambling roses and delphiniums, intertwined, growing down to the sward. The sound of spilling water, mist in the air, almost as thick as spray. Delphiniums, the garden, poison—someone at the inn poisoning the guests! She would focus on the garden. Footprints in the flower beds leading to the French windows. It hadn't begun to rain until after ten. The beam of the flashlight on the footprints leading to the body in the garden. Over there with that light! Shine the beam down over there! A dead man, the first of many. Lying face down in the herbs. The back of his clothes was dry, though. It had stopped raining around midnight. Miss Cavanaugh in bathrobe peering over the body, Miss Cavanaugh taking charge. Miss Cavanaugh attending the autopsy. The verdict: poisoned with belladonna. Hadn't Sarah heard that belladonna was a deadly poison? It was hard to believe that those blue delphiniums in the vase before her could be so beautiful and yet contain so dangerous a drug. She shuddered, imagining the poison passing through her system until she felt and knew nothing but the failing consciousness of her brain.

The next time she encountered Stargaard, she told him she was about to begin her new mystery. What did she care if she was patronized; she knew who she was, she had nothing to lose. She confessed to having drawn up a rough outline and a crime map, and that she had changed the setting to England.

He was in a playful mood and when he found out she didn't have a name for her village yet, he had some suggestions of his own. "How about Loose Chippings?" he said.

"That's a highway sign," she protested.

"Lost Mitten, then? Or maybe Bishop's Bedpan? Sotted Major?"

When she outlined her plot, he suggested a title: *Murder in the Herb Garden.* That was a good title. But she had come up with a title of her own. She liked *The Delphinium Affair.*

"I suppose you've noticed that the classic mysteries show a good deal of knowledge about the subject that's central to the mystery," he warned. "Such as tides, sailing, university life, railroad schedules, paintings or, as in your case, poisons, I suppose, and herbs. You ought to check out your background information with Kubilius."

Gradually the physical description of Miss Cavanaugh began to change. She grew taller, slimmer, more stately, she always held her head high. Her character became less flighty and eccentric and more authoritative. Her name changed, too. Now it was Mrs. Cavanaugh-Villiers. And she didn't walk through the countryside; she drove with a chauffeur in an old limousine.

But the more Sarah toyed with her mystery, the less interested she became in character and plot, or even in the writing of the book itself, and the more fascinated she became by the map and the many possibilities of the village she had drawn. The place was so tucked away that it was as good as lost. You could date the years by remembering the strangers who had called. Calamitous news from the outside world would take months to reach so forgotten a village, and would have no effect upon the place at all. Here you would hear only ancient storytelling and the usual fare of local gossip. Everyone was known to you, and everything that needed to be known was knowable. The same hilly pastures and bottom farmland through which coursed the familiar country lanes that led eventually to the same village green where the market was held on Saturdays. The world of your forebears, it would be the world of your children. Centuries would pass before you would see a change. What would Toby, with his office full of blueprints and topographical maps rolled up like scrolls, understand about such a village? Or Allan Orlovsky, who traveled as easily from America to an international conference in Venezuela as other men drove from a city to its suburbs, and who viewed human problems in global terms. "For better or worse," he had been heard to say, "the city is still the home of civilization. If you want art, education, social consciousness, cosmopolitanism, humanism and modern liberalism, you've got to live in or near a big city—the bigger the better. The small towns and rural areas would be in the dark ages if it wasn't for the countereffect of the cities. And I say this even though I prefer the countryside and towns."

"That all depends on what you mean by civilization," had been Auden's answer.

The next time Auden stopped by the house, Sarah brought up the subject of preserving small towns and farms as a prelude to announcing she was about to write about an old-fashioned village, certain that he, more than anyone else, would prove sympathetic to such a world. "It's only the setting for a mystery story," she confessed. "But I've learned a lot about the possibilities of such a peaceful place."

Which meant that once again she listened to Auden elaborate

upon his theory. Ten thousand years ago in the prehistory of the Near East there had been an irrigated oasis in a fertile delta in which grew orchards of olives, apricots and figs tended by a race of orchardmen who lived in peace with one another in unprotected villages. They had worshiped the great fertile goddess, the Earth Mother of us all. But then nomadic marauders had arrived on horseback, and advances in technology had permitted the manufacturing of efficient weapons of war, and masses of men began to move about, murdering and enslaving one another, and stealing the other man's land. We were still living in this human stage. But the instinct, or the recollection, of that Eden was still there in our memory banks, and you had only to let a small toddler wander through an apple orchard in springtime when all the trees were in bloom to bring it forth.

He spoke with an edge to his voice, and he seemed in an irritable mood. His heart, he confided, had been bothering him lately. Nothing to be alarmed about, but it had him worried. Sarah thought he looked frightened all the same.

She suspected that he didn't care for mysteries or detective stories. Even so, she explained the nature of the plot, how the murders would be committed with the deadly belladonna the murderer would extract in secret from the delphiniums in the garden.

"I must have missed something," he interrupted. "Because you can't be telling me that you think belladonna delphiniums and the poison belladonna are one and the same."

"But they are, aren't they?" she stammered. And when he shook his head, she said, "Oh, come on. The next thing you'll tell me is that delphiniums aren't poisonous." And she tried to disguise her apprehension with a pert little smile.

"No, I won't tell you that," he said. "I suppose if you ate a big mess of them they might kill you. I don't know of any commercial poison extracted from them, though. Come to think of it, I don't know if delphiniums rightly belong in an herb garden, either."

"I know digitalis comes from foxglove," she said, trying to recover. "I thought belladonna came from delphiniums."

"You get larkspur lotion from delphiniums," he said. "Belladonna delphinium, that's an old-fashioned variety of the flower. But the poison you have in mind comes from *Atropa belladonna*, also called deadly nightshade. It has small star-shaped flowers and small red berries. A relative of the tomato, incidentally, which it resembles. Which was the main reason people used to believe that tomatoes were poisonous. It grows on the roadsides and around the foundations of old houses, I dare say you've seen it. The poison atropine comes from the plant. No, no, delphiniums and atropine, they're different plants, different belladonna entirely. By the way, *bella donna* means 'beautiful woman' in Italian." Oblivious to the effect his lecture had upon her, he refused to let the subject drop; he just could not understand how anyone could make so preposterous an error. He added, "And I don't know why anyone would want to waste their time writing a detective story in any case. I don't read them myself, and I don't understand why anyone would want to read them. If people didn't read them, then others wouldn't write them, would they now?"

In the days that followed, Mrs. Cavanaugh-Villiers, the misty Welsh mountains, the narrow street of crooked houses, the border with delphiniums behind the inn, all disappeared forever.

Sarah no longer drew the little maps. She thought about the village, though.

At night she came to be possessed by dreams that were less images and narratives than physical sensations, mortal in their depths of despair and pain. She could feel herself suspended in the death struggle of an execution; she was tied up in a sack and swinging at the end of a rope; she was hooded and strapped in an electric chair. Or what was worse, she was in her cell or on the scaffold in those moments just before the execution was scheduled to begin, and she was sick and limp with the remorse and terror of such a horrible and reprieveless fate.

36   *The Mountain*

ONE midsummer evening after dinner at the Foxes', the women congregated in the kitchen and planned an all-women's hike into the mountains. They were to go the next Saturday bright and early, and if promises for the expedition were slow in coming, they were extracted. An Appalachian Mountain Guide was hunted up, and Mount Moosilauke was agreed upon; they would make a circuit, ascending the Gorge Brook Trail and descending on the old carriage road. Adele Fox, who had taken up hiking in the White Mountains with a passion in the past two years, had climbed the mountain earlier this summer; Sarah had climbed it, too, but that must have been fifteen years earlier and in the company of her brothers. Because they all knew that Sarah was the most experienced hiker, she was informally designated as their guide.

After the Kevilles had gone home, some of them had reservations, and asked Kubilius if Sarah should go. "Why not?" he said. "Does she want to go?"

"Seems to."

"Why not?" he repeated.

"Will it do her good?"

"Probably not," he said.

That night as they undressed for bed, Toby said to Sarah, "If you're not satisfied with Durr, why not see someone else? Let me know, and I'll call tomorrow down to Mass. General and set up the appointment for next week. What do you say?" But she was so tired she fell asleep before she could tell him, Don't.

She went climbing with the women on the mountain instead. The party was made up of Adele Fox, Pokey Kubilius, Pokey's oldest daughter, Colleen Orlovsky, and Janet Angle and several of her young friends, including, to the surprise of Sarah and everyone else, the infamous Miranda Sales. Alexander, who had promised to come only after she had been badgered into it, did not show up, and they decided they would go ahead without her. "I hope you didn't bring any salty food," Sarah warned. "Once we leave the brook there won't be any water until we reach the top. And I don't remember there being any water on the way down."

Sarah was in awe of Miranda Sales, and found herself staying back so she could watch her on the trail ahead. She had heard more about her recently. Her husband had filed for divorce but was asking custody of her two children, who were already in their early teens, Miranda having had them when, apparently, she was a teenager herself. Two camps had formed around her, one judging her conduct scandalous, the other, which included, amazingly, Janet Angle, insisting her actions were only those of a liberated woman who had the courage to be the equal of a man. The blow-up over the affair she had had with John Angle, Janet herself would tell you, had been talked out and resolved peacefully by all concerned, and Miranda was again baby-sitting for Janet. What the arrangement was between John and Miranda wasn't clear to anyone. It was hinted that Stargaard had had a casual but intense romance with her. She was said to know how to use men to her advantage, and that usually she was straightforward, asking or demanding what she wanted without pretense or nonsense, although she was not above using wiles, subterfuges and soft words. Adele couldn't get over how she actually called Renzi "honey" and how Renzi would lap it up with a blush and a big smile.

Everything about Miranda had been set high—shoulders, cheekbones, breasts—and if she was not so beautiful as Sarah had been led to believe, she was certainly sexier. She seemed to suggest that, like some wild she-beast, she could only show herself as lazy or aggressive, and in either case, sensuously so. She had come alone in her own car, wearing a brand-new pair of lederhosen, rolled up at the thighs. She had never climbed before.

They crossed a river and hiked at a leisurely pace through forest, the trail paralleling and switching back across a fast-flowing brook that seemed to descend in shelves. The path was steep and muddy, and the world around them was shaded, humid, splashy, green. Mist blew down through the hemlocks from above, seeming to fall with the water, and here and there the sun broke through with light. As they climbed they were infected with a sense of fun that bordered on hilarity, and they clowned for photographs, posing on a log that had been felled across the brook, or along a swaying rope bridge. "Save the film for the top," Adele counseled above the sound of water. That would be the most important picture, the gang of them standing on the summit against the sky in their sunglasses and windbreakers, arms around each other, looking like the conquerors of Everest. At the start they shouted to each other above the noise of spilling water and waterfalls about what their children and husbands were up to, the marvels of Chinese cuisine and the small gourmet restaurant with a French chef that some of them had discovered in a local inn, but now the topics turned to conservation and ecology as more and more people were encountered along the trail, far more than Sarah could remember seeing in the past. Some carried such huge packs on their backs that it seemed they must be doing the whole Appalachian Trail from Georgia to Maine, or planning to stay in the mountains at least a week.

For a while Sarah, Adele and Pokey kept together, talking about climbing. Sarah thought of herself as a mountaineer of the old school: she had climbed before any of the others, and she carried the proper equipment, and it wasn't new. Adele had taken up hiking to keep in shape, and she had already written a pair of articles on the mountains. Sarah was surprised at how many four-thousand-foot mountains she had climbed, and she seemed to know all the famous trails. Sarah thought: I don't think I know as much about the mountains as she does. She certainly hadn't climbed anywhere near as many peaks. Maybe she hadn't climbed as often with her brothers as she remembered. Pokey, it turned out, hadn't climbed in years, but had apparently roamed in the White Mountains when she was a girl. She had hiked in Europe, too, and although she didn't say where, Sarah was certain she had climbed the Matterhorn. "But don't you think we might do this?" she would say if there was a question as to how they were to proceed, or if she doubted the decision of someone else. Her daughter had gone to camp last year where she had climbed all summer. Janet and some of the others were new to climbing, and those who were more experienced, like Adele, slowed down the pace, calling out to Colleen, who, although a neophyte herself, was always ahead, to wait up.

Sarah fell behind. She was sweating, light-headed, she had a touch of vertigo though she wasn't near a precipice or in country where there was yet a sense of height. She carried

only a sandwich, an orange, a Swiss army knife, a compass, a
light windbreaker, a small first-aid kit and a collapsible drinking
cup in her nylon backpack, but the weight had grown heavy
on her shoulders. The damp woods were like a rain forest,
and her knees were muddy from the times she slipped and
fell along the trail. She often paused to rest under the guise
of fetching a drink of water from the brook. "I like to keep
up the rear!" she shouted to one of the others waiting on the
trail above. Another time she admitted, "I'm out of shape! I
haven't climbed in years!" She would soon catch her second
wind. After that she would do fine. If only she could climb
out of this oppressive forest and above the tree line onto the
bare ledge of the top and into a blast of wind. She longed
for the sight of green lichens and mountain cranberries. She
remembered the ruins of an old stone hotel on the summit,
and a high pasture from which, on a clear day, you had the
best panoramic view in the mountains. Several times she lost
the others to the mist above. Then Miranda Sales fell back
and kept her company. "You do this to have a good time?"
Miranda wondered. "You do this on your day off? I'd rather
lie on the beach."

Even older women and small children passed them on the
trail, along with novices in tennis shoes, tourists with Southern
accents and cameras, and a man in an Aussie hat, many of
whom encouraged them to continue, they could make it, it
wasn't so difficult from here on.

At the first lookout, a ledge that hung over a sheer ravine
of scree and forest, Sarah and Miranda caught up with the
others, who were already rested and anxious to move on. "You
mean this isn't the top?" Miranda said. The guidebook was
consulted. The lookout was barely halfway to the summit, with
the steepest climb to come. The direction of the summit was
pointed at in the distance behind a ridge. It looked ten miles
away. "You're kidding," Miranda said.

"Well, the summit itself is actually beyond what you're seeing," Adele reluctantly confessed. "And unless the mist burns off I'm afraid the summit will be socked in with clouds. It will be like Wuthering Heights up there."

"Lovely!" Pokey said.

"You mean we won't be able to see anything once we're there?" Miranda said.

Sarah slipped off her pack. She took out the orange, but instead of peeling and eating it, she just looked at it. It could have been a small globe, for all the appetite she felt. "I can't get my second wind," she said. "I must be coming down with something." She was fatigued, she couldn't breathe. Where was she, in the Himalayas, twelve thousand feet up instead of three? Then she began to feel the pain. Even so, it probably wasn't all that physical, she told herself. It was mental, spiritual, a case of mind over matter. Maybe her heart was no longer in the effort, and she was without compulsion to reach the top. Maybe she knew too much to expend herself on so meaningless a goal. She was so pale they took her pulse. "Not pregnant, are you?" Colleen joked.

Adele recalled that she had looked a bit peaked when they set out, and Pokey and the others were quick to second this observation. Sarah confessed to not having slept well lately. "Why don't you people go ahead?" she said. "I'll take my time going back to the car. You'll probably catch up and pass me on the way down."

"Sure you can make it by yourself?" Adele wondered.

"I'll go with her," Miranda said.

On the way down, Miranda said, "I guess we both made mistakes today. You're sick and I'm bored." They didn't have much in common, as it turned out, and said very little to each other after the first leg of the climb down.

Sarah wondered where Miranda got that healthy glow, seeing she was not interested in athletics or the outdoors. Sex, probably. She thought Toby would be attracted to someone like Miranda. She recalled her Swamp Yankee aunt had been obsessed with the idea of "the second wife," even though she was still the first. One of her favorite remarks was: "The second wife gets everything the first wife didn't." She would give numerous examples from among her family and friends to prove her point. One second wife received a new washing machine and drier, whereas the first had to make do with an old wringer type and clothesline for years. While others had received new cars, a new house, a new oven, a fur coat, a live-in maid.

The lower part of the trail, now that it was later in the day, was sunlit and hot. Uncomfortably hot, and they were no longer near the water. As Miranda, who walked ahead of her, rounded a curve in the trail, Sarah was amazed to discover that the woman's breasts were bare. She couldn't believe her eyes! Miranda had removed her halter-bra, and her breasts were bare. High, firm, large breasts that bounced, ever so slightly, as she descended, her shoulders held square. What an act of arrogance and innocence! It almost took Sarah's breath away. And she was singing, too, a popular folk-rock song about leaving your love. And she never stopped singing or covered up her breasts when she encountered, face to face, those new climbers who, embarrassed and amazed, made way for her along the trail, stepping off the path so that she could come down between them. Then, after watching her descend, they would turn to Sarah, who followed, with their mouths still gaping, looking as though they would like to query her as to the meaning of the apparition that had passed.

Sarah slept in the car until the others returned in the late afternoon. She slept on the long drive south, too, her head resting on Adele's shoulder. Even this was not enough to satisfy her, and she slept for almost fifteen hours when she came home.

37 At the Death of Art Ball

NOT long after a visit to his old friend Stargaard, the little artist who went by the name of Cambria drove up and bought the first farmhouse he happened to see for sale. It was just down the road from the Angles, but he had been living in it on and off for several months before he told anyone that he was there. Sarah's friends assumed he was at least moderately successful as a painter, for Adele had shown them the advertisement in a recent New York magazine for a three-man show at a gallery in Manhattan.

> CAMBRIA
> ROTHSTEIN
> MAGYAR-SCOTT

it read.

He was best known, though, for a one-man show that had been featured in the national news magazines a few years earlier. The exhibit had featured a series of portrait photographs of himself and friends along with a variety of famous people, all of which he had redesigned by scribbling on their faces with colored pens and pencils, much in the fashion of a child defacing an advertisement in a magazine. The President had been given a corkscrew of purple hair and a red Stalin-like mustache, while on his own portrait he had scratched out the face with a rainbow of cruel and careless strokes that in places slashed the paper until there was almost no head left visible upon the shoulders. This had only been a stage, however, not so much in the development of his art as in the development of his theory behind his art, and he had quickly passed on to other things.

Usually he painted in a style that had become known as abstract eroticism, and many such large canvases had been hung on the walls of his farmhouse home, the eroticism relying more on color—the evil violets, pornographic mauves, perverse greens, deviant yellows, as he labeled them—than they did on form, the colors blending into one another until they had the appearance, almost, of water-damaged watercolors.

To celebrate the decoration of his new house, he decided to have a party, and invited a number of his friends from New York and Boston to come up for the weekend. He also invited a selection of his new neighbors and hoped for an interesting clash or mix, he didn't care which. Only a masquerade party, he decided, would do justice to the occasion, and the costumes, he announced in his invitations, were to be based on the theme "The Death of Art."

Since no one in Sarah's crowd could remember attending a costume party as an adult or would have felt comfortable in a costume of any sort, not all of them planned to come in masquerade. And even those who did paid no attention to the orders of their host, finding it impossible to dress in keeping with so eccentric a theme. "How do you go dressed as a slashed painting?" Parker Fox wondered. "Or as a burning book?"

Toby said to Sarah, "We're not going, are we? I'm not that keen on it, and I don't think you're up to it, either."

"No, I want to go," she said. "But I don't want to dress up. I don't want to go as anything." That didn't prevent her from insisting that Toby dress as he did in college. She dug out an old crew-neck sweater and a pair of stiff white bucks that were charcoal gray with age, and a pair of baggy flannel slacks. In response he suggested she go in the antique finery of a *grande dame.* As Mrs. Jack Gardner, say. In a sardonic moment of self-mockery, she was tempted. After all, she told herself, it was her big chance to play the role.

But she wore a low-cut blouse and full-length flowered skirt and sandals instead. It made her look like a peasant girl. Possibly Mexican.

"Hey, *Señorita,"* Toby said.

"La Señora," she corrected.

Although many of the women came to the party in old-fashioned dresses of one sort or another, it was Pokey who wore her costume best. She was outfitted handsomely in ankle-length skirt, a blouse with puffed sleeves and a great plumed hat, which she removed. She was the Gibson Girl reincarnate, Cambria said. It was a marvel how she managed to look youthful and matronly all in one.

Chaz Kubilius came in the traditional black tie and tails that were left over from the days when he played in an amateur orchestra. He could have passed for a distinguished symphony conductor. "I tried to talk him into wearing the straw hat and blue smock of the French peasant farmer," Pokey said.

Renzi arrived in the tie and tails he still wore, as a member of the old-guard faculty, to the university president's ball each fall, and the two men confronted each other like two women at a party wearing the same dress.

"And here I expected to see you in toga and laurel wreath," Adele said. "Or dressed like a Renaissance prince."

Orlovsky, they joked, with his velvet jacket, flower in the lapel, big bow tie and huge beret, fitted in best with the page-boys, courtiers in powdered wigs, ballet dancers and spray-painted women who were Cambria's artist friends. Adele had predicted that Cambria would dress as Harlequin. Instead he wore an embroidered cowboy shirt, a large Stetson and a small black mask.

The clique of old friends quickly formed a small party of their own, which they said would probably be their last party in a long while since so many of their number were leaving for Europe soon. Pokey was taking the children for a year in France, where Chaz was to join them as soon as he could leave his practice in other hands. Renzi, of course, was off to Greece, and Stargaard was making noises that he would like to leave soon, and just might possibly go abroad.

"Who knows, maybe we'll all meet somewhere," Toby said. "We're planning a trip ourselves."

"I'd like to go to Europe, too," Alexander said. "Will you take me?" She had turned suddenly to Cambria, at whom she blinked her eyes.

"For me that would be taking a big step backwards," Cambria confessed.

"You mean you came from there originally?"

"Meaning I tried living with a woman once."

"What about you?" she asked Stargaard. And she slipped her arm around his waist. "Before you answer, I have to tell you, I could only live in Paris."

"My French isn't that good," Stargaard said.

"I'll be your guide, then," Alexander said, winking, squeezing close. "Stay close to me; I'll speak it for both of us."

It occurred to Sarah that Alexander lived her life by means of repetition. She had stood still while Sarah, in comparison, had raced ahead, too fast, perhaps, for her own good. She felt so much older than her friend.

She passed through the crowded rooms, moving sideways as often as she went forward, smiling, always moving. With a drink poised beneath her lips. She didn't know half the people. She didn't want to be with her old friends, didn't want to meet new people. She thought Kubilius and Alexander were avoiding her, that Renzi was cool to her, that Stargaard was embarrassed by her.

She pretended to be interested in Toby's telling some woman that delphiniums were heavy feeders and that if she would cut back the stalks after they blossomed in the summer and fertilized them, they might bloom a second time come fall; she overheard a recipe for a sauce that someone else said was in the *Cordon Bleu;* also the tail end of a Mexican chicken dish cooked with chocolate and peanuts; and someone asked Adele Fox if she had seen that tripe with mustard that was mentioned in *The Taming of the Shrew;* she paused long enough to hear the beginning of a story about a father who discovered that the burglars of the family cottage last winter were his own son in the company of his girl; also heard about a recent D and C; and the opinion that if we had spent one percent of the money cleaning up New England rivers that we had thrown away in the jungles of Vietnam . . .; listened for a while to a tongue-in-cheek argument by a woman of women's right to orgasm and a man's tongue-in-cheek reply that they had no such right, men had to have an orgasm to procreate whereas women did not, which made their orgasms perverse. . . . She moved on, though. Smiling. Turning sideways. Sidling through. A fresh drink to her lips. Saying, Pardon me.

She came across Toby hunched over Miranda Sales in a crowded corner. His cheeks were big and florid, and his neck was being strangled by his collar. Miranda was so much the woman on the outside, it was all the same to her whether she was naked or in clothes. They looked larger than life, and so physical it seemed that at any moment they might embrace and mate. She got close enough to overhear them talking real estate, a topic so much at odds with the uneasy passion in their looks. She was certain they had met before. And in private, too. When they hadn't talked entirely of real estate.

The lights were on in the backyard, and she watched Renzi cartwheel in a swirl of black tie and tails across the lawn to the applause of numerous other would-be acrobats and gymnasts. This was followed by a Mozart, after first removing his powdered wig, standing on his head. When she returned indoors she passed John Angle and Miranda Sales in the kitchen. She had her back to the refrigerator. They had been quarreling.

In the living room a drunken crowd of all ages in a hodgepodge of costumes and ordinary clothes was dancing to the deafening repetition and incoherent rhythms of electric guitars and organs. The dancers were inept but uninhibited, heavy-footed, tireless, whirling. Indians on a warpath, jitterbugs, go-go girls, Martha Graham devotees, belly dancers, soft-shoe shuffles, conga lines, and in the middle of it all, Janet Angle in stocking feet performing her own slow-motion mime-like dance, oblivious to the beat, one of her hands twirling an imaginary bola or lasso above her head.

Across the room a group was lifting a gypsy woman into the air. She lay on her back and appeared to be in a trance, her body stiff as a board. She was hoisted high up and held there by a host of upright arms. "Ooooom!" the body-lifters chanted in bass voices as the woman began to sway above their heads. The music sounded Oriental now.

Sarah saw Parker Fox and Chaz Kubilius dragging deeply, their eyes shut tight, on a smoked-down butt they passed along. Haze and bright lights and the din of a still louder electronic beat and twang. She was not a party to any of this, she was beyond it all. On a different plane.

"Ooooom!" they chanted, lifting a Prince Valiant.

"Ooooom!" Lifting the long-legged Janet Angle, whom they had seized and, because she continued to dance, only with some difficulty subdued.

"Ooooom!" Up with a willing Cambria, his second turn.

Someone said, "The *señorita*'s next! She hasn't had a turn!" Before Sarah could protest or retreat, strong hands were laid upon her, forcing her down. *"La señorita!"* the cry went up. She was lying on the floor at the bottom of a well of legs and faces leaning in and laughing. Then the hands slid beneath her back and waist, took her by the legs and shoulders. She closed her eyes and crossed her arms, mummy fashion, upon her chest. She felt the sensation of rising while swaying, with the rippling effect of the many hands supporting her making her feel she was borne upon a wave. She was weightless, lifeless, she was relaxed, on air, levitating. "How light she is," a man beneath her said.

"Ooooom!" the other voices said.

She felt timeless, prehistoric, Oriental; she thought of India, the Ganges, funeral pyres, prayer wheels. She was being man-handled, mourned, celebrated, sacrificed, cured, restored; she was part of the ancient ceremony; she was the dead and sacrificial maiden passed overhead from hand to hand through the teeming, grieving, chanting throngs who tried desperately to touch her corpse as it was passed along.

"Oooom!" said the hypnotic bass of several men, chanting. She could hear the drone above the screaming music and the pounding feet that did the dancing.

She knew now who she had been, and would never be. She had been deluded—all of her life deluded. She had longed for wisdom because she had known she was not wise, believing it would come to her in her old age. But she had been given another gift instead. It wasn't that she was great or good or wise or meaningful or useful or respected, because she would never be any of these things. It was only that she would see the truth, and always had.

"Ooooom!"

She had seen her mistakes, pretensions, falsehoods, delusions, self-deceptions—what a miracle to have seen them all! She had seen herself without exaggeration and distortion, with the clarity of spring water in the mountains—had seen everything! She was the dreamer who could not help but see the truth. She had seen, accepted, forgiven, saying, ultimately, This is who I am. Or was. Because how wonderful and forgivable her foolish acts and dreams had been. This, then, and no more, had been her gift. And what a wonderful gift it was! How could she ask for more?

"Ooooom!" the voices said.

I was never anyone, she said, I was never myself or anyone else. This was the sort of paradoxical nonsense that flashed brilliantly through her head. Being who I was not, I was myself. I am insignificant, but I am also unique. But that was a thought difficult to reconcile, mingling, as it did, the example of the East with the essence of the West.

Someone below jostled her, jolting her awake, and she opened her eyes to the smoky swirl of yellow light and saw two children in pajamas looking down upon her from above. The children of one of Cambria's houseguests, they stood on the balcony of the stairwell, one with his arms folded on the newel post, the other turned sideways with his elbow on the railing, looking down upon the noisy, costumed dancers and the body of the woman held aloft on the hands of her supporters. They looked too thoughtful to feel privileged or amused. For a moment she saw them as stand-ins for her own children, and reached out to them with a maternal passion she could never have summoned up for those who were her own. My children, she thought. And was seized with an impulse to rush home and check up on Ned and Jessie, who she imagined were troubled and restless in their beds, wondering where their mother was. She wanted to turn on the lights and wake them up and play with them or read to them; wanted to climb in bed with them and feel their body warmth. At the same time she imagined them grown up and living a life without her, glad to be on their own.

But what was this? She was being lowered, she could feel the small sensations of her descent. Those who had been kind enough to raise her up were trying to make her stand on her feet, they were telling her, Open your eyes. But she did not want to see or stand alone, she wanted to sink back and be lifted up, and while the hands were still trying to keep her steady, she fell back in a swoon. By the time she sat up, she was crying apologetically, beating her fist on the floor. Those around her tried to console her, saying they didn't mean to frighten or embarrass her, they would have stopped if they had known the way she felt. But they didn't understand, the body lift had been a wonderful experience. Even if they had taken a turn in the air themselves they could not begin to know the nature of what she felt. She had learned a great secret, had been given a great gift, and she had something important she wished to say to each of them, perhaps something only she, among them all, could ever know. She wanted to seek out Renzi, wanted to tell him that the secret of her life was not in becoming but in being; not in making but in knowing. Because what good was becoming, she would ask him, if you didn't know? It was enough for her to have been, she would tell him, and to have known. And would tell him, too, that one could learn the truth that maybe linked you with that universal All not only by becoming but, as in her case, by simply being—even if that meant being destroyed. But she couldn't find him anywhere among the crowd, although several times she mistook Kubilius for him, both men having dressed alike. So she went up to other people at random, including those she didn't know, saying, "I've had such a wonderful experience—" But when it came to naming that experience, she could only shake her head and smile. Her eyes glistened and her sleeveless low-cut blouse was off one shoulder, was off both shoulders now, and her full skirt was twisted around, almost sideways, on her hips; she had lost her sandals and her hair was undone. If anyone cared enough to listen to her, they patronized her, and the men put their arms around her waist. Some thought she was drunk or trying to be seductive. Most thought that she was both.

38   *My First Nude*

"THESE days there are only two kinds of painters," a drunken Cambria held forth toward the end of his party. "Those who paint with their head and those who use their penis, and the penis painter, in my judgment, is the far more interesting of the two. He takes it in hand, like so, see? And holds it just like he would a brush. Then he dips it into his palette, like so—"

"Thank goodness he's only miming," Adele Fox said.

"I hope this isn't his way of saying women can't be artists because they haven't penises," Alexander said. "Which explains their penis envy."

Cambria ignored them. "And there's a difference between its being soft and erect," he continued. "The brush strokes are different."

"And the big moment of the painting?" Stargaard wondered.

"Exactly," Cambria said. "No varnish splash, bad painting. You know the artist didn't put everything he had into the work."

Alexander whispered to Stargaard, "Do you paint?"

"Not like that."

"Could you paint a model?"

"You mean a real person, like in an art class?"

"Could you paint a naked model?"

"Female?"

"Would you like to paint me?"

"Naked, you mean?"

"Isn't that the way of models," she said, "always taking off their clothes?"

"I'd like to try," he said.

But once they were alone inside her house in the woods, she made them still another drink and didn't bring up the subject again. She said she was sleepy, and offered to make them coffee. But he embraced her, began to undress her. "I'm only calling your bluff," he said. She demurred, twisted away, tried to back out. "I feel the artistic urge," he said, untying her scarf.

They went into her studio, where she set him up with an artist's board on an easel. She cleaned a brush for him and squeezed out an array of colors on a palette, giving him some notion as to how he might mix them. "You're certain you're up to this?" she said.

"To this and more," he said.

While he watched she removed blazer, blouse and slacks and underclothes with so perfunctory a coolness that she might as well have done it while her back was turned. It was like watching a fashion model making a change between poses. However, it pleased and excited him far more than any provocative striptease.

He wanted to pose her astraddle a cushioned bench so that he could imagine her on horseback, but she suggested that she face him sitting cross-legged on the edge.

"Maybe you could use some props," she said. "How about some bananas, or a bunch of grapes? I think I know where I could put a rose. . . ." She tried to sound confident and in control, but Stargaard was certain that unless she fell asleep first, the advantage belonged to him.

His clumsy hands looked like bear's paws, the way they held the brush. And what a mess he made of the palette. Best sketch her in as she suggested. He noticed that she was posing with her eyes closed, unable, apparently, to watch him while he looked at her as closely as he did. She asked for a cigarette, and puffed on it, still with her eyes closed, even though he knew she didn't smoke. "Anything to do something," she said. She was growing cold, he could see the goose bumps along her flesh. She was yawning, too.

"It won't be long now," he said. He had rendered her flesh tone tan and muddy, with a streak of purple, and was trying to lighten it up somehow. In a moment of supreme confidence, he brushed in the pubic hair. Then he backed off from the canvas and was surprised to discover he was tolerably pleased with what he had done so far. After all, it was the first time he had ever painted with oils in his life, and the first time he had painted with anything since high school.

"How is it coming?"

"See for yourself," he said.

She came over with the striped blazer thrown across her shoulders. "That's not bad," she said. "Anyone can tell you don't know how to paint, but that you have an artist's sense for things. It shows."

He believed her, too. Granted the work was all a slapdash smear performed in ignorance, but for an oil sketch it wasn't bad. It was probably true that an artist would show his colors, no matter what he did. He could forget about the necessity of technique and skill; he would trust in the spiritual and intuitive power of himself. He kept at it, thinking: If only I could paint a perfect landscape, catch a pasture at some hour of daylight in a certain season; imprison it forever in an unfailing light.

He kept up a patter of talk while he worked. "Did you hear the story Cambria was telling just before we left? About the artist who used his own body as his canvas—tattooed himself for years until he covered every inch of his body. Did the work himself, too. Must have been painful; imagine inflicting that kind of pain on yourself. But then, art is supposed to be a painful process—didn't someone say that?" He tried mixing a yellow with some blue and made a mess he dabbed at with a rag. "Unless he was a contortionist, there must have been places on his body he couldn't reach. Cambria didn't think of that. . . ."

"Maybe he only made the designs for those, and had a tattoo artist put them on," she said.

He suspected she was being sarcastic. He went on anyway. "Not much chance for repainting and revision; he'd have to get it right the first time. . . . Cambria claimed the man looked all blue, like a blue man from the distance. But when you got up close, you could make out these narrow, wriggling lines, like white inlay. In some spots you had to use a magnifying glass, there was that much detail." He had picked up the painting knife and was wondering how you painted with it. He would try plastering some red on the section of wall he was attempting to render behind her head. "He wants to enjoy a great landscape, all he has to do is open his shirt and take a peek at his chest. A seascape—he rolls up his sleeve. Portraits— takes a mirror to his back. The whole world, it's all there on his skin. He's his own Garden of Eden, the ride to Canterbury, the Last Judgment, the Inferno, the Ship of Fools. . . . And he's not only created a masterpiece, he's the masterpiece himself. Renzi said a man like that was bound to be a boon for all those biographers who think the artist is more important than his work." He got close to the canvas, squinted at it and, putting down the knife, dabbed his brush into a fresh squirt of blue. "And when the man dies, his art dies with him. It rots, it disappears from the face of the earth. That was the point Cambria was making. . . . So I asked him why they couldn't skin him, preserve the skin and hang it on a museum wall like a tapestry? It would look something like a stretched- out bearskin in shape, I'd imagine. . . . So he said that wasn't the same as the skin being on a living body that breathed in and out and rippled its muscles and walked about. Besides, that was missing the point, he said. Which was that the artist is his art, and vice versa. . . . They live and die together. . . ." Suddenly he threw the brush down in disgust. What was wrong with him anyway? He had become more interested in the problems he was facing in his wretched painting than he was in its long-suffering model, who was now not only sleepy but pale and visibly shivering. He was a dimwit. She was so much better than the messy plodding of a drunken amateur.

In bed she seemed, if not exactly reluctant, then hesitant, and excited far more intellectually than physically. She embraced him as though he was her best chance to get warm. He felt like a schoolboy realizing a brief lifetime of romantic and erotic dreams. His sense of privilege and good fortune and even gratitude far outweighed the pleasure of any purely physical sensation. He didn't feel he had taken or given much of anything. Instead he had received a gift he wasn't certain he deserved. Maybe he was in love. Maybe he had made a choice of sorts, even if he didn't know precisely what that meant. He seemed to have aligned himself with some philosophy, or force—or maybe lack of force. Maybe the driftings and meanderings of the past years had, for better or worse, come to an end. He rose up on an elbow, and in the bar of moonlight that came through the window when he lifted up the corner of the shade, he watched her sleep, feeling better about himself than he had in weeks, months, maybe years.

On his way home the next morning he pulled his car over when he passed a small pond and bounded down to the shore, where he took off his cap and gave out with a whoop, pumping his arms in a cheer. He was in a playful mood and wanted to talk back to the world in a big voice. He wanted to brag, show off, act silly, behave like a nuisance; if others didn't share in his luck and happiness, by God, they could at least be made to witness it! He couldn't resist stopping to see Cambria, who lived along the way.

The driveway was full of large expensive cars with New York license plates, and in the country kitchen he found half a dozen houseguests wearing bathrobes and reading newspapers around a noon-hour breakfast of instant coffee and toast. He didn't remember them from the party and had decided they had only just arrived this morning, until he recollected that last night they would have been in costume. Cambria was still in bed.

No one spoke to Stargaard. He sat among strangers who talked among themselves of Provincetown and Manhattan and exotic people he didn't know. He felt awkward and ignored.

Cambria never did come downstairs.

39   Visiting Hours

DR. Durr put Sarah in the hospital for a week of examinations and tests, but when the week was up, he kept her on. For still more tests, he said. "Our hotel isn't so bad," he advised her. "We give you a room with a view, maid service and a menu that lets you order à la carte." Last week Sarah had overheard him say the same thing to the woman in the room across the hall.

But other than the taking of her temperature and pulse rate and feeding her vitamins and regulating her diet, nothing much was done. Durr looked in on her almost daily, saying, "We'll get you home one of these days. I want a little better color on you first." He understood that she didn't want to hear or talk about her health. Toby tried once to talk to her about it, but she wasn't interested, and he looked grateful that she had relieved him of his responsibility on this account. She was certain he knew the true nature of her illness now. Durr or Kubilius had told him, they would have had to tell him how she stood by now. Her friends knew, too, she could tell they knew. One day Durr said she might have to have an operation. To see how things were.

She found the ceiling alternately boring and as fascinating as the stars; she rarely spoke to anyone unless spoken to. As early as midmorning she would look forward to Toby's nightly visit. As early as midafternoon she would wonder why he hadn't come. Didn't he know how desperate she was? How could she make it through the long night if, for whatever reason, he failed to come? And when she awoke from a nap it was all she could do to keep from weeping when she learned so little time had passed, that visiting hours were still so far away. He always came, though. He would enter on tiptoe, afraid to wake her if she slept, and would tell her first about the children, what they had done that day, what they had allegedly told him to tell her.

She did not think that much about them, though, except for those moments when, envisioning them alone in the world, she pitied them and, at the same time, felt sorrow for herself. She did not miss them, either. She understood why children were not allowed to visit hospital rooms, cruel as that would seem when the patients were their parents. You didn't want to see your children. You wanted to see your husband. And yet she did feel she should be home looking after them. She sometimes wondered how they could possibly feed and dress themselves without her help. Toby brought them to see her one Sunday and, in her bathrobe, she went out to meet them in the lounge. But the meeting was awkward, and as formal and uncomfortable for the children, who were in their Sunday best, as an afternoon in church. She felt so much taller than they were, stooping over them like a stick figure using her cane. She seemed so distant from them, and so much older, too. She could have been their grandmother. Or remoter yet, their great-aunt.

Strange how her neighbors and acquaintances in the town visited her more than her old friends.

Two women became steady visitors. One was a roly-poly middle-aged lady, new to town, whom Sarah had spoken to several times in passing at the post office. She had spotted Sarah in her room while visiting a neighbor who was recovering from an operation next door, and had returned to visit Sarah long after the neighbor had gone home. She had a narrow hawklike nose and eyes that looked crossed behind the lenses of the pince-nez she wore on a chain, and she was exceptionally buxom, having what Sarah was accustomed to call "a bosom" instead of breasts. She came to help out more than to visit, and to this end she would wear a white dress and shoes that approximated a nurse's uniform. She fussed about Sarah, breaking water glasses, bumping into things, rolling the bed up in the middle instead of at the head, handling Sarah roughly as she made her shift unnecessarily about the mattress, and then apologizing for her clumsiness. Her name was Mrs. Munson, but Sarah, to herself, referred to her as "Munson-Bumbler." Sometimes her incompetence would so irritate Sarah that she would frown and beat her pillow, or even speak sharply. Afterward she would feel bad, fearing that the good-hearted woman had read her impatience as ingratitude.

Eileen, the second visitor, was a tall unmarried girl, close to Sarah's age, who claimed to know Sarah from high school in Massachusetts, where she had been several years ahead of Sarah. But try as she might, Sarah could not recall her. Sarah had no idea how Eileen learned that she was in this hospital, or why she had come to visit her that first time. Nor why she had continued to visit her several times a week thereafter, when the drive was forty miles each way. She had trained as a nurse, and performed nursing chores for Sarah with an effortless efficiency that the regular staff could not match. She came to work, and she took command. She knew how to handle Sarah—quite likely she could handle anyone! Once she had confided that her own mother had had a liver condition and that she had nursed her herself. Sarah assumed the mother was dead. Sometimes after Eileen left, Sarah would notice that the pamphlets of a fundamentalist Christian sect had been left on the nightstand beside her bed.

Whereas Mrs. Munson's back rubs were punishing and unskillful and given while the little woman stood, huffing overhead, Eileen's were athletic and sensual, and were performed while Eileen hummed and sang to her affectionately as she sat beside her on the bed. Eileen knew how to comfort Sarah when she cried, and could be sympathetic or authoritative as the moment required. In comparison, Mrs. Munson, at the first sight of tears, would flush with the color of a sunburn and clasp and unclasp her hands while repeating, "Dear, dear."

It occurred to Sarah that she had never seen the two women in her room together. How was it then that they came so faithfully on alternate days? Wasn't it reasonable to assume that they knew about each other and had agreed to share her between themselves? Grateful for their presence, she was nevertheless bewildered by the intimacy they had presumed. She could not see how she deserved the charity of their compassion. In her darker moods, she explained their interests in her by reason of their being busybodies, or ghouls; or because they were unoccupied and friendless and had nothing more interesting or sociable to do. Poor friendless women, then! There were times when their presence irritated her, but neither woman stayed beyond the point where, by showing her weariness, Sarah expressed a wish to be alone.

When autumn turned as cold as winter, she was surprised by the sight of Stargaard in her doorway. He was the classic Christmas caroler with his rosy cheeks, open coat and scarf he was in danger of trampling as it dragged across the floor. He brought her half a dozen English mysteries in paperback, each gift-wrapped separately. He had thought up some new names for her storybook village, and tried out Pressing Matter, Common Medley and Bedding Down. She forced a smile and dismissed them with a wave of hand.

"And Alexander sends her best," he said.

That he was embarrassed for Alexander's sake did not escape her notice. He wanted her to come herself, and probably had told her as much. He made no excuses for her, though.

"Sick people frighten her," Sarah said. "I've heard her say so. More than once." Maybe something of this same feeling explained the absence of the otherwise dutiful and sympathetic Parker Fox. Several years ago Kubilius had gashed himself with a hunting knife while deep in the woods, and Parker, his sole companion, whom he had asked to dress the wound, had turned white instead and fainted at the sight of so much blood. As for the absence of her other friends, maybe it was as Eileen had suggested: it was their very closeness to her that made it difficult for them to see her often and, in some cases, even to see her at all.

"I think hospitals do depress her," Stargaard said.

"Have you two gotten together yet?" she wondered.

"Well, we're still more far apart than together," he confided. "However, fate may be about to intervene. I'm being kicked out of my apartment—"

"Then you'll move in with Alexander?"

"Either that or back to the open road," he said. "And I'm broke."

A few days later Sarah awoke to the sight of Renzi reading a magazine at her bedside, so unexpected a visitor that she could not place his face at first. "No one told you I hadn't gone to Greece?" he said in disbelief. "No wonder you're surprised to see me."

"And here I thought any day now I'd be getting a card from Athens," she said.

"Believe me, I thought I'd be sending one," he said. "Unfortunately, I never realized, until the last minute, what a project the whole trip really was. I simply wasn't ready to go. I suppose, in a way, I'd been training for this trip for a lifetime, and I finally couldn't see any sense in going off half-cocked and playing it from one day to the next by ear. Then it occurred to me that I couldn't very well travel in Greece without my car— I don't know why I didn't think of that before—and by then it was already too late to have it shipped over in the fall."

Of course, Sarah thought, his car. For years he had driven an old English Humber, black as a London taxi, which he babied, confessing to having put more miles on its body with a chamois and wax than on the speedometer. Fortunately, he had been able to postpone his appointment in Athens until the spring.

Then the Angles came by and caught Sarah up on all their latest news. John had resigned his post at the experimental regional high school! The federal grant money to support the innovative curriculum he had introduced had run out, and the town, under the advice of the school board, had refused to pick up the cost on its own. "What choice did I have except to protest the decision by resigning?" he said. "Can you see me heading up a program dedicated to the teaching of the three R's?"

The times were bad, Janet said. Money was not only tight but the towns, which were already conservative, were becoming more so. Too many old and retired people, for one thing;

they ran the show. And with abortion and birth control, the school population hadn't grown as they had forecast only a few years ago. John was getting out of education entirely. They were branching out from their wood stove business into wind and solar energy systems and pursuing that full time. That was where the future lay. For them, for all of us. They were calling their business Natural Energy Resources, Unlimited. They were so optimistic and enthusiastic. They left her literature on solar greenhouses and solar fish farming that John had written and had printed up, along with their company's latest brochures.

How wrong she had been about John Angle. And wrong about Renzi, Toby, Auden, even Stargaard, and so many others, too. They had appeared before her with the shamelessness and innocence of boys insisting they were men, demanding admiration and pity simultaneously, and revealing an impotence and a self-interest that she, with all her private and inconsequential daydreams and delusions, had not possessed. Until now she had accepted them as they had shown themselves: as active, decisive professionals pursuing a lifetime of useful work. But behind the show, they were delicate and tentative, and their work was as inconsequential as killing time, and they knew it, too. Poor men! Compelled to lay claim to the stars when all they had eyes for were the snakes breeding around their feet! More than they knew, they were brothers to poor Cullenbine. There was a man who had been worn brittle and wafer thin as a cup of old bone china. And in the end he had smashed himself into a thousand little pieces.

One Sunday afternoon Vita Cullenbine paid her a visit in the company of a retired army general, a widower in his late sixties whom she introduced as her "boyfriend." A Southerner with a tropical tan and an old-fashioned white mustache, he was good-natured and surprisingly informal. He told Sarah stories of the Canal Zone, where he had once been stationed, and of Turkey, where he had served as some sort of attaché. They had just come from church, Vita said, whispering in an aside that Luke (the General) was an avid Presbyterian and that she had to be on her best behavior at all times. Both the General and Vita winked. Vita certainly wasn't keeping company with the sort of man Cullenbine had accused her of favoring in times past.

Unquestionably life was easier and gayer for Vita now that Cullenbine was gone. The General seemed in awe of her. How much younger she looked, too. Cullenbine had done her a favor by taking himself out of her life. She didn't miss him, either.

But strange to say, Sarah missed him. She saw him in baggy tennis togs with some roadside flower drooping out of his pulled-down tennis hat and bouncing as he walked along, his face lit up with that rosy energy and prissy impatience to corner someone with the effervescence of his slander. He was mythical to her now. The perpetual suitor in straw hat and summer blazer strumming a tennis racket while he made attempts to croon. Or some leafy and light-hearted personification of a green but malicious spring.

One evening a crowd of Sarah's old friends descended on her unexpectedly. On the strength of a whim they had decided to move their party from the house where it was in progress to Sarah's room, piling into their cars like teen-agers on a spree. They would be together again, they had reasoned, as in the old days, the good old days. They arrived after visiting hours were over—which suggested the presence or connivance of Kubilius—because Sarah had already received her drugs and was snuggling into that safe and selfish nest of twilight sleep. Suddenly there were blinding lights, shouts of greeting and "Surprise!" and "Look who's here!" and the crowd noise of a party in full swing which, in the surrealism of Sarah's mind, became a carnival of clowns pounding big drums and revelers blowing party favors and New Year's Eve horns. Squeezing all at once through the doorway of her room, they trooped in around her bed, investing her immediately with their atmosphere of sleigh rides and song and that cocksure hilarity of comrades who have successfully smuggled liquor to a prisoner in her cell. But bright lights, noise, presence, all brought her back reluctantly from her favorite dreams. She was confused and cross. She put her hands up over her eyes and shook her head from side to side. Why couldn't they know she preferred sleep and privacy and dreams? They were quick to apologize, backpedal, leave. From the corridor Sarah caught the undercurrent of recriminations from the embarrassed Adele Fox, who claimed she had counseled from the beginning that they should have stayed at home.

Sarah was never certain of all who came.

40 Champion

IN the weeks ahead in the world outside the hospital, powerful interests of industry and politics suddenly emerged to threaten the local landscape and way of life, and even those people who had been apolitical or indifferent were aroused enough to man the barricades. Sarah was kept abreast of her old friends' new preoccupations and activities by Toby and Kubilius, and occasionally by Adele Fox when she found enough free time from her busy schedule to pay a visit. They had all become maniacal about meetings. Telephone polling. Planning committees. Position papers. Adele talked to her of nothing else.

For years there had been a rumor of a plan to construct a six-lane scenic highway through the mountains on a course that would take it a mile north of the Angles' house and less than two miles from Auden's orchard, and apparently for no better reason than that the state had the federal funds to build it. Mountains would have to be cut through, old houses demolished, the wilderness itself violated from one end of the state to the other. Suddenly the local newspapers took to writing about the plan as though the Department of Public Highways was about to haul gravel and cut the timber off the land. Toby's feelings about the project were ambivalent. "A lot of people are saying that the people from New Jersey and New York will just use the highway to shoot up to the coast of Maine," he told Sarah, "and that it won't do us any good at all. Still, you'd think that some of them would pause along the way and buy themselves some land and second homes."

The Angles, of course, were active in the fight against the highway, and even Cambria, who would live as close to it as they would, joined in the cause. But the real leader of the local opposition emerged as Archie Auden, and the support he gathered from both the old-time Yankees like himself and the newcomers made some inroads statewide. He wrote learned and literate letters to the newspapers, and delivered a series of expository lectures at several of the local schools, firehouses and town halls. He even addressed the state legislature, in whose body he had served as a member in terms past, where he presented at length his theory of those orchardmen in prehistory whose oasis had likely served as the source for the myth of the Garden of Eden. He called on the representatives to make every attempt to return to a Jeffersonian notion of the small farm and the rural way of life. Adele, who went to hear him, said some of the older representatives maintained they hadn't heard that speech since Auden refused to stand for reelection twenty years before. When the state finally announced that the highway was only in the most preliminary stages of the drawing board, and was fifteen years away from being built, if it was built at all, the outcry against it gradually died down.

But the latter stages of the campaign against the highway had been overlapped by a rumor that a Greek shipping tycoon who owned a fleet of oil tankers was secretly picking up land options in a nearby town as a prelude to building the largest oil refinery in New England in the valley between the twin humps of a small mountain, with a large pipeline running from the port facilities to the refinery. When it was later reported that no less than the governor himself had not only welcomed the Greek but invited him in the first place, and that the big American oil companies were smiling on their venture, the people in the area became enraged. Adele Fox, who belonged to numerous conservation and political groups and had the advantage of receiving advice from a husband who was a lawyer, was the earliest to organize the resistance against the scheme. But to the surprise of everyone, it was Colleen Orlovsky, a member of no organization other than her country club, who emerged not only as the spokesperson of the resisters but as the symbol of their cause. Week after week her picture appeared almost daily on the front pages of the state's newspapers. There she was, the handsome former state women's golfing champion, whose photo in times past had appeared only on the sports pages, taking on the governor, the oil industry, the famous Greek tycoon, her words not only reported but quoted. Sarah herself had witnessed that triumphant moment when Colleen emerged for the first time from the crowd and received the spontaneous acclamation of her fellows, which elevated her to star status. It had occurred on television, the local educational network having broadcast the most important of the public confrontations between the antirefinery group and the representatives of the oil and shipping interests, and Sarah had watched it on the set her hospital roommate, like the one before her, kept on from dawn to midnight, oblivious to her wishes. At some point the public relations man for the refinery had displayed on a large easel an architect's industrial watercolor of the projected refinery, a neat cluster of silvery oil tanks of a high polish interlocked with a harmonious network of pipes and stacks, the whole complex set off by itself in an otherwise unspoiled valley between two small mountain ridges and overlooked by slopes of evergreens. It could have passed for some ultramodern university, sanitarium or space observatory. "It looks pollution-free," the spokesman said. "And it will be pollution-free. The trouble with you people is that when you hear 'refinery' you think of New Jersey. Well, get the stink and smog of New Jersey out of your heads. This is the space age. You people haven't kept up on things. Refineries don't have to be like that, and this refinery won't be like that, we can guarantee you that. Our model is the refinery in Bantry Bay in Ireland." He held up a photograph of what appeared to be a cluster of inconspicuous metal cylinders on an island off the fjordlike coast of Cork.

Then the camera was on the audience, where Colleen was standing before the microphone. "You're right," she said, "there is no pollution in Bantry. And there's a reason for it, too. It's the same reason why we'll have no pollution from a refinery here. It's because there is no refinery in Bantry! Or anywhere else in Ireland! Those tanks in your picture are only storage tanks. For weeks now we've heard nothing from you people except the wonders of this modern refinery in Bantry. Well, just to be sure, I sent a telegram to my old auntie who lives in Cork, and here is her reply." She held up an airmail letter.

The spokesman on the stage didn't appear to be concerned. "Your old auntie could be wrong," he said, amused. And his face said he had just set the weight of the governor, oil industry and Greek tycoon on the other side of the scale from Colleen's old aunt.

"Do you think so?" Colleen said. "Well, you may be right."

She paused, dramatically. "But what about the Irish minister of transport? Because I wrote him, too. And in my other hand I have a letter I've received from him." She was shouting now above the cheers, foot stomps and laughter. "Did you think we were such sheep that you could feed us lies like that?" she said. "Did you actually believe we wouldn't do our homework? Well, mister, I'm here to tell you that you, with all your agencies and studies and consultants, haven't done yours. You're just not up to me and my old auntie!"

It was at that moment that the audience, sensing victory, rose in one body to their feet and applauded and cheered without letup until the men on the stage turned to each other and shrugged and smiled with raised eyebrows, admitting defeat.

But Colleen was in no mood to give them quarter. What would be the effect of an oil spill on the tourist business along the beaches? she wanted to know. On the lobster fishing? On the clamming? What, they didn't have a study? Well, did they have a study then to show what new industries would grow up around that isolated refinery in the drawing, and another of the increase in heavy truck traffic in the area, and what effect that would have on the maintenance and enlargement of existing roads? And did they know anything about the housing developments that were bound to spring up around this pocket of industry and what the effect would be on the local school systems and the tax structures of the communities? And who would get the jobs in these industries, out-of-staters or local people, and she meant in the construction of these industries, too? By now the audience had become her constituency, and their cheers were as firm as votes.

Then one evening on the national news a piece on the refinery was featured, and there was Colleen on the screen being interviewed by a well-known newscaster. It was just after she had left still another meeting at which, as the film clip showed, she had hurled passionate questions and charges at a mumbling and finally incoherent governor, whose last response was a brief temper tantrum before he stamped out of the room. "The question is, Don," she said to the reporter, "are we going to allow the governor to say to a foreign company, You can build a refinery in such and such a town whether the people want you there or not, or are the people of that town going to have a say on a matter as important as this that can't help but drastically affect the quality of their lives." Only after the news had gone on to another report did Sarah realize she had seen the bearded Allan standing behind Colleen, so much overshadowed by her presence that she appeared to have the little man in tow. He had looked not only proud of his wife but a bit bewildered by her, too.

Later Sarah learned that Colleen had appeared on an early morning news-talk show and had more than held her own against the industry spokesman, who had been given little opportunity to speak, the interviewer having sided blatantly with Colleen although he had focused less on the issues than on her golfing championships and the marvel of an ordinary housewife's becoming the spokesperson of a groundswell of grass roots democracy—and what did her husband and children think of her sudden push to fame?

But Sarah could no longer maintain an interest in an affair as remote as this. She wished she could have performed important and worthwhile deeds for others and that, in her lifetime, she had done so from the beginning. She should have worked in that direction, should have tried harder, she saw that now. She should have helped people like the well-meaning but hopeless Mrs. Munson. Now Mrs. Munson was helping her.

Colleen Orlovsky and Mrs. Munson were not what mattered now. Achieving, creating, doing—they didn't matter either. Only existing mattered now. She dreamed about the big creaking cottage on the rocky coast; a fog bell ringing; fog blowing in, blowing out, blowing in again, there was a big bank of it, poised like an army, just offshore; a pot of tea, a comforter and a crackling fire of driftwood and the laths of smashed-up lobster pots. This was what she saw and saw again until at some point on the change of tide and fog she fell asleep.

41 Sandman

MOST evenings Kubilius would look in on Sarah, entering her room like a jewel thief who had been waiting in the adjoining suite for the drugged victim to fall asleep. If she stirred and murmured when he entered, "Shhh," he would say. "Don't worry, don't trouble yourself, go back to sleep, it's only me." He didn't like to see her uncomfortable or to find her awake but drugged, and these, along with sleep, were pretty much the conditions in which she passed her days. No, he didn't mind her sleeping. A painless if not entirely restful sleep. And when the night nurse came in, he would greet her with his forefinger to his lips.

Now that he shared his work load with the young Chinese anesthesiologist who would replace him when he joined his family for the rest of their stay in France, he had more time to himself than he had had since he was a boy. The unfamiliar silence of his empty house had been quick to haunt him, and any air he played on his viola echoed so forlornly through the rooms that they seemed empty not only of people but of furnishings, while the music itself was so lonesome a sound that he could believe his family was not merely gone but dead. In these moments he would lift his bow from the strings, the back of his neck feeling as though it had been touched by ice. He longed to hear the melodies of his oldest son's recorder, of his daughter's piano, and to catch sight of Pokey reading to the children before the fire, or, as she had done lately, teaching them some French. Without knowing it, he had taken to strolling through the house and throwing open doors at random, then gazing thoughtfully into the empty rooms, seemingly lost or confused. Nor could he interest himself in the herb garden he would soon leave untended for half a year, knowing how it would suffer in consequence. Its presence was funereal to him, while its wildness bespoke a place that had been abandoned. He dutifully sent his family letters, but the recitations of his doings were uninspired, and the act itself became a chore. He spent evenings brushing up on his French, and teaching himself Spanish in preparation for the trip he hoped to make to Galicia. He didn't seem to be able to get the pronunciation right, or to keep the phrases in his head.

Usually he spent his lunch break with Sarah, eating a sandwich and sipping lemonade from a cardboard carton through a straw as he stood leaning against the wall beside her bed. He had been known to call at any hour of the day or night, and would make sure to look in on her when he was called in on an emergency, at which time he would say to the nurse, borrowing her flashlight, "Shhh, I'll just have a look." Sometimes when he was settled down at home for the evening, he would suddenly put aside his phrase book, throw on a jacket and drive off to the hospital with the same urgency he would have shown if he had been called. Gradually he came to think of his visits as appointments he had to keep. The feelings of affection and protection he had, until recently, reserved for his own family, he began to show for Sarah.

He brought her bouquets of herbs almost daily, and would

dispose of yesterday's bouquet himself, rinsing out and refilling the vase, then arranging the new flowers. He brought a large bouquet of mints, which he bruised before he left the room, and one of gray and green artemisias. Once he came with a nosegay of thyme and lavender, and Sarah said that, thanks to him, she dreamed she was in Provence.

The nursing staff on Sarah's floor was aware that Sarah was a personal friend of the doctor, but was amazed all the same at the amount of time he found to spend with her, and at how faithful and concerned a friend he was. He let them know it, too, if he thought bed, room or patient wasn't up to the highest standard of housecleaning and nursing care.

He resented the presence of Eileen and Mrs. Munson, whom he occasionally encountered when he stopped by mornings or afternoons. He had been known to play the doctor with Mrs. Munson, asking her to please leave the room while he examined the patient. With the more formidable Eileen, whose professionalism he admired, he didn't dare to pull a stunt like that. Besides, she had only to glance at him out of the corner of her half-closed eyes to let him know she wasn't fooled by his "doctor mask," but understood, better than he did, what he was up to and exactly what he was feeling. He sensed the antagonism between them, emanating equally from each. He was jealous of her, and viewed her as a rival, which was how she saw him. It was as though they both knew they were frauds making a play for the inheritance that came with the hand of the delirious but infatuated girl—and may the best cheat win! Once she had the temerity to throw out his flowers, a job that, until then, had been his alone. His admission that the flowers had about gone by did not make him less angry at her presumption. He took it out on the nurses, asking them to make certain that visitors were not allowed to perform nursing chores and that they didn't stay so long, or come so often, that they tired the patients with their presence. He trusted they knew whom and what he meant. Later he came to question his pettiness, which, for the life of him, he could not understand.

He tried to arrange his visits so that they would not coincide with Toby's, for some part of him resented the husband's presence and that pathetic pleasure Sarah showed on seeing him, a welcome that touched Kubilius all the same. The conversations between husband and wife would be brief and warm, and Toby would hold her hand. He would, however, be quick to suggest she needed something from the commissary or that she ought to sleep, and he would wander out into the corridor, where he would chat with patients or a young nurse. Sometimes the outbursts between them, in which she was certain to ask him to take her away from here to a summer cottage on the sea, would become too painful, and the sentimental and beleaguered Toby would have to leave her bedside and pace about the room while Kubilius himself, if he chose to stay, would turn away.

When Toby started to come less frequently, Kubilius knew he had reached the point where he could not take much more. Whatever the reason Toby gave himself—business, children, fatigue, anguish, girlfriends—he had already begun his final leavetaking. As if to take his place, Kubilius came even more often than before. He did not suffer like Toby. He could sit and stare at the sleeping Sarah for so long a time at one stretch that the scene resembled that of the old-fashioned physician's death watch through the long and perilous night of crisis at the patient's bed. He looked pensive, unhappy and strangely satisfied. Maybe his concern was as much professional as personal, and he couldn't help but be fascinated by the puzzle of her disease. Every so often he would lean over and put his palm on her brow, or take her pulse, after which he would collapse in his chair with his head bowed, his hand on his own brow, his thick fingers widespread. Whenever she nodded, her weak eyes suddenly wide and frightened at the sight of him, for he must have reminded her immediately of where she was, he would say, "Better go to sleep, then. I'll get you something if you need it."

He could only make small talk with her, he could meet her only on that level.

"It's raining out," he said. "Can you hear it?"

A rustle in her bedclothes, the turning of her head. "I think so," she said.

"I opened the window a bit. . . ."

"Yes."

"A nice fresh smell," he said.

"A breeze," she said.

"Too cool?"

She shook her head, swallowing.

"It is a bit cool," he said.

"Smells like melting snow. . . ."

"It does at that. The snow's pretty much already melted now. . . . A few patches left in the woods, in the shady spots . . ."

Such was the profound nature of their conversations. Most of them were whispered, too, and in the dark, which gave them a secretive and intimate nature.

He could not explain his compulsion to visit Sarah, nor could he resist it. For years he had planned new projects with his free time: he would reread Tolstoy and Balzac, he would learn any number of new pieces on the viola, he would study the history of anesthesia and possibly write a paper on its practice in New Hampshire, he would acquaint himself with jazz, he would at last straighten out his garden. But he had neglected the garden, hadn't so much as touched the viola lately, giving Sarah the allotment of that time instead. His visits, in which he played the dumb witness, had become obsessive. He was like a voyeur looking through a woman's window, if a voyeur could be imagined sedated and not excited by what he saw.

The bedside vigilance was new to him. Except for the brief conferences he had with patients the night before their surgery, when he explained to them the nature and action of the anesthesia he planned to use, he did not have much personal contact with patients. Perhaps a remark or two on the operating table before he sent them off to sleep. He might as well have visited his patients in spirit only, so little was he known. He was the invisible shaman who held in his hands the power of sleep and wakefulness, pain and painlessness, life and death.

Maybe he was in love with sleep, euphoria, forgetfulness, with the gentle facsimiles and simulations of death itself. Maybe it was neither so profound nor so perverse as all that. Maybe she simply called up the reservoir of affection and compassion his cynicism could not always mask, and in this sense, she was his secret love.

Among themselves, the nurses had long ago concluded that his attention had gone beyond the call of duty and the simple pull of friends. What they suspected, exactly, he didn't care to name. He was certain they were talking, and that the rumors had spread among the staff. Those nurses who were accustomed to show him deference and, in some instances, fear now eyed him with a gloating, fish-eyed suspicion, and he could sense how they felt they had the upper hand. One evening as he sat with Sarah in the dark, he reached out to feel her forehead just as an autocratic nurse who had always reminded him of some huge cartoon hen that wore a pince-nez on her beak, and to whom he had spoken sharply more than once, turned on the light. She must have seen his reflex of guilt, how he pulled away his hand and fell back into the chair. "Oh, excuse me, doctor," she had said. "I hope I didn't interrupt anything."

God, he thought, do they think I climb in bed with her?

He was not an exuberant or a passionate man, and he could not explain the depth of his sympathy, nor did he know how to show it, except as he had. He was the sandman, and nothing more than that. It was what the children called him when they were little, encouraged by Pokey, who thought it appropriate and touching. When he came home late he made it a point to look in on them, one by one, standing in the half-dark above the beds in which they slept. To the children he was that silent shadow that came to haunt their doorway; close at hand, he was the face that smelled of tobacco and the hands with the rolled-up sleeves that smelled of medicines that the scrubbings could not dispel. And when they could or would not sleep, Pokey would say, Sandman's coming! Or the children would themselves call out, Send the sandman upstairs! We want the sandman! It's sandman time! And he would dutifully climb the stairs and by the time he reached the landing he would have transformed himself into that myth that made him more than just a man and father. If it was not too late, he would tell them a story in his soft voice of magic potions and transformations and the fantastic possibilities of the world of sleep and dreams, which would always end with the firm but gentle adjuration, "Now go to sleep." With that, he would pretend to throw a handful of invisible and magic sand into their eyes, which they would shut immediately. As often as not, they would be sound asleep before he reached the door.

42   The City of Pericles

AFTER Renzi had driven all day from New Hampshire to New Jersey, he decided that, worn out as he was, he would visit the Port Elizabeth docks, where he was scheduled to deliver his car, the notorious Humber, for shipment to Greece the next morning. It was a good thing he did, because the docks turned out to be as large and confusing as a city with streets of warehouses lined with tractor trailers and container cars and parking lots of brand-new, brightly colored European cars, thousands of them in neat rows. Not once did he see the water he knew was there, but several times the superstructures of freighters loomed up before him, looking, among the jumble of buildings, as though they, too, were on land. With the help of the map they had given him at the gate, he found his dock, and hoped he could relocate it in the morning. After that he spent half an hour driving up and down a freeway, boxed in by trucks, before he discovered how to turn off on an exit that would lead him to the Holiday Inn he could see standing off by itself, looking like a control tower in the middle of an airfield, its isolation made all the more fantastic because of its proximity to Newark and New York and the nearby congestion of airport, highways and refineries.

In the hotel room, he could not relax but found himself still clutching his briefcase and camera bag like some courier entrusted with state secrets. He was himself to fly to Greece the next afternoon, and the thought of the flight made him apprehensive and queasy. So did the odyssey he would have to make to get from the docks to Manhattan and the airport. A series of buses and taxis. He wished Karla, his ex-wife, was with him. Or another wife. Or some woman. A girlfriend or assistant, he didn't care which. She would handle the documents and money, make all the arrangements. She would talk to that army of nameless porters and waiters that would confront him from here on in. Someone who spoke German, like Karla. Or better yet, French. He recollected Alexander and Sarah sitting around the former's kitchen, speaking French. Lucky Stargaard, who was already in Europe, to have Alexander as his friend and guide. His own French was only passable, chiefly because he never had an opportunity to really practice it. He was spending a year alone in a country whose modern language he couldn't speak, and he doubted if many of the people he would meet would speak English. Maybe I can use my smattering of Italian, he told himself. He wondered how he could have waited until the last possible moment to worry about the multitude of practical and mundane problems that were sure to plague his journey. A year ago they had seemed like such minor considerations and inconveniences.

He was overcome with the fear that he had forgotten something. On the bed he laid out for his inspection passport, international driver's license, visas, traveler's checks, bill of lading for his car, address book, two hundred dollars in Greek currency, camera equipment, Greek phrasebook, airline tickets. So far so good.

It didn't reassure him, though. He felt not only apprehensive, but deprived. Left out, somehow. He didn't want to go to Greece alone. He didn't want to spend the night alone. The eve of his long-awaited journey, and all the emotions he could have felt had come down to loneliness. Unhappily he recalled those films of another era when the great ocean liners sailed out of New York bound for Le Havre and Southampton, and the first-class passengers would throw champagne parties in their staterooms for their friends who came aboard to see them off. There would be steamer trunks, pretty girls, ice buckets, popping corks, bon voyage bouquets; then a camera shot of steam blasting in a basso profundo up the ship's horn, followed by that of a uniformed purser rapping on the cabin doors ("All ashore who are going ashore!"); the crowd of well-wishers streaming down the gangplank, the crowd waving handkerchiefs and blowing kisses up from the wharf; the passengers, high up on the ship's deck, hanging over the rail and waving back; the big ship, guided by its tugs, easing away from the pier, black smoke pouring out of the three gigantic smokestacks; the orchestra in the first-class lounge striking up "Give My Regards to Broadway". . .

He would write to Sarah. He and Sarah were kindred souls, and he would have been satisfied with himself if she were at his side. He wanted desperately to write to Sarah; it was his duty to keep in touch. He would sit down and dash off a post-card. Unfortunately he hadn't bought one yet. No matter; he would write on hotel stationery and transfer the message to the card.

Dear Sarah, he wrote, I'm in Newark on the eve of my year in Greece and guess what? I'm feeling low and blue. And maybe just a little frightened, too. I'm well aware that the unknown might turn out to be far different from what I've expected, but I don't mind taking my chances with that. But loneliness is always the same, always unhappiness and desperation. I know what that's like already, we all know about that. . . .

He seemed to have exorcised the worst of his apprehensions in even this small act of writing, and his pen stopped. He read what he had written. I can't send her that, he said. That's not me. No one wants to read that crap. He crumpled up the paper.

He needed a drink. Not only to unwind but to celebrate. He ought to show himself a good time. After all, it was a big moment in his life, and he ought not to let it happen while he was alone. . . . He would go down to the bar and try to pick up a woman.

The hotel did not appear to be crowded, and the corridors and elevators were empty except for the occasional salesmen in pairs, usually dragging a sports coat wrapped up in plastic over a shoulder. They looked to him like former Southern college football players who had gone overnight from crew cuts to styled and blow-dried hair; most of them wore necklaces and leisure suits.

More salesmen were in the darkened bar, as were truck-drivers, whom he overheard talking about the cargoes they had delivered at the docks and how they were now waiting for a flight home to Florida and Texas. They wore neither ties nor jackets, and seemed to know each other from previous stays. He envied their camaraderie. He wanted to join in their conversation, tell them who he was, that he was on his way to Greece, that he would live there for a year.

The man next to him was one of several in matching tuxedoes. His bow tie hung untied around his collar, and he wore his blond hair in a ducktail. They were auctioneers, he told Renzi, and had just come from three grueling days of auctioning art in Newark, which was why his voice was hoarse. Their auction company hadn't been able to rent a hall in the area, and so they had held the auction in an automobile showroom, thousands of paintings on the walls behind all those cars.

"What kind of paintings did you sell?" Renzi wondered.

"American, European, modern, nineteenth century, old masters, you name it. We even sold a Winslow Homer."

The man's home was in Denver and he was heading there for a three-day rest. After that he was off to Portland, Oregon, to auction real estate, and then all the way to London to sell the machinery from a bankrupt bicycle plant.

"I'm off to Greece myself," Renzi said.

"Back to the old country, eh?"

"I'm sorry . . . ?"

"Returning to your birthplace?"

"Oh, no, I'm not Greek."

"On one of those tours, then, are you?"

"No, business."

"Then you've been there before," one of the other auctioneers said, leaning across the bar to get a better view of Renzi. He was older, puffy-faced and almost bald.

"No, first time."

The man nodded knowingly. "In most foreign countries,

even if you don't know the language," he said, "you can pretty much figure out what the signs mean on the stores. The trouble in Greece is that goofy alphabet. You don't know whether a place is a drugstore or a whorehouse until you step inside. It's the same in those Arab and Oriental countries."

Renzi didn't know how to respond to this, and so he said nothing, and the conversation lapsed.

At the restaurant he asked for a menu from the maître d', and returned it straightaway, amazed at the outrageous prices. Maybe he would pay such prices in Rome or Venice, but hardly here. The snack bar, although it was supposed to be open, was closed.

A wedding reception was being held in the large banquet hall where an orchestra was playing dance music, and some of the guests and wedding party had spilled out into the lobby. It was a large Italian affair composed of people about whom one said "New Jersey" before "Italian." The men reminded him of Mafiosi and dentists, while the women were trying, unsuccessfully, to imitate Californians or Swedes. The maids of honor wore skirts like ballerinas, and the groom and his ushers could have passed for dancers in an old-fashioned minstrel show in shiny baby-blue tuxedoes with ruffled shirt fronts and cuffs, and big bow ties, while their top hats were out of Dickens's London. My God, he thought, who would want their wedding in such a godforsaken place?

He bought a package of crackers and a cup of hot soup from the vending machine that was, oddly, in the hall outside his door, then sat on the edge of his bed, dipping the crackers into his soup. What an impersonal and sterile room! It seemed machine-made and as plastic-coated as a credit card. He could not imagine spending more than a night in such a room. One could either sleep in it, fatigued with traveling, or watch television, too travel-weary to sleep. Apart from that, it had no use.

He went to the window. Was there a fire smoldering deep

in the layers of refuse somewhere? He thought he could trap the air in a jar and see it, held up against the light. What appeared to be a marsh, and was possibly a landfill or a vast area where all the buildings had been demolished, stretched from the hotel for what seemed miles to the lighted skyscrapers of downtown Newark, making the city appear to have been built on the edge of a vast swamp. The hotel swimming pool was directly below, with cattails growing just beyond its fence, and the marsh beginning after that. The pool was, surprisingly, full of water for so early in the year, deserted, and only dimly lit. Who would swim in such a pool in such a place? he wondered. Who would come here with a bathing suit? On the railroad siding that ran behind the hotel, a lighted diesel engine was banging together a long train of freight cars, a sound he would hear all night. Across the way was the broad and smothered glow of Newark Airport, where the colored lights of the rising and descending aircraft blinked as dull as gaslights in the smog.

Strange how he had never really considered the possibility that the antiquities of the classic world might be set among modern and crowded cities (although he knew that in many cases this would be so), but had imagined himself, he supposed, standing among those marvels of marble ruins with all the splendid isolation of Labrador. It came home to him then: he was actually going to Greece, and this time there was no turning back.

He looked with incredulity at the camera and range finder in their handsome cases, those purchases he had made only after exhaustive studies and comparisons that had lasted half a year, and he remembered Aristotle's definition of happiness: that it was the exercise of all man's vital powers in the pursuit of excellence.

Until now his Greece had been less a real place of marble stone, olive trees, blinding sunlight and blue Aegean than the spiritual home of the human will. Since he had been that poor schoolboy in Cleveland, he had carried such a Greece inside his heart and head. A Greece that championed liberty and action while proclaiming it was a man's duty to make the most of what he had been given in this life.

But what if that physical Greece didn't match his vision of a lifetime? Or what was worse, if he failed, somehow, to measure up to Greece—not so much *that* Greece, but his own?

43   *On the Mar Menor*

FROM his balcony, Stargaard watched the troubled biplane above the lake. "He's stalling out," he called back to Alexander. The engine was popping now, the plane itself enveloped in a series of pushed-out puffs of smoke. For a moment it seemed it would suspend itself miraculously, then as though it would fall like a stone. Finally, after a snap and jolt that suggested the engine might have caught, it started down in the direction of the airport and disappeared behind the buildings of the town below. He waited, tense, anticipating the far-off thud of an explosion followed by the silent curling up of smoke beyond those distant date palms that rose up with all the disproportionate exoticism of giraffes' necks above the jumble of tiled roofs and Moorish-looking walls. Nothing happened. Neither bang nor smoke.

When a second and then a third biplane repeated the noisy misadventure of the first, he suspected a training exercise.

"Never mind," he called out, not that she had heard him the first time. For the rest of the day every biplane in the sky stalled out above the lake. The noise was nerve-racking. Still, it wasn't as if they were interrupting any attempts of his to work.

In the past two weeks he had grown accustomed to the unmuffled racket of the ancient planes. He had a special fondness for them and felt privileged to see them daily in the blue skies above the Mar Menor where their maneuvers reminded him of some panoramic reenactment of a World War I dogfight he might have seen in a 1930s film. They were used as trainers by the Spanish air cadets, who wore modern blue uniforms and acted much like American college boys when they gathered in the restaurants and bars in town. The planes reminded him of the backward Spain of old, like those big black anachronistic sedans and taxis and horse-drawn carriages that had lined the boulevards of Málaga when he was in Spain a dozen years before. It was this Spain that he had searched for as they worked their way down the Mediterranean from the Costa Brava to the Costa del Sol and partway back again, staying for a week each in Valencia, Alicante and Almería. But the coast, which looked crowded with new jerry-built high-rise hotels and condominiums that already showed broken boarded-up windows and places on the exterior walls where the bricks of the facework had fallen off, was one long construction site, the outline of giant cranes seen monotonously against the horizon. Even the beaches where they picnicked were littered with newspapers and garbage, and when they returned to the roads they were chased by armadas of large trucks expelling an exhaust so black it seemed their fuel was coal. Sometimes they passed the trucks, overturned, burned out and abandoned beside the road.

Even with its resident air academy, their small village on the Mar Menor was less spoiled than elsewhere. A street of run-down and shuttered summer villas that looked as old as the last century, and a tiled promenade along the shore, which was colonnaded with palm trees; wooden docks that had to go far out into the shallow salt sea in order to reach a depth deep enough for swimming in, and small seafood restaurants built out over the water. And a surrounding landscape of windmills, orange groves and market gardens, with marguerite and poppies of early spring blooming beside the road. But immediately to the south on a narrow strip of land that served as a breakwater between the Mar Menor and the Mediterranean, the city of high-rise hotels of La Manga rose sheer from the sea like some space-age Atlantis. Even the capital city, of Murcia, which he had previously thought of as being as remote as Mecca, and which brought to mind such adjectives as Biblical and African, was now torn up in preparation for the construction of wider streets and newer buildings, with piles of rubble and gaping holes where once old stucco buildings with their grillwork and balconies had stood.

Alexander, who had never been to Spain, was almost as disappointed in the landscape as he was, despite her claim to have a feeling for Spain. She certainly had taken to the slow pace and seedy comfort of Spanish hotel life: the coolness of the large rooms and tiled floors, the immense matrimonial beds and the great shutters that kept the room in shadows, the schedule of the late rising and breakfast followed by the big midday meal and then the love-making and the naps before the drinking in the afternoon at a bar that was the prelude to the snacks and drinking in still another bar, and finally the late dinner and the promenading on the boulevards around the fountains and a last coffee at a café before returning to the hotel and that shut-up world of sleep. He, too, had fallen prey to such a life, but not without a sense of worthlessness and guilt.

He suspected she was going native in the hopeless way of northern Europeans in Spain, and her rounds of sleeping and sunbathing on the balcony annoyed him. She had promised to keep a sketchbook of their journey, complete with commentary, and had also mentioned the making of a photographic essay. But he had yet to see her use a pencil, and she had taken barely a dozen photographs, and those of the usual tourist subject matter, of himself posed before a Moorish wall or reading a newspaper in an outdoor café.

The maid often had to rouse her to make up the bed, and he thought meanly that he knew why her home in the woods had looked like the photographs in the best home and garden magazines. She had spent most of her time cleaning it. Now she had no such duties, and she slept and read in bed. He suspected her whole life was a self-made illusion of activity, accomplishment, sophistication, and that she had done little more than pedal the machine that parted the curtains and sent up the pretty show.

Now he had discovered she was hardly the sophisticate he had assumed. The other night in a bar in Cartagena he had watched a drunken Swedish executive trying to pick up a pair of teen-age soldiers. The Swede had asked Alexander to tell the boys that it would be all right for them to go to his room, he only wanted to be their friend, and in her halting Spanish she had, to Stargaard's amazement, done so. Worse, she had continued to do so despite his head-shaking and whispered "Don't"s. At first he thought she was deliberately perverse, but later, when he challenged her, he was convinced she was only naïve. A week ago she had let a Spaniard start up a conversation with her in the park. He informed her he was a matador, and she had believed him. She had let him buy her a drink and take her for a walk into the park, where he showed her off to all his friends. Then he put his arm around her and kissed her on the lips. When she related this to Stargaard, they had argued not so much over her letting herself be picked up by the man as over whether or not he really was a matador. She still insisted that he was.

Since he had nothing better to do, he brought out the wine flask and turned his deck chair to face the sun. He must have napped, because the next he knew the biplanes were gone and he was enveloped in a rush of twilight that foretold a night where one should listen to flamenco and fall in love. Greedily, he surrendered to the fatalistic feminism of the mood, and was thinking of guitars and wine and heartbreak when a huge jetliner, military-colored and outlined with lights, appeared suddenly to hover low above the rooftops, where it resembled some extraterrestrial spacecraft threatening to annihilate the town. Finally it landed in slow motion, its size disproportionate to the buildings it disappeared behind. He hadn't known the airport could accommodate so large a plane.

Inside he sat in the dark and convinced himself he was so hopeless and homesick that he ought to cry. What on earth was he doing here in the company of that woman whose naked limbs he could barely discern among the twisted sheets and pillows of the bed, both of them childless, homeless, stuffing themselves with sleep and food and performing a perfunctory and sweaty sex that seemed to come with the room and schedule? He would break free of his melancholy if he could only work. But how could he do that with her sleeping in their room? Still, if he were really possessed by demons, he supposed he would shut himself inside that mausoleum of a bathroom, turn on the light and go to work.

"I'd like to get out of here," he said, suddenly. "I wouldn't mind moving on to Granada." And when she did not pick up on this, he added, "I wish you'd arranged for Marco to send your money to Granada. Then we could have gone there to wait for it. Money will get to Granada a lot faster than it will down here. I told you in Alicante my money was coming here. We didn't both have to have money sent to the same place at the same time. I don't know why you didn't write to him. That way if we got tired of waiting here, we could have moved on to Granada and had my money forwarded."

"But we didn't know if we wanted to go to Granada," she said from the near-dark of the bed.

"How much is he sending?"

"How much are *you* expecting?"

"What if my money doesn't come?" he said. "The last time my bank sent it on by boat—"

"What if Marco doesn't send me anything? I don't think he has to, legally."

"All the more reason why you should have sold your house," he said. "I don't know why you didn't put it up for sale."

"It's none of your business what I do with my house. When I go home, I want a place to go to."

He could understand that. Still he couldn't resist getting in the last word. "Who knows, it might have sold while you were away."

She turned away from him with a thump of mattress and pillows as if in response to his approaching her, which angered him since he hadn't so much as taken a step.

"Complain, complain, complain," she said into the pillow in which her face was buried.

She was right. Why should he fault-find and complain? He feasted on artichokes and Seville oranges, drank his daily ration of wine from Jumilla, traveled with a woman strangers took for a movie star and who had money of her own even if she did show little inclination to spend it. He had wanted to give up the world of art for the superior world of life, hadn't he? At least for a while? He still found the events that had made this possible difficult to believe. He had sent a portion of *Ground Level* to his publisher on the slight chance that the editors there would like it so much they would willingly allow him to extract even more money from them. In the many years since his signing of the contract, both the owners and the editors of the house had changed, not once but twice, and the new people had not only refused to give him more money, they had told him that under no circumstances would they publish so tedious a book. His agent had then sent the half-completed manuscript to another publisher, who was so enthusiastic about the novel he advanced him five times the money of the first. Which meant he had at least two years in which to live comfortably while he finished the work. He had been given, unreasonably, still another reprieve. In the final hour, he could always count on the good opinion of the governor. He was the blindfolded prisoner with the heart pinned to his chest who heard, just after the calling out of "Ready! Aim!" the distant voice shouting, above the rapid fall of approaching feet, "Wait!"

He could hear the cadets singing in the bar up the street, and was tempted to go alone into the ancient city of Cartagena, where he would lose himself among the milling crowds. He wanted bright lights, shellfish, drunkenness, gaiety, the smell of confections cooked in oil, the Spain of old, dark striking girls with square shoulders and high breasts, parading in their best clothes. He would wander among those swarms of sailors and soldiers, so many of them they made the city seem like a place at war. Young soldiers with their shaved heads and outrageous boots, like GI boots only heavier and bigger, and brutal weapons in themselves. And he would see again those well-dressed dark men in dark glasses and dark suits who sat, reading newspapers, in the thronelike chairs of the private clubs that were cool and tiled and whose windows lined the promenade. Men who looked more Arabic than Spanish, and probably more Phoenician than Arabic, and somehow sinister and pitiless, as unfathomable to Stargaard as mandarins and Kafirs.

He threw himself face down on the narrow couch and, without sleeping or dreaming, came face to face with death. Come hither, Stargaard, it cried, and dealt him a soul pain so fierce he felt it in his bones. Death had its arms around him—it would

choke and crush him all at once! What an awful fate! More
gruesome than the worst of folklores! It was a charnel house,
a moldering shroud, a leering Carthaginian mask. It was violation and decay. He had never believed in an afterlife, but until
this moment he had never felt the anguish of its absence nor
understood with the full force of his imagination the truth of
absolute and utter nothingness. Not the horror of nothing in
the abstract, but that of having been and of knowing passion-
ately, with the most painful sense of disappointment, that you
would be no longer, that for you the universe and all creation
had reached its end. Where, among the living things of earth,
was there an anguish as great as that?

He sat bolt upright, heartsick and cold. What if the onslaught
of his passion meant that someone he knew had died, someone
as far away as several thousand miles? What if Sarah had died
and sent him, at the moment of her death, a final extrasensory
message, and he had experienced what she had experienced?
If so, he felt horrible for Sarah, for himself—for all mankind!
Such an explanation did not stay with him long. Sentimental,
superstitious fool, he said to himself, self-important to someone
else's last. Besides, they had heard only recently from Adele
Fox that Sarah had made a temporary recovery and seemed
to have a way to go before the end. He blamed the mood on
too much rich food and wine, along with too much sun and
sleep, which had dulled the lazy brain of an unhappy man
and opened it to the sunken chambers of primeval feelings.

Exhausted, he crept into the bed beside the sleeping Alexander and, careful not to rouse her, molded his shape to hers
and, without moving or sleeping that he could remember in
the morning, stayed that way throughout the night. Even she
who could not give him sympathy or understanding gave it
anyway. She had only to be human, and to be there. Such a
thought was probably a lie, he warned himself, but in the con-
text of his present desolation, it consoled him all the same.

44   *Last Illusion*

ONE morning after her return home for an extended visit, Sarah opened her eyes to see Ned and Jessie standing silently beside her bed. They looked perplexed and ill at ease, and on the verge of tears. The shades were drawn, the door closed, and the room in its cool chroma had the fixed neutrality of a snapshot turning gray. "What do you want?" she demanded, surprised she had woken to a world without color. In her own ears, her voice had sounded cross and accusative, and she hadn't meant it so.

"Daddy told us to come in," Jessie began.

"We had to," Ned said.

"What for?" she asked.

They shrugged and looked at each other. "I don't know," each said.

Sarah knew why, though. Because they had not visited her on their own, Toby had ordered them into her bedroom, thinking she was awake. But they had found her asleep and were afraid to wake her and, with their father somewhere outside the door, equally afraid to leave. And so they had stood dumbly, like patient little sentries who were being punished. She was so moved by their helplessness that she cried herself, which only increased their awkwardness and fear. She brought her arms out from under the covers and squeezed their hands, hoping this would reassure them. She reminded them of when they were little and they would crawl in bed with her and Daddy in the morning, snuggling up or roughhousing, depending on their mood—those were the times she liked best about their being little! But now those times were gone forever, they were too big for that. She had never loved or pitied them more than in this moment. Nor had she ever been more thankful that they were who they were, and were hers.

Later she became like some fussy old lady in bad health, and no longer cared if she saw the children. The smallest thing they said or did annoyed her. Her world had become too small to include anyone but Toby in it. The children, meanwhile, blamed her illness for their exclusion, which meant they blamed her, since, in their minds, her illness had become inseparable from herself.

Despite the demands of all his properties and plans, Toby spent many of her waking hours beside her bed. He kept assuring her that business was good, that he was successful, as though she worried about his investments and gambles, as though she cared. Recently he had purchased the entire summit of a small mountain to the north and his enthusiastic plans for its development were what he spoke of most. She noticed he was finally letting his hair grow in the fashion of the times.

When she felt up to traveling, Toby took her for drives through the country. She knew this pleased him, too, and they often ended up by driving along some property he owned or coveted. She was surprised how much the town and surrounding countryside had changed. Modular homes and house trailers were set out on almost every other acre lot, and the last of the dirt roads had been paved. The main highway had been widened, and the elms that lined it were all dead from the Dutch elm disease but had yet to be cut down. The few large maples that were left, Toby explained, were dying because of the salt put on the road in winter. The parking area of the town's general store had been paved over; and where there had once stood the town pump, from which, in a dry spell, the townspeople had hauled their water, there was now a catch basin, the runoff from the roads flowing down into what had been for two centuries a never-failing well.

One day early in that spring she decided she was strong enough to go outdoors and take a walk around the house. Toby offered her his arm, and she pretended it was an act of gallantry and not necessity. She felt bent, palsied, arthritic, wizened, old. No doubt about it, she was aging. Maybe she was already old. She could imagine Toby old, too, the pair of them, the old ones, walking arm in arm around the lawn. But when she turned to him, he looked so young, more youthful than he could have ever looked before. She felt betrayed. How could this be? She stole another look and saw that his face was worn and worried; his eyelids were heavy, his jaw sagged and his mouth moved ever so slightly but silently, as if he talked to himself. If he had aged, it was probably from taking care of her. Who knew what he had learned from the lesson of her illness, or what he had become because of it?

When she came to his delphiniums she found that he had Rototilled the bed. Her first thought was that he had dug up the plants in order to separate the crowns as a prelude to transplanting, but they weren't to be seen in the shade of any of the nearby trees. "Your flowers?" she said, stopping.

"I plowed them under," he said. "Finally gave up on the things. I didn't want to do it, but now that it's done, I wish I'd done it sooner. You were right all these years—it was an awful eyesore."

In the middle of the bed was a small mound of gray ash mixed with bits of charred stalks and flower heads, surrounded by a ritualistic circle of unburnt stalk ends. He had burned last year's growth to kill any mites that had carried over. "Will you start over?" she asked. "With just a few plants this time? And no hybrids?"

"I'm going to plant grass here."

"Grass," she repeated, nodding her head.

"And maybe some dwarf pear trees."

"What about an old variety of apple?" she said. "They have dwarf versions of so many of them now. And they taste so much better than the newer apples."

"Maybe," he said. But she could tell she hadn't budged him from thinking pear tree.

She had to be pleased, though. At last he had faced the truth and acted. It was a sign of his maturity. He had learned how to wait, how to admit failure and start anew.

On their second trip around the house she began to weep. She said, "You know, Toby, I think I really did want to be a *grande dame*, or someone like her, all along. It wasn't just a joke."

"You're a grand dame," he said, giving the words the English pronunciation. "And a *grande dame* you'll be." But he winced when he said it, and forced a smile.

No matter what he thought, she knew he spoke the truth. It would happen to her as he said. She had only to learn to take life as it came. She had only to survive and wait and see. And to try, in the meantime, to keep the very worst from happening. Delaying tactics were what was called for now. She had been lucky. The treatments she had been taking at the clinic were working fine. They would have told her and tried new treatments if it were otherwise.

She was no longer cognizant of the distance she had traveled nor of what she had learned along the way, much less of who she had become. Having gone so far, she had turned back and, in this final stage, returned to that dream that had been her point of origin. This time it was not so much the woman who dreamt it, for that woman was gone now, as it was her shell. Her world continued to shrink. It became an island. A big summer house on the rocky shore of an island. A sunroom in the house that overlooked the garden and beyond it, the little cove. Then it became the ringing of a bell buoy. And finally only the sight of the flat sunlit expanse of sea.

"Just curious," Toby was asking at her elbow, "but where am I in your plans for old age?"

The question caught her by surprise. She wondered whether his tone, which was kindly, was also patronizing, whether some small portion of him could acknowledge he was speaking to someone who was already partly gone. She had to give him credit. She was certain he had seen, better than she had, into the selfish secret of her lovely dream. He was looking beyond her, too, envisioning a time and a life apart from her that would not be lacking in new appetites and pleasures, and she thought she could catch the spirit of Miranda Sales shining in his face.

She tried hard to see him in her old age, tried hard to take him with her into her dream of accomplishment and worth. She supposed she must have expected him to accompany her. What else would she have done with him? She wanted him to age gracefully, and to become responsible and civic-minded, a patron of the charities and of the arts as he grew craggy, gray-haired, even more handsome. He would stand behind her chair at a Newberry Street gallery as they were shown a selection of Weirs and Twachtmans. He would still play tennis and sail his boat. She could picture them walking down some dusty lane on Nantucket or Islesboro. His face was tan and sported a white mustache and he was wearing his faded blue blazer, white trousers and his yachting cap with the sweat-stained band. He was pointing with his cane at wild flowers that grew along the roadside, or shaking it after the dust cloud of a speeding car. But she had to face the truth: she was ready to give him up. Because there she was, the great good lady strolling by herself in summer whites across the lawn that rolled down to the sea. She supposed she was a widow, that she had buried him. Certainly his death, difficult though it was bound to be for her, would offer her an even greater opportunity of freedom and authority. It would be an experience that would make her so much the wiser woman in the end. There was no way she could not admit the truth of that.

Her eyes were moist, but she knew how to keep him from seeing that. "You're in the garden," she lied. "Puttering in your old clothes. Among your old delphiniums." And for the first time she understood how lonely would be that life of the *grande dame* that lay ahead.

45   Hotel du Midi

AROUND the large table covered with the red-checked tablecloth in the restaurant of the Hotel du Midi, the Kubiliuses with their graceful air of relaxed formality must have resembled some early-in-the-century aristocratic family of white Russians spending a summer in France. Between courses the five children sat with their hands on their laps, leaning forward in their eagerness to speak. When they ate, they went at it with a fork and knife in either hand, putting their food on the back of their fork with their knife, in the European way. And what a meal M. Papillon, their proprietor, had set before them: baby mussels *vinaigrette, pâté de campagne* with *cornichons,* boned veal roast rolled in garlic, simple salad, and now fresh fruit and a tray of cheese. *Merci, M. Papillon! Salut, M. Papillon!* How good it was, Kubilius thought, that the family Kubilius was together again.

Pokey and the children had been living in Villefranche-sur-Mer, where Pokey's family had old connections, and the children had been able to go to school. He had met them in Nice, and they had driven up to tour the Dordogne, where in a few days' time they would move into a farmhouse they had rented for the next three weeks. Built in the sixteenth century of golden sandstone, it looked more like a chateau than a farmhouse, having both a square tower and a dovecote. It was set in countryside that was as green as Ireland, with fields of yellow mustard interspersed with pastures, and the surrounding copses were full of cuckoos that called all day. Pokey had made the arrangements.

He was amazed how the hair styles, the new French clothes and the manners of the children made them appear so European. He didn't know how to describe the change, unless it was that they were slimmer and more feline and, somehow, more childlike than before. How splendid they looked! And what poise and self-confidence they demonstrated at the table. Not only was there no letup to their spirited conversations, but no two people ever talked at once. Already they appeared to know a good deal of French, and even made a game of seeing who could be first to correct and laugh at their father's grammar, which, Lord knows, deserved both their help and their ridicule. Their French, he knew, was due to Pokey. What a good life she had given him, what a rich, complete existence; he had only to sit back and to watch and wonder, beaming.

Now they were all excusing themselves, and Pokey was steering them toward bed. After all, it was nearly ten. How well she handled those two older boys, whose remarks were coming close to insolence. Well, testing the waters anyway.

"*Bon nuit, Papa!*"

"*Bon nuit, mes petites filles,*" he said, delighted that the girls had taken to calling him *Papa*.

"How do you say 'sandman' in French, *Maman?*"

Pokey shrugged and smiled.

"*Bon Papa*, sweet *Papa.*"

"*Bon filles.*"

"Take it easy, old man."

"Goodnight, boys. Take care, old beans."

"Coming, *Maman?*"

"No, you kids go along," he said, answering for her. "I want to talk to your mother for a minute." And when she returned to sit across from him, he took her hand and kissed it. "Your humble servant and admirer," he said. "Sometimes I lie awake at night trying to discover what I did to deserve you."

Embarrassed, she mumbled something about clichés.

"Well, I know enough to stay out of your way," he answered, uncertain as to how he should take her response. "But listen," and he drew closer.

But the girls came out on the balcony and called for mother, and what it was he meant to tell her had to wait, as she left the table for the stairs. He didn't really care, though. He was accustomed to being left alone.

Wonderful man, this M. Papillon. He had asked him for his best *vin du pays*, as he had in every hotel in which he stayed, and he had been presented with a two-liter bottle of a dark and fruity Bergerac, the *vin du patron*, complimentary with the meal. Only two other parties remained at the few tables. The local basketball team, which appeared to be having its annual banquet, and was drunk and throwing bread balls at each other, and a pair of truck drivers in blue overalls, one with the bright flush of the happy alcoholic about his Gallic face.

Behind the inn a small stony stream, clear enough for the brook trout he had dined on at lunch, raced to the lowlands, and he could hear it without letup day and night, splashing beneath the ancient bridges, tinkling against the ancient foundations of the medieval houses. What a clear and purifying sound! For at least two thousand years, and for perhaps as long as forty thousand, people had lived in this one spot, listening, as he listened now, to that purling and splashing sound. And how dark and isolated the little village was at night, unlit except for the light post at either end, where it was already more country than town, delineating the length of your evening stroll. *"Très vieux,"* he said aloud. And poured himself another glass of wine. *"Très magnifique!"*

How absolutely right he was to enjoy his family while he could. He congratulated himself on his wise decision to take a leave of absence from his practice and travel with them in Europe. It would be an experience they would not forget. They would recollect it at dinners and later at reunions that would extend into a future that would find him no longer there. And as a bonus he would realize that special little dream of his that had kept him happy in the evenings, and see Galicia in Spain. He would not have the chance again. These days if you waited, the place changed for the worse. Either that, or you were changed. To dust. It had always been the case.

In Bergerac this morning they had picked up a week's accumulation of mail sent *poste restante* from home, and there had been a brief note from Adele Fox saying that Sarah had died the previous week. In the hospital, he gathered. She had lasted about as long as he had expected.

An attractive woman whose helplessness he had found appealing. Cut off in her physical prime, certainly. He doubted that mentally she would have significantly changed or broadened; or, to be brutally frank about it, that the character of the woman herself mattered much. However, he was not convinced that people really changed in any case. He doubted the efficacy of free will, and was convinced the science of genetics was on the threshold of proving this rather unpopular suspicion correct.

Still, he had shared with her some silent and secret moments, more like the intimacy of prayer, he supposed, than sex. In his morbid way he could admit to having shown a fondness for her that approached the state of love. The risk was not so much. The affair had been certain to remain a secret, and he had known from the beginning how it would end. A dangerous infatuation all the same. Like being in love with sleep. Or death.

An awfully modern death. American. Avant garde, he might have said. Struck down by a mysterious organism, or toxin, or combination of the two, wasn't exactly like breathing your last with old-fashioned pneumonia. One theory would have her the victim of some new life form, at least half man-made, born of the dump heaps of modern man's creations and destructions and perhaps, ultimately, more adapted to the human environment (which was becoming, unquestionably, the world environment) than was man himself. Certainly a creation of man himself—a microscopic Frankenstein's monster—there it was at long last, man becoming God! You needed a new sort of Aeschylus and Sophocles altogether to wrestle with a retribution the like of that. A student of biology and chemistry far more than a human observer or maker of myths.

Not much meaning in existential actions, so called, at such a time in such a place. Too many invisible and external forces over which you had no control, nudging you this way, weighing you down with this and that. Probably too many people, too. Their numbers would turn you into a fly speck if you thought about them. Pretty difficult to make your life meaningful, knowing what you did these days about how the old world's changed just in the brief course of your lifetime, much less to make others care. About anything.

Cullenbine, for instance. Poor silly Cullenbine. You wanted to make all of us no more deserving on this planet than a duck or stone. And yet you must have ended your crazy life believing it was as romantic and tragic as *Tosca*. But, to be fair, who could say? Maybe you were convinced it didn't matter what nonsense you tried to put across. Do it, or don't do it; it was all the same, and who cares in the end?

Once more he saw himself in Cullenbine's doorway, looking across the living room into the bedroom where the ashen Cullenbine lay on his bed. And he seemed to hear the myriad and overlapping voices of a thousand frightened patients whispering in his ear, Put me to sleep, doctor. I don't want to know what's going on. I want to wake up and find it all over. He saw himself, in the distortion of their ether dreams, insert the needle into their arm, slide the tube down their throat, place the mask upon their face. Count backwards, he was telling them, the man who was never more than that overhang of face, half masked, that came before their consciousness like the moon shadowing the sun. Beginning with ten, nine, eight . . . It will be over, all right, he thought. Soon enough.

Strange. He had begun by recollecting Sarah, and had so quickly and naturally drifted on to other thoughts. He supposed he was already on his way to forgetting her, and that he would have to work hard at making himself feel anything but a general sort of grief. He wished it were otherwise. Let her assume the natural place within your memory, he counseled himself, even if that means being consigned to near-nothingness. These days that was grieving enough for anyone.

He heard Pokey say good night to the boys for what she announced was the tenth and final time, and caught a glimpse of her on the balcony as she passed on to the girls' room, calling ahead that she was coming, they needn't fear the storm.

The thunderstorm had startled him; he had not heard it approach. Since they had arrived in the Dordogne, thunderheads had blown in daily from the direction of Bordeaux, leaving the air after the deluge as cool and thin as that beside the sea, but until now they had occurred in the late afternoon.

Thunderclaps rolled along the hotel roof, the windows flashed, rain cascaded all around the eaves. Papillon was busy fastening the banging shutters. What electricity! What timpani! What a deluge! What a show! Theatrical, almost. Mythical, too. Some giant of a Celtic god banging a tremendous cymbal in a sacred grove. He recalled for no particular reason that Beethoven had died in such a storm.

He looked forward to their three-week stay in the fertile garden that was the countryside around these parts. It could pass for old Archie Auden's prehistoric utopia come true. Slopes of vineyards interspersed with fields of sunflowers, tobacco and corn, and orchards of peaches, plums and nuts, along with an occasional stand of wood and small pastures with grazing cows and hedgerows of blackberries along the roads. Neat farmhouses with fig trees and pots of flowers in their courtyards, hotels trellised with wisteria, medieval chateaus on the limestone cliffs that overlooked the river. Thank goodness Pokey had sense enough to say, We stop here and go no farther. If he had had his way, they would still be on the road, looking for that perfect hotel or house for rent in the perfect setting. It didn't matter what idyllic place they happened on, he would still be haunted by the possibility of an even better place just a little farther up the road.

Even now he could hardly wait to cross the Pyrenees and enter Spain, making a beeline for Galicia. He took out the road map of northwestern Spain and spread it before him on the table, a cigarette dangling in the French fashion from his lips. He would follow the Costa Verde along the Mar Cantábrico, then head to La Coruña and go all the way to Vigo. On the way back they would spend a few days in Santiago de Compostela.

God, the wine was grand. He'd have another glass of that. He glowed. He wanted to yawn and sing. He wanted to call good M. Papillon over and have a chat. "*Très vieux!*" he would tell him. "*Très magnifique!*"

But the boys, now that Pokey had left them unattended, weren't settling down. They were making noise instead. A pillow fight, perhaps. Oh, well, children were often fired up after a meal, and this had been a late meal, and they had spent a long afternoon cooped up in the car, touring. Just simple horseplay, a working off of high spirits. Perhaps too much, though, in the line of roughhousing. Was he mistaken or had Tod just shouted at John in French? Something insulting, likely. He let them go on until he found himself saying, M. Papillon shouldn't have to stand for this. At which time he acted as he would have had he been at home and reading the newspaper in his slippers in his favorite chair, and rose up with the open map in hand. Reluctantly he went up the stairs and opened the door, his large shadow blocking out almost all the light he himself allowed into the room. "Go to sleep," he said.

46   A Fish Story

WITH the Kubiliuses away, it was the duty of the Orlovskys to look in occasionally on their house, and on a sunny day in early fall Colleen left the golf course and drove over to perform her small list of chores. The battle against the oil refinery had been won, temporarily at least, and although the governor was more determined than ever to see the fruition of his plan, the Greeks and oil men, surprised and then intimidated by the vociferous outcry against them, had backed off. Apparently the refinery would be built somewhere eventually, and if not here, then where? Well, that would be the problem of some other area. And Colleen Orlovsky, having won this one battle, resisted all entreaties to lead her legions in the support of less immediate environmental and political causes, and like that Roman general of old who broke his sword and returned home to plow his fields, she returned to the links, where she played daily, weather permitting, and to that social and mildly alcoholic life of the clubhouse, which she loved almost as much. She was ready, however, Allan maintained, to come to the aid of her fellow citizens whenever their call for help was heard again.

At the Kubiliuses' house she encountered three young women of the type the locals had at first called "hippies" out back in the overgrown herb garden. She knew they lived in the camps and old abandoned houses up the road where Pokey had once pointed out to her the marijuana plants they grew brazenly in their dooryards. Here they were busy cutting long woody stalks of flower heads with what looked like rusty scissors and piling them in large swaths on the sunny path of unmown grass. They wore full skirts that dragged along the ground or baggy denim coveralls, with their hair in railroad bandannas, and one carried a baby in a sling across her breast. A pair of small children toddled close to their feet, and a friendly but scraggly dog wandered, his tail between his legs, in and out of the bushy herbs. Colleen was content to stand in sunlight and watch them for a while, still in her green golfing visor and miniskirt, her skin Mexican-colored this time of year. She thought the women reminded her of slaves working in the cotton fields. Finally the women saw her, waved and smiled.

"Hello there," Colleen said. "What's going on?"

"We're herb-gathering," one of them said. "Dr. Kubilius, before he left, said we could help ourselves."

Their faces had a well-scrubbed look and seemed incapable of registering an expression that was not a smile. Two of them wore old-fashioned wire-rim eyeglasses, and one of them displayed several original if crude tattoos. "Good for you," Colleen told them. "I'm sure he's glad someone is getting some use of them. Did he tell you what was what?"

"He gave us a guided tour and made out a kind of map, but it's still confusing," the girl with the baby said. "Before that I couldn't tell parsley from chives."

"Well, I'd be careful, all the same," Colleen said. "I'm sure he has plants here that are poisonous, or full of drugs."

As though to reassure her, the women took her through the garden, pointing out the yarrows, marjorams and camomile that they had picked for their herb teas, along with the sage, hyssop and peppermint the doctor had told them to use in an infusion for coughs and colds, for they were interested in preparing their own folk medicines. Colleen, who followed after them, smelling and tasting each, confessed, "I don't know a thing about them. In flower gardens they're all daisies to me. And in this garden, they're all weeds."

She left them to their harvesting and played with a baby that had been set down on a towel in a shady place, then she went inside the house and watered the plants. When she came out she had a drink in hand. A pair of young men had walked down the road to meet the women. Both wore their blond hair long and had bushy beards. One of them wore nothing but bib overalls. He had naked shoulders, naked arms, naked feet—he was naked beneath those overalls. He had a superb physique, and reminded her of a proud little boy in a brand-new pair of overalls, sticking out his chest. Wouldn't I know what to do with you if you were mine, she thought. She watched the bunch of them walk up the road to their camps, the men carrying the children on their shoulders, the women with their arms full of the weedy herbs.

After that she had to hurry home. It was their turn to have the Foxes over after supper for what had become their weekly night of bridge. She hadn't made anything special for a snack, and she got out the crackers and a wedge of "store cheese," remembering the plates but forgetting the knives and napkins.

Adele showed up a few minutes late, explaining she didn't know where Parker was, he had said he might go flounder fishing off a bridge, but they knew how Parker was, he couldn't be counted on for anything. She had left a note reminding him of their engagement, and she expected he would be along soon enough. In the meantime the three of them fooled around with a dummy hand, which put the usually sunny Allan, who had been a consistently crusty bridge player since he first played the game in college, into an impatient mood. Only the night before he had returned from a conference in Salzburg, where he had found the hotel rooms so expensive that he had taken a room at an inn thirty miles out in the country and ridden the bus back and forth each day. And he was supposed to be one of the top two American representatives. Home again, he wanted the security and solace of family, Americana, suburban house, the company of neighbors and a rubber or two of friendly bridge.

An hour later Parker Fox came striding into the room, still excited, if worn out. He had to sit down and catch his wind! What a story he had to tell! He had gone for a drive by the sea, where he had seen crowds of people with rods in their hands casting off the rocks into the waves, and naturally he had stopped and taken out the pole he always carried in his trunk and hurried down to the shore, putting it together on the run. They were catching bluefish, so many bluefish that most were fishing for the fun of it and throwing the vicious monsters back. The warm water, it was said, had brought them in, the first time anybody could remember in a dozen years.

"I don't know when I last had bluefish," Colleen interrupted.

"Bluefish is quite a delicacy," Orlovsky added, interested now and suspecting the skillful and occasionally generous Parker had caught and kept perhaps a dozen.

"You could have had all you wanted!" Parker said.

"Bravo!" Orlovsky said. "That's what I want to hear. How many did you get?"

"I didn't get any."

What, no bluefish? Orlovsky thought.

"Why didn't you get any, you silly man?" Colleen said.

"I didn't fish for bluefish," he said.

What was this Orlovsky was hearing? Parker had completely ignored the running bluefish? Instead he had become hysterical at the sight of the teeming herring and mackerel the hungry bluefish had trapped, as the tide turned, in a small cove close to shore. Parker had never seen a sight like it! What a massacre! The tops of the waves were alive with thousands of small desperate splashes, while the world beneath the surface turned and swirled with thousands of small frightened shadows. There were more fish than there was sea! He had thrown down his rod—literally cast it aside—and waded fully clothed and in his good leather shoes into the surf, where, stooping with outstretched arms, he had tried to catch the small fish the waves thrust toward him in writhing heaps, looking as he did so, he surmised, as though he were trying to embrace the sea. All around him the water boiled with the shadows and flashes that were maneuvers of attack and escape. Mackerel swam with their tails bitten off, with death gashes in their streaky sides. What a slaughter! But no matter how he lashed out and grabbed and splashed, he couldn't catch a thing!

He had taken a cue from a group of children who had waded out to catch the fish just down the beach, and raced back to his car in his soaking clothes and driven to the nearest hardware store, where he bought a plastic laundry basket and laundry pail. Then while the others continued to cast for bluefish from the rocks and a huge oil tanker passed on the horizon and a sailboat race took place around the bell buoy just offshore, he waded out into the water and on every third try or so brought

up a dripping laundry basket containing up to a dozen mackerel
and herring. At first he simply turned around and pitched the
catch as far as he could onto the shore. What did he care if
half of them fell into the sea, or that he was hit from the blind
side by a big wave and knocked to his knees; there were more
fish where they came from, and he couldn't get wetter. He
sat down with fatigue in the waves; his head bobbed, his feet
left the bottom. He was exhilarated, laughing, he kept throwing
the fish upon the shore. He supposed he went mad in those
moments; he wanted to catch every fish in that cove, wanted
to scoop them up like silver coins. He was like a crazed miser
who had stumbled on a treasure horde. But then he noticed
that the fish he had been throwing on the beach were not
content to stay put until he came ashore to pick them up,
but were struggling by means of flip-flops and leaps to return
to what had become for them the life-giving and lethal sea.
He hoped the bellowing he had done in that moment had
been drowned out by the surf. Immediately he had floundered
out of the water in his heavy clothes and chased them up and
down the stony beach. ("Come back here, you! . . . Oh, no
you don't!") They were all trying to escape his clutches! Most
were making it, too! For every fish he caught, ten escaped.
Even the mutilated mackerel slapped and quivered in his hand
with a strength that seemed equal to his own until, as often
as not, they shook free. While the herring were small and quick
and slippery, and just when you thought you had one, you
were left fishless, with herring scales upon your hands. He
fought them along the rows of seaweed that had been washed
ashore and made a last-ditch stand against them at the water's
edge until his back ached from bending over and he was gasp-
ing, like the landlocked fish themselves. After that he changed
his tactics and with great effort brought each dripping laundry
basket full of fish ashore and dumped it into the pail. Even
then most of the fish spilled onto the beach or leaped out as
soon as he went back for more.

He had changed his clothes at home but hadn't time to shower. Look at his hair, will you, it was thick with salt. "We'll have to leave early, Adele," he said. "I'll be up half the night as it is, cleaning fish. I more than filled the pail. Too bad I didn't buy a trash barrel."

"Your bid," said Orlovsky, who had long since dealt.

"Two spades," Adele said.

"Your bid," Orlovsky said to Parker, aware that he had yet to look at his cards, had yet even to notice them before him on the table. Allan was not all that entertained by the story, especially when the man held up the game by telling it. Besides, he could be certain he would hear the adventure narrated almost verbatim a second time at their bridge game next week, unless, of course, he ran into Parker before then, which would make next week the third time.

Well, there wasn't much in the way of alternatives. With so many of their old friends in Europe, or interested in other things, the Orlovskys and Foxes were left to each other and had reverted to the bridge games they had played together years before.

Vita had never really been part of their crowd, and Auden was a bit stand-offish, and had been more Sarah's friend in any case. Adele said she had heard that the orchard had become too much for one man to manage and that Auden was renting out its operation to another orchard next year and might have to sell it after that. The last few times that Orlovsky had seen him he seemed to be in a depressed and morbid mood, and had spoken with a resignation, not entirely free of fear, of death—his own. No one had seen much of Toby, and most had yet to meet his new wife, whom they knew about but had seen only in passing. Because he had remained a widower for only two months, there was speculation that an affair had begun during Sarah's illness. His supporters pointed out, however, that with small children to look after, and taking into consideration the stress he had been under during the length of her failing health, what else could the poor man do but marry the first solid woman who came along and made her play? He hadn't married Miranda Sales, as someone or other had once predicted, or anyone remotely like her, but a young woman in town with two small children of her own who had only recently divorced her husband. She had a mind for business, and some said she was quick and shrewd. She had obtained the local distributorship for a cosmetic company, and she made her rounds in her own new car with her own name and that of the company she represented emblazoned on the driver's door. She was studying for her real estate license and was already a notary public. The Angles had drifted away from their old friends, and were associating with a much younger crowd that seemed to have formed around a philosophy of "open marriage." They played tennis and practiced yoga together, and had been seen singly or in tandem jogging in their sweat suits along the highway in the early morning. They drove twin Thunderbirds. She had the KAMA on her vanity license plate; he had the SUTRA on his.

"Your bid, Parker." It was Adele Fox, echoing Orlovsky's own earlier entreaty of her husband. With as much success as he had, too.

While Orlovsky waited for Parker to shut up long enough to look down and discover he had been dealt a hand, his thoughts sailed hither and thither until, by means of transitions and connections he couldn't recognize, they traveled ten years or so in time and settled on the wedding day of Auden's daughter. The ceremony had been held out in the middle of the orchard, the date having been set to catch the apple blossoms at their peak. But there had been a heavy rain the night before, and petals were on the ground as well as on the trees, and what the rain had not knocked down, the wind, that had come up to clear out the rainy weather, was threatening to blow away. He remembered Auden in something like an old frock coat that seemed too large for him and was threadbare and glossy, and the son-in-law, the fair-haired Mississippian, in, of all things, a white suit, and the two of them walking through the orchard with Auden telling him that he sprayed his apples as little as possible, and that he could remember when he was a boy and his father ran the orchard, and they never sprayed, and the apples were perfect anyway. That was because they kept cows they turned out into the orchard in late fall, you see, and the cows ate up all the old drops in which the diseases and insects would otherwise have wintered over until the spring.

How bright and windy the day had been! And he remembered how, at the onset of the simple ceremony, as Auden was reading a short poem he had himself written for the occasion, a small toddler had wandered away from the gathering. As though summoned by an unheard voice, he staggered down the wide, blossom-strewn avenue between the trees. When it was apparent he was not about to go only so far and no farther, Janet Angle, who had been keeping her eye on him, casually went after him, her arm extended to call him back. (Orlovsky couldn't believe it, but that toddler must have been the oldest of the Angles' boys, who was almost as tall as Orlovsky now.) But the boy had wanted none of his mother and had started into that stumbling run that made him look as though he were running downhill, out of control. That was when Orlovsky turned his attention from Janet, whom he had been eying during Auden's recitation, to Sarah Keville—that day was the first time he had met her. She was blond and already had a summer tan and was wearing a big straw hat and something like a white, old-fashioned muslin dress. Behind her, the unfocused background of apple trees suddenly rustled with a great flourish of sweeps and bows. Too late she reached up to hold down the big hat, which the wind blew off, and her blond hair had come immediately undone and seemed to explode upon her head, sailing up as though to pursue the hat. It was he, Orlovsky, who had been first to give chase to the hat. But it sailed, disklike, so much farther than he expected, and forsook the orchard altogether for a ridge of open pasture, where it rose and fell like a kite trying to gain the upper air. Thrice he came close enough to see the ribbon wound around it and the nosegay of apple blossoms in the band, but each time he made to seize the brim, the hat took to somersaulting and escaped him as though it had a life of its own or was jerked by an unseen string. Farther and farther away from the wedding it traveled until he felt he must look laughable and ungainly and as though in pursuit of some gigantic elusive butterfly. But Sarah would have gone after her hat, too, she wouldn't have stayed behind, and the thought of her behind him made him cavort and skip a bit while continuing to push on. She would be running as best she could across the field in her long white dress, the hem held up in her hands and her blond hair spiraling around her head. But when he looked back, she wasn't there. Only grass and woods and sky. He and the hat were in the field alone. Way off among the trees, he could see the wedding, a circle of pastel people in a mass of pink and green. They had reached the point in the unique ceremony where everyone was singing, sounding together like some rustic church choir concertizing in the out of doors. The strains of an old pacifist song—"Michael, Row Your Boat Ashore" or "Down by the Riverside," he couldn't remember which, although they may have rendered both—were blown his way, and if he were not still on the run, would have moved him to the brink of tears. By then the hat had taken a turn for the orchard and seemed certain to outdistance him when, miraculously, the wind died. He had picked it up at last and was holding it to his chest in both his hands as though he had himself just doffed it in reverence to some landed gentry or shrine, when the young Angle boy ran out into the open from between two gigantic apple trees, followed by his mother who, on his heels at last, snatched him up from behind. Twice she turned him upside down as she spun him around, treating him like a baton. The boy was laughing and struggling and still kicking his little legs, pretending to run along on air a foot above the ground. . . .

With that, Orlovsky came to, seeming to struggle himself. In an action that had nothing to do with his fellow cardplayers, whom he surprised, and without knowing why he did it, he threw down his bridge hand with a slapping sound, pushed back his chair and stood up. "Too bad, too bad, that was too bad," he said, shaking his head.

Dark Harbor, 1972
York Harbor, 1979